To Eden.
If I included all the reasons why,
I'd have to cut the whole book for word count purposes.
Thank you for loving me, friend.

Advance Praise for *Not That Kind of Proposal*

"Full of hilarious banter and sizzling tension, *Not That Kind of Proposal* weaves laugh-out-loud scenes with quiet, thoughtful moments of reflection on grief and self-discovery in a poignant, beautiful, and tender way. . . . Victoria Lavine is at the top of her game, and I adore everything she writes!"

—Chelsea Curto, *USA Today* bestselling author of the D.C. Stars series and *In Stormy Weather*

"Full of charm, wit, and heart-squeezing moments, *Not That Kind of Proposal* is everything you can ask for in a romcom. . . . This book will make you laugh, cry, swoon, and blush past your bedtime—I know I did!"

—Lana Ferguson, *USA Today* bestselling author of *The Nanny*

"*Not That Kind of Proposal* is touching, heartwarming, and HOT! Victoria Lavine wrote a sparkling love story that every romance reader will adore."

—Joss Richard, internationally bestselling author of *It's Different This Time*

"Victoria Lavine has done it again! Heartwarming and sweet with full, well-rounded characters, I loved following Gracie and Jude's journey!"

—Naina Kumar, author of *Say You'll Be Mine*

"I adore everything about this book. . . . The perfect read for inextinguishably hopeful romantics (like me), *Not That Kind of Proposal* is a knockout. Gracie and Jude have a permanent home in my heart."

—Ellen O'Clover, author of *The Heartbreak Hotel*

"I fell in love with this book the moment Jude put on that party hat. . . . A romantic comedy that's tender and hilarious and gorgeously felt. I loved it."

—Georgia Clark, author of *It Had to Be You* and *Play It Again*

"Clear your schedule, throw out your TBR—this book is charming and funny, clever and crazy hot, and soulful in a way that grips your heart and won't let go long after you reach The End. If Victoria Lavine writes it, I'm reading it, I'm underlining whole passages, I'm making it my entire damn personality. I love this book!"

—Laura Piper Lee, author of *Pot Shot* and *Doomsdate*

"These pages are infused with everything I need and love in a book—comedy, complex human emotions, and a ubiquitous sense of hope. Get ready for Victoria Lavine to be your new favorite romance author."

—Tarah DeWitt, *USA Today* bestselling author of *Left of Forever*

NOT THAT KIND OF PROPOSAL

A Novel

Victoria Lavine

ATRIA PAPERBACK

New York Amsterdam/Antwerp London
Toronto Sydney/Melbourne New Delhi

An Imprint of Simon & Schuster, LLC
1230 Avenue of the Americas
New York, NY 10020

This Atria Paperback edition July 2026

ATRIA PAPERBACK and colophon
are registered trademarks of Simon & Schuster, LLC

Interior design by Davina Mock-Maniscalco

Manufactured in the United States of America

1 3 5 7 9 10 8 6 4 2

Library of Congress Cataloging-in-Publication Data is available.

ISBN 978-1-6680-8329-1 (pbk)
ISBN 978-1-6680-8330-7 (ebook)

AUTHOR'S NOTE

Dear Readers. This story, while categorically a rom-com, also explores heavier themes that some readers may be sensitive to, including discussion of domestic abuse. While no abuse happens on page, the long-term effects and memories of growing up in an unsafe environment are discussed by adult characters, particularly in chapter 24. Please read with care.

While it will always be my goal to make you laugh and swoon, it's also my hope to shed light on issues that are close to my heart. Like so many, my life and the lives of some of my nearest and dearest have been impacted by domestic abuse in its various forms. By telling this story, it's my sincerest hope that those of you who have been through this experience (no matter what form it took or continues to take) feel less alone. A detailed list of content warnings can be found on my website, www.victorialavine.com.

1

GRACIE

Some unsolicited advice: when choosing your team for the zombie apocalypse, consider enlisting a wedding planner. I know, I know—at first glance, the two seem completely unrelated. But as both a wedding planner *and* zombie film aficionado, hear me out. Weddings, much like the zombie apocalypse, are extremely high stakes.

On the big day, every moment has the potential to be a cherished, lifelong memory or a disaster that's rehashed at every Thanksgiving in perpetuity. I mean, technically, no one's going to have to fend off the undead during cocktail hour, but I can name at least three of my brides (including the one about to walk down the aisle) who'd probably choose a fight with a zombie over the stress hives I had to cover up before their first-look photos. But thanks to Kit, it wasn't a problem.

Like a reflex, I rest my hand on the black leather satchel that may as well be an extension of my body. Inside are critical emergency essentials: a sewing kit. Eye drops. Boob tape. A nip of whiskey. Staple gun. Antinausea *and* antidiarrheal pills. There's a lot more, of course, all neatly organized into a color-coded warren of zippered pockets, but my point is that a good wedding planner is prepared for *anything* (just ask me how many uses there are for extra-strength hemorrhoid cream—I dare you).

From my hidden position under an ornate stone portico, I look out at the large crowd seated for this outdoor wedding ceremony and quickly glance at my watch. *Seven till. You're still early.* My earpiece is silent, which means my two assistants, Mark and Phoebe, aren't dealing with any emergencies inside. I let out a breath and force my shoulders down from where they're trying to get cozy with my ears. At this point, I'm usually like one of those overeager helper fish that cling to more majestic marine life, ready to clean up anything that might annoy my client. But my bride, Jasmine, asked for a moment alone with her mom, so I stepped outside.

I'm considering going back in to check on them when a flash of white catches my eye. I turn to see Jasmine striding toward me, her gown flowing like a Renaissance painter's dream. Golden hour sunlight streams through the rambling rose garden to kiss her skin and upswept hair. It's a moment dying to be put on the glossy cover of a New England bridal magazine, and it very well might be.

Larkwood Estate—where I both live in a tiny guest cottage and work—is a blend of architectural styles that I would personally classify as "Fairy Tale." Vines of ivy and climbing roses tangle in a romantic battle over the creamy-gray limestone walls, while turrets and leaded windows seem to guarantee the existence of a secret library.

It's the kind of place you dream of living in when you're six years old and *Beauty and the Beast* has been permanently burned into your retinas. Or, when you're thirty years old, still reeling from the worst breakup of your life, and desperate for a place to live out your dissociative Romantasy dreams. Not that I'm speaking from personal experience or anything.

"*Gracie!*" Jasmine calls to me in a half-whisper as she approaches. I shove down my souring thoughts and return her beaming smile.

"You look radiant," I whisper back, glancing at the seated crowd as she grasps my hands in hers. "How are you feeling?" I ask, pulling her deeper into the shadowed portico. "Ready to go?"

"Of course. Sorry I came outside—I just needed some air. I can't believe the moment is here." Jasmine's eyes well up, threatening to overflow, and my hands are already leaving hers to open Kit.

"You have nothing to apologize for. Here," I say, once I've found a dainty white handkerchief. "Dab—don't rub."

"Gracie, you think of everything." She chokes back a laugh, delicately dabbing at the corners of her eyes.

"That's my job," I reply with a smile, even as my regularly scheduled wave of sadness begins to swell. Jasmine tries handing back the handkerchief, but I shake my head. "Keep it. You'll probably need it again."

While Jasmine tucks it into the bodice of her gown, I press a button on my earpiece.

"Hey, Mark, we're nearly ready. Could you bring out the wedding party? I have Jasmine with me."

"You got it, on our way."

The next few minutes feel like the backstage of a Broadway show if all the actors were emotional wrecks, but with Mark's help, I can handle it. This is only my third year of coordinating weddings, but I'm a fast learner. I've had to be, ever since I planned my stepsister's wedding here, and the owner of Larkwood decided to bring me on permanently.

Her offer couldn't have come at a more desperate hour, and my gratitude—the undying, eternal variety—is why every single "big day" I've been entrusted with *has* to be perfect.

After directing the wedding party into formation, I send Mark to check in with the wedding band. As he rushes away, I make eye contact with Kyle, the lead violinist of the string quartet I always hire, despite his firm stance on not brushing his hair ("Bridesmaids love it, Gracie!"). I hold up a one-minute warning finger and press the button on my earpiece to check in with Sofia, my childhood best friend and lead photographer.

"We've got walkers," I say softly, knowing only she'll get my *Walking Dead* reference. "I repeat, we've got walkers."

"Roger that, Ring-Slinger," comes her familiar voice. "In position."

My palms begin to sweat, despite the perfect, June-in-Rhode Island weather. Have I mentioned weddings are high stakes? At any moment, the maid of honor's secret flame for the groom could combust. The four-year-old ring bearer could mistake his precious cargo for shiny Cheerios. The groom's questionable choice to pound a beer with his groomsmen right before the ceremony could manifest in an ill-timed burp.

But so far, everyone is holding it together. I take a breath. Giving Kyle the thumbs-up at last, I dart behind a pillar so I'm not in the photos as the first notes of Canon in D rise from the quartet. The crowd turns in unison toward the portico, and I signal for Jasmine's mother to start walking. The procession unfolds until it's time for the big moment. The crowd gasps as they catch sight of Jasmine and her father for the first time, perfectly framed within the carved stone archway covered in ivy. Right on cue, my eyes close.

After months of planning a wedding that would give Martha Stewart herself the warm and fuzzies, this moment should make me feel triumphant. But instead, it only reminds me of everything I've lost. The music swells, and my tear ducts launch a stinging Pavlovian response. It's not something I can control—trust me, as a double Virgo, I've tried. So instead, I hug Kit to my chest like it might be able to mend the ripped seam in my heart—sadly, the one thing it doesn't carry a remedy for.

There was a time, before Larkwood became my postbreakup fallout shelter, when the only wedding I thought I'd be planning was my own. Back then, I was starting a bridal wear line, ignoring my ever-growing mountain of debt, and happily hoping for *him* to pop the question.

So much has changed since those naive days. Now, as a single, debt-riddled, cottage-dwelling hermit who lives a hundred yards away from where she works, securing my own Happily Ever After seems about as likely as this particular groom not sweating through another shirt (he's on his third).

Before I'm too tempted to slide down this pillar and directly into the fetal position, I hear a voice I can only describe as crisp and crinkly (much like its owner).

"You better be reminiscing about the ménage à trois you had with that carpenter and acrobat and not moping over Kevin again."

A reluctant smile tugs at my lips as I look at my boss, Agatha. I'm fairly tall myself, but Agatha is taller. At a sprightly eighty-four years old, she's all sharp angles and long limbs, perpetually draped in eye-wateringly bright colors. Today, she's in a head-to-toe fuchsia ensemble that was probably shipped directly from Paris. Paired with poker-straight silver hair and her signature "just try me" expression, I'd probably be terrified of her if I didn't love her like a grandmother.

"It's Calvin, not Kevin," I remind her, even though saying his name feels like unzipping the contents of my chest and watching them plop onto the cold stone floor. "And I'm definitely not reminiscing about a ménage à trois I never had."

She squints an eye at me. "Are you sure you didn't? I swear you gave me the most *lurid* details about the acrobat's—"

"No, Agatha, I didn't," I whisper nervously, taking a quick peek at the wedding guests. Thankfully, they're too enraptured by the bride to hear her. Agatha isn't exactly in the habit of lowering her voice. Ever.

"Hmm. Must be a memory of my own. Forgive me, dear. Going senile," she says with a wink.

"Agatha, if you're senile, then the rest of us are hopeless," I say distractedly. Jasmine and her dad are halfway to the spectacular Victorian arbor covered in white roses, and no one has vomited or started sobbing uncontrollably. *We're almost in the clear.*

"I never get tired of this," Agatha comments softly, pulling my attention from the ceremony. "Seeing my home become the starting point of someone's Happily Ever After." She pauses before saying, almost to herself, "Larkwood was meant to be a place of *hope*. Of new beginnings."

My heart squeezes. A new beginning is exactly what Larkwood and this woman have given me.

The night of my stepsister's wedding, she found me crying in a corner of the ballroom while my whole family cha-cha'd real smooth across the dance floor—fully unaware that I was in the middle of a quarter-life crisis. Between my breakup with Calvin and the swift death of my business, which followed, the bottom of my life had officially fallen out and caught fire.

But after confiding in Agatha—a sympathetic stranger I had no expectation of ever meeting again—she offered me a job on the spot. And even though she isn't in touch with modern costs of living and nearly every precious cent I earn is swallowed by the black maw of my debt, Agatha is the only reason I'm not still sleeping on the lumpy pullout in my mom's basement.

"It really is," I agree, trying not to let the sigh that escapes sound too woe-is-me. Reflexively, I slide my thumb down my unadorned ring finger.

Agatha's eyes cut to mine, and the look she gives me is too all-knowing for my comfort. "He was never going to be your happy ending, sweetheart," she says, like it's a simple fact. "That's something you'll need to make for yourself."

The tightness in my throat turns into a full-fledged lump. Our relationship has always been this way—she might be my employer, but there are times when I suspect she wanted a granddaughter more than a wedding planner when she hired me. Maybe she knew I needed her, too.

"I know that," I say gently. "But sometimes I just . . ."

Her features soften with understanding. "Want to get laid?"

I can't fully repress my surprised laugh, and the cellist nervously glances in my direction.

"*No*, Agatha," I whisper once I've composed myself. "I was going to say that sometimes I wish I could find my person, too."

Admitting this to anyone feels humiliating, but Agatha has already seen me in my rock-bottom sweatpants and helped me remedy my DIY bangs decision, so it's only up from here.

"The only way you're going to do *that* is by forgetting about Kevin and meeting someone new," she says.

I don't mean to snort, but my nose does it anyway. Unless my meet-cute happens in the Sad Food for Wishful Singles aisle at the local Stop & Shop, meeting someone new seems highly unlikely. "I'm not like you, Agatha." I look down at the simple black dress and blazer I wore specifically to fade into the background. "I don't emit a homing signal for the single and fabulous."

"Oh, tosh. You look like Audrey Hepburn with an ass," she says succinctly. "Who doesn't love an Audrey with an ass? Nobody *I'd* associate with." She sniffs. "You're smart, hardworking, and far too kind for your own good. Kevin has no idea what he's missing."

"His name is Calvin, but . . . thank you, Agatha," I say, more than a little touched. "He definitely doesn't know what he's missing."

I say this with confidence because we haven't had any form of contact since we split. Not unless you count the one—fine, *three* times—I've snuck onto his Instagram to torture myself with photos of him bonding with his fellow finance bros over happy hour drinks.

"That's the spirit, honey," Agatha says, rubbing my back. "You know, come to think of it, my grandson is outrageously handsome and single . . ." She trails off, like this thought is occurring to her for the first time, and not the five-hundredth time since I've known her. "He lives—"

"In Providence and doesn't visit nearly enough," I finish for her, thinking of the few glimpses I've caught of him from behind my cottage windows. I know he's tall. That he has carefully schooled, dark wavy hair. He's also always in a suit, he always brings her peonies, and Agatha flat-out refuses to introduce us until I ask her to. Which will be exactly never.

She gives me a wicked grin like she can tell I'm replaying every look I've ever gotten of him. "I'm not pushing," she pushes. "But just say the word and I'll accidentally bring him over while you're scantily clad."

It's not . . . the worst idea. Not the scantily clad part—that *is* terrible. But maybe meeting him. The truth is, I haven't tried dating anyone since Calvin, and yes, I'm *well* aware of how pathetic that sounds.

My phone starts vibrating, and quickly, I peek around the column to see Jasmine and her fiancé clasping hands while the officiant speaks. "Sorry, Agatha, I'm getting a call."

I take my phone out of my pocket but immediately drop it onto the cold flagstones after seeing the caller. Because it's not Mark or Phoebe. It's a video call . . . from *Calvin*?

"Oh my god," I say, crouching down and gingerly picking the phone up like it might detonate. My heart becomes a helicopter in my chest. *Calvin* is video calling me. *Why?* Is this the world's most tragic butt-dial? Or is my secret hope—that he'd grow up a little and realize he let go of the one person who loved him best—about to come true?

Remnants of our last conversation come back to me like darts to the chest. *We're just in different places right now, babe. I'm not ready for the picket fence. Maybe when we're older . . . who knows?*

"Well, are you going to pick it up and give him the finger, or should I?"

Agatha's voice is crisp and businesslike, yanking me back into reality. I try swallowing nonexistent saliva. "I'm going to pick up. Please, Agatha. Keep an eye on the ceremony and let me know if something, I don't know"—I flap a hand—"catches fire."

She harrumphs something about what she'd *like* to see catch fire as I speed walk farther into the shadowed portico. With a last anxious ruffle of my short bangs, I take a deep breath and accept the call.

2

GRACIE

Gracie!" Calvin's handsome face fills the screen, and ten thousand memories I've tried to keep buried claw their way to the surface. He's smiling, his dark blond hair slightly damp, like he's just showered. I inhale and swear I can almost smell his scent of sandalwood and mint. "It's been forever, how are you?"

Speaking. Words. Conversation. The last three decades of experience in these fields are suddenly insufficient. "Cal, hi," I say eventually. "This is unexpected."

He pulls an apologetic face, eyebrows pinching above deep-set blue eyes. "I know, I'm sorry—I didn't catch you at a bad time, did I?"

I glance toward the wedding ceremony I've been hired to ensure goes perfectly, and then to where Agatha is blatantly eavesdropping, looking every inch like a bad-tempered flamingo.

"Um, it's fine! Great, I mean. I'm coordinating a wedding right now, but I have a minute. Is everything okay?" And by that, I clearly mean, *Are you calling to reveal the unwavering torch you've carried for me all this time?*

His grin is back, this time wider than before. I'd forgotten the way it gives him those smile lines around his eyes and—

"Everything's good, good! I'm calling about a wedding, actually. I know we fell out of touch—totally my fault, you know how bad I am at that stuff—but I pop onto your socials once in a while and know you're planning weddings these days. You look fantastic, by the way."

At his completely unembarrassed admission to some light social media stalking, sparkling possibilities spring into my mind like foregone conclusions. I imagine him telling me his sister is getting married, and would I be interested in planning it? Maybe discussing it over dinner and a bottle of red?

"Thanks, Cal, you look really great, too," I say a little too earnestly. "Whose wedding are you calling about?"

His grin slides into something sheepish, and he rubs the back of his damp hair in a gesture I remember all too well. "The thing is . . . well, believe it or not, it's mine." He looses a nervous laugh, as though he can hardly believe it himself.

For a long moment, all I can do is stare, hoping I've misheard him or that this is some kind of punishment nightmare for finding finance bro vests remotely attractive. Absently, I realize my jaw has dropped, right along with what feels like a bowling ball, into my stomach. I'm pretty sure it's my heart.

"I know." He chuckles, oblivious. "I'm the last person anyone expected to get engaged, but I guess when you find the right person . . ." He lets out a sigh, and I swear his eyes go heart-shaped. "You're done for."

"Right person," I repeat through numb lips. All this time, I told myself I was letting go and moving on. But now, all I can think of is the single sentence I've been grasping onto since he ended things. *Maybe when we're older . . . who knows?* Six words. Six words that have fueled my most pathetic fantasies. I've never felt so fucking embarrassed. I begin to shake, and suddenly, getting off this call is more important than my next breath. "Congratulations, Cal. I . . . I'm happy for you," I manage. Barely. "But listen, I have to go. The ceremony is finishing up and—"

Calvin sits up, his relaxed posture disappearing. "Gracie, wait. I haven't even gotten to why I'm calling. The thing is, Brooke and I are in a pickle."

Brooke. Suddenly, my worst nightmare has a name. *Why couldn't it be Mildred?*

"The thing is," he goes on, "we're looking to get married in early August. Maybe even at the end of July, if possible."

My wedding planner brain auto-calculates how long he'd have to plan. "That seems doable," I say. "Fifteen months is more than enough time."

"No, not next August," he corrects me. "*This* August. As in, a little over two months from now."

I blink. "Cal, that's . . ."

"Aggressive?" He chuckles. "I know. But the venue you work at is stunning, and I swear we'd be the easiest clients. Brooke and I don't have time to plan this anyway, so you'd have complete creative control."

"*Me?*" I ask, tempted to look around in case there's another wedding planner hiding in the rosebushes. Until now, it was plausible that he was calling for advice or a recommendation. But at the revelation that he thinks *I'm* the woman for the job, my body temperature quickly begins to climb.

"Look. I wouldn't have asked you, but we *have* to get married in August, and I don't know anyone else who can, or *would*, help us."

For one unthinking millisecond, my traitorous heart has the urge to swoop in and save the day, just to have him back in my life. Just to get the approval I've always craved from him. But the indignity of this task quickly smothers the feeling and then whacks it with a hammer.

"But why the rush?" I ask, redirecting the conversation away from me and the outrageous suggestion that I'm going to help him with this. If he were to set a reasonable date, then he could have his pick of venues and planners—specifically, anyone but *me.* His *ex-girlfriend.* "Surely you both want to enjoy your—" I pause, getting control of the sudden urge to vomit. Or rev a chainsaw. "Engagement," I finish.

This time, I'm not the only one who looks a little queasy. "Ah, well, the thing is . . ." He pauses, looking down at his knees before meeting my gaze again. "I'm going to be a dad." He lets out that disbelieving laugh again, his face turning pink with wonder and nervous joy.

A rogue tear escapes down my face. "Oh my god," I say faintly. I blink down at myself, trying to clear my eyes and half expecting to see a well-aimed spear sticking out of my chest. "A baby. C-congratulations."

The words are automated. A knee-jerk nicety, as all my thoughts are shot down midflight.

"Aw, Gracie! Look at you getting all choked up. That means a lot," he says, like he has no recollection of my own dreams of having kids with him someday. To create the stable, affectionate family I never had myself. He smiles, and the first spark of anger in my chest feels like a flame trying to catch in a drizzle.

"Brookey is only a few weeks along," he goes on, "but she wants to tie the knot before she pops. She's got a *really* conservative family." He grimaces, and I consider ending the call in protest to that nauseating nickname alone. "A big wedding is important to her, so . . ." His voice softens. "It's important to me, too."

It's too much. His audacity is beyond the pale, and before I can stop myself, the words slip past my defenses in a quiet tremor of hurt and disbelief. "Is this some kind of cruel joke?"

He looks aghast. "Gracie, no. God, of course not. I didn't mean to—" He sighs and runs a hand through his hair.

"You didn't mean to what?" I demand as anger begins to burn through my shock. "Ask the ex you completely ghosted to *plan your wedding*?"

To his credit, he looks appropriately ashamed.

"Gracie, please," he implores. "I'm sorry. I know you're the last person I should be asking, but I've never met anyone as organized or creative as you. You're the only person I know who could pull this off, and I'm desperate."

At his flattery, the old, familiar urge to please him rears its head again like a Whac-A-Mole dummy I'm too slow for. This time, it takes more effort to remember that he *knows* I've never been able to say no to him. But even I can recognize that what he's asking is ridiculous to the point of absurd. There isn't a wedding planner in the universe who'd be willing to take on a two-month timeline.

Patience finally snapping, I say, "Why don't you just elope? I'm sure there's an Elvis out there more than happy to do the job."

Calvin shakes his head. "Absolutely not. Brooke's parents would never forgive us, and I won't have them shaming my wife."

My wife. It's another spear to the chest, but at this point, I'm basically an Edible Arrangement sans the fruit. What's one more barren skewer to the heart?

"I can't do this," I whisper, half to Calvin, half to myself.

He shakes his head and leans forward. "Listen," he says desperately. "I know I fucked things up between you and me. I ran away when I shouldn't have, and you didn't deserve it. But neither does Brooke, and neither . . . neither does my kid." He stares deep into my eyes, vulnerable in a way he's never been with me before, and my heart turns over like an engine failing to start. "I love her, Gracie. I love them both, and I want to do this right. *Please*, help me get it right this time. You're my only hope."

I swallow around the softball lodged at the back of my throat as misguided sympathy renders me speechless. He's asking too much. I have enough on my plate as it is without the added trauma of helping him marry the woman I'd hoped to be one day. Of course I'll say no. I have to.

But at his desperate face, careful compliments, and the first hint of an apology I've ever gotten from him, I'm somehow *not* mashing the End Call button when I know I should. Instead, I'm biting my lip, losing a desperate fight against the ingrained urge to avoid disappointing anyone—including Calvin and his pregnant fiancée, who only want the same things I've always wanted. *Safety. Security. Happily Ever After.*

Already, justifications for my bad decision are swirling in my mind. Haven't romance novels taught me that everyone deserves a happy ending, even if they've made mistakes? Calvin and Brooke are never going to find another wedding planner or venue willing to work with this timeline. I honestly don't even know if I'd be able to pull it off. I let out a caged breath. I need to say no, and yet—

"Can you give me a few days to think about it?"

His blond head pops up like a meerkat's. "Yes! Of course! Gracie, you have no idea what this—"

"I haven't said yes," I tell him. "I need to check my calendar and . . . things." And by *things*, I mean my sanity.

"That's fine, take all the time you need. I mean, don't take too long." He laughs nervously. "But thank you, Gracie. From Brookey, too."

I repress the urge to gag. "Goodbye, Calvin."

I end the call and promptly collapse against the cold stone wall. I close my eyes and hear a cheer go up, like 150 people are applauding my idiocy. *The ceremony is over*. From pure muscle memory, I press my earpiece and check in with Mark and Phoebe. When they give me confirmation that they're ready, I know I've got approximately two minutes to pull myself together before I need to make a thousand carefully timed details flow seamlessly together.

I crack open my tear-stung eyes, telling myself to stand up straight, only to find Agatha striding toward me in a fury of pink. I expect a reprimand. Maybe a small slap to the face. But instead, she pulls me from the wall herself and hugs me. The scent of Chanel No. 5 engulfs me, and I let out a small sob.

When she whispers into my hair, her voice is soft. "That man deserves castration."

I gulp down a small laugh. "Agatha, don't—"

She pulls back to hold me at arm's length. Her dark eyes scan my face as she purses her bright red lips together. "But you're still going to help him, aren't you?"

When I don't confirm or deny it, her face softens. "Well, he was right about one thing. You *are* kind. A little too kind for your own good sometimes."

"I could tell him no if you're against it. I could tell him we're completely booked," I say, even as the guilt I know I shouldn't feel begins slinking through me.

"The decision is yours, Gracie. Larkwood is open to them, but only because I think this might give you the closure you need. If you do this, you *have* to promise me you'll try to move on."

Closure. The elusive word that's been outrunning me for the last three years. Maybe this is the way I find it at last. "I promise," I tell her.

She smiles and pats my cheek. "That's my girl. Now dry your tears and go after that bride and groom before they trample my rosebushes. I'm going up to drink champagne in my bathtub."

I can't help my smile. "Of course you are."

The look she gives me is long and tender. "You're going to be okay, sweetheart. You took it on the chin today, but getting back up is what's going to make you stronger."

"Do you think I'll find it, Agatha?" I ask in a quiet voice. "My own Happily Ever After?"

She smiles. "You'll find your great love, Gracie. Something tells me he'll be the *last* person you suspect. But remember what I said earlier. Your Happily Ever After is up to you. Not me, not the future love of your life, and certainly not *Kevin*."

I nod shakily, feeling an almost irrepressible urge to tell this woman, who has been more nurturing to me than my own family, that I love her. But then she's gone, striding off in a twinkle of jewels before disappearing behind the heavy wooden door.

I'm . . . not okay. I'm whatever the opposite of okay is to the power of infinite *Brookies*. But I wasn't okay the night Calvin left me either, and I managed, didn't I? I built a new life for myself, and right now, Jasmine and her family are depending on me. I wipe my tear-streaked face and straighten my back with the confidence of someone who knows that—at the very, *very* least—her day couldn't possibly get worse.

And that's when one of the beautiful white doves released at the ceremony flies beneath the portico, becomes confused, and shits directly on my black blazer.

3

GRACIE

They say when you think things couldn't possibly get worse, that's when they do. Actually, I have no idea if "they" say that at all, but it's the waking nightmare I'm currently living in, so I guess it must be true. Because Agatha . . . is gone.

I blink rapidly, trying not to cry again as the third funeral speaker drones on about Agatha's generous charitable donations. Nearly everyone here is a politician, since Agatha's daughter is the attorney general of Rhode Island. But in this sea of sensible pantsuits and manufactured condolences, grief is a fist slowly crushing my rib cage. Nobody mentions the way she would throw her head back when she cackled or how Elizabeth Taylor used to call *her* for dating advice. None of them know how much she meant to me.

She was found in her bathtub last week, the day after Jasmine's wedding. Heart failure, of all things. Even now, it seems ludicrous to the point of impossible that the woman I knew—with her zero-tolerance policy for bullshit and unflappable belief in the power of love—would succumb to failure of the heart. In the wake of her loss, the organ beating in my own chest feels enfeebled. As though it's suddenly wondering what chance it stands against the battering ram of life if *Agatha Larkwood's* could simply give out? I suck in a calming breath, smoothing out my handmade dress.

In the last week, I put aside all the complicated feelings sewing brings me and re-created the only black dress Agatha would have approved of. It felt like a way to honor her, since she continually asked to see my work from Grace & Veil—my failed bridal wear design business that cheerfully lowered me into the ninth circle of hell (also known as high-interest debt repayment). Sewing after so long had been cathartic, and even though I couldn't afford the genuine satin of the original design, I think I did it justice. I think . . . I think Agatha would have loved it.

The politician steps away from the podium, and I'm hoping it's the last colorless speech I have to sit through when someone from the front pew stands up. Immediately I recognize the hair. The height. The perfectly tailored suit. *Agatha's grandson.*

He walks slowly up to the podium, head bowed. In the cool, dim light of the church, his carefully tamed waves are nearly as dark as his suit. An irrepressible curiosity to finally see his face, and perhaps a hint of Agatha's, has my stomach muscles clenching.

He turns, facing the room at last, and the hinge of my jaw goes slack. The first look I get is of his pale profile. Dark brows, ruler-straight nose, and a soft mouth. His clean-shaven jaw looks like it was designed with a T square and blueprints. The words *outrageously handsome* float back to me in Agatha's voice, and that's before he even turns to face us completely. When he does, I lose any pretense of gazing politely and segue neatly into ogling.

Without looking at anyone, he places a wooden box on the podium and raises the mic by about a foot. He opens the box, and for a wild moment, I think I'm about to see Agatha's ashes. But then he pulls out . . . *a party hat*?

I lean forward, sure I'm mistaken, but no—it's a metallic gold paper cone with a pink pom-pom on top. The church goes silent. No rustle of fabric, no covered coughs, *nothing*, as with complete seriousness, this solemn man in his solemn suit stretches the elastic band and carefully positions the hat on his head at a jaunty angle. He follows this spectacle by reaching back into the box and pulling out a shocking pink feather boa, which he loops precisely behind his neck and over one shoulder.

Then he looks up. His eyes are startling, but not just because they're the color of burnt caramel. It's the way he's glaring at all of us with distinct disapproval while wearing a children's party hat and matching feather boa. Like *we're* the ones acting inappropriately.

"Good afternoon," he says in a voice that's deep and serious. "My name is Jude Larkwood, and I was lucky enough to be Agatha's grandson." Emotion briefly tightens the muscles around his eyes, and he visibly swallows. *Jude.* I turn his name over in my mind like a ruby, realizing only now that Agatha exclusively referred to him as *my grandson.* I never asked her for more details. Never wanted to show interest in him when my heart was so firmly elsewhere. But now, as I see him muster control over grief as unwieldy as my own, the urge to somehow connect with him—with someone else who loved her—is overwhelming.

"As others have mentioned before me," he goes on, "my grandmother was a remarkable woman, known for her generous patronage of the arts and her commitment to preserving Larkwood Estate—one of Rhode Island's greatest architectural treasures. But these are facets of her life that mattered little to me as her grandson." He swiftly brushes a hand beneath his eye. "You may be expecting me to speak about her tenderness. The warmth of her embrace. Perhaps about the cookies she'd bake for me as a child. But she was never that kind of grandmother. The truth is, the nana I grew up with was far more likely to sneak me into a cocktail bar with her theater friends and keep me behaving with sips from her dirty martini."

A small whoop goes up at the back of the church, where those late-arriving theater friends have gathered. Disapproval ripples through the crowd, but all I feel is an invisible rope and grappling hook launch itself directly from my chest toward this man. He *knew* her. Really knew her.

"I don't tell that story to disparage her character," he goes on, "but, instead, to celebrate it. And to also partly serve as an explanation for the last part of my eulogy." He removes a folded piece of paper from the box. "I was one of the lucky few who visited her in the weeks leading up to her passing. When I did, she insisted she didn't know when the world would be deprived of her sparkling presence but gave me firm orders to wear these . . . accessories at her memorial when the day came to pass. She also instructed me to read a poem she'd written to—and I quote—'breathe a little goddamn life into the affair.' So without further ado," he continues, unfolding the paper before him, "the words my grandmother chose to be remembered by." He clears his throat, raises his cleft chin, and says in his resonant voice:

"There was an old girl from Larkwood,
who was often misunderstood.
Except when she lifted
her fine skirts and insisted,
that handsome gents take a tour of her goods.

"Now she's gone and it's shocking
for all the blokes who came flocking.
They'll miss her sweet smiles,
her money and wiles,
but mostly how she had their boots knocking."

He finishes in a tone more appropriate for reading Sylvia Plath, reaches into the box one last time, and pulls out a party horn. He blows it once, the paper unrolling with a loud *toot*, and the laugh that rockets out of me in a spasm of joy and heartache is uncontrollable.

Jude's eyes snap to mine, and I realize with dawning mortification that the rest of the church is completely silent—even her theater friends managed to keep their respectful silence. His eyes widen slightly as he gets a good look at me, and my face becomes the new primary heat source for the Earth. But then, he smiles. It's just the smallest quirk at the corner of his wide mouth, but it transforms that invisible cord between us into an electrical conduit, pulsing with unexpected connection. A corner of my own mouth twitches upward, like a tug on our string.

Jude blinks like he feels it, then drops his lashes. "Thank you, everyone, for coming." Without looking at me or anyone else again, he gathers the items on the podium, removes his party accessories, and walks back to his seat.

I let out a breath when he sits. A woman with dark auburn waves and a similarly square jaw, who I assume is his mother, rubs his shoulder as the priest returns. He closes the service, but I barely hear any of it. My eyes are locked on the back of Jude's head, and I'm already plotting the best way to corner him at the canapé table later. It's probably—no, definitely—a terrible plan. He's grieving, and I'm sure he doesn't want to be accosted by a stranger who basically wore a Halloween costume to his grandmother's funeral.

But in the week since Agatha passed, there hasn't been anyone I could really mourn with. And maybe I'm just desperately projecting my own need for connection, but the way he held my gaze in mutual understanding felt like passing a note in secret. And more than anything else, I need to unfold it.

Entering Larkwood's ballroom in a stream of other funeral-goers, I'm a woman on a mission. Since leaving the church, my need to talk to Jude has condensed into a sharp and specific hope—that maybe if I tell Agatha's grandson how much I loved her, the regret of never having told her myself will feel a fraction less crushing.

Thanks to his height, he's not hard to spot. He makes his way slowly through the crowd, responding to greetings with a reserve that strongly encourages people not to chitchat. But I refuse to be deterred by this, *or* by his cheekbones, which seem biologically designed for intimidation.

Dodging other guests who stare openmouthed at the room's frescoed, velvet-draped splendor, I position myself behind a tall, tropical-looking plant near the bar Jude is headed for. It's the wrong move. The line moves surprisingly fast, and before I can extricate myself and casually sidle up to the bar, Jude is being handed a drink and turning away. He's moments from being greeted by another group of guests, and I stumble quickly from where I'm lurking.

"Jude?"

He turns at the sound of his name, but naturally the spiky plant I've brushed against in my haste decides it wants to hold on to me forever. The long, blade-shaped leaves catch in my carefully swept-back hair, and I rear back a step. Something sharp jabs into my scalp.

"*Shit*," I curse under my breath as I reach up and discover razor-edged leaves that are fully capable of ruining both hair and lives. Desperately trying to unsnarl myself while somehow looking completely chill, I execute a spectacular double-fail. I'm the picture of grace, half bent over with my arms over my head as Jude abandons his drink at the bar and strides toward me.

"Here, let go, you're going to—"

"Ow!" I cry as one of the leaf edges slices across the pad of my thumb.

"Hurt yourself," Jude finishes. I automatically suck the shallow cut between my lips, and then he's standing right next to me. Close enough that I can smell his cologne, which reads explicitly like a fall breeze rustling the crisp pages of a book beside a glass of whiskey. Which is ludicrous and— "Do you mind if I try?"

His voice is deep and soft. Like the kind of feather pillow that seems like a good idea until it swallows your head whole. I release my hurt thumb and raise my eyes to his. As my gaze travels up—and then up some more—I clock every detail of his suit. The expertly cut wool, the elegant roll of his lapels, the perfectly dimpled gray tie. A small, bright pink feather rests on his collar. It nearly makes me smile despite the plant situation, but when my gaze reaches his face, all brain activity dissolves.

Because Agatha's grandson is beautiful. From a distance, it was hard not to stare. Up close, it almost feels awkward *not* to comment on. Like when you're faced with a friend's terrible haircut, only the exact opposite. My gaze stutters up to his eyes, but they're half-shaded as he makes his own curious perusal. It takes me *way* too long to realize he's politely waiting on my answer to his question. *Dear lord.*

"Um, yes," I manage. "That would be grelpful. I mean, helpful. And also great."

Kill me now, Agatha. Take me with you to that infinite bubble bath in the sky and then drown me for good measure.

A corner of his mouth pulls upward, right along with the blood rushing to my face. I want to explain that I don't get out much. That some exposure therapy to handsome men who love their grandmothers would probably do me some good.

"Okay, hold still," he instructs, before lifting his hands to gently explore my tangled strands with a touch I feel in my toes. He sinks perfect white teeth into his bottom lip.

"I'm sorry, there's no saving it," he says after a moment, looking down at me. "Do you mind if I take your hair down?"

I am a guppy. Unable to do more than blink and open my mouth several, pointless times. Finally, I nod, but it pulls at my scalp, and I wince.

"Don't move," he murmurs, eyes back on my hair. He takes a step closer, and then his hands are pulling pins from my chignon, one by one. The bottom half falls heavily around my shoulders, where it isn't caught by spiny leaves. He hesitates a moment, and then his fingers are sinking into my hair, scraping my scalp and freeing the bladelike leaves. I try not to moan. I'm at a *funeral*. But in my defense, the last person who touched me like this was my hairdresser, and her face doesn't make my brain feel like melted cheese.

"Oh my God, thank you," I say, when I'm free.

"Anything to be grelpful," he responds with a smirk, holding out his hand.

At first, I have the bewildering impression that he's about to twirl me into a dance. But then I see the bobby pins in his palm and flush. *Right*. Because I'm not an eloquently spoken debutante at a ball. We're at his grandmother's funeral, and I'm a woman who gets caught in potted plants and invents brilliant new words. I take the pins and put them in my clutch.

"I'd say you surpassed grelpful," I tell him, feeling no choice but to lean into my word vomit. "That was almost neroic."

One of his dark eyebrows lifts. "And that's some variant of . . . *neurotic*?"

"No!" I blurt. "No, it's a combination of *nice* and *heroic*. *Neroic*,"

I repeat, like saying it again might somehow make the situation any less humiliating. It doesn't.

He smiles kindly at me. Like maybe he's used to people completely losing their ability to speak naturally in front of him. "And here I thought you already had an accurate read on my personality."

It pulls an unexpected laugh from me. "I'm sure you can't be too bad," I tell him. "You're Agatha's grandson, after all."

His smile falters and my heart trips over its feet. "You knew her well?" he asks hopefully.

Behind my eyes is a quicksilver montage of my most cherished moments with Agatha. The day she insisted I move into the guest cottage and stop commuting from Providence. The first time she excavated the story of Calvin and assured me that *Every great life needs at least one great heartbreak, darling*. The last time she hugged me, when I missed my chance to tell her how much I loved her.

A tear slips down the side of my nose. "Yes," I whisper. "I knew her."

The step Jude takes toward me is almost imperceptible.

"I could tell," he says quietly. Fervently. "When you laughed at the church."

My shoulders creep toward my ears. "I'm so sorry about that—"

"No, don't be," he says, eyes wide and earnest. "It was such a relief to know I wasn't the only one who—"

"Knew she would have preferred to be scattered at sea on a *Chicago*-themed booze cruise?"

This time, he blows past all the smirks he's given so far and blasts me with a smile so wide and warm, I feel like a cat curling into a patch of sunlight. It cuts smile lines into his cheeks and creases around his eyes, and I'm . . . perfectly fine. Ambivalent, even. Totally neutral over these face-related developments. "Exactly," he says with a laugh that turns into a soft gaze. "I should have known from your dress that you were close with her."

I look down at my careful copy of the world's most iconic little black dress, and a warm buzz begins building inside me. "You recognize it?"

"Of course. Nana made me watch *Breakfast at Tiffany's* anytime I was in a shitty mood."

"It was *Roman Holiday* for me!" I beam, half joyous, half bereaved. *This.* This was exactly what I'd hoped for—a connection with someone I could share my memories of Agatha with. What I didn't expect was this constant fluttering in my chest after years of whatever the opposite of fluttering is. Sputtering, maybe. His gaze skates over my silhouette.

"It's a lovely replica," he says, eyes lingering on the high neckline resting just beneath my collarbones.

I brush a nervous hand through my bangs. "Thank you," I say. "It was fun to sew."

His eyes snap to mine. "You *made* your dress?"

I lift a shoulder. "I've always loved to sew. It seemed like—" I pause, calming the upsurge of emotion. "Like a good way to honor Agatha."

Jude swallows. "She would have loved it. But you're missing your pearls." His gaze traces down one of my bare shoulders, all the way to my hand, and I suddenly feel like a repressed Victorian, scandalously flashing a little too much elbow. "And your gloves."

Something small and shameful squirms in my stomach. I don't want to admit that after buying the fabric, I couldn't afford the costume jewelry or gloves. "I thought people might take offense if I showed up looking like I'd come for a costume party," I say instead.

"I'm honestly surprised Nana didn't stipulate that everyone come dressed in costume."

My eyes drop to the tiny pink feather still on his collar, and before I can think better of it, I reach up to pull it off, my fingers grazing the soft wool of his jacket. I hold it between us, heart thrumming from my daring move. Since when have I made *moves*? The only moves I make are from the safety of my own mind when I've had a little too much wine and think about drunk-dialing Calvin.

Calvin. With a jolt, I realize he hasn't crossed my mind once since Jude saved me from hell's houseplant. It must be a record, but I suddenly realize I've managed to forget not only my ex, but also where I am—at my dear friend's memorial. Guilt is like a hard pinch to my heart. There's got to be some kind of karmic penalty for flirting at a funeral, right? But then I think of Agatha, and a tingle at the back of my neck makes me feel like she's here, eyes sparkling with delight as she watches us. If *anyone* would approve of me flirting at their memorial, it would be her—especially if it was with her grandson.

And so, gathering my courage, I twirl the feather between my fingers as I raise my eyes to Jude's. "I think your costume would have stolen the show no matter what."

He looks dazed, absently raising a hand to where I removed the feather. Then he shakes his head. "I'm so sorry. You know my name, but I haven't gotten yours."

I smile. "Is this when I tell you I have to leave, and then accidentally-on-purpose lose a glass slipper?"

"That depends. Do you have any scary stepsisters? Because you should know, as an only child, I'm completely unqualified to handle an evil stepsibling dynamic."

I grimace, hoping he doesn't pick up on how close he's hit to home. When my sports-obsessed mom remarried, she gained my football-fanatic stepdad and the kind of daughters she always wanted. If I had to sum up Brianna's and Josie's personalities, it would be with the cheer, "Be *AGGRESSIVE*! B-E *AGGRESSIVE*!"

"Unfortunately, yes. They're both division one volleyball champions and could easily wield their muscles for evil."

He sighs. "Well, shit. Guess I'd better practice my serve."

I'm grinning stupidly and try reining it in. "Or, I could just go easy on you. My name is Gracie. Gracie Holland."

"Gracie," he repeats softly. "That fits like a glove."

My chest fluttering promptly turns into a chest rave, and I'm suddenly nervous he'll be able to see a strobe light pulsing beneath my skin.

"And how did you know my nana?"

I exhale. An easy question. "Actually, I work here. I'm the estate's wedding coordinator. Your grandmother hired me three years ago," I tell him.

At this, all the warmth drains from his expression. "*You're* the wedding planner? The one who lives on the property?"

The sudden alarm in his voice is edged with distaste, and I fumble to respond. "Um, yes? Does my reputation precede me?"

Jude rubs his jaw, staring at an unfixed point over my head like he's either mentally shredding his good opinion of me, or wondering if I'll fit in the body bag he keeps in his trunk. *What the hell?*

"Is there a problem with my . . . existence?" I ask, half joking, half desperate to get back to where we were before.

Finally, he looks back down at me, frustration tightening every line of his handsome face. "Frankly, yes."

I step backward, and suddenly, being closer to the sword plant doesn't feel nearly as threatening as Jude. *And this is why we don't flirt with strangers!* a singsong voice chirps inside me.

I rise to my full height. "Well, since I'm so bothersome to you, I'll go find somewhere else to take up oxygen."

He lets out an exasperated sound. "Wait, no," he says as I begin walking past him. He places a hand on my elbow, and I stop, shaking him off. He lets go at once. "I'm sorry. I was just—" He closes his eyes for a moment. "What I meant to say is that your *job* and living situation are the issue. Not you."

My eyes narrow at the bitter way he emphasized the word *job* because that *job* is basically my whole personality these days. The first tendrils of panic begin curling in my stomach. After Agatha passed, I'd naturally wondered what it would be like to work for Larkwood's new owner, but keeping my job wasn't a question. Not when sharing Larkwood as a wedding venue was *so* important to her. Just like the estate's gardeners and maintenance staff, who have continued going about their business, I'd assumed I was essential. My mouth goes so dry it could be a fire hazard.

"What's wrong with my job and living situation?" I try to demand, but it comes out like a croak.

For a moment, he looks apologetic. But then his features firm up like he feels completely justified in dealing the coming hammer blow.

"The issue is that your job and living situation are about to disappear. Larkwood never should have been a wedding venue to begin with, and moving forward, it no longer will be. Your termination notice was going to be given on Monday."

It's unclear if the roaring I hear is from the surrounding crowd or the blood rushing in my ears. *No.* This has to be another joke. Any moment now, he's going to grin and say *GOTCHA!* Because after the week I've had—after what happened with Calvin and losing *Agatha*—losing my home and livelihood on top of it all seems too catastrophic to be allowed.

"No," I blurt, when the pressure inside of me builds to a whistling heat. "No, you must be mistaken. It was Agatha's greatest joy to share her home as a wedding venue."

Jude's mouth tightens. "Well, it's no longer her home, unfortunately."

"Who is even making this decision?" I demand, looking around the room at funeral guests, like I might see someone casually leaning on a pitchfork. "I'd like to have a word with them."

Jude frowns. "You are having a word with them. I'm Larkwood's new inheritor."

My eyes go round, and I'm almost positive the dramatic *DUM-DUM-DUM* sound wasn't just in my head. He isn't carrying a pitchfork, but my eyes immediately jerk to his dark waves, searching for horns.

"But you can't do this!" I exclaim. "I have weddings lined up into the fall. Clients who booked us well over a year ago!" I don't voice the more personally pressing matter of depending on this job to pay off my debt and generally avoid living under a bridge.

He looks around the opulent ballroom we're standing in, and there's no mistaking the bitterness in his expression. "I'm sorry, Gracie, but I'm canceling all upcoming weddings. The person interested in the estate needs it by August, and I need to prepare the property for the transfer."

Tears spring to my eyes. "But our clients have signed contracts! Is it even legal to cancel their weddings?"

Jude straightens. "Since Larkwood is also a private residence, there's a clause maintaining the right to cancel all events during a family crisis."

"So, that's that? Your grandmother's gone for three seconds and you've already decided to turn her beloved home into . . . into luxury condos, or something?"

"No, not condos," he says, with the decency to look slightly ashamed. "Not exactly."

"Oh, 'not exactly'? How comforting. And what's going to happen to all my clients who expect to get married here? Do you even *know* how stressful this will be for them? No one needs their marriage to start off on that kind of rocky footing. Relationships are hard enough as it is!"

At this, he's cold and impassive. "I'm aware that it's an inconvenience, but I'm happy to break the news to them and issue refunds if you're not up to the task."

"Not up to the—" I sputter, infuriated. "Don't even *think* about contacting my clients, I'm perfectly cap—" I stop with a gasp, because I've just realized something else. "You understand that if you fire me," I say with mounting horror, "you're also firing dozens of local wedding vendors who rely on Larkwood, right? We have exclusive relationships with so many incredible people who would be devastated to lose that income." I take a choked breath as I think of Angie from The Love Notes, supporting her little girl with special medical needs. My friend Valerie from Sweetly Ever After Cakes, who's just finding her footing after becoming a single mom, and so many more. "This can't be happening," I say, feeling faint.

Jude shifts his weight in the universal sign of guilt. But before I can get my hopes up that maybe he *is* a decent person, he doubles down. "I assure you, it's happening."

"But what about your grandmother?" I say, grasping my last ace. "Don't you even *care* about her wishes?"

Jude's eyes harden, and I wonder if I just imagined all their warmth before. "Unfortunately, Nana and I never saw eye to eye on the best use for the estate."

"Best use?" I repeat incredulously. "Larkwood was *made* to be a wedding venue—it's one singing candelabra away from out-fairy-tale-ing the Disney castle! Your nana intended Larkwood to be the place all our clients will think of when they remember the best day of their lives."

Instead of having the impact I want, my impassioned speech only elicits an epically bored eye roll. "Until they're at each other's throats in mediation, fighting over who gets custody of the Peloton."

His bitter words make my jaw go slack. Agatha was romance incarnate, and this grouch is supposed to be her *grandson*. If it weren't for the dead ringer height and can't-be-bought bone structure she passed on to him, I wouldn't believe it.

"You're . . . you're a *cynic*," I finally say, aghast.

He tucks a hand into the inner breast pocket of his jacket. "I'm afraid that doesn't quite cover it." He pulls out a card and hands it to me. "Here. In case the road proves too rocky for your clients."

Numbly, I take the weighty card.

JUDE LARKWOOD, ESQ., CA
Divorce and Family Law Attorney

"You have *got* to be joking."

"Unfortunately not. Take care of yourself, Gracie. I'm sorry we couldn't meet under better circumstances."

But I'm barely listening to his false platitudes. His slimy apologies. This man is my natural nemesis, and I'm already busy plotting how to fix this because one thing is certain: I'm not giving up my home, my future, and Agatha's legacy without a fight.

"Oh, this isn't the last you've heard of me," I threaten. "You may not care about this estate, but *I* do, and so did Agatha. If there's any way to save Larkwood from your . . . your *clutches*, then that's what I'm going to do. And you can keep your card." I fling it at him and notice I'm also still gripping the tiny pink feather I'd shamefully planned to keep. "*And* your feather." I flick this at him, too, but it has the projectile force of . . . a feather.

He's speechless as they both fall to the floor, and I take the opportunity to march past him, shoulders bunching around my neck.

The sooner I'm in my cottage—my *home*—the better. Then I can figure out how the hell I'm going to save this place—not just for myself, but also for my clients, my vendors, and for Agatha's memory. Because if there's one thing she taught me, it's that fresh starts and fragile hope need a home, too. Larkwood gave me mine, and I'll be damned if I let him lock those doors for good.

4

JUDE

The first time I saw my best friend, Henry, he was passed out and upside down on a children's slide with a dick drawn on the side of his face. It was his nineteenth birthday, and his first time drinking. You'd never guess it's the same man I'm looking at right now, though. Not with his horn-rimmed, *numbers-are-fun!* glasses or his somber, this-is-going-to-hurt expression.

"Just tell me," I intone as we walk into Larkwood's warm and cluttered kitchen. When I was growing up, it used to be one of my hideouts, since it was one of the few rooms that didn't feel like it should charge an admission fee.

Henry tosses the thick leather folio that contains my grandmother's will onto the kitchen island with a slap. "I'll make you a PB and J first," he says, moving toward the walk-in pantry.

I repress a sigh. There's no point trying to stop Henry when he wants to feed you. He'll only tell you that you're making his Indian and Italian genetics hurt until you eat.

He returns with ingredients before looping around the island to the refrigerator, which is still covered in a humiliating gallery of every buck-toothed, cow-licked, pimpled phase of my childhood. I don't have the heart to take it down, despite knowing I'll be living at Larkwood every weekend for the foreseeable future. The thought gives my stomach a sloshy spoiled milk feeling, but there's no way out of it. Nana named me as her executor, and there's no one else I'd trust to manage her possessions and final wishes. I close my eyes as the pain of losing her rises in me so fast that I feel vertigo.

Why didn't you tell me you were dying, Nana? Why couldn't I get over my bullshit and visit you more when I had the chance?

"See? You're dead on your feet." My friend tuts like a mother hen. "You need some nourishment." He sticks four slices of bread into the toaster.

"You don't need to toast the bread," I grumble.

A patient smiles stretches over his features. "You'll be thanking me in a minute, asshole."

I flop onto a barstool. I'm too tired to argue. Between finishing up my current cases, fighting with my mother over Nana's wishes, having to be in the same fucking zip code as my father, and losing one of the painfully few people I truly love, it's been two of the shittiest weeks in recent memory. And that's not even counting what happened with the wedding planner. *Gracie.*

Shame and anger needle the back of my neck at the memory, and I automatically glance at the nearest window. She still lives here after all. But beyond the glass, the lush kitchen garden is empty. What does it say about me if I'm disappointed? That I wouldn't mind getting glared at again by those dark eyes?

Probably that I need to get laid.

The sound of the toast popping up makes me jolt, and Henry makes a soft tsking sound. "Did you even hear what I just said?"

I jerk my eyes away from the window. "Sorry. It's been a long two weeks."

"Forgiven." Henry lays the toast on the cutting board before digging into the jam with a knife. "I was saying that you have your work cut out for you. Your grandmother gave direction for the major things, but there's a lot of antique sorting and last request management ahead of you."

If I were more naive, I'd hope this was the worst news awaiting me. But when Henry starts making comfort food, it generally means I should schedule something with my therapist.

"She didn't contract the estate out to *Dancing with the Stars*, did she?" I say darkly.

Henry chuckles, now layering the two sandwiches with potato chips. "Good guess, but no."

"Who puts potato chips on a PB and J?" I ask him, distracted.

"Unappreciated saints," he answers, before starting on the peanut butter. "How's the Rocher case, by the way?"

I drop my forehead to the butcher-block counter, slowly rolling it back and forth. "I thought you were trying to make me feel better," I say, voice muffled against the wood.

"That bad, huh?"

Yes, that bad. For a good portion of my job, I'm able to work with people who don't suck. Ninety-nine percent of the time, those people are my pro bono clients. I can't say the same for the ones who pay my bills. Thankfully, my team was incredibly understanding when Nana passed, and this is the last billable case I have to finish before taking a six-week break to handle the estate. But until then, I'll be mediating disputes over who gets Hay Girl Hay—the thoroughbred neither my client nor her soon-to-be ex-husband ever sees, but are willing, apparently, to duel at dawn over. Reluctantly, I sit up and look at him with dead eyes.

"Eat your sandwich," he says, pushing the plate toward me. "You'll feel better."

I take a bite, and somehow, he's right. The warm, gooey filling is balanced perfectly by the salty crunch of the chips. "Fuck." I groan with my mouth full. *When was the last time I ate?*

"Dude, gross. If I wanted to hear your *O* noises, I would have brought you a Neiman Marcus catalog," he says, throwing a cloth napkin at me before taking a bite of his own sandwich.

I shrug. Henry has been giving me shit for dressing well since I met him. But underneath it all, I know he's grateful I helped him outgrow the tucked polos and khakis I've come to think of as his Golf Period.

He also knows it was Nana who taught me to appreciate companies that actually pay their workers a living wage and make clothes that last longer than six months. At the realization that I'll probably never get to nerd out over French seams with anyone else, my heart tumbles a little deeper into the hole that opened up when she passed.

And then I remember a little black dress, perfectly tailored to hug every gaze-demanding curve it accentuated. *Gracie.* Gracie, who loved my nana. Gracie, who gave me breath enough to laugh when my grief was suffocating. Gracie, who'd be thrilled to see me roll around butt-naked in poison ivy. I push the now-empty plate away, disgusted with myself. Did I *actually* give her my business card?

Yes, you did. Because she asked if you even cared about Nana's wishes, and you just had *to lash out.* Regret tightens my chest, but I've had to field the same goddamn question from my mother at every turn, and unfortunately for Gracie, I'd finally hit my breaking point. Because Nana meant more to me than pretty much anyone, and while I'm 90 percent sure she would support my plans for the estate, the other 10 percent is riddled with doubt. But I can't ask her about it. Because she's gone now, and all that's left is this *fucking* house that has only ever felt like a monument to secrets and lies.

"Christ, Judy. What did those crumbs ever do to you?"

I glance up from my plate, which I've been glaring at. I let out a slow breath. "Sorry. It's been—"

"A long two weeks," Henry finishes for me, putting our plates in the sink. "Well, I hate to say it, but it's about to get longer."

"Let's have it," I say, sitting up straighter.

He unzips his folio to reveal a hefty stack of paper, fringed with color-coded tabs. "So, the good news," he begins, leafing through some pages, "is that Agatha left you the main estate and its grounds outright. Because it was privately owned and she declined having it listed on the National Register of Historic Places, Larkwood isn't subject to preservation laws, in the traditional sense."

I nod. *Thank fuck.*

"However."

Never mind.

"She did set up her own preservation clause. It's quite detailed and stipulates a number of specific contractors who specialize in historic restoration, and one carpenter who is, and I quote, 'finer than a thirty-two-year-old Patrick Swayze.'"

I pinch the bridge of my nose as the headache that's been my constant companion for the last two weeks pulses in friendly greeting. *Christ, Nana.* I think of the person interested in the estate. It won't be news to them that ownership will mean putting up with certain maintenance burdens, but with a preservation clause . . . I chew my lip. It'll be another hurdle to cross, but not impossible. Not when I'm prepared to donate any organ they may need if it means ridding myself of this place.

"Okay. That's fine," I say, waving a hand for him to continue.

"Are you sure you're not still hungry?" he hedges.

"Come on. It can't be that bad."

He sighs and pulls off his glasses, carefully folding them.

Shit.

"Okay. The bad news is that while the majority of the estate *was* left to you, there's a small piece of it that wasn't. I know you had plans on selling to a buyer whose privacy is of the utmost importance, and this development . . . complicates things."

"What the hell are you talking about?" I ask calmly, despite my slowly rising panic. Privacy isn't just important to the person considering the acquisition—their interest *hinges* on it.

Henry clears his throat, shuffling the pages of the folio until he finds the right one, marked with a red tab. *Fitting.* The color of emergencies and Satan's ass. "It says here that the guest cottage has been bequeathed outright to one Gracie Holland." Henry looks up. "No idea who that might be, do you?"

All at once, I feel like I need to sit down. But I am fucking sitting down. Head swimming, I struggle to form words. To form thoughts.

"Jude. Hey, man, are you okay?"

When I don't answer, I hear him quickly walk off somewhere and then the sound of running water. Moments later, I'm being nudged. "Drink."

Numbly, I do as I'm told, but when the glass is drained, I still haven't accepted the incomprehensible fact that Nana left an essential piece of the estate to her *wedding planner*. *Why?* My prejudices against the entire institution of marriage gather like an acrid film at the back of my throat, but my personal opinions don't matter. What *matters* is that the person willing to take on this behemoth money pit will *not* accept it if someone else is living on the grounds. *Fuck, fuck*, fuck.

"Talk to me, Judy."

Henry looks about three seconds away from making me a stress lasagna, so I do my best to sit up and answer him. "I know Gracie Holland. Or at least, I've met her."

"Okay, that's a start," he says, clapping and rubbing his hands together like my own personal positivity coach. "Was she a friend of your grandmother's? If she's elderly, she may not be up for moving. She might be willing to sell it to you."

I think of Gracie storming away in her snug little dress, her glossy, dark hair a mess around her shoulders. Heat creeps up the back of my neck, and my hand jerks up to loosen my collar. "No, she's definitely not elderly."

Henry's eyes narrow, assessing me. "You mean she's hot."

"That's not what I said."

"And *that's* not a denial," he drawls with a shit-eating grin.

"Acknowledging whether or not she's attractive has no relevance to this conversation or the issue of getting her to sell the cottage to me," I snap.

Henry's mouth turns down as he weighs this. "Not necessarily. You could always just seduce her for it."

I know he's only joking, but the thought spins images of touching her again in my mind like cotton candy, obscuring all reason and sense. Until I remember what happened. A bitter laugh spools out of me. "Not likely. I haven't mentioned the best part of all this."

"Which is?"

I pull a hand down my tired, scratchy face. "She can't fucking stand me."

Henry lets out a long-suffering exhale. "What did you do?"

So I tell him. Not about her bell-like laugh at the church, or how it made me feel like I wasn't alone for the first time since Nana had passed. I definitely don't mention what pulling bobby pins from her hair did to me during my grandmother's memorial luncheon, of all places. Nope, I don't tell him any of *that*. Instead, I tell him about her unique work and living situation, and how I've ruined any chance of getting the cottage by destroying her life and making myself less likable than an ingrown toenail.

"Christ on a bike," Henry mutters, rubbing a dark eyebrow until the hairs are sticking out in every direction.

"Not helpful, Hen."

"*I'm* not helpful? I beg to differ! *I* break bad news with peanut butter and jelly sandwiches. I don't go full *Terminator* on innocent, grieving women who happen to be the key to all my future happiness."

He makes a point. In my defense, I didn't *know* she was the key at the time, but I somehow doubt Henry will give two shits. He walks back around the island and begins aggressively shuffling papers back into his folio. I rarely see him angry, but right now, the frustration rolling off him could kill grass.

"You're right. I was a dick," I say, hoping the admission might calm him. "I regretted what I did the second she walked away."

"Then *apologize*. She lives on the grounds, right?"

At the thought of seeing Gracie again, even if it's to beg for forgiveness, I feel like I've swallowed a lightning bolt. But no. I need time to—

"I'm going to see her," Henry announces.

My head snaps up as he begins walking. I practically knock my stool over in my haste to follow. "No, wait. Stop."

But he's striding toward the kitchen door that leads to the garden, which isn't far from the cottage.

"Henry, please," I say as he opens it, letting in a swirl of rose-scented air and sunlight. "Let me apologize to her on my own."

He finally turns to look at me. "Jude, as the probate lawyer on the case, I need to tell her about the will. Also, if you want any hope of selling Larkwood to Bono or whoever it is, you're going to need that cottage. Just do yourself a favor and let me handle it."

"I can handle it just fine," I say through my teeth.

His gaze turns pitying. "Listen. I stopped expecting you to tell me why you hate this place so much a long time ago. It's fine. Keep your secrets. But I *do* know you're going to be seriously considering arson until it's off your hands, and I want to keep you out of prison."

"And how exactly are you going to convince her to sell the cottage to someone she'd love to push off a cliff?"

"Easy. Property taxes."

He begins walking again, and I put a hand on his shoulder. "Wait."

He stops, and I take a breath, trying to find the words to explain feelings I hardly understand myself. "I know I fucked up. She didn't deserve to be let down so hard, and I want to make amends if I can. At the funeral luncheon, before I—"

"Gave her your divorce lawyer card to pass on to all her newlywed clients?" Henry says dryly.

I wince. "Yes. Before that, we . . . connected." The word feels foreign in my mouth and mortifying when Henry's eyebrows shoot up. He knows I don't typically *connect* with anyone unless it involves swiping right and sending them a photo of my driver's license. I push through. "Gracie knew Nana really well. I think telling her the news myself could help repair things. Maybe."

Henry is eyeballing me doubtfully, but before he can come to a decision, we both spot someone on the far side of the garden. It's Gracie.

"Shit, is that her?" Henry whispers, and suddenly I feel like we're a couple of middle schoolers spying on a girl.

We watch as she walks along the sunlit garden path that winds through much of the grounds, pausing occasionally to stretch. She's wearing running shoes, faded blue yoga pants that show off every inch of her long legs, and a cropped white T-shirt that does almost nothing to conceal her hot-pink sports bra.

I try clearing my throat, but it's gone so dry it makes no difference. "Yeah. That's her."

"Gracie!" Henry promptly calls out, and I have to physically restrain myself from pushing him into a bush and diving in after him.

Alarmed, Gracie's head snaps toward us, her thick, dark ponytail swinging. Even from here, I can tell the moment she spots me. Her wide eyes narrow as she crosses her arms over her chest.

"Gracie, do you have a second?" Henry calls out again, already striding toward her. I have no choice but to follow.

When we reach her, she's every bit as lovely as she was at the funeral, even in worn-out leggings with holes at the knees. Suddenly remembering the estate's payroll I've been reviewing, and the pitiful salary my well-meaning but out-of-touch Nana paid Gracie, I frown. She frowns right back.

"Let me guess: you're here to evict me," she says, dark eyes flitting from me to Henry and back.

"No, of course not," Henry answers with a smile. "Jude just wanted to say hi since we saw you passing. He said that you, ah, *connected* at Agatha's funeral."

I'll murder him. It's actually the perfect solution—I'll go to prison for life and never have to deal with this clusterfuck again. Gracie shoots me a look that says she knows very well that I would have chosen a tax audit over saying hi.

"In a manner of speaking," she mutters.

"I'm sorry, but we haven't been introduced. I'm Henry Khan," he says, holding out a hand.

Gracie takes it dubiously. "And you're the person he's selling Larkwood to?"

Henry laughs handsomely while I continue to lurk next to them like a tree with anxiety issues. "No, definitely not. For one, my pockets aren't that deep, and two, a place like this deserves better than a bachelor with a secret Bagel Bites addiction."

At this, Gracie's lips quirk into an almost-smile, and an unexpected twinge of jealousy has me speaking up for the first time. "Henry is my best friend. He's also the probate lawyer handling the transfer of the estate. Henry, this is Gracie Holland, Larkwood's wedding planner."

"Don't you mean *ex*–wedding planner?" she says, leveling me with a gaze sharp enough to slice through my button-up. "Or have you decided that you actually care about preserving your grandmother's legacy?"

Henry shoots me a nervous look. Some small, rational part of my brain is shouting at me not to take her bait. But all my hurt, grief, and anger roar louder, and I may as well be a dragon she just poked directly in the eyeball.

"The responsibility of preserving my grandmother's legacy is exactly that: mine. And while you may think you knew her, I'd thank you for trusting that I was a *little* closer to her than an employee."

At this, Gracie stands straighter, the light flush of her cheeks deepening to a color so pretty, I notice it even in my state of ire. Until she says, "That's funny, because I only ever heard her refer to you as the 'grandson who doesn't visit enough.'"

Her words burrow deep as daggers, and I struggle to recover. She has no idea. *No* idea how difficult it is for me to even stand in this house's shadow, let alone enter it. She has no idea how cowardly I felt every time I turned down an invitation to visit, or how the shame of every missed opportunity now drags behind my every step.

She goes on. "If you were *actually* close with Agatha, then you wouldn't be dismantling everything she worked so hard to establish."

At this, the guilt she stoked in me at the memorial burns to life, but my fury flares hotter. I step closer, nonnegotiable anger urging me forward until she has to tip her head back to look at me. "You think I don't know that she loved turning this place into a wedding venue?" I bite out. "Of course she did. She was sentimental and lonely, and frankly, it was good business." Her eyes go wide and indignant, but I keep going, unable to stop. "But if there's *any* silver lining about her passing, it's that I can finally find a use for Larkwood that doesn't feed some commercialized fantasy of *Happily Ever After*."

She blinks, unable to hide the hurt my words have inflicted. My guilt is instant, even if everything I've said is true. Considering the current divorce rate, it's ludicrous that people spend so much on a single day they'll probably have to legally untangle down the line anyway. In my admittedly unpopular opinion, the wedding industry is a callous, exploitative machine, and hopeless romantics like Gracie just perpetuate it. And no, I'm not fun at parties either.

"Well, at the very least, now I know who I'm up against," she says, staring at my face like she's finally got the right measure of me, and it isn't impressive.

"You mean the most qualified person to make decisions regarding the estate?" I clarify.

"I was going to say the Scrooge of weddings, but whatever helps you sleep at night, Ebenezer," she tosses at me.

From my left, Henry snorts, and Gracie and I both startle, having totally forgotten his presence. Gracie looks flustered and says, "Anyway. If you aren't here to frog-march me out of my home yet, then I'm going on my run. Henry, it was nice to meet you."

And with one last glare at me, she takes off. In an effort not to run after her to either argue some more or grovel, I turn to Henry, who's covering his grin with his fist. At the look I give him, he lowers his hand, forcing his face into a semineutral expression he's able to maintain for less than three seconds.

"Well, it's a good thing you handled that so tactfully. Really could've screwed yourself if—"

"Please shut up," I groan, turning to walk back to the house.

He falls into step beside me, still grinning. "You know, I'm more than happy to take over negotiations, Ebenezer."

"No," I snap. "Just let me deal with it."

Henry gets to the door first and opens it for me, but mutters, "Just trying to help, man."

I exhale, digging a hand into my hair. "I'm sorry. I know."

"Look," Henry says as he closes the door behind him. "It's obvious you're both hurting over Agatha. *Use* that, Jude. Connect over your mutual loss instead of bickering over who knows what's best for Larkwood."

"But I *do* know what's best."

Henry sighs, grabbing his folio from the kitchen island and walking toward the exit. "Good luck, Judy. Text when you need me to save your hopeless ass."

He walks away without waiting for a response, hand lifted in a wave. Miserably, my gaze swings to the window, looking at where Gracie literally ran away from me.

Earning her trust again won't be easy. But if I want any chance of getting that cottage, I'll need to find a way back to her good side—even if it's just a sliver of a ledge that I'm destined to keep falling off.

5

GRACIE

Seven Weeks Before the Wedding

So who do we need to hex?" are the first words out of my best friend's mouth when I let myself into her apartment and collapse on the transient Marketplace couch I suspect has cushioned half of all the butts in Providence. It's been two days since my run-in with Jude and Henry, and almost nothing could have tempted me to leave my home when I'm half expecting an eviction notice and a roll of trash bags to show up on my stoop—*except* Sofia's dad's empanadas.

"No one," I answer her firmly, not in the mood for a candle wax burn or a tarot card reading that guarantees my future suffering. Sofia and I went through a witchy phase at RISD, the art school we attended for college, but while my own belief in magic was crushed beneath the weight of adulting, hers remains intact. My muscles relax as I take in the familiar decor—half candles and crystals, half organized business owner. On top of moonlighting as my wedding photographer, Sofia also runs an arts community where creatives rent studio space.

"Anyway, aren't there repercussions for hexing people?" I ask. "Like seven years bad luck?"

Sofia comes back from the kitchen with a plate piled high with flaky pastries I know are stuffed with slow-cooked pork in cinnamon-laced tomato sauce. My mouth waters. Mr. Morales doesn't make them often, but when he does, he knows to make enough leftovers.

"See! I knew I could bring back the witch in you," Sofia says delightedly, setting the plate down on her coffee table. "But no, seven years bad luck is the mirror thing. What you're referring to is the Law of Threefold—whatever energy you put into the universe gets returned to you three times over."

"And you're willing to risk getting the threefold shaft by hexing people for me?"

"*The Threefold Shaft* sounds like every erotica book I want to read," she replies, folding her petite frame to sit cross-legged on the couch next to me so that her knee is digging into my hip.

I snort as we simultaneously grab empanadas. My first bite of warm, tender pastry feels like an explosion of nostalgia in my mouth. I close my eyes and I'm back in the Morales kitchen—my favorite place on earth besides Larkwood.

When I was growing up, Sofia's house felt far more like home than the two houses my parents used to shuttle me between like an inconvenient house guest. After school, I'd soak in the love and comfort of people who would load my plate with second helpings and fuss over me like I mattered. I would watch Sofia's dad twirl Mrs. Morales in the kitchen despite her rolling eyes, and ache for the kind of everlasting love and stability they had. Even now, they're the reason I still believe Happily Ever Afters exist.

The inner corners of my eyes prick, and I know I'm seconds away from falling apart again. Sofia rests her head on my shoulder, her dark curls tickling my cheek. "Tell me what's going on, Gracie. And don't leave anything out."

I blink away the sting in my eyes. "Well, the long story short is that I'm about to spend my every last penny on a billboard that has the words *ASS WIPE* printed over Jude Larkwood's forehead."

At her raised eyebrows, I sigh and launch into my tale of woe. Once I've updated her on everything that's happened, Sofia's delicately tattooed hand comes up to cover her mouth, brushing her small silver septum ring. "Gracie, that is just . . . so much. Like, the motherload of shitty luck, especially after Agatha's passing. But listen." She grabs my empanada-free hand, squeezing tight. "Once the dust settles and you get a plan in place, I think it might be for the best."

"For the *best*?" I repeat. "In what realm of possibilities is this not the worst-case, apocalyptic scenario for me?

Sofia winces but goes on. "I'm not saying that this doesn't suck in a completely monumental way. But it's been three years," she says, leaving the past unspoken. *Three years since Calvin left you. Three years since your business imploded and you ran away from the world.* "I know you love Larkwood, but I don't think it's healthy for you anymore."

When I struggle to get words out past my hurt feelings, she quickly goes on. "I mean, I think everyone has the right to float around in long nightgowns and lick their wounds in an enchanted cottage after something like that but . . ." She sighs. "Maybe it's time to leave the cottage-core life behind and try your hand at Grace & Veil again. You know I'd make room at KILN for you."

Throughout this entire speech, my spine has gotten stiffer and stiffer. At the name of my failed business, it could support a concrete dock.

"So, you're saying I shouldn't even fight this?" I ask. "And just reopen a business that'll cost me *another* mountain of money I don't have?"

Sofia's lips press together as her hand leaves mine. "There are always startup costs to a new business."

I shake my head, suddenly exhausted. "I couldn't take that risk again even if I wanted to. No bank on the planet would give me a loan right now. At this point, I doubt they'd even lend me a hand if I fell flat on my face in their lobby."

"Okay, but what about *Randy*?" she demands, pulling out the big guns.

Something pinches in my chest. Named for the host of *Say Yes to the Dress*, my middle school obsession, *my* Randy is a bedazzled keepsake box, stuffed with sketchbooks, fabric swatches, and broken dreams. Thinking of it now is like a swift kick to my inner child.

"I still sew!" I insist. "I sewed my dress for Agatha's funeral."

"That's great," Sofia allows. "And when was the last time you made anything before that?"

"I made that custom bunting for my sister's bachelorette party, remember?"

Sofia gives me a flat look. "Sewing the words *SAME DICK FOREVER* onto little triangles for your scary stepsister doesn't count."

I make an exasperated sound. "I know you're trying to be supportive, but not every childhood dream is destined to work out, okay? Maybe mine was supposed to be a stepping stone into some actual stability for once in my life."

Sofia tucks her hair behind her ear with an impatient flick of her hand. "A stepping stone, my ass. I think all the bullshit Calvin used to say about getting a 'real job' finally sank its claws in. I think you were on the cusp of making a name for your brand, and then the breakup destroyed your confidence."

"Calvin wasn't wrong, Sof. Being able to pay my student loans on time and more than the bare minimum on my credit cards . . . it's been a game changer. I just need to get back on my feet, and I want to do it at Larkwood."

"But, Gracie," she says slowly, "how on earth do you plan on fighting this? If Agatha's grandson wants to sell the estate, what can you do to stop him?"

I shift on my seat and grab my empanada again to avoid eye contact, mumbling, "Well, I do kind of have a plan."

I'm about to lift the pastry to my mouth when it's snatched away. "Nuh-uh," Sofia scolds. "No treats till you spill this so-called *plan*."

I groan, forcing myself to turn toward her. "You're not going to like it."

Her eyebrows lower. "On a scale of one to this-calls-for-an-intervention?"

"Probably closer to the range of 'this-calls-for-a-lobotomy,'" I warn.

Sofia closes her eyes and takes a deep centering breath. With an empanada in each hand at her knees, she looks like a meditation leader with excellent taste in snacks. When she opens her eyes again, she's ready. "Okay, hit me."

With no comforting pastry to clutch, I pull down the faded baby quilt Sofia's abuela made from the back of the couch and just rip off the Band-Aid. "Calvin called me."

"WHAT?" Sofia's voice is so loud in the empty apartment that I almost throw the blanket over her head to muffle the noise.

"I haven't even told you the bad part yet!"

"Oh my God, okay." She stuffs the empanada into her mouth and takes an enormous bite, which I'm assuming is supposed to serve as a scream-preventative.

Before I lose my nerve or she has a chance to swallow, I say, "He's getting married, having a baby, and he asked me to plan the wedding at Larkwood."

In an instant, the scream-preventative bite turns into a life-threatening air blockage as Sofia starts choking. "Sofia, oh my God!" I say, scrambling to my knees on the couch. "I don't know the Heim-licher!"

But then she starts coughing, her face bright pink. I sit back down and put my hands on her shoulders, needing to know she's okay. To my surprise, she starts laughing.

"The Heimlicher?" she wheezes. "I think you mean the Heimlich."

My own face floods with heat. "Stop laughing—you almost died, and you *know* I misspeak when I'm nervous!"

Mortifying memories of *grelpful* surface, but I don't linger on them. Not when Sofia's mirth quickly fizzles and she says, "What the hell, Gracie? Why did you even pick up his call? He's the king of vest-wearing, finance-bro douchebags!"

Cheeks still pink, her eyes look ready to shoot lasers at anyone who dares to wear a vest in her presence. "I know," I say, too cowardly to admit that I've been crying to sad girl breakup ballads every night for the past two weeks. "I was really angry when he called, too, and at first, I told him absolutely not. But he begged me to reconsider, and then Agatha passed, Jude . . . happened, and I had this idea for how to save Larkwood."

"Okay, let's hear it," she says grumpily.

"Well, as I've established, Jude is trying to ruin my life. But *be-fore* I learned his plans for the estate, we kind of . . . bonded over Agatha," I say, deciding not to mention the initial fluttery feelings and attraction he promptly fly-swatted to death with his business card. "He loved her, but I just don't think he understands how important Larkwood was to her. And yes, maybe he happens to be a jaded divorce lawyer," I go on quickly, ignoring the way her eyes bug at this inconvenient detail, "but I also *know* he feels guilty about all the vendors he's screwing over—you included," I point out. "He was practically squirming in his loafers when I mentioned everyone who would be devastated by Larkwood closing."

"Okay, but how exactly does this relate to planning your ex-dickwad's wedding? Why not just beg him to keep one of the weddings he canceled to prove your point?" she asks.

"Because showing up to a wedding that's already been planned is just going to a party," I explain. "But if I can convince him to let me plan Calvin's wedding, then I can bring him into the process and have him meet all the vendors who would be impacted. And who knows. Maybe he'll even grow a heart along the way."

For a moment, she just stares at me, while irrational hope practically beams out of my pores. "Gracie, he's a divorce lawyer," she finally says. "Your natural predator."

"All of my brilliant scheming, and *that's* what you decide to focus on?" I demand, taking my empanada back and biting into it.

"Well, yes, since this entire ridiculous plan depends on you convincing a man who literally ends marriages for a living to suddenly see the romantic side of life and keep an estate he doesn't want because *weddings are magical.* And that's *if* he lets you plan it, period."

Desperation wells inside me. "You're forgetting the brilliant part where I guilt him into it!"

Sofia's features soften. "Okay, Gracie. I know you're going to try this no matter what I say, so I'll be in your corner. I promise I won't even photoshop eye bags and pimples into Calvin's wedding photos if you pull this off."

I smile, relief ballooning inside of me. "Well, maybe just one pimple."

She smiles before her face clouds with concern again. "But if he agrees, how are you going to plan a wedding in less than two months? You usually work with clients for a year or more."

This conundrum has occurred to me as well. "I'll manage. It'll be like finals week, but for like, two months."

"And what about your mom's birthday thing? Isn't that happening around the same time, too?"

Shit. I hadn't thought of that, but now that she's mentioned it, yes: the sixtieth birthday extravaganza my family has roped me into planning is also happening at the end of July.

Sofia must see my realization playing out across my face because she says, "Oh no . . ."

"It'll be fine!" I insist as my brain already begins prioritizing tasks. "I mean, obviously I'll need to cut some corners," I say as my inner perfectionist purses her lips and gives me a severe look, "but I'll manage."

Sofia gazes at me with something like pity. "Okay, but doesn't this seem like the perfect opportunity to say no to them for once?"

"It's her sixtieth," I reason. "You know if I don't help, I'll be written out of the will."

"And miss out on all those inflatable lawn ornaments?" she asks dryly. "Say it isn't so."

"Sof, please," I say. "They're still my family."

"Gracie, they literally only get in touch when they need something, and you *never* say no."

"Well, not all of us grow up with perfect parents like yours. It doesn't mean I want to cut them off," I respond, hurt darkening my insides like a bruise.

When we were children, it was impossible not to wish that my own parents were as emotionally available as hers. And even as I got older and realized that was never going to happen, it didn't stop me from trying to be seen and appreciated by them.

Looking chastened, Sofia blinks several times as her legs cross a little tighter. "I'm sorry," she says. "I know how lucky I am, but they're far from perfect, you know," she says in a subdued voice. "They have issues, too."

Her expression becomes closed off as she looks away from me, and my heartbeat accelerates. "What do you mean?" I ask, going still. "Is everything okay?"

She glances up at me and takes in my expression. "Yeah, it's fine. Same old, same old," she assures me, but her smile is tight. "So, what do you think we should watch tonight?"

Well aware she's changing the subject, I eye her before saying, "*Evil Dead*?"

She gives me a smile—a real one this time—and relief blooms through me.

"You're probably the only hopeless romantic in the world who wouldn't rather watch *Bridget Jones's Diary* right now."

"Gotta have balance," I say, taking another bite of empanada. "I'm like a chocolate-covered potato chip. Sweet *and* salty."

"You are my favorite weirdo, Gracie Holland."

I lean over and kiss her cheek. "You're mine, too."

She smiles, and for the rest of the night, there's no more talk about my impending career crisis, Jude, or my questionable family dynamics. With Sofia's tenuous support, I know my next move.

Even if it might just break me.

6

GRACIE

Seven Weeks Before the Wedding

Agreeing to plan my ex-boyfriend's wedding is something not even my wildest nightmares have prepared me for. *If only*. I could have used a hint on how to endure this. But after leaving Sofia's house last night and weighing all my options (no, I haven't ruled out chaining myself to the cottage), I haven't come up with a plan that feels morally better than this one.

Obviously, the more *conventional* path forward would be to just accept what's happening and start scouring job sites while I resist the urge to toilet-paper Jude's car. But after years of struggling with my business, I've finally found something I'm great at with people I love working with.

And still, as I tossed and turned last night, I *tried* to convince myself to go quietly. I know this plan is ridiculous and will probably be shot down by Jude in an instant. But *not* trying leaves me with an image I can't shake. Larkwood, languishing as some celebrity's rarely used fifth home while Agatha looks on from above, cursing their love of bland neutrals and wall-to-wall carpeting. So while my odds of saving Larkwood might be worse than a cockroach finding true love (and by "a cockroach," I mean Jude), I'm not ready to give up yet.

I open the video call app on my phone. On the screen, my dark eyes, dark hair, and sun-fearing skin make me look like an anemic vampire. I'll bet anything Brooke is naturally blond, tan, and *so full!*

after her daily green juice breakfast. But since the universe is a *kind* and *benevolent* ruler (did you hear that, Universe?), I probably won't have my suspicions confirmed on this call. *Right?*

Swallowing hard, I hit the Call button.

"Gracie, hi!" Calvin says, picking up after one ring. "I was beginning to think I'd never hear from you!"

I force my face not to reveal how lovely that alternative would have been as I'm confronted by the same kitchen I used to make coffee in, wearing just his T-shirt. "Hi, Cal. How are you?"

"Completely depends on you, I guess," he says, flashing me a nervous grin. "Have you made your decision?"

"Right to the chase, huh?" I ask, reaching for a small zombie toy on my desk. Its cute little eyes and brain pop out when you squeeze it, like the world's weirdest stress ball.

"Sorry," he says, running a hand through his straight blond hair. "This call is all I've been thinking about."

A flutter of unthinking pleasure takes flight in my stomach at the idea of him wanting to talk to me. I squash it. "Of course," I say, hoping I come off as understanding and not like I want to throw darts at his butt. *Here goes nothing.* "Well, I've given it a lot of thought and decided to help you and Brooke out, if the new owner approves the wedding."

Calvin exhales like he's been holding his breath for the last two weeks. "Oh, thank God. You're really saving my ass here, Gracie."

"Nothing is set in stone yet," I warn him. "Larkwood is in the middle of changing hands, and the owner doesn't want any more weddings here. But I'm going to talk to him and see if he'll make an exception."

"Goodness," he says with a worried tilt of his sandy brown eyebrows. "Do you have any idea when you'll know for sure?"

"I'm hoping to see him sometime this week. But it will also depend on my vendors—this would be an extremely tight turnaround for them." *And me*, I mentally add.

He nods with a guilty expression. "I totally get that. But I'll do anything to give her the day she deserves." His eyes go glassy and desperate. "She's the love of my life, Gracie."

Can hearts get nauseous? The answer is yes. "Do you have a rough guest count yet?" I ask in a tight voice.

Again, he winces. "Probably around two hundred." At this, I *feel* the little color I have leech away from my face, while my little zombie's eyes and brain get stuck in bulge-state from my grip. "But I know if there's anyone who's going to pull this off, it's you—"

"I haven't given you my terms yet," I cut in, my voice turning as shrill as any self-respecting spinster's.

He sobers at once. "Anything," he says. "Just name your price."

I blink, startled by his blank-check offer. Calvin has never hurt for money. He grew up with an actual, God-as-my-witness pony, which later molted and became a series of increasingly larger Land Rovers. Knowing this still doesn't make asking for what I need any easier, though—I've become an expert at not making waves, or even ripples, for that matter.

But even people pleasers need to pay their bills. So after telling him Larkwood's standard fee for a five-hour event, I sit up straighter, spine buzzing, and force myself to look into his eyes. "Because I'll need to coordinate vendors on such late notice and do the same amount of work in a fraction of the time it usually takes, I'll need an additional ten percent rush fee. Up front. Not including gratuity," I tack on quickly.

It's a physical effort not to apologize, but in the end, I have nothing to worry about. Calvin looks a little taken aback by my unusual display of assertiveness but then nods with a casual shrug of his shoulders. "No problem. And do I make that rush fee out to you directly or to Larkwood?"

My armpits are basically sprinkler systems when I stammer out, "Just me. Please."

"Sure thing," he says with a smile. I hear a door close in the background of his house, and Calvin looks in the direction of the noise.

"Babe, you're home early!" he calls out, and the affection in his tone is an uppercut to the stubborn bit of my heart that still wishes I were the one walking through his front door. "Come meet Gracie—she's just given us the best news."

My brain is repeatedly smashing an Emergency Eject button as I blurt out, "Oh shoot, I'm getting a call from my . . . dermatologist!" Obviously, a lie. Even if doctors' offices made calls at seven thirty at night, having a dermatologist would suggest having both health insurance *and* a budget for skin-care products. "I'll be in touch soon, thanks, Calvin!"

I hang up before he can say anything else, my heart pounding. What the hell is wrong with me? It's not like I'm never going to meet Brooke—she's my client now, too, just like Calvin.

Calvin is my client.

The full implications sink into me like a flaming shipwreck. If Jude agrees, I'll be helping my ex say "I do" in the slimmest, barest hope of saving Agatha's legacy, my vendors' incomes, and my own future here at Larkwood.

I cover my face with my hands and try not to cry. Honestly, I don't have time for it. With that call, my deadline to cobble together a two-hundred-person, black-tie wedding has officially begun to count down—*if* Jude lets me. I glance at my beat-up laptop with its duct-taped power cord. What I should do is get a head start and create a new client file. But then my eyes slide to my tiny kitchen, where a dusty bottle of suspiciously cheap wine labeled BIG RED calls to me with a siren song. *You just agreed to plan your ex-boyfriend's wedding*, it seems to say. *You deserve to wallow just a little bit.*

I swallow hard. Tomorrow, Operation Save Larkwood begins. But tonight, I'm listening to Big Red.

7

JUDE

Seven Weeks Before the Wedding

The first rule about nervously pacing outside a woman's door in the dark is to just knock like a fucking adult. I exhale but still can't stop my feet. Ever since I told Henry I'd "handle" telling Gracie the news about the will, I've become the foremost expert in avoidance. But tonight, when I got to Larkwood for my weekend stay and saw lights on in the cottage, I was out of excuses. It's time to tell her about Nana's bequest and somehow convince her that selling the cottage to me—her least favorite human on Earth—is in her best interest.

Goddamnit, Nana—what were you thinking?

Exhaling again, I summon all my self-control and stop in front of Gracie's door. It's knowing that I might actually scare her with my loitering that finally makes me knock. From inside the cottage, I hear indistinct music get quieter and my heart picks up speed. I quickly push my glasses up my nose and try not to look like I'm sweating in the evening chill.

When the door opens, spilling light onto the darkened garden path, it takes a second for my eyes to adjust. As they do, my brain registers the mournful tones of "All by Myself" from inside the cottage. Then Gracie comes into focus. She's holding a bottle of red wine and wearing almost nothing but an oversize T-shirt with the words NICE TO EAT YOU over a cartoon zombie. Above the shirt, her face is slightly obscured by . . . a *wedding veil*? It's extremely sheer and does nothing to disguise the slightly glazed look of disgust she gives me.

"I'm sorry. You look like you're busy," I say quickly. "I'll come back when—" My eyes drop involuntarily to the hem of her shirt, where it brushes the tops of her very long, very bare thighs. *Fuck.* I force my gaze away and start to turn. "Another time. Sorry."

To my surprise, she lunges, slightly off-balance, and grabs onto my sleeve. "I don't think so, buster."

"*Buster?*" I repeat, amused despite myself.

She ignores this, but that may be because she loses her balance slightly and stumbles into me. She smells like sun-warmed flowers and red wine, but the overwhelming nearness of her is undercut by my worry. *How much of that bottle has she had?*

"Why are you here?" she demands, glaring up at me. "Did you think you could just show up wearing glasses and kick me out in the middle of the night? Did you think it would stop me from making a scene?"

"It's barely eight thirty," I point out, steadying her with the arm she's gripping. "And I'm not sure how my nearsightedness is relevant, but I didn't come here to kick you out." *Not yet*, I think grimly.

"Not yet," she retorts like an echo of my guilty thoughts. Needlessly, I push my glasses up again, and her eyes clock the nervous movement. She swallows. "If you're not here to evict me, then what do you want?"

I let go of her shoulder when I'm convinced she's not going to fall over and clear my throat. "I wanted to talk. I have some news to share with you about my grandmother's will."

For a brief moment, her dark eyes lose their accusatory glare, and our gazes meet. I don't think I'm the only one who stops breathing as the shared grief that tethered me to her at Nana's funeral tugs tight. Then she shivers, and I want to kick myself for keeping her outside. When you live this close to the ocean, even a summer's night can be cold. "You're going to freeze out here," I say. "I can wait if you want to get something warmer on or—"

She blinks, seeming to realize only now that she's barefoot and pantsless. I half expect her to argue, but then she sighs. "Just come inside," she says in a defeated tone. She turns unsteadily away while maneuvering the wine bottle beneath her veil to take a swig.

Come inside? That . . . wasn't part of the plan. Something acidic spreads unpleasantly in my chest. I haven't been inside the cottage since I was a kid. But any second now, Gracie is going to turn and wonder why the hell I'm just standing here like I can't get past a force field for idiots. I let out a difficult exhale. *It's just four walls and a roof,* I tell myself firmly, before following her inside and shutting the door with all the stilted grace of a rusty wind-up toy. As I force myself to breathe slowly, I begin noticing things.

For one, the room doesn't smell like dust and neglect but like *her*. Warm honey and the last of the apple blossoms outside her windows. The room itself is tidy but lived in, with an alarming number of scattered romance novels, an incongruous collection of zombie-themed paraphernalia, and mismatched furniture that looks cast off from the estate. Against the living room window sits a desk, and beyond it are several plastic-wrapped bolts of fabric, a dress form, and stacked boxes.

My shoulders lower. Somehow, without doing any of the exercises my therapist has recommended, I feel my heart rate begin to slow on its own. This isn't the same dark cottage I remember, crowded with ghostly, sheet-covered cabinets. It's . . . a home.

My attention is caught when the music cuts off. I see Gracie drop her phone on the kitchenette counter before coming back toward the living room with her wine bottle still in tow. Her pouty lips are stained red from the wine, and the wedding veil she's wearing is askew. It's such a stark contrast from her meticulous appearance at Nana's funeral, and I can't help feeling like I'm to blame.

"I'm sorry to barge in on your . . ." I trail off as she passes by and flops onto the old, crushed velvet couch.

"Pity party?" she finishes for me. "Don't worry, Big Red and I are happy to host as long as you don't need anything." She attempts to take another swig from what I assume is "Big Red" but forgets that her mouth is covered by a veil. At the press of sheer fabric between the bottle and her lips, she puts the wine between her knees and reaches up to unpin the veil. But clearly, this requires more coordination than she currently possesses.

"Goddamnit," she whimpers, attempting to yank the veil from her tangled hair with no success. After a few more tries, her arms lose strength, and she drops them by her side before looking up at me. "Help?"

She looks about a minute from crying, and I automatically sit by her side, despite knowing the *last* thing I need to be doing is removing an article of clothing from this woman.

"I think you've got it. Just pull that left pin, and—"

She turns toward me on the couch, and the white cotton of her shirt slides so high up her thighs that I can almost see— *STOP LOOKING*, I mentally bark at myself. Like a *saint*, I raise my eyes to hers, but their dark, liquid depths behind the veil are no safer. "Are you trying to make me beg?" she asks.

"No," I blurt loudly, wishing I had a paper bag to breathe into. "Please don't do that."

She rolls her eyes as I reach up to untangle the veil. I keep my movements as clinical as I can, removing pins that have become stuck on the comb tucked deep into her hair. Once the veil's loose, I don't let my hands linger in the act of pulling it free, but it doesn't matter. Watching the sheer white fabric slide away to reveal her chestnut waves and the pale expanse of her long neck still sends an almost painful bolt of longing through me.

"Here," I say, tossing the veil at her like it's stung me.

Her long lashes lift sleepily, and I notice her cheeks are flushed peony pink. *It's just from the wine*, I tell myself. There's no way she enjoyed—

"Thanks," she says, mercifully tugging her shirt down her lap. "If you wanna do me one more favor, you could never ask, mention, or think about the veil . . . ever."

"I wouldn't dream of it." *Liar*.

"Or Big Red."

"Obviously." I hesitate. "But can I ask if you've had any water lately?"

The way she squints as she tries to remember gives her away. Relieved to put some space between us, I go to the kitchen to retrieve a glass of water. While I'm at it, I open the cupboards to see if she has some crackers, but I'm confronted with nearly bare shelves. Maybe she eats out a lot? It seems unlikely, given Larkwood's isolation from civilization.

I continue my search in the fridge, but like the cabinets, there isn't much inside except some lunch meat and a quart of—I shudder—coffee milk. My concern is punctuated by another hiccup from the living room, but luckily, I find butter and a mostly finished bag of sandwich bread.

When I come back with a glass of water and buttered toast, she eyes me suspiciously. "Why are you suddenly so nice?"

Shame prickles down my back. "No danger of that. If I were being nice, I would have dumped out your coffee milk."

She makes a face of outrage. "Coffee milk is Rhode Island's beloved state beverage."

"It's also the home of 'clear chowder' in case you're a fan of watery clams, too."

"Aren't you the attorney general's son? You should be enjoying coffee milk with every meal."

"Thanks, but I prefer my drinks *not* to be sourced from Satan's teat."

She groans in exasperation and lifts her wine bottle.

"Speaking of which . . ." I say, "I don't think that particular vintage is doing you any favors either."

She frowns. "You know, snobbery was something your grandmother couldn't stand." She takes a pointed sip. "Then again, it doesn't seem like upholding her values is your top priority."

Defensiveness flares bright but quickly winks out. After our clash in the garden, I made the effort to see past her accusation that I don't care about my grandmother's wishes. It wasn't hard to do—at least, not after a few punishing, slightly angsty laps in the pool.

Honestly, it shouldn't have taken me so long to get past my misplaced anger at Gracie. She's raised valid concerns regarding my plans, and that doesn't give me the right to lash out at her—not when I'm the asshole ruining her life.

With a pit in my stomach, I sit back down as she takes a delicate bite of her toast.

"I understand why it might seem that way, and I'm sorry my decision has been so stressful for you," I tell her quietly.

Her wary eyes meet mine, but when she doesn't snap back, I go on.

"It was shitty of me to break the news to you so harshly, and I have no excuse for being so rude. You'll probably find this hard to believe, but I'm not actually rejoicing over the loss of your job."

Her eyes get brighter. "So, is this apology toast then? Did something in Agatha's will make you reconsider selling Larkwood?"

I shake my head. "Unfortunately, no. My mind is made up on that." The hope in her expression dies, and for one, logic-flinging moment, I want to promise she can stay in this cottage indefinitely. Which brings me straight back to reality, because technically, under the terms of Nana's will, she can. That is, until I use every legal intimidation tactic in my arsenal to scare her into selling it to me.

God. She only thinks she hates me right now.

"Then what on earth did you want to tell me?" she demands. "Have you come to offer me a replacement job as your henchman? Or inform me that I've been living with asbestos for the last three years and can win BIG in court with you if I call 1-800-OMG-FML?"

I only barely manage not to laugh. "Pretty sure that number's missing a digit and no. I'm not that kind of lawyer, Gracie."

"Oh, right. I forgot. You're the kind that charges five hundred dollars a minute to dance on the graves of dreams and happiness."

I can't help my smirk. "I can assure you that my grave dancing services are entirely complimentary."

She glares at me and takes another bite of toast. Meanwhile, I try not to acknowledge the alarming satisfaction of seeing Gracie eat food that I've made her. Instead, I use the opening to bring up the reason I'm here. "But I do have some news about the estate that's relevant to you. You remember my friend Henry, who's handling the probate process?"

"The handsome guy with the dimples?" She nods, swallowing her toast. "He was sweet."

Does Henry have dimples? If he does, they've never fully registered. Disconcerted, I continue with an off-balanced "Right. Well, after going through Nana's will, he discovered that in an act of misguided generosity, she bequeathed this cottage to you." I take a breath before continuing. "I say misguided because, unfortunately, ownership comes with a number of significant financial demands, including property taxes on a historic site, as well as a preservation clause that would require you to finance the restoration and upkeep of the property to an exacting standard." Here, I pause, allowing the gravity of my words to sink in while gauging her reaction.

Gracie blinks rapidly, tears quickly welling in her dark, expressive eyes. *Yes, good*, I think, fully aware that I may as well be twisting an evil villain mustache.

"I know it's a hard pill to swallow," I say, adopting the gentle tone I use with clients after a loss in court. "At first glance, it seems like owning the cottage would solve all your problems, but selling it to me would actually—"

Gracie's tremulous voice makes me stop short. "Agatha remembered me in her will?"

Mentally, I backpedal. "Uh, yes. The cottage has been left to you, along with the financial responsibilities of ownership."

A little clumsily, Gracie puts her plate of half-eaten toast and the glass of water on a side table. I'm about to suggest (or beg) that she finish them when she knocks over the wine bottle by her foot.

"Dammit," she says. Quickly, we both reach down to grab the bottle, which thankfully (and worryingly) is too empty to have spilled. Our hands accidentally brush, and the brief sensation of her skin against mine violently elbows every one of my thoughts out of the way.

"Sorry," she mumbles as I pick up the bottle, hugging herself like she no longer trusts her limbs. "I'm not usually—I don't do this all the time, or anything," she says, and I'm horrified to hear her sniffle. "It's just been the worst week, and everything feels worse without Agatha. Now she's left this place to me and I . . ." She pauses, and I watch the profile of her full bottom lip tremble. "I'll never get to thank her," she squeaks out, voice tight. "Just like I never got to tell her how much I—"

She stops speaking and puts her face in her hands. I can only tell she's crying from the silent sobs shaking her back. My hand moves to hover above her tense shoulders, but I hesitate. Right now, I'm fairly sure she'd prefer a back rub from a cactus.

"I'm keeping it," she whispers as I silently draw away.

Gracie's voice is quiet enough that I hope I've misheard her. "Excuse me?"

She sits up, mascara blurred beneath her defiant eyes. "I know you're trying to scare me into selling it. But if Agatha left this place to me, then I trust her judgment. She wouldn't have given it to me if she thought it would be a burden."

No. Fear slips a cold hand around my throat at the thought of my deal for Larkwood falling through. In a flash of overwhelming frustration, I wish I could explain everything to her. Closing my eyes, I take a much-needed breath.

"I have no doubt my grandmother meant well," I say with forced calm, before looking at her, "but she was also extremely out of touch with today's cost of living for people without her means. So, unless you explicitly told her what salary you needed, I can't imagine she was paying you that well."

Trying to spare her dignity, I don't mention that I know *exactly* how little Nana paid her. But even if I didn't have access to the estate's ledgers, Gracie's empty cupboards and her flush of embarrassment at my words would have given me all I needed to know. What's less clear is why she never advocated for herself. Loathing myself, I press my advantage.

"I'm talking about tens of thousands of dollars in yearly property taxes and historic preservation costs here." She visibly gulps, and the squeeze of my airways relaxes the tiniest bit. "But the good news is, I'm prepared to take the cottage off your hands. You wouldn't need to bear any of the financial responsibility of owning a historic site. Plus, you'd never have to see me again."

At this, her eyes flick toward me. "Out of everything you just said, that's the most appealing thing on the list."

Ouch. But beggars can't be choosers, so I say, "Have I mentioned I'll be here all the time until it's off my hands?"

She wrinkles her nose. "Ew, why?"

"Because I have approximately thirty rooms of shit to sort through and restoration projects to oversee before the transfer," I say, taking off my glasses and rubbing my eyes.

"Why not just hire someone to do it?"

I look over and catch her gaze aimed at the loosened tie and collar I neglected to redo before coming here. Her eyes jump up to mine, and the honest answer slips past my defenses. "Because I miss her. And as much as I don't enjoy being here, it feels like . . . like a way to say goodbye."

Gracie stares at me for a long moment. "I don't understand you. How can you love her like this and not want to save what was so important to her?"

My jaw tightens as a rush of pain, family pressure, and love for my nana grates against this golden opportunity for Larkwood. "It's complicated."

"Is that grump-speak for 'mind your own business'?"

"I guess so, yeah," I say, losing a little of my patience. I shove my glasses back on my face in time to see her frown.

"Well, unfortunately for you, it is my business now. And while no, I can't afford to pay those kinds of taxes or fees immediately, I don't see why I should rush to sell to you while I'm figuring out how to avoid living in my mom's basement."

"You don't understand," I grit out. "The person who's interested in the estate is looking to acquire a property in August, no matter what, and I intend for it to be Larkwood."

"And why is it so important that they're the ones who buy it?" Her eyes skim my outfit, and her mouth hardens. "You're clearly not strapped for cash. I don't see why you can't just make my life the tiniest bit less shitty and wait a few months for another buyer."

I accept the jab about my privileged financial situation and shake my head as she edges a little too close to the plans I can't tell anyone about. There's a reason Larkwood has to go to this particular party and why the transaction has to be made with the utmost discretion, but I've already said too much. "I can't tell you why, but it *has* to be them."

"Then I guess I'll have new neighbors," she says sweetly. "I'll make sure to bake them some welcome cookies to go with my mile-long list of reasons why Larkwood should continue being a wedding venue."

"Gracie, please," I nearly growl. "Privacy is crucial to them, and this deal won't happen without the cottage included."

She crosses her arms over her chest, brushing my side in the process. *When did I move this close to her?* "Then I guess we're at a stalemate because I haven't given up on saving Larkwood yet."

"There's no point in trying to '*save Larkwood*.' I'll find a way to sell the estate with or without your cooperation."

"Unless I can change your mind," she says with a determination that should be punishable by law.

"I'm not following," I snap.

"Unsurprising, but listen. I want to make you a proposal."

I give her a deadpan look. "Don't you think we're moving a little fast, darling?"

"Not *that* kind of proposal," she huffs, color flooding her cheeks. "I had hoped for a better moment to have this conversation—like, a fully sober, not-in-my-jammies moment," she says as she stands, wobbles slightly, and then walks to the other side of the living room. "But I guess it's now or never."

I don't register what she grabs off her desk. I barely register what she's said, because my gaze has zeroed in on the two black bow tattoos just above the backs of her ankles. They're small, delicate, and there's a good chance I need to be defibrillated.

When she sits again, she's holding what looks like a scrapbook. She exhales. "So, I have a new client who wants to get married at Larkwood before August, and I need you to agree to let me plan their wedding."

My mouth is already forming the word *no*, but then she lays a gentle hand on my knee. I not only stop but nearly swallow my tongue while I'm at it. "I know you're just *itching* to shut me down, but hear me out for a second, okay?"

When I barely manage a nod, she removes her hand. Oxygen returns to my brain.

"The past few days have been . . ." She bites her lip. "*So* hard. I've spent countless hours on the phone comforting my clients over their canceled weddings. I honestly feel like I should have a license to practice therapy after those calls," she mutters, and guilt is a rake down my back.

She goes on. "I'm doing what I can for the clients who were going to be married the soonest, and they're mostly set with new venues. Public parks and apple orchards and whatever else I could come up with," she says. "But this new couple is . . . well, they're desperate. They're expecting a baby, and they need to get married as soon as possible in a place like Larkwood, due to family expectations." She looks up at me with a pained expression that's difficult to read.

"Usually, I'd *never* agree to a timeline this tight. But when you told me you wanted to get rid of the estate, I had an idea. That maybe, if I were to plan this wedding before you sell, then it could be an opportunity to show you exactly why weddings at Larkwood meant so much not just to me, but also to your nana, our clients, and all the vendors who work here."

I look down as Gracie opens the scrapbook in her lap. My chest constricts painfully as I take in the collage. Gracie clinking champagne flutes with Nana at the end of a reception, their faces tired but alight with a job well done. Nana holding a grinning bride by the shoulders, her wrinkled face rapturous over the beautiful wedding gown. Photo after photo of my grandmother in her element, radiant with happiness.

"There was nothing she loved more than this," Gracie says in a choked voice, and I reluctantly lift my eyes from the photos to meet her gaze. "I know you were close with her, but I worked with Agatha for years, Jude. She really believed Larkwood was meant for this. And I realize you have other plans for the estate, but I wouldn't be able to live with myself if I didn't at least *try* to convince you to keep it.

"Which is why," she says, before taking a steadying breath. "If you want this cottage, you'll need to let me plan this wedding. You'll also need to meet with all the vendors—my *friends*—who will be financially devastated from the loss of Larkwood. With any luck, seeing this couple exchange vows might even prove to you that true love *does* exist." She swallows, and there's that complicated look again, somewhere between distress and resignation. "But if I still can't change your mind by the wedding, then I'll consider selling to you."

My eyebrows draw together as I try to get control over the guilt and grief she's fanned to life. "Let me get this right. You want to try guilt-tripping me into keeping Larkwood by making me plan a wedding with you?"

She sits up straighter and attempts to look down her nose at me. "I prefer to think of it as helping you rehydrate your shriveled little raisin of a heart, but yes. I'd like you to fully understand the scope of your actions before you pull the trigger. Even if I can't stop you, at least you'll know what you've done."

Well, fuck. When I walked into this cottage tonight, I was convinced I'd be the one comforting Gracie—preferably with a large offer on her cottage—but now I'm the one who needs a goddamn hug. If I had to pick the *last* way I want to spend my limited free time, being guilt-tripped for destroying my grandmother's legacy while planning a stranger's wedding would be the winner. But unfortunately, Gracie has the upper hand. I need this cottage by August, and if she told me I had to be her personal doormat to get it, I'd probably just ask if she wanted me face up or down.

"I can't believe I'm saying this . . . but okay," I finally respond, unable to help admiring how determined she is. Unfortunately, she has no idea that while I respect all the points she's made, my reasons for getting rid of Larkwood take priority over anything else—no matter how awful I feel that there will be collateral damage. Which is why I say, "But if you don't change my mind, then you have to sell me the cottage. No maybes."

Fear washes over her features, and self-loathing makes a prickly lap inside my stomach as I consider making her sign an actual contract.

But then she lifts her chin, holds out her hand to shake, and says, "Winner takes all on the day of the wedding. Deal?"

It's a terrible idea. Not least of all because it means spending more time with a woman who inspires frustration and fixation in equal measure. But somehow, I know she'll be true to her word when I eventually win this bargain. All I have to do is run down the clock. So, with Larkwood's future hanging in the balance, I take her hand in mine and get the spooky feeling that Nana is looking on, kicking her feet and cackling as she tosses popcorn into her mouth. "Deal."

8

GRACIE

Seven Weeks Before the Wedding

Brianna: Gracie, Mom wants to know if you can get us a free bounce house.

Mom: Ask her if there are any Patriots-themed houses. Extra large.

Josie: Mom, you're in the group chat. Ask her yourself.

Mom: Gracie, can you get us a Patriots bounce house? We need a BIG one.

Brianna: I still think we should roast a whole pig. What are your pig connections like, Gracie?

Mom: Are we final on the football theme? Maybe a Bruins bounce house instead.

Brianna: Mom, the theme is PASS THE PIGSKIN. 🏈

Josie: It's Mom's bday, Bri.

Mom: Let's talk about it when Gracie brings the favors over.

Brianna: Are those done yet, Gracie?

Gracie: Working on it! I'll see about the pig. How important is this bounce house?

Josie: We have 19 kids under the age of 10 coming. You tell ME how important it is.

Mom: CRITICAL.

Brianna: She was asking Gracie, Mom.

Gracie: I'll see what I can do.

9

GRACIE

Six Weeks Before the Wedding

It's only 10 a.m., and today's theme is already "The Worst." Actually, apply it to the whole past week. After striking my bargain with Jude and exchanging numbers with him last Saturday, it's been a nonstop juggle of helping my panicked ex-clients and planning my mom's sixtieth under threat of disownment.

It's why I spent my morning at her house, convincing my stepsisters that hiring the Patriots' team mascot *isn't* happening, and why I'm now late to a meeting with Calvin, Brooke, and Jude to sign contracts. Normally, I'd handle this over video call, but after getting a text from Calvin saying that Brooke wants to meet in person (and the three-mile stress run it inspired), I decided this was a good thing.

For one, it forces me to rip off the Band-Aid of seeing Calvin with his fiancée. Secondly, it's a chance to ease Jude into the wedding planning process—something I'm still shocked he agreed to help with while I lacked the full use of my faculties or my *pants*. And while I may only have his cooperation because of my unexpected leverage from the cottage, I can't help the surge of hope I feel anyway.

After parking, I lock my car and start jogging down the street. I *tried* to leave on time, but Brianna physically blocked me from the door until I helped them source the football bounce house of their dreams. By the time I escaped, I was already late.

Smoothing my freshly de-bird-shitted blazer, I take a deep breath and turn down Westminster Street, trying to calm myself before this meeting. Probably an impossible task without, say, a horse tranquilizer. And yet, I'm determined to make the most of this opportunity.

After Jude revealed that Agatha left the cottage to me and I was able to overcome the emotional shock, my mission to save Larkwood suddenly felt divinely validated. It was as if Agatha *knew* her grandson would try to sell the estate and knighted me as its valiant checklist-wielding defender. And while I doubt that a contract meeting will be the thing to thaw Jude's heart, I am holding out hope that seeing Calvin and Brooke together will bring out the softer side I know he has deep (*deep*) down.

When I finally make it to the café, I'm panting as I pull open the glass door with a tinkle of bells. It's packed inside, and it takes me a moment to spot Calvin, Jude, and a woman who—no shit—looks like a young Brooke Shields, sitting at a table near the back.

My spine feels like a lightsaber that just got switched on, neon bright and electric as the full gradient of human emotions pulses through me. I watch as Calvin throws his head back and laughs in seeming slow motion. It's been three years, but longing sprints ahead of everything else, with shame nipping close at its heels. *Why can't I get over him?* Are some hearts just more stubborn than others? Incapable of moving on, even when there's no hope or reason to keep clinging on?

I glance at Brooke, who's holding his hand on the table and smiling indulgently at him, her engagement ring glinting from across the room. I'm half considering making a run for it when my gaze slides to Jude. He's watching me intently, a look furrowing his brows that could either be concern or annoyance. *Dammit.*

I force myself to start walking and feel Jude's unsettling eyes on me the entire time. Why do they have to catch the light like that? It isn't natural or appreciated. But at least he isn't wearing those glasses again. *Small mercies.*

When I get to the table, I pull out a chair and quickly say, "Sorry I'm late, everyone, my last meeting ran over." *Technically the truth, even if it was because I nearly got into a slap fight with my stepsisters.*

Calvin and Brooke begin assuring me that they just arrived when

Jude stands quickly, accidentally hitting the table and making the dishes rattle.

"Sorry," he says, meeting my surprised gaze. "Can I grab you a coffee, Gracie? Some food?"

Taken aback, I think of the toast he made me. I'd assumed he was just buttering me up before asking me to sell the cottage, but maybe he just has some kind of bizarre radar for whenever I'm undernourished and undercaffeinated. I could definitely use some sustenance, but as I glance at Calvin and my nerves zing to life, I respond, "That's okay, I'll grab it myself."

"It's no problem," he parries, grabbing his nearly full cup. "I'm going up for a refill anyway."

I narrow my eyes at him in suspicion, and suddenly, it clicks: Jude can't stand being around a lovesick couple.

I try not to let all my hope deflate. The whole point of bringing him along was so that he could see the excitement of a couple ready to tie the knot and maybe consider the possibility that marriage *isn't* lifelong incarceration. Well. His plan might be to take every chance to leave the table, but I'm not ready to give up yet.

"Then I can refill it for you," I counter sweetly, attempting to take the cup from him but only succeeding in awkwardly putting my hand over his.

He blinks at the contact, and for several seconds, the feeling of his warm fingers beneath mine sends my train of thought right into a ditch. His grip tightens, and he says in a lowered voice, "Please. You must be starving if you're coming straight from another meeting. I can get you a latte and madeleines. They're the best—"

"In the city," I finish for him. For a moment, we just stare at each other, and I've forgotten what we're fighting over until Calvin clears his throat and stands as well.

"Gracie! Let the man get you a drink and get over here. I haven't seen you in ages!"

Jude's eyes flick to Calvin in surprise and then back to me. Then a closed-lipped smile pulls across his face that might be construed as warm if I didn't know it was smug with victory. *So much for Mr. Nice Guy*. I let go of the cup.

"Okay, thanks. A latte and madeleine would be great."

"Good choice," he comments before leaving me to face my own personal version of hell. I want to flick the back of his head.

"Calvin, hi!" I say, giving him a little wave instead of walking into his now outstretched arms.

He doesn't get the hint and walks toward me before I can sit. And then I'm wrapped in his arms, breathing in mint, sandalwood, and what I'm positive is the stale ghost of my dignity as I suck in lungful after lungful. He lets go far too soon or far too late—it's hard to decide. But then I'm being turned bodily by Brooke and blasted full in the face by her outrageous, thick-eyebrowed beauty.

"Gracie, you angel! It's so wonderful to meet you at last," she says in the sort of British accent that belongs in Jaguar commercials and Jane Austen adaptations. *Naturally*.

"You, too!" I attempt to say, but it comes out sounding much closer to *You chew!*

She graciously ignores this, but I get the feeling everything she does is filled with grace, including tripping and burping. As we sit, I see Calvin glance between us excitedly, like he's thrilled we haven't automatically challenged each other to a cage match.

"Cal, you never mentioned how beautiful she is, you sly dog," Brooke teases, poking him in the arm with her tasteful cream manicure. While I wrestle with whether to be flattered or flattened by this, she goes on, "I feel rather lucky you let go of her at all."

The smile plastered on my face goes wooden as I change the subject with the delicacy of a brick through a window. "I owe you two a congratulations!"

On cue, Calvin shoots Brooke the most adoring look I've possibly ever seen on a human face before resting his hand on her still-flat stomach. "Thanks, Gracie. We couldn't be happier."

Brooke flashes me a shy smile, and my own falters. "Right! Yes! The baby," I say heartily, before glancing over to where Jude is waiting for his order and desperately wishing I weren't alone. "How are you feeling, Brooke?"

"Honestly, I'm embarrassed to say I've been fine," she says, lowering her voice conspiratorially. "I know so many people have nausea at this stage, but I think this little one knows not to come between Mummy and her spreadsheets!" she jokes, and my laugh is robotic.

Calvin throws an arm over her shoulders. "Brooke is a partner at the wealth management firm mine competes with." He makes a grimace. "And while I'm glad she's feeling great, I could have really used a little break from her snapping up all our best clients."

"Wow, so you're work rivals," I say faintly, winded by this further revelation that Calvin's love story is straight out of a romance novel. But I'm saved from the urge to ask them if they ever found themselves in a one-bed scenario at one of their Successful Hot People conferences when Jude returns with a steaming latte, two madeleines, and what looks like half a baguette stuffed with more veggies than I've probably eaten in the last week.

"Um, thanks?" I say, taken aback. "I didn't need the five-dollar-foot-long, though."

He shrugs but doesn't meet my eye as he sits. "Save it for later, then."

What in the freshly baked hell? I mean, I'm not necessarily opposed to chivalry when it's of the nutrient-dense variety, but I'm still not entirely convinced Jude isn't trying to poison me.

"What have I missed?" he asks, and even though he sounds like he's hoping to hear "*Everything! We're actually all finished up here!*" I can't help feeling a little less alone.

"Only that Calvin is counting on his fiancée's sick days to compete with her at work," I say, earning a guffaw from Calvin and a delighted "I knew I was going to adore you!" from Brooke.

I glance over at Jude, whose face is carefully neutral as he takes a drink of coffee. I take a hasty sip of my own before reaching into my bag to retrieve the contract and Larkwood welcome package I give to all my clients.

"I'm kidding, of course. I was delighted to hear from Calvin again, and we're thrilled you've chosen Larkwood for your wedding venue." Jude makes an indistinct sound of dissent, and I kick the side of his leg. "Right, Jude?"

"I didn't realize this was an old-friend situation," he says, side-stepping the question. "No wonder Gracie was so insistent on making this happen."

He says it with a smile that's so offensively charming, there's a good chance they don't detect his displeasure with the whole situation.

"'Old friend' is one way to put it," Brooke says. She leans forward like she's sharing a hot piece of gossip with Jude. "Cal and Gracie dated years ago. But he swears that's all ancient history."

Calvin meets my eyes for a moment so brief I think I've imagined it before he drinks from his cup. He smiles at no one in particular. "It's true. But you know how it goes. Everyone has that old college flame that inevitably goes out. Then you realize you're better off as friends. Right, Gracie?"

Jude must sense that I've turned to stone because it's his turn to bump my foot under the table.

"Right," I hear myself agree. "Ancient history."

Jude nudges the plate of madeleines closer to me. "Should we get down to business?" he asks, saving me from any further emotional torture. "I'm sure you both have a thousand questions for Gracie."

And that's when I feel something for Jude I never saw coming—gratitude.

10

GRACIE

Six Weeks Before the Wedding

In a surprise turn of events, I make it through the meeting without quietly slipping off my chair to lie down and hoist a white flag. Even more surprising, I'm almost sure it's because of Jude. While no one except maybe a boulder would describe him as chatty, his quiet, intimidating presence kept the meeting from venturing back into personal territory, for which I am both begrudgingly and eternally grateful. Calvin even refrained from hugging me goodbye, but that may have had more to do with Jude looming close beside me as they left.

"Thanks for coming today," I say a bit awkwardly when he comes back from having my giant sandwich wrapped in paper. "And for lunch," I add, taking it from him.

"Anything to hear you say the words 'five-dollar-foot-long,'" he says, surprising a laugh out of me.

"Oh yeah?" I ask, untucking my hair from my blazer. "That's what does it for you? Vaguely inappropriate sandwich slogans?"

His eyes track my hand as I adjust my necklace. "Are you trying to kink-shame me, Gracie Holland?"

Despite his deadpan delivery, my cheeks heat like he just whispered it in my ear. Trying to recover, I say, "That depends. Are you admitting to a kink involving deli meats and their adjacent marketing strategies?"

He snorts but then hesitates. "If I were divulging any kinks, it wouldn't be in a café."

Okay, not where I expected this conversation to go, but I surprise myself by replying, "So I guess that scratches exhibitionism off the list."

Jude's eyebrows shoot up. "I didn't realize you were making those kinds of lists about me."

The flush that's been building since our left turn into this bizarre conversation intensifies, and I try pulling back into a realm I'm more comfortable with: antagonizing him. "Anything to figure out an opponent's weaknesses."

His lips quirk. "I'm beginning to think we may be more alike than I'd originally thought."

"We are *nothing* alike," I say, shouldering my bag with the freshly signed contracts and, most importantly, my payday. "I'm a wedding planner. You're a divorce lawyer. We're like . . . like a butterfly and a murder hornet."

"Huh. I've never thought of myself as a butterfly," Jude says, absently rubbing the annoying cleft in his chin as we head toward the café door.

My mouth drops open with indignation before I point a thumb to my chest. "No, *I'm* the butterfly. *You're* the murder hornet."

He tilts his head, studying me as he buttons his charcoal suit jacket. "I don't see why I'm the de facto murder hornet here," he says. "You're the one giving me psycho-killer eyes."

Against my will, my gaze flicks to the mirrored wall behind him. And fine, maybe my eyes are a *little* murdery. But whose wouldn't be, talking to this misery monger? This prenup peddler? This—

"Gracie."

My name in his soft baritone yanks my gaze back to his.

"*What*," I snap.

He stares at me, a look of almost angelic innocence in his wide, honey-colored eyes. "If you're a murder hornet, I'm a murder hornet."

At his blasphemous misquotation from *The Notebook*, I groan. I will *not* let this man be the death of me. I take a breath and try to remind myself that he just helped me through a meeting I gave myself 60/40 odds on surviving. He bought me a sandwich. And even if it's a dubious kink sandwich, now I won't have to eat boxed mac 'n' cheese for dinner.

"Anyway, I'm headed back to Larkwood," I say. "I'll text you about meeting the band I usually work with. I want to ask them in person to do the wedding, and they have a gig this weekend."

"So that's the next task you've got in store for me? Enduring a wedding singer?"

"Only if you're not too busy doing unforgivable things to a Subway sandwich. Otherwise, you can look forward to meeting some of the kindest, most talented people I know."

He holds the café door open for me, grimacing as we step outside under the overcast sky. "Transmission of guilt received." He looks up toward the clouds. "It's going to storm. You're not planning on going back right now, are you?"

I begin walking toward my car, and he falls into step next to me. "Well, considering I still live there, yes."

"Does your car have four-wheel drive?"

"It's a little rain, not a monsoon."

"You didn't answer the question."

I think of my dinged-up 2005 Toyota Camry with its rusted bumper and Can't-Stop-Won't-Stop engine. "Yes. It has four wheels and drives great."

He mutters something I don't catch because his head is too far above mine. I'm about to argue that rain wasn't even in the forecast when there's a crack of thunder. *Great*. I honestly hate driving in the rain, or the snow, or the dark (yes, thank you, my eightieth birthday *is* coming up), but there's no way I'm admitting this to Jude.

"Isn't there someplace you can stay in the city?" he asks.

I think of Sofia. She'd definitely let me crash at her place, but I happen to know her on-again off-again situationship is currently on, and I have no desire to intrude. I bite my lip as I consider asking my parents, but quickly decide I'd rather drive in torrential rain and lightning. "I'll be fine," I say. "I need to get back and work on this wedding."

Jude looks over at me. A single fat raindrop lands on one of his high cheekbones like Mother Earth herself is weeping over them, and I'm unprepared for the abrupt subject change he makes.

"So you and Calvin, huh? That sounds . . . complicated."

He says this last word carefully, like he's trying to say *horrific* in a different language. I cross my arms over my chest, hugging myself tight. "It's the least complicated thing in the world, actually."

"Because he has the personality of a Styrofoam peanut?"

An indignant sound squeaks out of me. "How could you say that? You have no idea who he is."

"No?" he asks, squinting at the darkening clouds ahead. "So, if I guessed that he went to Brown after a well-timed alumni donation, began his career with a nepo-baby internship, and works for Daddy with the plan of taking over the firm within the next fifteen years, you'd tell me I'm wrong?"

When the disturbing accuracy of his assumptions prevents me from responding, Jude sighs. "I work with men like him all the time, Gracie. They glide through life expecting things they don't deserve and feel validated as supreme rulers of the universe when they push people over to get their way."

"That's rich coming from you," I huff. "Seeing as you're about to inherit an *estate* and plan to—how did you phrase it? 'Push people over to get your way'?"

It's Jude's turn to look indignant as he says, "It's different. I take no pleasure in disrupting your life, or any of the wedding vendors you've mentioned. It's why I'm here, attempting to make amends with you instead of keeping the lunch meeting I had planned with one of my clients."

"And here I was thinking it was because you want to get your hands on my cottage."

"Can't it be both?"

I glance up at him, but his gaze is still focused forward, giving me an entirely too-convenient view of his structured jawline, which could probably work as a rain shelter in a pinch. His words give me pause, but my questionable compulsion to defend my ex is still yanking at me. "Either way, I don't see why you feel the need to attack Calvin.

I wouldn't have taken on his wedding if he were an awful person or if there was anything lingering between us."

Jude shoots me a shrewd look. "Considering how your scheme to save Larkwood hinges on planning a wedding," he drawls, "I think it's safe to assume you would've been willing to plan Cruella de Vil's nuptials, dalmatian puppy dress and all."

"That's not true," I sputter, but he keeps going.

"If I were a betting man, I'd wager Calvin called you out of the blue for this massively insensitive favor because he knew he could take advantage of your kindness." He looks over at me, and I endure the sensation of being x-rayed. "Did you go to RISD and fall for him doing Jell-O shots at a Brown frat party or something? You know—the whole quirky art student falls for WASPy golden boy thing?"

And that, I decide, *is enough*. I stop in my tracks, and people on the rain-flecked sidewalk are forced to swerve around us. "It *wasn't* at a frat party."

"Let the record reflect that there *were*, in fact, Jell-O shots involved," he murmurs.

There's another flash of lightning, but I'm pretty sure my temper is hotter.

"Let the record reflect that it's *none of your business*," I parrot back at him.

"You made it my business when you roped me into helping with this wedding," he retorts, and I note with annoyance that the wind has loosened his neatly combed hair so that glossy dark waves are falling into his face. *Ugh*.

"I asked you to help me with wedding tasks, not psychoanalyze me."

He shrugs. "Old habits die hard."

"Because invasive insights into relationship dynamics are a favorite pastime of yours?"

"No, but they're a pretty critical part of my day job."

"Must be nice to spread love and joy wherever you go."

"If you'd like to count the forty-something holiday cards I received this year as proof of character, just let me know."

"No thanks; unlike you and your vampire brethren, we humans are sensitive to anthrax."

He laughs, and an unwilling thrill shoots up my spine at the sight of his wide smile and the vertical lines on either side—like his face has to make special accommodations for it. I quickly look away and start walking.

"You know, we vampires aren't as heartless as you'd like to think."

"Right. So, you just think the institution of marriage is pointless, romance is dead, and kittens should be drowned on principle."

"On the contrary, marriage has excellent tax benefits for those willing to risk it, I think romance is entirely possible and maybe even inevitable with the right person, and I happen to be the indentured servant of my feline overlord, Taco."

I can't help the laugh that skips out of me. "You have a cat named Taco?"

"She looks appealing but gives me heartburn. It's the perfect name for her."

"I'm more shocked that you have a cat, period."

"Do I not strike you as a cat person?"

I frown, considering. "Actually, you're sort of the quintessential cat person. Moody, unaffectionate, snobby . . ."

"Intelligent, good-looking, independent," he continues to list, pushing his disheveled hair back from his forehead. We round a corner, and I spot my car at last. But despite the rain, I find myself wanting to stay.

"This is me," I say, pointing at my Camry with the sandwich I'm still carrying.

Jude frowns at the maroon eyesore parked in front of us. "Your tires are bald," he notes.

I sigh. "Yeah, well, he's still got great stamina."

Jude shakes his head and glances at the sky again. "You really don't have a place to stay for the night in Providence?"

"I do have a few people I could call, but you're missing the point. I *want* to go home and sleep in my own bed."

He bites down on his bottom lip and glances at the small park ahead of us. "Would you be willing to wait out the rain with me? If it gets worse, you stay and call a friend. If it dies out, you go?"

I look down at my heels and then up at the ominous clouds. I should just get on the road, but for reasons that have *nothing* to do with the bite marks in his lip, I say, "Fine. But I don't want to get soaked."

The smile he gives me is wolfish as he opens a compact black umbrella I didn't notice he was carrying. "And here I thought wedding planners were supposed to be prepared for anything."

"Anything but *you*," I shoot back, but somehow, it feels less like a retort and more like a confession. And based on his smug smile as he tugs me beneath the umbrella, he knows it.

11

JUDE

Six Weeks Before the Wedding

Umbrellas are available in all kinds of sizes—some for couples, some for kids, and some for chronic loners like myself. I'm sure there are depressing statistics on what sells best somewhere, but right now, none of it matters because Gracie has transformed my lonely, party-of-one umbrella into an undersize shelter for two.

I exhale as we cross the street to the park. I need to get a handle on myself. I know I have a habit of being overprotective of the people I care for. In my one-night-only relationships, those tendencies manifest in ways that my therapist has a lot to say about. But with Gracie . . . it feels different. She's pulled me into her orbit, and now I spend all my time wondering if she's gone grocery shopping, or if she's sewing something new, or if she's busy plotting my demise.

"So, now that I know you're an animal lover who believes romance is 'inevitable' under the right conditions," she says as raindrops begin to fall more heavily around us, "I think it would be best if you just give up pretending you're not a secret cinnamon roll and agree to renovate Larkwood's greenhouse as a new wedding reception area."

I can't stop my incredulous smile as I look at her. "I'm sorry—a secret *what*?"

Her dark eyes flick to mine, and I wish for the millionth time that I didn't find her *quite* so beautiful. The rain begins to fall fast and hard outside our small bubble of protection, and she moves closer to me.

"A secret cinnamon roll," she repeats. "It's basically a way of describing a fictional character who seems prickly on the outside but is secretly soft and gooey on the inside."

"Wow. And here I was, thinking those were just my internal organs."

"Don't sell yourself short, Jude. I'm sure you've got a feeling or two rattling around in there."

"I'm flattered. But you prefer what? Overexcited blond lapdogs?"

Her shoulders bunch slightly, just like they have every time I've thrown a verbal dart at Calvin. I should stop, but the urge to discover whether her defensiveness is purely platonic or coming from something deeper eggs me on.

"If you're referring to Calvin—"

"Yes."

"Then I'll repeat what we both said earlier: it's ancient history. If you didn't notice, he's getting married, and not to me."

Her thick lashes cast downward, and the fact that she feels anything other than dislike for him is utterly confounding. Annoying, too. *Deeply* annoying.

"I did notice and feel it's my right as the reluctant fourth wheel to be briefed on any history that might complicate dealings with our clients."

"Is this just the way you talk? Like you eat contracts sprinkled with binder clips for breakfast?"

"I never claimed to excel at casual conversation. The whole lawyer-by-day, vampire-by-night thing really limits my range of social skills."

"To spreading misery and suffering?"

"Almost exclusively."

A laugh bubbles out of her, and it's almost the same one I heard in the church. *More.* The thought is voracious and I realize with a jolt that I'm not just attracted to her—I like her. I *like* the way she holds up a mirror to all my faults and makes me think twice about them. I like the way she was professional and kind in the face of whatever personal turmoil that meeting with her ex obviously caused. I know from daily experience that separating your personal shit from work can be challenging, and Gracie did it flawlessly.

"No wonder you don't see the point of keeping Larkwood as a wedding venue," she says, brushing against me as we sidestep a puddle. "Have you never been in a serious relationship?"

"Now who's asking the intrusive questions?"

She bites her bottom lip. "Sorry, you're right. Too personal."

I shrug, and—trying not to look too deeply into my sudden urge to be a sharer after avoiding the topic my entire adult life—say, "No, you're right. I'm your standard, emotionally unavailable one-night stand expert with baggage of every size, shape, and hazardous material class." I pause, trying to articulate decades of avoidance into one sentence. "I guess as someone whose job primarily involves helping people decouple from walking red flags, I figure I should probably keep myself off the market until I'm not one of them."

Gracie is silent for so long, I look down at her. She's staring up at me with an expression I haven't seen on her face before. But then the heel of her shoe catches on something and she stumbles into me. A haphazard second later, I'm holding her against my chest and fumbling to keep the umbrella above us.

"You okay?" I ask, but even after she feels stable, I can't force myself to let go. Not with her looking up at me like this. Not with rain pouring all around us like *this* was the whole point of the sky opening up.

"I think the strap of my shoe is broken," she says, eyes still wide and startled.

"Hold this," I instruct, handing her the umbrella as guilt takes another swing at me. *What was I thinking, suggesting we walk in a downpour? What if she'd hurt her ankle?*

I barely hear her halfhearted "You really don't have to . . ." as I drop to one knee to examine her shoe. Water soaks through my pants where I'm kneeling and down my back where the umbrella doesn't cover me, but it hardly registers as I take in her bare legs and delicate ankles, slick with rainwater. A muffled swear escapes me, but I don't think she can hear it over the deluge. Thankfully, the strap isn't broken, but it has come undone, and the prospect of refastening it sends a burst of heat through me. I swallow hard before raising my eyes to hers.

"Not broken, just undone. Can I?"

She nods, her lips slightly parted, and I can feel my heartbeat in my fingertips. My hands get to work, slipping the thin black strap of her shoe into its minuscule buckle. My body is chugging dopamine with every brush of my fingertips against her wet skin, and it's indecent, what a simple act like this with her can do to me. If she knew, she'd probably kick me away, and I'd deserve it.

When I discover a little black bow at the back of the strap, I have to stop myself from crawling on my hands and knees to see how well they go with the ones inked above the backs of her ankles. *Christ, what's wrong with me?*

With effort, I finish the job as quickly as I can and stand back up, praying she doesn't notice exactly how much I enjoyed that.

"You're all set," I say, voice hoarse.

"Thanks," she says, looking a little flushed herself. "I didn't plan on going full damsel-in-distress there."

"Well, to be fair, I didn't save you from a dragon or anything—just an undone shoe," I reason to her *and* myself. "But I do feel like I should be acknowledged for my self-sacrifice."

"Oh yes, the trials of buckling shoes should never go unrecognized."

"I was actually referring to my ass, which *somebody* neglected to cover with the umbrella."

She gasps as she grabs hold of my arm and looks down behind our shoulders to see my sodden pants. "Oh my god, I'm sorry! I swear I didn't realize."

"It's okay," I say as all my focus snaps to her grip on me. Knowing I shouldn't, I loop her arm through mine. "I know you secretly wanted to make me explain to my colleagues why it looks like I pissed myself."

She laughs. "I'd like to point out that *you* were the one who insisted on this walk in the first place. If it were up to me, I'd already be halfway back to Larkwood."

Discomfort squirms in my stomach. "If you'd driven with those tires in this weather, you'd be in a ditch right now."

"Wow, worry much?" she says as the rain begins to let up as quickly as it came.

I let out an exhale. "Trust me, I'm well aware of my capacity to overthink things."

She's quiet for a minute. "You know, you're surprisingly . . . self-aware," she finally settles on. "And kind of tragic."

"Some would say anxiously considering every possible outcome is a superpower."

"Sure, but I don't just mean your overthinking," she muses. "What you said earlier. About choosing not to be in a serious relationship because you don't want to saddle anyone with your issues? It's weirdly considerate but also . . . everyone has baggage, Jude. Relationships are meant to help us grow, and I'm a firm believer that everyone deserves to find their person. I'm sure there's *someone* out there who'd be willing to, you know . . ." She swirls her sandwich in the air. "Deal with you."

"Thanks for the vote of confidence."

"I'm serious! I'm beginning to think these wedding planning tasks are exactly what you need to see what's possible if you just open yourself up a little." She gently hits my shoulder with the sandwich. "A hoagie fetish doesn't need to be your only option."

"Please—don't start feeling sorry for me. I'm not celibate, if that's what you're thinking, and I have more than enough on my plate between work and my family."

"That's right, your mom is a pretty big deal," she says slowly before smiling at me. "I can't imagine what that's like. The only thing my mom is famous for are the teenie-weenies she microwaves for Patriots games."

"Can't say I've ever tried a teenie-weenie, but that honestly sounds nice. The obscurity—not the mini hotdogs," I clarify.

Gracie's eyebrows pinch together. "Trust me, feeling obscure isn't all that it's cracked up to be."

The way she says it feels like a knot in a thread that I want to untangle. "So, you'd rather have notoriety?"

She lifts her shoulders. "I don't crave fame, if that's what you mean. But I wouldn't hate it if I were someone's most important person someday."

I think of Gracie, holed up in that cottage day in and day out. How fiercely she's trying to hold on to it. Something's not adding up. "I hate to break it to you, but living in an isolated cottage probably isn't the most direct path toward a Happily Ever After. Maybe you should get out more."

"I get out!" she protests. "I'm out right now, aren't I?"

"A work meeting doesn't count as 'getting out,'" I respond. "That's like listing laundry as a hobby because you technically do it in your free time."

Her gaze narrows. "Staying at Larkwood isn't just about living my best homebody life. It's about fighting for what one of my closest friends wanted for their home and trying to protect myself and my colleagues from losing our jobs."

"Gracie, my grandmother left the estate to me. She knew my views. If she wanted it to continue running as is, she could have left it to my mother."

"So, your mom thinks it should remain a wedding venue, too?" she asks, eyes going bright with validation.

"She thinks it should be kept in the family," I confirm. "She's not a huge fan of change."

Understatement of the century. For a moment, the lid covering every messy feeling I have about my mom is lifted, and I have to force it back down. This isn't the time or place, but I make a mental note to call and check on her later.

"Well, I guess that makes two of us," Gracie responds. "If Agatha really didn't care what happened to Larkwood after she passed, then why would she have left the cottage to me? She clearly wanted me to continue working there."

We're approaching her car, but the rain has started back up again with a fresh roll of thunder. I stop in front of it with a fresh twinge of doubt about my grandmother's wishes. "I don't pretend to know what Nana's grand plan was. But now that it's mine, I know what I intend to do."

Gracie glares up at me. "Only if I don't change your mind first."

"And what if I said staying with a friend overnight would put you on my good side?"

"I would say you're lying," she replies, opening her bag to fish out her car keys, which have a key chain of the pretty zombie lady from *Corpse Bride* attached.

"Gracie, please. I have a spare room if you need somewhere to stay."

"Wow, I tell you to open your heart once, and you're already propositioning me."

Heat scrapes up my neck. "That's not what I'm doing."

"Then just let me risk my life and good driving record in peace, okay?"

"At least let me follow behind you. If you break down, you'll have a ride."

"No need for that, I've got a kayak right here," she says, waving the sandwich.

"I'll get my car. It's not far away."

"Stop. You're going to give yourself an ulcer. I'll text you when I make it back."

I bite back another argument, knowing I'm edging away from concerned and into controlling. "Fine."

"See? Was that so hard?" she asks, opening the driver's-side door.

Yes.

"I'll text you when I make it," she assures me again when I don't answer her.

"Bye, Gracie."

She closes her door and starts what sounds like a hamster-powered engine. As she drives away with a wave, I grab my phone, check the GPS, and set a timer for fifty-six minutes—the exact amount of time it'll take her to get from here to Larkwood.

12

GRACIE

Six Weeks Before the Wedding

Jude: You should be back now.

Jude: Are you not responding on purpose?

Gracie: Too busy hailing a long-haul trucker with my sandwich. Do you think flashing some leg would work better than flashing pastrami?

Jude: Tell me you're not broken down and hitchhiking.

Gracie: I'm home! Just pulled into my driveway, you psycho. Go pet your cat or something.

Jude: I'd prefer to keep my fingers, thanks.

Gracie: Your own cat won't let you pet her? Sad.

Jude: Taco is more of a "look with your eyes, not your hands" companion.

Gracie: Like a museum exhibit?

Jude: Like a land mine.

Gracie: Aw. I'm sure it's just you she doesn't like.

Jude: I think you forgot the word "not" before "just."

Gracie: Nope. Just you. ♥

Tuesday

Jude: *Video message*

Gracie: The only thing this footage proves is Taco's wise, instinctual mistrust of lawyers.

Jude: Henry still has scars!

Gracie: Scars build character! Also, a responsible owner would make sure their pet's nails are trimmed.

Jude: Yes, she's quite militant about enforcing my personal hygiene habits.

Gracie: Good to know where you rank in the scheme of things.

Jude: Definitely below treats, but somewhere above kitty litter.

Gracie: And don't you forget it!

Gracie: Btw, do you have time to meet tomorrow at my florist's? It's called Daphne's Petals. I need to beg her to do this wedding, and you definitely haven't had your weekly recommended serving of guilt yet.

Jude: I'm practically wasting away. Can you do 12?

Gracie: Yes, it's a date!

Gracie: Not like a date, date. You don't even do those, obviously.

Jude: Obviously?

Gracie: Am I not texting with the Grim Reaper of Relationships? Yes, obviously.

Gracie: . . . right?

Jude: Why, are you interested?

Gracie: Kb N

Gracie: oops, I mean, NO.

Jude: You sure, butter fingers? I've been told my scythe is really big.

Gracie: I'm blocking you! See you tomorrow.

Jude: I'll be the one in black.

Gracie: BLOCKING

Wednesday

Gracie: Are you okay? You seemed a little shell-shocked when we left.

Jude: I'm fine, just sweeping up the pieces of my shattered soul.

Gracie: I never said this was going to be easy.

Jude: You also never said you'd be breaking the news about Larkwood to your friends in front of me. Are all of them going to cry like that?

Gracie: Probably? I tried to tell you how much Larkwood means to everyone. I wasn't kidding.

Jude: Consider me chastened.

Gracie: And convinced?

Jude: I'm sorry, no. But that doesn't mean today didn't have an impact.

Gracie: Then I guess you can consider me hopeful.

Jude: I can't imagine you as anything but.

Thursday

Gracie: I see you typing. Is this about the chance of rain in the forecast?

Jude: It's over 80 percent. That's practically a threat.

Gracie: Shouldn't you be busy unaliving a marriage or something? I have a weather app, you know.

Jude: Do you have new tires, too?

Gracie: No, but I do have a handy predisposition for never leaving my house unless forced.

Jude: We're still on for tomorrow night, though, right?

Gracie: Do I sense the tides shifting? Are you looking forward to wedding planning events?

Jude: I'm looking forward to having an excuse not to join Henry's pickleball team.

Gracie: That *almost* makes me want to cancel. But we're still on—unless it drizzles, of course.

Jude: With those tires, you should take hydroplaning seriously.

Gracie: I think it's time for your prune juice and a nap, Grandpa. ♥

Jude: See you tomorrow, Gracie.

13

GRACIE

Five Weeks Before the Wedding

Sitting in my dark car in downtown Providence under a streetlamp, I check my lipstick one last time. Tonight, I'm dragging Jude along to hear the band that plays at nearly every Larkwood wedding, hoping three things: (a) they won't be able to resist my sad-puppy eyes when I beg them to squeeze Calvin and Brooke's wedding into their packed schedule, (b) Jude meets an amazing group of people who would be seriously set back if Larkwood stopped hosting weddings, and (c) he miraculously changes his mind about selling. And while *maybe* it's a little too soon for C, after our meeting with Daphne this week, my hopes have never been higher.

I don't want to admit that I'm nervous. Not just about guilting him into keeping Larkwood, but also because prior to last week, my feelings for him were black and white. He was Jude: the heat-seeking missile aimed directly at my life. Now though, he's Jude: devoted but unappreciated cat guardian, excessive worrier over my bald tires, and sender of texts I look forward to *way* too much.

It's more than a little unsettling. Admitting that I enjoy talking to him (or worse, that I've taken to rereading our text conversations when we're *not* talking) feels wrong. But the fact is, I've stopped crying in my shower to Celine Dion, and that's a silver lining I'm not quite ready to give up. So, with nerves crackling in my stomach, I get out of my car and walk to the bar.

Inside, it's snug and crowded with a 1920s Art Deco theme and jazz that runs like a current just below the hum of conversation. Across the dim room, I spot Jude seated on a dark-green velvet barstool. An electric pulse goes through me at the sight of his large, graceful body leaning with one elbow on the bar, like he was born to slouch in elegant rooms. Rolling my eyes at the thought, I make it to the seat he's saved for me.

"You didn't bring Taco?" I say in greeting.

Jude smirks as he turns toward me. "She's out back with the band, drinking bathtub gin and flashing her knees."

"This place definitely makes me wish I'd worn something with more fringe," I say, slipping my light trench coat from my shoulders. His eyes follow the garment, dropping down as my clingy maroon dress makes its appearance.

"You look lovely," he murmurs, eyes meeting mine again.

I look away as the compliment, free of any of his usual snark, makes all my pulse points flutter to life.

"Thanks!" I say lightly, hanging my bag and coat under the bar before sitting down. I don't mention that, as usual, *he* manages to make a boring white button-up look borderline pornographic. Instead, I say, "No sign of the band yet?"

"Not yet, but the drinks are strong." He slides a cocktail menu over to me. "Anything look good to you?"

My eyes instantly zero in on the prices, which, at seventeen dollars per drink, make me want to rear back and rub my eyeballs.

"My treat," Jude says, like he can hear the mental list of groceries I could buy for the price of two of these concoctions.

"No thanks," I say primly. "Unlike Taco, I don't require treats."

"Please. It's the least I can do after being . . . what did you call me the other day? The world's most apologetic life ruiner?"

"That title could be revoked, you know. We still have weeks to go before the wedding, and every moment you spend with me is a moment you could change your mind."

"Have you ever considered that I might change yours?"

I look over at him. In a slight departure from his usual straight-from-the-office appearance, he's got a dense five o'clock shadow, and his collar is unbuttoned and tie-free. His rolled shirtsleeves reveal a pair of distressingly toned forearms that I have *no* business staring at. But there are veins and muscles and—*is that what I think it is?*

A dark tattoo peeks out from the underside of his left arm and draws my gaze like water going down a gutter. It's the last thing I would expect from Mr. Lawyer McContracts, and my brain can't stop itself from remembering the way Calvin barely tried to hide his disappointment when I came home with tattoos of my own. *It's just not what I'm into, babe.*

But maybe Jude is. The thought flies through my mind before I can stop it, and I force my eyes away from his skin. I think I do need that drink after all.

"Impossible," I finally respond. "I'm extremely stubborn and fully committed to your emotional makeover."

"Haven't you ever heard that saying about embracing change, since it's all we can ever count on?"

"Oh, I've already filled my Abrupt Life Changes bingo card. This year, I'm signing up for the Peace and Predictability package."

"I didn't realize the life of a wedding planner was so tumultuous."

I look back up at him, ignoring the way my blood fizzes under his unwavering gaze. "Well, it's not. Choosing the quiet life of a cottage-dwelling event planner calmed the tumult, but now you're threatening to throw me back out to sea."

For the first time since I sat down, he takes a sip of his drink, his searchlight eyes scanning my face over the rim of his glass. He lowers it and says, "You look like a pretty strong swimmer to me."

My heart lurches to a stop before resuming its job.

"I'm surprised you have any confidence in me after your visit to my cottage," I admit, curling the corner of the menu in front of me. "I was definitely treading water that night."

He lifts a shoulder and takes another sip of his drink. "We all need to drown our sorrows once in a while. And anyway, I take full responsibility for driving you to make that particular life choice."

"Oh, you don't get to take all the credit, trust me."

His dark eyebrows rise in faint surprise. "Who on earth is making you more miserable than me? I'll need to try harder."

My smile is halfhearted at best when I think of Calvin embarking on family life with Brooke. But instead of the usual pang of longing, I'm hit with a flare of unexpected anger: at Calvin for asking me to plan his wedding, and at myself for agreeing to it, no matter what opportunities it opened up for saving Larkwood. But there's no way I'm getting into all that with Jude, who probably wouldn't understand unrequited love if the dictionary definition got up and did a pole dance for him. I sit up a little straighter. "Unfortunately for you, that's a secret I won't be divulging."

He turns more fully toward me, and I'm trapped like a fly in his dark, honey-colored gaze. "I could take a guess."

My eyes run away from his, landing on the tattoo peeking out from beneath his rolled shirt sleeve. I can only see half of it, but the distinctive forked tail feathers are instantly recognizable. *A swallow*. It's simple, all black linework. I force myself to look away. "It's cute that you think you know me so well."

"I'm picking up on little things." His gaze flicks to my nervous hands, curling my menu. "I bet I could order your new favorite drink."

"Does that mean you missed my aversion to unrequested food and beverages?"

"Stop pretending you didn't love that sandwich."

"'*Didn't?*' You make it sound like that sandwich exists in the past tense and won't continue to feed me and my future grandchildren for generations to come."

"Then you admit it's the gift that keeps on giving and won't argue if I order something for you here." I only realize how close we've gotten when he sits up straighter and flags the busy bartender. It's like she's been waiting for his subtle hand raise all night.

"Everything good here, handsome?"

I can't tell if she's committing a little too hard to the speakeasy bit or simply hitting on Jude, but either way, I am not bothered, because this is *not* a date.

"Could I get a Corpse Reviver for my date?" he asks. "Also, do you know when the band is coming on?"

The bartender glances over at me like she's just now noticing that I'm not a particularly dense collection of air molecules before smiling apologetically. Meanwhile, I begin what I know will be an ultramarathon of overanalyzing the word *date*, the tone in which he said it, and where the moon was in conjunction with planet Whatthehell.

"They got a flat tire," the bartender answers as she grabs a coupe glass from under the bar, "but I'm about to put the karaoke machine out while we wait. I'll get you that drink first, though."

She hustles off, and I'm left staring at Jude's profile.

"I hope you didn't mind being called my date," he says, without looking at me. "She was coming on a little strong earlier."

Oh. So, I was just his decoy. That's . . . fine. Great, in fact. No astrological charts or mental flagellation necessary. I clear my throat. "No problem. But she is really pretty. No need to deny yourself a good time on my account. That is, if you're even single, or interested in humans of the female variety."

A smirk tugs at his full lips as he swivels back toward me. His knee brushes the outside of my tightly closed thigh, and I realize if I were sitting any more rigidly, I could probably put out a hat and earn a few bucks as a living statue. That's when I see the inside of his other forearm has a twin swallow. *Why, God, why have you cursed me with a deep appreciation for symmetry and inked skin?*

"I think you know I'm single," he tells me. "I also prefer humans of the female variety, both as partners and generally speaking. But she's not my type."

"Hmm. More of an O-negative kind of guy?"

His sharp-cornered grin sets off a chemical chain reaction that starts low in my belly and ends . . . well, we'll see where it ends. "If only it were that easy. These days, my tastes seem to tend toward everything I can't have."

I'm saved from having to respond to *this* information by the bartender, who slides me a yellow cocktail in a frosty coupe glass. I nod my thanks, and she winks at me.

"So, a Corpse Reviver. You think this will be my new favorite drink?" I lift the glass and take a sniff. It smells delicious, but I say, "I didn't realize our conversation made me look that desperate for resuscitation."

"You could never be mistaken for a corpse, Gracie."

"Wow, I'm blushing," I say dryly, except I think I might be.

"I've noticed you're pretty into them."

"What, corpses? So, I accuse you of an admittedly weird sandwich kink, and you retaliate by immediately jumping to necrophilia? That seems extreme."

"If you want to play Guess My Kink, I'm game, but I was actually referring to your equally weird zombie fixation."

"How do you know about my zombies?" I say defensively.

"Were they supposed to be a secret?"

"Well, no, but I thought only my best friend and Cal—" I stop. "I didn't realize I was broadcasting it."

He leans in close and says in his pillow-soft voice, "Well, I hate to break it to you, but you were wearing nothing but a NICE TO EAT YOU T-shirt when you answered the door for me the other night. It left an impression." He leans back, and I hope the dim lighting is doing a sufficient job of disguising the flush I feel pulsing in my cheeks.

"Well, congratulations, Sherlock, you found me out," I say unsteadily. I hesitate a moment. "I spent most of my time at my best friend Sofia's house growing up," I tell him, not entirely sure why I'm sharing this. "After her parents would go to bed, I'd sneak downstairs with her and her siblings to have these all-night zombie movie marathons." I smile as some of the best memories of my childhood send a tender ache through me. "They used to terrify me, but now, they remind me of hiding under blankets with my best friend and popcorn fights with her brothers and sisters."

Jude's eyes are on me like he wants to absorb every word I've said. "I'd probably love them, too, if I'd grown up like that."

"So, not a fan of blood and gore?"

"Not unless I want to pass out. Could be handy on a sleepless night, though."

"Cheers to that."

He lifts his glass to clink it against mine, and we both take a sip. I can't remember the last time I had a fancy cocktail, much less one that was zombie-themed, and this one has everything I love packed into it, including the novel sensation of being seen. I close my eyes in pleasure, letting the cold, sweet-sour liquid swirl in my mouth before swallowing it. When I open my eyes again, Jude is looking at me—more specifically at my lips.

"You're welcome," he says preemptively, but his usual velvet baritone has a sandpaper texture that makes me think of early mornings and tangled bedsheets.

Stop it, Gracie. The only tangled bedsheets in my future are the ones I'll tangle myself in during sweaty nightmares about losing my home and job.

I'm about to give him a belated thank-you when the sound of microphone feedback cuts through the room. Swiveling on my barstool so that my back is to Jude, I see our chipper bartender standing on the low platform and velvet-curtained backdrop that serves as the bar's stage.

"Hello, everyone! I know you've all come out to hear the Love Notes perform, and I promise they'll be here soon. But until they get some car trouble sorted, I'm opening up the stage to karaoke. If you'd like to sing, just sign up at the bar!"

There's an automatic increase in chatter around the room as everyone begins cajoling their dates and friends into embarrassing themselves. At this point in my life, Sofia has dragged me onto so many karaoke stages, I've become numb to the requisite humiliation. But something tells me Jude hasn't. I turn back to him with a wicked smile on my face.

"No," he says, before I even open my mouth to speak.

I pout and say, "Is Broody Jude afraid I'll destroy him at karaoke?"

Jude shifts in his chair and averts his eyes from me, opting for a long sip of his nearly empty drink. Eventually, he says, "I'm already threatening your livelihood. I didn't want to crush your ego, too."

I let out a delighted laugh of disbelief and wave down the bartender, who lets us sign up first. After scrolling through a list on an iPad to find my go-to song, I grab my drink and—without letting myself overthink it—his hand, before dragging him up to the stage.

"What are we singing?" he asks.

"You think I'm going to give you a heads-up?"

He smiles, while above us a disco ball turns on and begins

refracting its sparkling, swirling light. "You know, most people who sign up for a duet don't want their partners to suck."

"I guess I'm not most people then."

He shakes his head, his gaze softening. "I guess that's one thing we can agree on."

The slipped-down-a-step feeling in my stomach is back, but I don't have time to acknowledge it because the bass starts thumping from the karaoke speaker. I lift my drink to take a last sip for courage and then bring the mic to my lips.

Jude immediately recognizes the iconic sounds of "Ice Ice Baby" and starts to laugh. Not a sardonic chuckle but the real deal, complete with a mile-wide smile and possibly the most adorable nose scrunch I have ever witnessed. I blink, wondering how he managed to hide it from me this whole time, but then it's time for my opening verse.

I don't need to look at the lyrics on the screen in front of us, so instead, I keep my eyes on Jude, reveling in his shock and pleasure at my perfectly executed rhyme, complete with some well-timed hair tosses and a poke at his broad chest when the chorus breaks loose and is sung by the entire bar. With one last smirk, he snatches the mic from me when it ends and launches into the second verse, shocking me down to my pinched toes when he doesn't bother sparing a glance at the screen either. Instead, he knows every word as well as I do. By now, the entire crowd is cheering or singing along, and Jude is standing so close that I have to arch my neck to keep looking at him.

We may be in front of a crowd, singing about 9's and Lamborghinis, but suddenly, in this cocoon of his whiskey scent and whirling, mirror-ball light, I feel suspended in a world of our own. Once the second chorus is finished and the grin on my face begins to hurt, it's time for the last verse. When he leans down and holds the mic out for us to share, it's the most natural thing in the world to slip my hand over his to center it between us.

Joy and something new and sparkling fizzes in my stomach like I've swallowed a whole packet of Pop Rocks in one go. His skin is so warm and electric beneath my own, and as we launch into the final verse, I don't attempt to create distance between us as he leans in closer to me, his eyes crinkled at the corners from the smile he can't seem to get rid of either.

I'm breathless when we finish, and it's like someone has turned the volume back on the cheering crowd. We make our way back to our seats as the new singer begins an incredible rendition of "Killing Me Softly." When we sit, I take a thirsty drink of my Corpse Reviver, which seems to travel directly to my brain and blocks its capacity for rational thinking. Because that was *fun*, and for a moment under the disco lights, all I wanted was for Jude to kiss me.

"So," he says, taking a sip from the fresh Old Fashioned that's waiting for him at the bar. "A wedding planner with a secret passion for fine tailoring, zombies, and 90s hiphop. What other secrets are you hiding from me, Gracie Holland?"

I take another sip of my drink, trying to look enigmatic and not like he's just summed up my whole personality in a thimble. "Where's the fun in spoiled surprises?"

For the next few songs (some wonderful, some wonderfully terrible), I pretend that Jude's knee isn't touching mine beneath the bar. He pretends not to notice the way my gaze keeps falling into the vertical crevice of his bottom lip like it's a canyon I leaned too close to look at. I'm on my second cocktail when the band finally shows up to a round of applause.

"Wow, I kind of forgot they were coming," Jude says.

"You mean you forgot the whole point of this outing?" I ask, even though I've had the same memory lapse.

"I think the 'whole point of this outing' is up for debate."

"The *whole point* is the guilt trip I'm taking you on when we talk to my friends later."

He raises an eyebrow. "And here I thought the *whole point* was for you to lure me in with strong drinks, your charming quirks, and red dress until I had no choice but to do your bidding."

He says "red dress" like it's a swear, and a shiver goes through me that feels like a rush of power. I take a slow sip as the band hurries through a sound check. "And is it working?"

"Feeling guiltier by the second." His voice is a rasp.

It's definitely the alcohol, and maybe also the way his eyes make me feel like I'm standing too close to a furnace, that makes me lean in and whisper near his ear, "Then maybe you should just give up now and give me what I want."

His cologne must wrap silken fingers around me because I can't move when he turns his face toward mine—so close that I can feel the warmth of his breath while my own hitches. His eyelids are heavy, like they're suddenly tired from holding up such a wealth of eyelashes. My heartbeat is less of a beat and more of a vibration in my chest when his thumb comes up to brush the underside of my jaw. My lips part, and—

"*Hellooo*, and thank you for your patience! We're the Love Notes and we do *not* know how to change a flat tire!"

I rear back at the loud interruption and wish I could say that I nearly fall off my stool. Instead, I *actually* fall off my stool. My heels are hooked over the footrest, and the rounded edge of the bar is too wide and slippery to grip easily. I'm going down, ready to kiss the sticky floor, until Jude catches me by the shoulders and I cling onto his forearms for dear dignity.

"Wow, what did they put in those drinks?" I say with an embarrassed laugh once I'm stable.

I look down and realize my fingertips are digging right into his swallow tattoos. I jerk my hands away like they might be nipped for the intrusion, and Jude's hands leave me just as quickly.

"I'm sorry," he says, eyes wide. But I can barely hear him over the opening notes to the jazz standard "I've Got a Crush on You," which, *great*.

"It's fine," I hurry to say, even though it's not clear what he's apologizing for. Is it for almost kissing me? Being the best-looking problem of my entire adult existence? Or for leaving handprints I'll likely feel for the rest of my life?

I try swiveling away from him to watch the band—*the reason I am here in the first place*, I pointedly remind myself—but Jude grabs hold of the bottom of my stool. He swivels me back, and this time, my legs are trapped right between his as I'm forced to come face-to-face with him.

His features are as grave as his voice when he repeats himself. "I'm sorry."

"Don't be," I say, attempting lightheartedness. "Pretty sure you just saved me from getting too friendly with the floor of this establishment."

No smirk, no flicker of amusement. "I'm sorry for almost kissing you," he says baldly. Like my super mature plan of pretending it didn't happen would never enter his mind as an option.

"Oh," I say, waving a hand, like almost kissing someone you can't decide is your biggest enemy or biggest crush happens all the time. "That."

"I'm . . ." His eyes take on a tortured look, honey darkening to molasses as black pupils blot out everything but two starved rings. "Very attracted to you."

The words land like a bomb in my stomach, making my ears ring. He goes on. "But it's no excuse for making you uncomfortable, and I promise it won't happen again." A deep V forms between his eyebrows. "I'd never want you to think I'm trying to manipulate you to win our bargain or take advantage of you in some way."

Our bargain. Right. It hadn't occurred to me as a possibility, but now that he's said it, I can't be sure that this isn't just another part of his strategy. Suddenly, every mean inner voice that enjoys reminding me that I was never enough for Calvin, my business, or my family pipes up. *Why* would *he be interested in someone whose life is such a wreck?*

All at once, I feel ridiculous. For Jude, a self-admitted "one-night-stand expert," everything that's happened tonight is probably run-of-the-mill. Maybe he momentarily lost sight of our unique situation in the swirl of lights and strong drinks, but he quickly steered us back on course. Meanwhile, I'm developing feelings for a man who terminated my job and wants to evict me, because apparently, I'm *that* desperate for a little affection. *God*. I need to call Sofia and have her knock some sense into me.

Taking a breath, I put my guard back up. No matter what his intentions are, I need to start thinking with my brain again instead of my lonely heart and lonelier vagina. I pick up my drink and slowly turn it in the light.

"You could make it up to me," I say without looking at him.

"Go on."

"Tell me what your plans for Larkwood really are."

Even without touching him, I feel him tense. "I can't do that."

I take a sip and look up at his wary face. "Why not?"

He rubs absently at the side of his bristled jaw. "I would tell you if I could. But the person who's interested—"

"Requires absolute privacy. Yeah. You've mentioned. But why is *this* buyer so important? Is it Vanilla Ice or something?"

He stalls by taking a drink of his Old Fashioned and placing the glass down slowly. When he speaks, his words are careful. "No, it's not Vanilla Ice. Let's just say their aims for Larkwood align with values that are close to my heart as well."

Rolling my eyes at the lawyer-speak, I respond, "I didn't realize you had one of those."

A smirk appears as he holds a hand to the center of his chest. "Just updated my software last night."

I narrow my eyes at him. "If these 'aims' are so meaningful to you, why not share them?"

He rotates his sweating glass a quarter turn on the bar. "It's personal," he says shortly.

"Does Henry know who the buyer is?"

He pushes dark waves that have become increasingly unruly from his forehead. "No, Gracie, he doesn't, but he *does* understand the concept of privacy."

I sit back at the sharpness of his tone, realizing I've gotten a little too close to something he doesn't want me—or apparently even his best friend—to see.

He rubs a hand across the lower half of his unshaven face. "Look, I'm sorry I can't tell you. Their privacy isn't something I'm just respecting out of the kindness of my heart. It's something I'm legally obligated to ensure."

My brow furrows. "Does that mean they're your client?"

He stares at me, worrying the side of his bottom lip for a moment. "Not in the traditional sense. But I'd feel more comfortable if we stopped talking about it. They've placed their trust in me, and confidentiality is something I take very seriously."

The guarded look in his eyes is gone, replaced by a silent plea for understanding. Finally, I nod. There's no lie in his voice, and I can't help admiring his commitment to his client's privacy.

"Okay," I finally say. "I'll stop pressing. I appreciate you telling me what you could."

His heavy shoulders visibly sag in relief. "Thank you for understanding. I realize it must be frustrating for you."

"Has Henry given you shit for this, too?" I ask.

Jude takes a sip of his drink with a shrug. "He's an attorney. He gets it. But yes, as a rule, giving me shit is Henry's favorite pastime."

I smile. "I knew I liked him for some reason."

Jude rolls his eyes, and for the rest of the evening, we listen to the band, who are amazing, as usual. Even better, after their set, they agree to perform at Calvin and Brooke's wedding, and Jude is forced to meet more of the wonderful people he would be financially hurting if Larkwood closes its doors. From the band's reaction to the news that the rest of the season's weddings have been canceled, there's no doubt in my mind that he's beginning to understand the scope of his actions.

He's somber when we leave the bar—more somber than I realized was possible after an "Ice Ice Baby" duet—but it's impossible to tell what he's thinking. Is he reflecting on the people he'd hurt if he continues with his plans? Our almost kiss? Or the cause that's *so* close to his heart that he can't tell anyone about it?

I don't ask—not as he walks me to my car in silence, and not after I promise him I've sobered up enough to drive. There's no sparkling, tug-of-war conversation between us, just a quiet goodbye before he walks off into the night with his suit jacket slung over one shoulder. And maybe that's because he's not the only one lost in thought. For the first time, I consider the possibility that Jude's reasons for wanting to get rid of Larkwood aren't as selfish as I believed. That maybe there's more to this—more to *him*—than I ever imagined.

14

Five Weeks Before the Wedding

Henry: Is it or is it not true that you were at a bar last night, participating in Vanilla Ice karaoke with a mysterious woman and NOT with the best friend you promised to play pickleball with?

Jude: How the hell do you know where I was last night?

Henry: This is Rhode Island, Jude. She suffers no secrets. Also, my friend Astrid was the one pouring you and your self-described DATE drinks. Did she enjoy her Corpse Reviver btw?

Jude: You are intolerable.

Henry: And YOU will be coughing up every last detail Astrid couldn't glean on our Sunday fun run tomorrow.

Jude: Fantastic. Can't wait.

15

JUDE

Five Weeks Before the Wedding

Feet pounding the dirt, I round a corner of the woodland path that cuts through Larkwood's carefully contained wild acreage and catch a glimpse of the ivy-covered house I'll be sorting antiques in for the rest of the weekend. Its dark windows glare back, reminding me that what I'm *not* here to do is trade my preferred workout of swimming for running, just because Gracie happened to jog on these trails that one time. And yet, here I am, sweating it out in woods I haven't entered in years.

I take a deep breath as Henry catches up. I've been pushing us harder than usual to keep thoughts exactly like this out of my head *and* to stave off his interrogation.

"Jesus, Judy, there isn't a bear chasing us." He slows his pace to a jog.

So much for that plan.

"Those Bagel Bites finally catching up to you?" I ask breathlessly, slowing my pace to match his.

"*Fuck*"—he pants—"*off.*" He wipes sweat-dampened curls off his forehead. "I know what you're doing, and you're not getting out of this. Tell me about your mystery date."

"It wasn't a date," I say.

"Astrid said you specifically used the word *date*."

"That's because Astrid was trying to burn my clothes off with her retinas."

"Oh, to have your problems, ye of perfect face and stick-up ass."

"I don't have—"

"Who were you with, then?"

I pause, not sure why I'm hesitant to admit the truth. "Gracie."

The astonished look on Henry's face would be comical if it didn't reveal exactly how low his confidence in me is.

"You're telling me you managed to unsink the *Titanic* and get her to grab a drink with you? Was it bribery or kidnapping?"

"Neither," I say, pushing sweaty hair back from my face. "It was her idea."

"Explain."

We keep jogging, and I tell him about the night I apologized and told her about Nana's will. How Gracie used her newfound upper hand to make the absurd proposal I found myself agreeing to.

"So let me get this straight. Gracie thinks she can convince *you*—the founding father of fuck boys—to keep the place you hate most in the world by forcing you to plan a *wedding* with her? I feel like I should tell her she'd have a better chance if she just ransomed Taco."

I snort. "Are you kidding me? Taco would ransom *her* if she got too close. Also, Gracie doesn't know me like you do." Guilt slinks through my stomach. "She thinks she has a chance."

"Does she also think you have an entirely different personality? Have you taken up method acting?"

"She knows it's a long shot. But she also knows I'm selling it no matter what, so she figures she may as well put all her chips on the table."

"So now you're planning a wedding. *You* are planning a *wedding*."

I wipe my brow, squinting as the sun breaks through the trees. "I'm happy to jump through whatever hoops she's got for me as long as I get that cottage by August."

I don't mention that those hoops have been flaming with guilt. Meeting with each new vendor has felt like stomping on a butterfly.

"And you're willing to go through this for the all-important mystery buyer you won't give me a single hint about," Henry says.

When I let silence stretch between us, he says, "It's Dwayne 'The

Rock' Johnson, isn't it? Did he threaten to crush you between his pecs if you tell anyone? Blink twice if I'm right."

My laugh is half groan as I shake my head. "*Please* stop asking me."

"Okay, fine. I get it," he says, slapping a bug off his shoulder. "Confidential. How does your mom feel about all this, by the way? She must be pissed Agatha skipped over her in the will. She hardly left her anything at all."

The question, which I'm only surprised he hasn't asked sooner, is another one I don't want to answer. Because my mom isn't pissed—she's heartbroken. Nana understood that anything she gave to my mom would inevitably benefit *him*, too. My father. And that was simply out of the fucking question.

"It's complicated," I grunt.

Henry sighs. "Ah, yes. The hallowed words from your family's crest."

"Every family is complicated."

"Yeah, except yours could be the inspo for a BBC miniseries."

"Why do you think I'm trying so hard to get rid of this place?"

"Getting cocktails with a gorgeous woman doesn't seem like too much of a hardship, if I'm being honest."

No. It wasn't. In fact, I've spent most of the last thirty-six hours replaying every moment in that bar with the feverish intensity of a horny teenager who's just discovered new uses for soap. Every time I close my eyes, I see her dark cat eyes tracing my tattoos like a fingertip. Feel her unwavering conviction in love-everlasting tighten its chokehold on me. It's as incomprehensible and irresistible to me as any villain who secretly craves the one thing he claims to despise.

I pick up my pace like I have a hope of outrunning my own thoughts, but they just snarl beside me. *How could I have let myself almost kiss her?* It's bad enough that I'm stringing her along, letting her think she has a chance of winning me over, when I know there's only one way this is going to end—with zero chance of her not hating me.

By the time Henry catches up again, our exhalations are harsh as we adjust to the faster cadence I've set. He glances at me. "So, on the topic of drinking with beautiful women, I was thinking of asking her out. Gracie, I mean."

At this, my head snaps to look at him. He flashes that stupid dimple at me, and I don't see the tree root but feel it against the toe of my running shoe. *Fuck*.

Arms pinwheeling in a way that should come with a slipped-on-a-banana-peel sound effect, every prepubescent year of my youth flashes before my eyes in a kaleidoscope of too-long limbs and sweaty humiliation. I fall fast and I fall hard, barely saving myself from a mouthful of dirt with my outstretched hands. Head pounding and still panting, it's a moment before the sting hits my palms and ego.

"Shit!" Henry shouts, skidding to a stop next to me. He crouches down in the rising dust, shouting at top volume, "*Judy!* Judy, speak to me!"

He grabs my shoulders, but by now, I'm pushing myself off the ground, sucking in gulps of air. I wave him off, sitting back on my heels and closing my eyes. *Jesus*. Why the hell didn't I see—

And then it comes back to me. Henry wants to ask Gracie out.

"You're bleeding," he says, grabbing my wrist to look at the mess I've made of my palms.

I snatch my hand back. "I'm fine," I say, forcing my legs to stand me back up.

"Man, I haven't seen someone bite the dust that hard since . . . ever. Are you okay?"

I brush myself off and try not to feel as shaken as I am. "Yeah. I'm okay, thanks."

He looks at me for a long moment, biting the inside of his cheek. "You don't look okay. This isn't about what I said about Gracie, is it?"

Slowly, I limp back into a jog, unable to look at him. "You only met her the one time, right? How do you know if you'd even like her?"

At this, Henry hesitates. "Actually, I came to see her the other day to discuss the transfer of the cottage and sign paperwork."

"You visited her? Here? Why didn't you tell me?" I ask, feeling inexplicably affronted.

Henry shrugs. "I was doing my job. You don't tell me about every meeting you have, do you?"

I have nothing to say to this, because he's absolutely right. "I've never heard of the probate process finishing so quickly," I point out instead. "You must have set a record."

At this, he looks a little abashed. "I may have prioritized her case."

No need to ask why. Henry wouldn't dream of asking a client out because of ethical reasons, but with the cottage officially transferred to Gracie, he's technically in the clear. Suddenly, I feel completely winded.

"So, you like her," I manage, even though it's a foregone conclusion. Who the hell wouldn't like Gracie? But Henry—who openly talks about his desire to find "the one"—has a habit of testing the waters with most, if not all, of his female acquaintances.

"There's something about her, man," he says, shaking his head. "After she stood up to you in the garden, I couldn't stop thinking that I'd like to get to know her better—no offense. Then when I stopped by, she was just so . . . I don't know. *Lovely*." He laughs at himself. "You know what I mean, though? She's fucking lovely."

Yes, I do know. I know she smells like flowers drowned in honey and is the only reason my grief over losing Nana hasn't suffocated me. I know I've never felt this way about anyone, and unless I'm wildly mistaken, neither will my best friend.

"So what do you think?" he asks, punching my shoulder lightly. "Should I ask her out?"

I bite my tongue as my entire brain vibrates with a resounding, illogical *NO*. I'm not okay with Henry asking Gracie out, even though I should be. She already told me she thinks he's handsome, and I know better than anyone that he's the whole package. Smart, successful, funny, relentlessly kind. On top of all this, he's looking for exactly the same thing she is—Happily Ever After. They'd be perfect for each other, and if I were a decent friend and human being, I would have already suggested the match.

But I'm not a decent friend or human being. I'm a greedy, possessive asshole, hung up over someone who doesn't and will never belong to me. The simple truth is, I'm not capable of giving her a fraction of what she needs or deserves.

It's this depressing thought that finally makes me say, "You don't need to ask me for permission, Hen. You should go for it if you like her."

"I know I don't need your blessing." He keeps his eyes ahead on the trail as he says, "Just making sure all the I-Hate-You energy between you two isn't more like I-Hate-You-Let's-Fuck-It-Out energy."

I will my feet not to stumble again because suddenly, I'm back in that bar with the warmth of her citrus exhale on my lips. One inch and one bad decision away from sinking my fingers into the flare of her hips in that fucking dress and ruining the tentative truce we've established. But I know she was just caught up in the moment. She might be attracted to me, but there are about ten thousand good reasons why she should stay away from me. So I say, "Absolutely not. Don't let me get in your way."

"Well, it wouldn't be the first time, would it?" Henry's voice is deceptively light, and he's still not looking at me.

"What are you talking about?"

"Oh, come on. Every time we go out, I may as well be a coatrack next to you."

"Bullshit," I argue. "That's not true."

He shoots a flat look over at me. "Jude, I've been trying to get out of the friend zone with Astrid for months. Then you sit down at her bar *once*, and the next thing I know, she's texting me, asking if the buddy I always mention, Jude Larkwood, is taken or just casually dating, and would I give her your number just in case."

For a moment, I'm at a loss for words. "Shit, I'm sorry, Hen. I didn't realize."

He waves my apology away. "You never do, but as your shorter, less-chiseled best friend, let me assure you that it's a pattern."

I hardly know what to say to this, partly because I feel like a dick, and partly because in my own mind, I'm still the gangly kid with dental headgear and glasses on my nana's refrigerator.

"I'll try to be more self-aware," I promise him. "And I won't stand in your way with Gracie. You're both sickeningly romantic and stunningly naive—a perfect match."

Henry grins at me. "Then let's head toward her cottage. Never know if we'll run into her."

"You go ahead," I tell him, knowing I won't be able to safely watch him ask Gracie out to dinner without risking a burst blood vessel. "I need to shower before the plaster-repair person gets here."

"Okay," he says. With a nervous grin, he adjusts an invisible bow tie. "Wish me luck."

I give him a weak salute before he turns away, running down the path toward the kind of woman he deserves. A woman who deserves him, too. Chest aching, I tell myself it's from the run. The fall. Anything but the pain of losing something I never had in the first place.

16

GRACIE

Five Weeks Before the Wedding

It's eleven thirty on a rainy Tuesday night, and I should be asleep, but instead, I'm staring up at my ceiling in the dark, thinking about Jude. Not productive or wise, especially after the things he said and *didn't* say to me at the bar the other night, but I can't seem to help it. I spent the day following up with my ex-clients and was prepared to cry alongside them again. But with every conversation, I was stunned to discover that each of them had managed to find gorgeous new venues to squeeze them in at the last moment. When I asked them how they managed it, they all had the same answer: Jude Larkwood.

Apparently, Jude used his connections among the Rhode Island estate community to pull strings for all my former clients, securing them locations that usually book over a year or two in advance. I clutch my blankets to the center of my chest. *Was he ever going to tell me?*

I've been thinking of texting him all day, despite the awkward way we left things at the bar. Not just because of what he did for my clients, but also because today is Agatha's birthday. My own heart has felt bruised since I woke up this morning, and I can only imagine what he's feeling. So many firsts are celebrated . . . first steps, first days of school, first anniversaries. But there are also the firsts that follow the loss of a loved one. Birthdays, holidays, and special moments that are quietly passed in pain as we tend to the missing pieces of our hearts, wishing they were still here.

The only sound in my room is the rain on my roof, but it seems to whisper ideas I should definitely ignore. Instead, I roll over and look at the dark outline of my phone on my bedside table. It's so late. Texting now would be completely—

The screen lights up the room, stopping all my thoughts. I know it's probably Sofia ordering me to look at the full moon so that my inner goddess doesn't shrivel, but that doesn't stop me from lunging across my bed anyway. But I lunge too hard, and instead of grabbing my phone, I manage to knock it off the table along with my latest romance novel.

Groaning, I haul myself over the bedside, legs tangling in my sheets, but stop moving when I see Jude's name.

Stomach summersaulting, I swipe open his message, which turns out to be a picture of him and Agatha, both wearing the same kind of party hat he wore at her memorial. It's candid, with Agatha blowing out enough birthday candles to start a bonfire. Jude, meanwhile, is captured reaching out a blurry hand to pull her silk scarf out of the way of the flames, terror etched across his handsome face.

I can't help the laugh I let out, even as my nose and eyes begin to sting at the sight of Agatha in her element. Then a second text comes in.

Jude: Missing her.

My heart rises inside my chest until it's blocking my throat. *Jude*. Pulling myself back into bed, I start typing the words "me too," but stop. Bite my lip. The same feeling I had at Agatha's memorial is churning in my chest—the need to be closer to him when the loss feels too big to bear alone. *He's up, right? And talking is easier than texting*, I reason. Before I can second-guess myself, I call his number.

"Hey," he says, sounding surprised when he picks up. His voice is low and hoarse, like he hasn't used it in hours. "Sorry, I didn't mean—"

"I miss her, too," I interrupt, my heart beating far too fast for someone sitting in bed.

He's quiet on the other end of the line. "Yeah?"

"I was about to text," I admit. "It felt . . . I don't know. Weird to let the day pass without acknowledging her birthday?" I say, rubbing a hand under my bangs. "I mean, I didn't have a priceless photo of Agatha nearly setting fire to the entire Eastern Seaboard to share, but I was going to say something."

His chuckle is soft and exasperated. "You know she did that every year? Wore something highly flammable and dangly?"

"Just to keep you on your toes?"

"Or incinerate them. Hard to tell."

I smile as I lie back down, tucking into my covers. "Are your man feet *that* horrific?"

"Unspeakable. They've made children cry."

I laugh as the weight that's been on my chest all day begins to lift. "Should I be concerned that you're showing your bare feet to children?"

"Jesus, Gracie, no," he says with a laugh. "I swim a little. Subjecting innocent strangers to my feet at the public pool is just collateral damage."

"Will the horrors never cease?" I ask, even though my mind is now a slow-motion film of his broad chest and shoulders emerging from chlorinated water. "Tell me you don't wear a Speedo, at least."

I hear a rustle of bedsheets on the other end of the line before he says, "Leopard print."

"Honestly, I think Agatha would approve," I say, laughing again, and *God*, why is it so easy to talk to him? How does he make me grin like this when I've been on the verge of tears all day? After shutting me out of his decision about the estate (again), I told myself that I'd stop this kind of thing. No more texting about Taco or anything that isn't strictly wedding related. But now I've called him, practically in the middle of the night, and the truth is, I don't want to let go of this invisible tether between us. Instead, I want to wrap myself in it and *pull*, until he's so close that neither of us will have to face this pain alone again.

He's silent for a long moment before saying, "Thanks for calling me, Gracie. Today was . . . shitty."

His voice sounds different over the phone. Somehow farther away and more intimate at the same time. Cradling my phone a little closer, I say, "Same, except . . ."

"What?" he asks, and if I close my eyes, it's almost like he's lying right beside me in the dark. I know I shouldn't picture it, but it's so hard to resist the feeling of being less alone.

"You made my day a lot better than it could have been," I admit.

"Did I?" he asks, his voice surprised but pleased.

"I called to check on my former clients whose weddings were canceled," I explain. "They told me what you did for them."

"Ah," he says, and I can hear him shift his weight, like he's suddenly uncomfortable. "I didn't realize you would follow up with them."

"Of course I did, I've been worried sick about them."

"Some of their weddings will need to be on weekdays, but—"

"It's fine. More than fine. They're over the moon, Jude. I can't thank you enough," I tell him, hoping he can hear how much I mean it.

He's quiet again before saying, "It was the least I could do." And even though he never expected me to find out, and even though the favors he pulled were for my clients, the way he says those words makes me feel like he did it just for me.

We're both silent for so long, and the rain is so soothing in the pitch-dark, that I don't realize I'm half-asleep until he wakes me with a soft, "Hey."

"Mmm?"

"Did Henry ever stop by your place?"

I yawn and stretch my free arm above my head, but don't open my eyes. "Yeah, he came by with the cottage paperwork a few days ago. I guess it's officially mine now."

"No, I mean more recently. Sunday."

My eyebrows scrunch together as my sleep-fogged brain struggles to remember. "Sunday? I don't know, I was at my mom's house all day. Why? Does he have more paperwork for me?"

"No, nothing like that," Jude says, and I hear the rustle of his sheets again. They sound nice, like they'd be crisp and cool around his large, warm body. My thighs press together and— "We were on a run, and he said he might stop by to say hi."

"Oh," I say, a little surprised as he interrupts my sleepy, wayward thoughts. "What a sweetheart."

"Yeah," he says stiffly. "Anyway, I should let you sleep."

"And what about you?" I ask, unwilling to let him hang up just yet. "Shouldn't your man feet get some beauty rest, too?"

"Unfortunately, they're beyond help, and I'm still working."

"You're working in bed? Isn't that a no-no?"

"How can you tell I'm in bed?"

I shrug a shoulder and hum a sound like *I dunno*. "Just can." I can also guess that he probably isn't wearing his starched white button-up or any pants. His dark hair is probably a mess, and he's mostly likely wearing those hot librarian glasses. I try not to linger on the image I've created, but it's hard to shoo away when I'm this tired. "What are you working on?" I whisper instead.

"You really want to know?"

I yawn again, my eyelids too heavy to lift anymore. "Mhmm. As long as it's really boring."

"Gracie, are you using me as a sound machine?" he chides.

"You have a really nice voice," I say without thinking, too sleepy to care. "You could narrate romance novels."

"Your reading material of choice." It isn't a question, and I vaguely wonder what else he noticed while he was in my cottage.

"Don't knock it till you try it," I say, pulling the covers almost completely over my head. "They could teach you a thing or two."

"Why would I need romance novels when I have you in my life?" he asks softly, and there's no sarcasm or annoyance in his tone.

"Having me as a friend isn't enough, Jude," I mumble, half asleep. "I'll prove it to you."

He doesn't respond to this, and as the rain falls harder, I slip into the embrace of sleep, knowing he's on the other side of my dreaming. Because that's what I must be doing when I hear him quietly say, "You already have."

17

GRACIE

Four Weeks Before the Wedding

In a thrilling first for me, I've been tasked with tasting wedding cakes on behalf of my clients. Who gives up free cake, you may ask? Beautiful power couples with no time for sugary carbohydrates, apparently. But while Calvin and Brooke have truly left every detail of their wedding up to me, I'm not complaining about this errand—even if I am a little nervous about spending the afternoon with Jude.

My stomach twists as I rush to finish my makeup. After our late-night phone call, we haven't talked other than confirming today's outing. I'm not *saying* that we're pretending it didn't happen, but something about falling asleep to the voice of your supposed enemy after grief-bonding with them makes it seem a lot like they're not your enemy at all.

Which is why, when Henry showed up at my door the next day to ask me out, I said yes.

Partly, it was shock. I couldn't remember the last time I'd been asked on a date. And not in some algorithm-based, look-at-me-pose-with-this-fish way, but face-to-face. With windswept curls and a dimpled smile, he took his shot, and it had felt . . . simple. Not in a bad way, but in a refreshing I'm-not-actively-trying-to-ruin-your-life kind of way.

Which is why I *won't* think about how Jude secured new venues for all my former clients. Or our almost-kiss. Or even *those* words. The ones I'm desperately trying to forget.

I'm . . . very attracted to you.

"*Ow!*" I quickly press my hand to the eye I've just stabbed with my mascara wand. *Dammit*. This has been happening all week. That single strained sentence will pop back into my head, and suddenly I'm running into doorjambs, or struck speechless when I should be answering simple questions like "Can I help you find something, miss?" *Yes, helpful grocery store employee, can you help me find my goddamn MIND?*

Quickly, I redo my makeup. *Henry, Henry, Henry*, I silently chant, like it might point my thoughts in a safer direction. It works for a few minutes, but as I leave the cottage with a slightly throbbing eyeball and barely a minute to spare, I'm immediately confronted by the source of all my troubles.

Jude is in my driveway, leaning against a shiny black Mercedes SUV that makes my Camry look like it emerged from the primordial ooze. In dark sunglasses, cream slacks, and a navy linen button-down that's open at the throat and rolled at the sleeves, he looks like he should be drinking wine on the French Riviera. Or I guess rolling up to the turn-of-the-century estate he's just inherited? Either way, it's the first time I've seen him in anything other than a suit. When he takes off his sunglasses, I gulp.

"Hey," I say, silently asking myself *why* I let him pressure me into carpooling. But I know why. Today's forecast has a 20 percent chance of sprinkles, which in Jude's mind translates to a 90 percent chance of raining lava and . . . I guess I didn't want him to be anxious.

He opens the passenger door for me. "Hello," he says, sounding reserved in that particular Judish way I'm learning means he's nervous, too. How the hell are we going to survive the next hour trapped in this car? Maybe I could suggest an audiobook he'd love. Like *Crime and Punishment*. Or *The Dictionary*.

"Is it too cold?" he asks when we're both in. "I'll turn down the AC." But as he twists to buckle his seat belt and adjust the thermostat, I'm too overcome by his cologne to respond. He somehow smells like every up-against-the-stacks, after-hours librarian fantasy I've ever had, and my thighs pinch together on the leather seat with a needy squeak. *I'm . . . very attracted to you.*

"It's, uh, very clean in here," I say, hoping my bland commentary disguises my sordid thoughts. *You should be thinking of Henry,* I scold myself. *Remember him? The man you just agreed to date?*

"Why do you sound so nervous about cleanliness?" Jude asks as I fumble to clip my seat belt. "Would you rather sit in a ball pit of take-out cups and gym socks?"

"Honestly, if it gave me something to poke fun of you for, then maybe," I mutter, disarmed as usual by how perfectly put together he is.

"Good to know you'd willingly martyr yourself for the chance to give me a hard time," he says dryly.

I take in more details of the car. "It's almost *creepily* clean in here," I observe. "Are you one of those guys who polishes his tires on the weekends, or did you just dispose of a dead body and bleach the evidence away?"

"Definitely the latter," he says, putting the car into drive with a soft chiming sound. "I couldn't possibly have had it detailed because I knew I'd have a guest in my car and wanted them to be comfortable."

This pulls me up short. "You got your car detailed? For me?"

His shoulders tense like he's been caught red-handed. "I bring Taco with me to Larkwood on the weekends. I didn't think you'd appreciate sitting in a car that smelled like anxious cat."

"That's . . . really thoughtful of you," I say, touched by yet another display of above-and-beyond concern for me, "but I'm not that high maintenance. I'm pretty sure my floorboard mats are more crumbs than mat at this point."

He lets out a long-suffering sigh. "You and Henry really are perfect for each other."

It's like an ice cream scoop has reached in and hollowed out my stomach. "He told you?" I ask after a moment. "That he asked me out?"

Jude turns onto the main road without looking at me, but a muscle jumps in his jaw. "I encouraged him to do it."

I'm unprepared for the sting I feel at discovering that my ill-advised crush on Jude has been completely one-sided. I was almost sure he felt the same way. But that's kind of my track record, isn't it? Falling for men who aren't as interested in me as I am in them. I try not to get swallowed by embarrassment.

"He also told me you said yes," Jude says into the silence.

His voice is neutral, but his knuckles are white on the steering wheel. *Why?* If he's encouraging his best friend to ask me out, then he certainly isn't interested in me himself—at least, not beyond basic attraction.

"I'm excited," I say decisively. "He really took me by surprise."

"Why should you be surprised?" Jude asks, sounding vaguely offended.

"Um, maybe because the last time I was asked out on a real date was when 'camera phones' were the hot new thing?"

At this, Jude gives a skeptical snort. "I find that hard to believe."

His easy dismissal of my lack of dating history registers like a compliment he didn't intend to give, and my heart does an illegal skip. "Do I need to remind you that I live alone, in an isolated cottage, in a town with a significant geriatric population? Not exactly a hotbed for dating, unless I decide to start strolling the yacht marinas, hunting for a sugar daddy."

"Aligning with someone who has greater means than yourself is a perfectly valid and common dating strategy."

"For what? The Middle Ages?" I ask, unable to stop my smile.

"For anyone whose top priority is financial stability, rather than romance. I have plenty of clients who openly acknowledge it as their primary relationship aim."

"Wait, so you're telling me that if committed relationships weren't your worst fear, and someone told you that they'd like to 'align with you' for financial gain, you'd be open to it?"

He frowns, considering. "Why not? If there were sufficient compatibility and attraction, I wouldn't be opposed to taking care of someone that way. And I'd much prefer honesty to a charade."

"Is it honesty you're after, or do you just want someone to call you Daddy?" I ask, grinning over at him.

I'm definitely not imagining the brush of pink that appears on his cheekbones or the way he shifts in his seat at my joke. "Trying to pin down my kinks again, are you?"

This time, it's my turn to flush. "That is *not* what I was doing." I tack on an "Ew," just for emphasis.

He tilts his head and glances at me. "You could always just ask me to list them alphabetically."

"Is that confirmation you have some, then?"

"Are you *looking* for confirmation?"

"No!" I cry, resisting the urge to stick my head out the window for some fresh air and to possibly get sucked out.

His responding smirk reveals the line in his cheek that's too long to be called a dimple, but is, unfortunately, just as attractive. "Well, since you obviously spend all your time thinking about this . . ."

"I don't!"

"I do."

The tone in which he says these two simple words is so shaded in ambiguity, I want a translation app. But I'm also aware that clarity on this topic will only mean trouble. The silence between us stretches out like a path covered in warning signs. *Turn back now! Don't take the bait! Booby traps ahead!* But apparently, I'm illiterate, because I run right past all of them and say in a rush, "You do *what*, exactly?"

He lifts a shoulder. "Have kinks."

He says this so nonchalantly that it takes me several seconds to actually process it.

"Oh," is what eventually leaves my mouth as he stops at the last red light before the highway. I don't voice the obvious next question: *Which* kinks?

But it's like he hears me think it anyway, because he looks over at me, all traces of humor gone. I only realize my hands and skirt are pinned between my squirming thighs when his gaze drops to them. I freeze. For an indeterminable number of seconds, neither of us moves. Breathes. When his eyes finally drag back up to mine, what I see in them makes my stomach flip inside out and backward.

But then someone hits their horn behind us, and we both jump. Jude quickly looks away and hits the accelerator, shoulders rigid, hands tight. Meanwhile, the seat warmer I was enjoying suddenly feels like a griddle for my ass. I take a much-needed breath.

What the hell just happened?

My mind releases a deluge of panicked reminders that would have been *extremely* helpful about forty seconds ago. I am about to go out with this man's best friend. He's trying to sabotage my life! I have no business thinking about his bedroom preferences or the fact that the most adventurous sex of *my* life involved an impromptu can of whipped cream and a lot of regrets involving Monistat 1.

"I'm changing the subject," I announce. "Tell me about Henry."

His voice is an audible glower. "I have no idea if he has any kinks. You'll have to ask him yourself."

"I wasn't— I'm not asking—" I sputter before regaining my composure. "How are you two even friends?" I finally get out. "He's so *nice.*"

If I thought his spine couldn't get any stiffer, I was wrong. "I'm well aware. But somehow, I've hoodwinked him into thinking I'm decent company."

He says it cooly, but there's no mistaking the undercurrent of hurt in his voice, and suddenly I feel like the jerk. "You *are* decent company," I say. "In fact, I keep forgetting not to like you." I cut my eyes toward him. "I think under different circumstances, we could even be friends."

"Friends," he repeats, but I can't get a read on his tone. The leather of the steering wheel squeaks beneath his grip.

"Sure," I say brightly. "I mean, before I found out your plans for selling Larkwood, I even thought— "

I stop myself. If things get any more awkward in this car, I'll be left with no choice but to duck and roll out the passenger door.

"You thought what?" Jude presses, his voice scratched around the edges.

I think back to our initial meeting. How I knew he'd be someone I could find comfort with after losing Agatha. How my heart raced when he saved me from that plant, and he made me feel a spark for someone other than Calvin for the first time in years.

"I thought we shared a connection over Agatha," I admit, looking out the window at the highway rushing by. "I thought we could help each other through the grief."

He's quiet for a long moment until, finally, he says, "What do you think the other night was?"

It feels like acknowledging something off-limits, and the atmosphere between us immediately changes to something softer. Heavier.

"You're right. And I meant to say thank you," I tell him, tugging on the hem of my skirt. "I mean, I know you probably have your parents to talk about her with, but for me . . ." I stare down at my hands. "You're the only person I can really reminisce with."

Out of my periphery, I see him shake his head before saying in a low voice, "It's the same for me. My father isn't in my life, and my mom . . ." The exhale he makes is almost inaudible. "There's family history that makes grieving together complicated."

At this, my heart feels like it's just come face-to-face with its long-lost twin. Our gazes catch for a moment, and before I can stop it, a question I've been wondering for a while voices itself.

"Is that why you use Larkwood as your last name? Because it's your mom's and Agatha's instead of your dad's?"

His shoulders shift beneath his shirt. "Yeah," he says shortly. "I changed it when I was old enough."

"I'm sorry," I whisper, overcome by simple, painful understanding. "My father isn't in my life either."

He looks away, but not before I see something like anger in the set of his mouth. "His loss."

"*Their* loss," I correct him.

He keeps his gaze fixed on the road. "Maybe. But at least we found each other," he says quietly, before pausing to weigh his words. "Remembering Nana with you confirms every one of my best memories, Gracie. Like, as long as I know you, I don't have to doubt that they actually happened."

Despite all my efforts to stay emotionally detached from this man, I feel a sharp tug on the cord that has connected us ever since Agatha's funeral. The question rises inside me like a breath I don't want to let out. *What would make you question your best memories, Jude?*

I already know how he'd respond: *It's personal.* But I want him to know that even if we're nothing more than two people in mutual grief, thrown together by circumstance, he can still count on me to share this loss. So, I say, "I guess that means you're stuck with me, then."

He lets out a ghost of a laugh, keeping his eyes on the road. "Trust me, Gracie, you're the one stuck with *me*. I fully plan on sending you traumatizing pictures of Agatha on every major holiday."

I can't help the grin that stretches across my face. "I keep meaning to ask—did she ever mention me to you?"

His full lips hitch into a rueful smirk. "Oh yeah. You were always the cute, single wedding planner she wanted to introduce me to."

"Hmm. Kind of jealous that she chose to go with 'cute' when your designation was always 'outrageously handsome.'"

His eyes find mine for a moment. "I may have downplayed what she actually called you. For the sake of propriety."

"Screw propriety, I want compliments!" I laugh.

"Good thing no one would accuse you of being demanding."

Smacking his arm, I say, "What did she call me?"

He clears his throat, and then, in an uncanny impression of Agatha's crinkly old-lady voice, says, "'Just tell me when you want me to introduce you to my gorgeous wedding planner, Judy. You'll love her—she's smart as a whip and looks like Audrey Hepburn with an ass.'"

Laughter shoots out of me the same moment nostalgic longing weaves through my chest. I never thought I'd hear those words again, but listening to Jude repeat them in the same cheeky tone Agatha always used feels like casting them in gold. He was right earlier. The memories I've cherished alone somehow feel more real when they're shared with him. No matter what else happens between us, the love we shared for Agatha will always be there, linking us with a bright, unbreakable thread.

Still grinning, I say, "I don't know who to be more mortified for—me, because she shared her Audrey comparison with other people, or you, for that nickname."

"Definitely feel sorrier for me. 'Audrey with an ass' is a fantastic compliment, whereas I'll have to endure a lifetime of Judge Judy jokes and bobbleheads from Henry."

I laugh, and despite the barb of discomfort I feel when he mentions his friend, I find myself slipping back into the now-familiar current between us, letting myself get pulled irresistibly along. We keep talking, sharing our precious Agatha-isms like trading cards, and somehow, the hour-long drive flies by. When we pull up to the familiar strip of small businesses, I'm snorting and begging for photographic proof of the time Agatha pressured him into wearing a purple sequined bolero at their ballroom dance lessons.

"Sweetly Ever After Cakes," Jude reads in a doubtful voice, squinting at the sign tacked between a pet supply store and a tanning salon.

"Don't be so judgy, Judy."

"You really went there. Wow."

I stick my tongue out at him. "Come on, and be *nice*. Val's doing me a huge favor with this last-minute order."

He opens his door before giving me a smile that cuts my breath short. "You have no idea how *nice* I can be, Gracie."

And with that, he gets out and walks toward the cake shop, leaving me to pick up the pieces of my scattered composure.

I know I made the right decision in saying yes to Henry. I know what I should want. But as Jude turns to open the door for me, I also begin to understand that some cravings have no regard for "should" at all.

18

GRACIE

Four Weeks Before the Wedding

Walking inside my friend Valerie's cake shop is an automatic dopamine hit as every pore on my body absorbs the scent of warm chocolate and vanilla beans. The tasting room is small and chic with a selfie wall, and below its neon-pink sign that reads *You Had Me at Cake* are hundreds of Polaroid pictures of couples kissing. Through an open doorway at the back, I can hear the hum of a mixer at work.

"Oh my God," Jude says, breathing in deeply. "Did I just get a contact high? From . . . sugar?"

"Quite possibly," I say as a short, stressed-looking woman bustles into the room with a streak of flour beneath her hairnet. She isn't anyone I recognize.

"Hello, hello," she greets us, tucking a stray piece of frizzy blond hair into place. "You must be here for the tasting?"

"We are," I say, glancing toward the back doorway. "Is Valerie here, by any chance?"

"No," she says in a surprisingly severe tone. "She had one of her headaches and left me to make three rush orders on my own and conduct two tastings."

Disappointment promptly turns into anxiety. Valerie is a vendor I really wanted Jude to meet, since Larkwood is one of her biggest sources of income during wedding season.

"Oh," I manage. "That's too bad."

"Yes. It is," she agrees with a frown. "And if you can believe it, I had to cancel the last tasting appointment, because the *wedding planner* came instead of the couple." She shakes her head. "What if she'd chosen a flavor they hated? I'll tell you what would have happened: someone would've gotten blamed, and that someone is *me*."

I'm immediately taken aback by how unprofessional Val's new assistant is, but unfortunately, it's not the biggest issue at hand. Dread settles like an anchor in my stomach as I realize I'll somehow need to reschedule this tasting on an already impossibly tight timeline *and* convince Calvin and Brooke to do it themselves. But then Jude steps forward and holds out his hand.

"That's unbelievable," he says as she takes it. "Who wouldn't want to choose their own wedding cake? I'm Calvin, by the way, and this is my fiancée, Brooke. I don't think we got your name though . . ." He trails off, letting her fill in the blank he's left. Meanwhile, I try not to look like I've just been smacked directly in the face with a pillow embroidered with the words *BAD IDEA*.

"Actually," I squeak, but our grumpy host has no eyes or ears for me.

"Betty," she answers, seeming to fully register Jude for the first time.

"Lovely," he responds warmly, before taking his hand back to tug my waist against his. The sudden feeling of his warm body against mine turns my stomach into an electric squiggle, and a nervous, nonsensical laugh ejects from me. Luckily, Betty barely spares me a glance.

"I can't imagine that dropping everything to do a tasting is very convenient with all your rush orders," Jude says to her. "If it's easier, you could just bring the samples and get back to work. We'll leave a note for Valerie about our choices."

At this point, Betty may as well be a pool of melted chocolate in the center of his palm. "Oh, it's no trouble. No trouble at all," she says, patting her hairnet. "Just give me a moment."

She walks off with a coy smile at Jude over her aproned shoulder, and I'm left gawping up at him, still snug against his hip.

"Okay, Casanova, this was *not* the plan," I whisper-yell. "I don't want to be fake-engaged to you!"

He smiles down at me. "You do if you want to check this task off your list, Brookey."

I clench my teeth. I do love checking things off my list, dammit.

"You are the most—"

"Charming improviser?" he finishes for me before leaning closer. His voice is a low whisper that travels along every one of my nerve endings. "How much do you want to bet she's going to bring us extra cake from the other tasting?"

But I don't get to tell him what I think because, for one, his grip on my waist has eliminated my ability to speak, and secondly, Betty is back. When she sets down a platter with eight hefty slices of cake on the table, I feel Jude's nearly silent I-Told-You-So chuckle against my ribs and discreetly kick his foot. He responds by leaning down to nuzzle my hair, which my body registers as a seismic event. My *brain* may know this is all for show, but my pounding heart sure doesn't.

"Young love," Betty says with a sigh, her crinkled blue eyes twinkling in a complete mood reversal. "I know you only ordered four samples," she goes on, "but since you two actually showed up for your tasting, you may as well have the other order, too."

"Betty, you shouldn't have," Jude says, like he's been getting extra helpings from her his whole life. "But my angel *does* deserve every option," he says, before booping me on the nose.

My jaw goes slack. *Angel?* I'm half-tempted to feel his forehead for a fever when he smirks at me. Just a tilt of his wide mouth, and I realize he's messing with me. No. *Challenging* me.

The game? Who can be more cringe. The prize? Not having to face the nightmare of rescheduling this appointment.

For a second, I nearly laugh, but then all my mental spiraling stops as I meet his gaze. Beneath the traces of humor, there's something else. A silent understanding that if we're only playing a game, then all of this physical contact doesn't have to mean anything. If it's just a game, then I can touch him, too.

And just like that, nothing seems more important than proving that *cringe* is basically my middle name.

"Now. As you know," Betty says, "Valerie is known for her unique flavors, but I can *always* tell what someone's favorite will be."

She squints an eye and slowly lets her gaze travel down the length of Jude. I have to wonder how she thinks his crotch is capable of communicating whether he's a Funfetti or lemon meringue guy, but when her gaze returns to eye level, she says decisively, "Valrhona chocolate and espresso. Complex, dark, and decadent."

Jude makes an approving hum I feel against my rib cage as Betty turns her gimlet eye to me with far less interest. Suddenly, I'm terrified of losing this game and all my dignity by being equated to fruitcake—*boring and universally disliked*. On an impulse that feels like a shooting star in my chest, I turn to press myself fully against Jude. Lying a hand on his chest, I look up at him with the most lovesick gaze I can muster and try to keep a straight face.

"How did she know, sugar bear?" At the stupid nickname, he has to pass a snort off as a cough, and I try not to grin in victory. Instead, I turn my head to give Betty a long-suffering look. "I can't keep any dark chocolate in the house. Or coffee for that matter!"

She chuckles, pleased that I've confirmed her guess, and I beam back at her as a sparkling, first-sip-of-champagne feeling goes straight to my head.

"Guilty as charged, rose petal," Jude responds, placing his warm hand over the back of mine and pressing it to his alarmingly sculpted chest.

I try to get a grip on reality, but it's slippery at best. When his thumb starts idly stroking my captured hand, a mental image flashes through my mind so vivid and inappropriate, I have to swallow a quiet gasp. Me, pressing my lips to his blunt fingertips; him, sliding them into my open mouth.

Heat surges between my legs, and I try blinking the image away, but apparently, it's been permanently branded behind my eyes. To make matters infinitely worse, Jude is staring down at me like he knows—like he's watching the same private movie as I am and—

"Now *you*," Betty says to me, snapping us both back to the present moment, "are citrus and rose Battenberg. Sweet and almost too pretty to eat."

I glance up at Jude and feel his heart kick beneath my palm.

"She is, isn't she?" he murmurs, lifting his hand from mine to smooth the collar of my blouse. His fingers dip between the fabric and my skin, brushing my collarbone, and game or no game, scorching heat draws a fiery line from the spot he's touching directly to my low belly. I draw in a shaky breath. *It's all just for show*, a distant voice in the back of my mind insists. *Just for show.*

Betty laughs and places the slices of cake in front of us. "Okay, let's see if I guessed right. Would the groom like to try first?"

Groom. The word lights firecrackers in my blood as I lose myself in the world's most reckless game of make-believe. Jude seems just as lost because he doesn't make a move. Telling myself it's just part of the game, I pick up the fork and cut a lush bite of chocolate cake. Rising onto my tiptoes against him, I raise the piece to his mouth.

"Open up, sweetheart," I say, barely registering how breathy my voice sounds. But he does as he's told, and carefully, I slip the chocolate cake into his waiting mouth. His lashes shudder.

"Christ, that's good," he rasps after swallowing.

I'm trying not to pant as he cuts a piece of Battenberg for me and raises the fork. "Your turn," he says, and obediently, my mouth falls open for him. The restless shift in his hips seems involuntary while his expression straddles the line between pained and hypnotized.

When he puts the fork into my mouth and I slide the cake off with my lips, a small hum of pleasure escapes me at the taste of the delicate sponge. All at once, Jude's eyes become hungry in a way that has nothing to do with cake.

"Good?" Betty asks.

"Delicious," Jude responds, eyes still on my mouth.

Betty laughs. "You look at her like she's the cake!"

Jude doesn't seem capable of replying, and I'm barely better off. I *feel* like a piece of cake, incapable of thought and ready to be devoured.

"You two *must* be on our Wall of Love," she says, gesturing to the giant collage of Polaroids behind us before grabbing the camera off a small table.

Immediate, nervous heat bolts through me as my eyes snap to all the photos of couples kissing. There isn't a single picture of a couple *not* locked at the mouth. I look up at Jude, heart thumping wildly. There's no way we're going to do this, right? But Betty is already holding the camera up to her eye. Jude quickly glances from me, to the door, and back, clearly asking, *Do you want to make a run for it?* I swallow hard, giving him the tiniest head shake to say that it's fine. I'll just give him a quick peck. Friends pretending to be engaged do this sort of thing all the time, right?

"Okay, on three, you kiss," Betty instructs with a smile behind the clunky camera.

"One . . ."

Jude's hold around me tightens. *Is this actually happening?*

"Two . . ."

My toes strain to lift me a little higher as Jude's hand comes to cradle my upturned jaw. *Is face-touching a form of foreplay?*

"Three!"

He leans down, close enough for me to reach his mouth, but pauses just short of my lips to give me a last, searching look. *Is this okay?*

It's his perpetual concern that finally breaks me. Body trembling, I tilt my face to brush my lips against his in a single, chaste kiss.

But I don't count on the way it feels. In an instant, I realize I've grievously miscalculated how warm and deliciously soft his lips would be. How precious and wanted his hand on my face would make me feel. I need to pull away, but then his thumb is stroking my cheekbone, his mouth pressing so tenderly to mine that my heart is convinced he's adored me this whole time. My arms come up to drape around his neck, and a low sound emanates from the center of his chest. It travels directly into mine, and I'm pressing closer, needing this to never end.

Vaguely, I hear the click of the camera, but it only occupies one percent of my awareness as all the feelings I've worked so hard to repress stage a mutiny. Jude breaks the kiss for half a breath before his lips are pressing back to mine at a new angle, like he needs to feel that moment of first contact again. My hand slides to the back of his powerful neck, and I realize I've never felt this kind of ache before—the kind that melts walls and denial like they've been tossed into the sun.

The camera clicks again, and Betty is saying something, but I don't hear it because Jude is pulling his mouth away, breath ragged as his bewildered eyes find mine. I can't let go of him. If I do, it means it's all over.

Betty's knowing chuckle reaches me like I'm hearing it underwater. "I'm going back to the kitchen, but call me when you've made your choices, lovebirds. I took an extra photo for you to keep."

She leaves, and my eyes shut as I try coming back to myself. But then Jude takes hold of my chin, and I'm forced to look directly at him. His eyes are desperate, and my vision goes dark around the edges when his other hand slides to my lower back.

"You've got a little something. Just here," he says hoarsely, bringing his thumb to the edge of my bottom lip. The stroke is slow and feather-light. When he brings the pad of his thumb to his own mouth, sucking off the offending jam, I cease being a person and accept my new identity as one giant nerve-ending.

I run my tongue quickly over the spot he touched, still tasting sticky sweetness. "I think you missed some."

He nods like a serious miscarriage of justice has taken place, and then the backs of his fingers are gently stroking the underside of my jaw, sending a ripple of need through my entire body. *Goodbye, breathing. You were fun while you lasted.* Somewhere in the depths of my brain, I know this is a bad idea, but when his fingertips trace down the line of my neck, my brain shouts *CONSEQUENCES, SCHMONSEQUENCES!* like it's rallying an army of bad decisions.

"I promised I wouldn't kiss you," he says, but it sounds like he's talking to himself, trying to summon any last vestiges of rational thought.

"But you already did," I remind him, leaving the rest of my argument unsaid. *What's one more?*

He nods, like my logic is irrefutable. "That's true," he agrees. "And Betty could come back. It would be suspicious if we jumped apart."

There are definitely flaws to this logic. But my eyes are fixed on his decadent mouth, and I find myself nodding in agreement anyway. "So suspicious," I whisper.

When his warm lips graze mine again, they're low and off-center as he licks away the last traces of jam. A small gasp escapes me, but then his mouth is lifting away. *No!* My hands tighten in his collar, and his eyes lock with mine in silent understanding. When I tug him back, he finally kisses me like I need him to and one thought obliterates all the others.

Chocolate.

He's ruined it for me. I'll never be able to eat so much as a single M&M again without becoming painfully aroused. My hand slides into the back of his hair—thick, silky, and made for tugging, and I'm lost. The hot, delicious slide of his tongue against mine is better than any secret fantasy, because I didn't *know*. Had no idea a kiss could be like this—an untamed, living wildfire between two people.

With a groan, Jude takes my hips and turns me against the table, and it's like every moment of frustration that's built between us finally has a release valve. I sink my teeth into the bottom lip that's driven me to distraction countless times, and then he's sucking my tongue, biting my lips, neither of us able to get enough. A grunt issues from deep in his chest as he presses his hips harder against mine, needing to be closer. When he lifts me onto the table, making room for himself between my legs, I whimper into his demanding mouth. The size and heat of him turn any lingering fragments of self-restraint into an explosion of powdered sugar, scattering on the wind.

His fingers are stroking down my neck, lips and teeth following the trail, and my head falls back. *What have I been doing with my life if it wasn't this and only, exactly, this?* With every hot press of his lush mouth on my skin, I feel more alive than I have in years. With every groan of my name, I know I haven't been the only one lying awake at night trying to deny what we clearly both want. He's completely wrong for me when I should be trying to find someone who wants the same things I do. Someone like—

"Henry!" I yelp.

Jude's teeth release the earring he's been tugging the same

moment I fully realize I'm sitting on the cake-tasting table, and—according to the moisture seeping through the back of my skirt—a slice of cake as well. He lifts his head to stare at me in dazed, hurt confusion.

"I'm not—" he begins to say, but then the bucket of ice water I was hit with seems to drench him, too. "Fuck," he rasps out.

We stare at each other, both mentally calculating how badly we've betrayed Henry. Guilt hits me like a ten-foot wave I'm not expecting, and Jude must see it all over my face.

"You haven't done anything wrong," he says quickly, but I'm pretty sure he's incorrect, because I can still taste the chocolate from his mouth. I start shaking my head, but he cuts me off. "*I'm* his best friend, Gracie. *I'm* the asshole here."

"Oh my god," I say quietly, panic setting in.

"I kissed you when I said I wouldn't," he goes on, backing away so I can close my wide-open legs and yank down my equally complicit skirt. "I'll tell him what happened. I'll tell him it's my fault." Misery etches every line of his face. His hair's a mess, and somehow, there's pink frosting on his cheekbone that my lizard brain still wants to lick off. "God, I'm so fucking sorry."

"It wasn't just your fault," I say, voice shrill. "In case you didn't notice, I practically ate your face!"

"Fuck," Jude says again, pressing a hand over his eyes. He encounters the frosting, looks at his hand, and says "*Fuck*" one more time for good measure.

Meanwhile, I get an unobstructed view of his crotch and nearly pass away. This was supposed to be a work errand, not the opening scene of a bakery porno! I bring a shaking hand up to brush my bangs into place, but it's covered in the same pink frosting that was on Jude's face. *Mystery solved.* I look down and see that I must have put my hand into the pink-and-white Battenberg that's half-crushed beneath my butt. *GREAT.*

Before I can get to my feet, Jude is coming back with a wad of napkins he found somewhere. "Here, let me," he says, making a move like he's going to clean me up. But frankly, the *last* thing I need right now is this man's magic hands near my ass, so I quickly take the napkins from him.

"I've got it," I say, hopping off the table onto wobbly legs.

"Gracie, we should talk. If this is—"

"I don't want to talk, Jude!" I say, trying to keep my voice down while shakily wiping cake off my skirt. "We just . . . took the ruse too far," I insist, trying to erase every moment my heart wanted to believe our kiss meant anything to him. Jude, the so-called one-night stand expert. Jude, who's *so* unavailable that he encouraged his best friend to ask me out. Regret fills my lungs till I can barely breathe, because now Henry, who's only ever been kind and *actually* interested in me, is going to find out what we've done and be so hurt.

"Ruse?" Jude repeats, like he's not following.

"To stop Betty from canceling our tasting! I—I just got caught up in the act. It's not like there's anything between us, right?" I give a slightly maniacal laugh. "I live for romance. You kill it for a living! We couldn't be worse for each other."

"You think I don't know that?" he snaps, tossing his pink-streaked napkin on the table after wiping his face. "Why do you think I told Henry he should ask you out? He's the best man I know, and you . . . you're so fucking perfect." At my startled expression, he looks away. "For him, I mean. I'm the last person you want anything to do with, Gracie."

I know he's right—he's the wrong choice for so many reasons, but it doesn't stop my heart from breaking at the way he automatically writes himself off. It doesn't silence the unthinking part of me that still wishes I were in his arms. But I have my future to think about, and the simple fact is, we don't want the same things.

"It was just a mistake," I whisper, on the verge of tears. "My date with Henry is tomorrow, and he's perfect for me, too, Jude. I *really* don't want to lose my first chance at a normal, healthy relationship in years."

When he looks at me again, he's so gorgeously distraught I want to shield my eyes.

"You're right. It was my mistake," he says in a deadened voice.

"I'm sorry for taking it too far. For pretending for a second that you wanted something"—his eyebrows slant together—"else."

At the quiet resignation in his voice, my heartbeat stumbles. For a moment, it's almost too tempting to interpret his words the wrong way—that he thought I might want *him* instead. But over the last few weeks, he's made it clear that a strings-free, physical connection is what he prefers. *That's* what he was pretending I wanted—the one thing he's comfortable giving. But I need so much more than that. Unfortunately, I may have just blown my best chance of finding it.

"I have to tell him," I whisper. "I'll do it before our date."

"No, don't."

I look up at him sharply. "Jude, he has to know. It wouldn't be fair."

"Yes, obviously, but this is on me, Gracie. You're free to kiss whoever you want, but I just betrayed my best friend. I need to be the one to tell him."

"And you'll make sure he knows that it didn't mean anything, right? It was just part of a stupid game."

He looks away, but not before I see something that looks alarmingly like hurt cross his features. "Of course."

I take a shaky breath. "And do you think he'll understand?"

Jude looks at me, his expression unfathomable. "I'll make him understand."

I nod, grateful and wretched. "Thank you, Jude."

He nods. "I'll go find some to-go boxes and say bye to Betty for us."

He walks off toward the back room, looking like he was just attacked by a dangerously sex-deprived woman. I let out a quiet, despairing groan. This entire outing has been one giant failure.

But somehow, the suspicion that I've hurt Jude feels worse than anything at all.

19

GRACIE

Four Weeks Before the Wedding

Is it possible to die from awkward silence? With my mortification still at potentially fatal levels after leaving the cake shop, I ask Jude to drop me off at Sofia's studio instead of braving the hour-long drive back to Larkwood with him. He doesn't argue. He only nods in what I assume is shell-shocked silence as I frantically text Sofia.

Thankfully, she replies that she'd love to see me, but there's a catch: I'll have to attend the community potluck that's being held at KILN. I sigh. Being pressured into taking a studio space is the opposite of how I envisioned spending my evening (in my Snuggie with my old pals, Ben & Jerry). But at this point, I'd happily skip out of an airborne plane to escape Jude's presence.

We pull up to the building, and after a flustered goodbye with zero eye contact, I eject myself from the car. Sucking in a merciful lungful of non-Jude-scented air, I don't think I've ever been so relieved to see Sofia in my life.

"Gracie! I'm so glad you came!" she says when I meet her at the studio entrance.

"You have *no* idea how happy I am to see you," I say as Jude drives away.

She takes me by the elbow and pulls me inside. "Come on. I can't wait for you to meet everyone."

I'm still getting my bearings as we enter a large, light-filled studio on the first floor, and a small spasm cinches my chest tight when I look around the crowded room. Lined with heavy printmaking equipment and all the telltale trappings of an artist trying to make a living doing what they love, this space is a reminder of a life I left behind.

Silently hushing that line of thinking, I hold up the hefty box of extra wedding cake that feels like evidence from a crime scene, and say, "Where should I put this?"

Her eyes light up. "Follow me."

The room is packed with what feels like the entire Providence arts scene—a moving gallery of carefully waxed handlebar mustaches, asymmetrical haircuts, and even a few babies sporting mullets.

Sofia responds to greetings as we weave toward the long tables at the back, straining beneath potluck offerings. Standing at the table serving herself quinoa salad is a well-dressed woman with long, straight black hair and utterly perfect skin. She beams at Sofia and me like she's been waiting for us.

"Hey, Sofia!" she says, holding her plate away to wrap Sofia in a one-armed hug. She lets go and smiles at me next. "You must be Gracie. I've heard so much about you! I'm Jae."

"I am *so* glad you two are finally meeting," Sofia says as we shake hands. "Gracie, Jae is also an apparel extraordinaire and rents the studio above this one. She designs the most to-die-for, all-organic children's clothing that sells out the *moment* she posts new products."

Jae nods and waves a hand, like breaking into the super-competitive luxury children's market is NBD. "Sofia told me all about Grace & Veil and showed me pictures of some of your designs," Jae says, excitement radiating from her. "I can't *wait* to have you as my studio neighbor. Maybe even collaborate on some flower girl sets?" she suggests, her voice trailing enticingly.

"I—"

But I can't complete the sentence because suddenly, the room is stifling, and standing next to this gorgeous, successful woman who is living a version of my failed dream feels like looking into a warped mirror of should-have-beens.

"Nothing is set in stone yet," Sofia hastens to say, laying a gentle hand on my shoulder like I'm a horse that might bolt. "Gracie put her business on temporary hold, and she's working as a wedding coordinator right now. But her situation might be changing in the coming months."

Jae's expression wilts a little, then brightens. "Well, I really hope you consider reopening Grace & Veil." She looks at Sofia and laughs. "Can you tell I'm desperate for someone in the building whose eyes won't glaze over when I start talking about vegetable-based fabric dyes?"

Jae and Sofia seem happy to carry the conversation while I contribute the bare minimum. Inside, I'm crumbling. Standing in this picture-perfect studio space, I'd give anything to turn back the clock and avoid all the mistakes I made the first time.

But now, with hefty student loans, an ocean of credit card debt, and a credit score that would make a lender's eyes water, the idea of restarting Grace & Veil isn't an idea at all—it's an impossibility. And even *if* I decided to sell my beloved but shabby, six-hundred-square-foot storage shed that calls itself a cottage, there's no way it would clear my debt. Which is why I forcibly kick the thought out of my mind.

The next two hours are a blur of keeping a smile on my face while trying not to think about the giant frosting stain on the back of my skirt *or* the damning Polaroid I snuck into my purse at the last second. I meet so many incredible artists who all seem convinced that I'm about to join their ranks, and my exasperation with Sofia and this entire day nears a breaking point.

As the event wraps up, Sofia walks over to where I'm boxing up some leftovers. "So," she says. "What do you think? I don't have a studio that's open *yet*, but I know everyone would be so excited to welcome you here."

She sounds nervous, which isn't like her, and the immediate urge to placate her wars with my frustration. I put down the take-out container.

"I know you only want what's the best for me, but I wish you hadn't made it sound like I'd already signed a lease and rented a moving truck."

She winces, tucking her dark curly hair behind an ear. "I knooow," she says. "I'm sorry I got carried away. But you're on the brink of a big change no matter what happens with Larkwood, and I just want you to keep your options open."

"But you know reopening Grace & Veil *isn't* an option for me," I remind her. "If worst comes to worst and I don't change Jude's mind, I'm going to need to find another job as quickly as I can."

She pulls me over to a couple of folding chairs, and reluctantly, I sit. "And how's that going?" she asks. "Any hint that he might be persuaded?"

In a flash, I'm back at the bakery with my hands tangled in his dark hair and his teeth scraping my neck. I put my elbows on my knees and my face in my hands, trying to breathe normally.

"Oh boy," Sofia says. "What happened?"

So I tell her. I tell her about our stupid game that relocated my brain between my legs. How I practically dragged him down to kiss me and, shamefully, how it was the hottest kiss of my life—or possibly anyone's life.

"I knew it. I *knew* this was going to happen! You can't have an almost kiss and then not follow through eventually. It's like, against the laws of sexual tension!"

"Not helpful," I say, tilting my head in my hands to glare at her.

"Do you like him?"

"Not the point."

"On the contrary, I'd say it's a pretty salient point, since you just traded bodily fluids with him."

"Ew, but again, liking or not liking him isn't relevant. He's got the relationship preferences of an oyster, he holds the nuclear codes to my life, and I'm going on a date with his best friend tomorrow!"

"*What?*"

"I know." I groan, wracked with guilt all over again. "His name is Henry, and he is literally *perfect* for me. Handsome, gainfully employed, emotionally available, and no known history of sending unsolicited dick pics."

"Wow," she says, her eyebrows rising over her gold wire-frame glasses. "Impressive."

"Exactly. Which is why kissing Jude was *not* okay."

She tilts her head and gives me one of her shrewdest looks. "Then why'd you do it?"

Without meaning to, I raise my hand to my mouth, which still feels branded by his kiss. I close my eyes, remembering how it felt to be the focal point of his hungry gaze and bossy hands. *I'm . . . very attracted to you.*

"Do you have any water?" I croak out.

Sofia gives me a knowing look and passes her water bottle.

"So, it's just physical?" she asks while I take a deep gulp. I swear I hear the water sizzle as it hits the bottom of my stomach.

"Definitely," I insist, not sounding definite at all. "He's trying to evict me. Fire me. Destroy my friends' jobs and stomp on Agatha's legacy." I rub the spot between my eyebrows and shut my eyes. "But he's also incredibly thoughtful, funny, and scared of his own cat, and when we talk, I completely forget that he's ruining my life! It's the *worst.*"

"So, you mean definitely not just physical," she says with a smirk.

"Did you even hear what I just said?"

"Did *you*? You obviously like each other, Gracie."

"I mean, I like him, but I don't *like* him," I say, wondering how many middle schoolers uttered the same sentence today.

She gives me a flat, disbelieving look.

Quickly, I say, "Jude has openly admitted to being a walking red flag who doesn't do relationships. Even if Larkwood wasn't at stake, that's not what I'm looking for. *Henry* is who I'm looking for."

I twist my hands in my lap, unable to help noticing the lack of conviction when I say it. But trusting my gut hasn't worked out for me in the past, and I'm not about to try again when all it seems to do is clap out the name *Jude, Jude, Jude*. So instead, I tell her, "It's the first time I've felt open to dating anyone since Calvin, but I'm afraid I've already ruined my chance with him by kissing Jude."

Sofia brings her legs up so that she's sitting cross-legged on her chair. "Gracie, you haven't even been on a date with this guy yet. It's not like you signed a contract to be monogamous with him. It's not ideal that they're best friends, but you have every right to play the field, and honestly, you *needed* a superhot kiss. Jude might not be the guy you build a life with, but at least he broke you out of your slump."

"So, you don't think I should tell Henry about the kiss before our date? Jude said he wanted to speak to him first, but I feel like I should address it, too."

"*Hell* no. You are a free agent, allowed to kiss anyone you want, anywhere you want, anytime you want, until you both decide to be exclusive."

"But they're *best friends*."

"Then let the *best friends* work it out on their own. You can't beat yourself up for being so hot that you've got competing suitors vying for your favor."

"You make it sound a lot more romantic than it is."

"Gracie, this is *peak* romance! What do you think the chances are of turning this into a why-choose throuple situation?" she asks, waggling her eyebrows at me.

I laugh, which definitely wasn't on my Bingo card tonight, and in my gratitude, I throw my arms around her. She hugs me back and says, "It's going to be okay, you know. Even if you lose Jude, Henry, *and* Larkwood, it's going to be okay. You'll move back to Providence! I'll have my best friend back!"

I sit up to look at her. "What are you talking about? You still have me."

She lowers her eyes to her lap and says, "I mean, yeah, but it's not like before, when you lived in the city."

At this, I take a better look at her. I came in tonight so consumed by my own troubles that I didn't notice the purplish tint beneath her eyes and the strained lines around her mouth. "Sof, is everything okay?"

She lifts a petite shoulder but doesn't meet my eye. "I'm okay. There's just been a lot on the plate."

"With work? With Sasha?" I ask, realizing I haven't checked in with her for too long. Her roller-coaster relationship with Sasha (a tortured artist who calls her his muse but insists on space every time she hints about exclusivity) is a perennial source of heartache for her.

She rolls her eyes. "Sasha went to Joshua Tree last week. He's probably trading portrait paintings for Quaaludes in a nudist colony somewhere."

"That tracks. And how are you feeling about him leaving?" I ask, knowing she's probably hurting more than she's letting on.

"Honestly, I hope he stays out there," she says quietly. "I know I always say it's just casual, but there's this part of me that's always secretly wishing he'll grow up and pay his studio rent on time. That and, you know." She gives a bleak laugh. "Love me."

It's so reminiscent of my own dashed hopes for Calvin that my heart breaks, knowing she's been suffering from similar disappointments. I lean my head on her shoulder. "I'm so sorry. You know I've been there, and it's the literal worst feeling."

"At least Calvin had the decency to break up with you face-to-face," she says dully. "I got an IOU on a greasy pizza box and an abandoned studio filled with masturbation paintings."

"Fuck that guy," I say, anger broiling under my skin.

"Yeah," she agrees, but without any of the heat I want from her. "Fuck that guy."

"I wish you had told me. I could have, I don't know, secretly rubbed lilies all over his paintbrush satchel. They give him massive sneeze attacks, right?"

She snorts. "Brilliant, as usual. But you've had enough to deal with."

"I *always* want you to tell me what's going on," I insist. "I want to help."

She turns to look at me. "Gracie, you don't have *time* to help me."

I'm about to argue that I'll always make time for her, but she holds up a hand. "Look. I've known you for nearly my whole life, and while you've got a lot of strengths, saying no isn't one of them. You give everything to the people you love, even when they don't deserve it. And yes, to be clear, I'm talking about your family and Calvin." She sighs. "I don't want to be another person in your life you can't say no to."

I swallow hard around the lump in my throat because she's right. I know I'm a notorious people pleaser, but I never imagined it would hurt anyone but myself. "I know I've been taking on a lot lately, but it doesn't mean you're any less of a priority to me."

"I know that," she says. "I guess I just miss you. I don't have anyone else to watch zombie movies with."

"I miss you, too," I say, feeling the words in my bones. "But promise me no matter how busy I get, you won't keep the big stuff from me, okay?"

She looks away. "I told you, I'm fine. But if you want to get on my good side, you could consider renting a studio if one of them opens up. Just for personal projects!" she tacks on quickly.

I try not to sigh. "I'll think about it."

"Perfect," she says, brightening. "Now spill the tea about Henry and this *date*."

I do my best to smile, wishing the change in conversation gave me the butterflies I know I should have. Instead, my stomach sinks lower, knowing the clean slate I've been hoping for is already a mess with frosting and lipstick. But with any luck, dinner with Henry will put me back on the right track.

All I have to do now is forget about the best kiss of my life and pretend I want nothing to do with the man who gave it to me.

20

GRACIE

Four Weeks Before the Wedding

Despite Sofia's insistence that I should play it cool with Henry, she seems to have forgotten that I am incapable of playing it cool, ever. As I walk toward the restaurant where he told me to meet him, "cool" feels about as foreign to me as Jupiter. This morning, after my daily stress run through the grounds, I got a text from Jude with three of the most panic-inducing words I've ever read: *I told him*.

I called Jude immediately, but he didn't pick up. Instead, I got another message.

Jude: Heading into a meeting.

Gracie: What did he say?? Is he okay??

Jude: He's pissed at me, but not at you. He still wants to have dinner.

Gracie: That's all you're going to tell me? What details did you give him? Do you think he's going to bring it up tonight?

Jude: I have to go. I hope you both enjoy yourselves tonight.

After that last text, he set his phone to Do Not Disturb, and I was left on my own to contemplate texting Henry or possibly flinging myself into the ocean. In the end, I did neither, instead opting to bury myself in work and party planning for my mom. But now I'm here, and avoidance-through-checklists is no longer an option. Taking a deep breath, I walk into the restaurant.

Looking around, I'm struck by how romantic and capital-*F Fancy* it is inside. The space is dim and tastefully modern in muted shades of pink with crisp white tablecloths. It smells like freshly baked bread and flambéed paychecks. Immediately, my guilt ratchets higher. It's been years since anyone wined and dined me in a place this nice. *But he didn't cancel*, I remind myself. *He wants to give this a chance, too.*

After the host greets me, I'm guided through the room of artfully set tables until I spot him. Henry stands immediately, dressed in an impeccable blue suit and white T-shirt, and I'm relieved to see him smiling.

"Hi," he says, coming over to kiss me on the cheek as the host vanishes. He only has an inch or two of height on me, which means less back-bending and tiptoeing than with certain very tall people who will not be thought about. Clearly a bonus. Henry draws away and says, "You look beautiful."

I feel color rise to my face as I get a hit of his spicy aftershave. "Thanks, so do you."

He grins, dimples on full display as he pulls my chair out for me. "Well, I did wax my unibrow just for you."

A surprised laugh escapes me as I tuck in my seat and Henry settles across from me. "Thoughtful hair removal before a first date should never go underappreciated."

"Especially when that hair removal is the only thing that makes me distinguishable from my eighty-three-year-old nonna."

I smile, but the elephant in the room may as well be perched on my shoulders. Thankfully, he notices and breaks the ice for me.

"So. You and Jude. I heard he took things to the next level at the cake shop."

Heat rises to my cheeks as all my excuses bubble up like magma. "It was a complete accident," I blurt. "The lady at the shop would have turned us away if she didn't think we were the couple and—"

"Gracie, relax," he interrupts, leaning forward to catch my gaze. "Jude explained the whole thing. Am I pissed that he didn't just kiss you on the cheek like a gentleman? Yeah, I am. But he said you made it clear you're not interested in him that way, and he's not the kind of guy who's *ever* interested in anything serious." He leans back, his eyebrows drawing together with concern. "But I did want to confirm what he said. That you're not interested in him, I mean."

You seemed pretty interested in him when you had your tongue in his mouth, a prim little voice points out. *Or when you fell asleep to his voice on the phone and woke up missing him.* But the truth is, my misplaced feelings for Jude are irrelevant. Like Henry pointed out, he isn't interested in commitment, and I need to give myself a chance with someone who is.

"What I'm interested in," I eventually say, "is finding someone who actually wants to be in a relationship. I want to see if there's a chance of that with you."

He stares at me for a moment, like he's trying to make sure I'm telling the truth. Finally, he says, "Then that's good enough for me."

Relief washes through my body, and I'm saved from having to come up with the next thing to say when a buttoned-up server comes to greet us. As we order drinks and Henry continues to charm me with his self-deprecating jokes and genuine interest in my life, the tension that's made my spine feel like a knotted rope for the last twenty-four hours relaxes. By the time our second course arrives, making conversation is easy.

"Do you like being a lawyer, though?" I ask when he says he used to dream of being a chef.

"Most of the time," he says, absently swirling his wine. "I've always gravitated toward work with lots of details to manage." He takes a sip and smiles ruefully. "My idea of fun as a teenager was teaching myself accounting software to help my parents with their small business, in case you wanted to know how much I *didn't* get laid during high school."

"Well, I happen to find a working knowledge of QuickBooks *very* attractive," I joke, only realizing how flirty it sounds after it comes out of my mouth. I'm about to backpedal until I remind myself I'm on a date. I *should* be flirting. But so far, despite his dimples and charm, all I feel for Henry is great friendship chemistry. The worst part is, I'm not sure it would have been an issue for me before meeting Jude. But now, there's something missing—a connection that goes deeper than a fun conversation and fills the cracks left by loss. If that weren't enough, the complete absence of any urge to get my hands up Henry's shirt feels like a missing puzzle piece Jude stole from the box.

"I love organizing details and checking off long lists, too," I say, trying to pivot. "Especially if it means helping someone with a big life event. I'm sure people are just as grateful for your help with the probate process."

"You'd be surprised," he deadpans. "Mostly, they wonder why it takes so long, but I do get a few gem clients once in a while. Like Jude," he concedes, while I try hiding my surprise that he brought him up again. "He understands the process better than most, and he's paying me a king's ransom for the Larkwood job. Wouldn't even listen when I offered my friends-and-family rate."

I take a sip of my wine, grateful that Henry can't hear my heart rate climb. "That's generous of him. Larkwood must be an enormous project."

Henry finishes chewing a bite and wipes his mouth with his napkin. "Understatement of the year. But Jude wouldn't dream of shortchanging anyone." He glances at me with something like apprehension. "I know yesterday wasn't his finest moment, and no, I haven't fully forgiven him for it, but usually, he's the most morally solid guy I know. Honorable, even, if such a thing still exists."

I drop my gaze, pushing the last bites of food around my plate. "My opinion of him has definitely been changing as I get to know him better," I say carefully. "But sometimes it's still hard to believe he means well when he's the main reason I might be out of a job soon."

"I get that. But trust me when I say he isn't doing it lightly. Whatever reason he's got, I know it has to be something unavoidable."

"So, you have no idea who his mystery buyer is, or why he's acting like his plans could trigger Doomsday if they got out?"

Henry adjusts himself in his chair and scratches the side of his neck. "Ahh, not technically. No."

"Not technically," I repeat, unable to help leaning forward in my seat.

Henry hesitates, slowly spinning his wineglass on the white tablecloth. "Well, if I had to hazard a guess, I'd bet his secrecy has something to do with his family."

"Oh," I say, surprised by his answer when all I've been able to picture is Taylor Swift adding Larkwood to her Rhode Island real estate portfolio. "Do you mean with his mom being attorney general? Like it could be a political thing?"

Henry leans back, his eyebrows pulling together. "No, I don't think it's political. Jude's family . . ." He glances up at me, and I try not to look like I'm an investigative journalist who's just smelled blood in the water. "I'll just say I've known him a long time, and I've never heard a single story about his childhood. I didn't even know he'd grown up at Larkwood until I met Agatha at graduation and she forced him to bring me over." He gives me a wry look. "Up until then, I guess I assumed he'd just emerged into existence, fully formed and wearing a suit."

"So, you think his reasons are purely personal, instead of work-related?" I ask, thinking of how he told me the buyer had certain aims "close to his heart."

Henry shrugs. "Well, with Jude, work *is* personal."

I snort. "You mean because his greatest joy is being the funeral director of his clients' relationships?"

For the first time all night, Henry looks defensive, which, after the kiss debacle, is a testament to his loyalty as a friend. "A lot of people marry the wrong person. And Jude doesn't just work with the Newport 'have-yachts.' He'd never mention this, but nearly fifty percent of his work is pro bono."

I pull up short at this. "He can afford to do that?"

"Well, the other half *is* the Newport set, so yes."

"I think as a wedding planner, it's been easy for me to judge him," I admit, feeling abashed. "A divorce lawyer kind of feels like my natural enemy."

Henry's easy smile returns. "I get that. And to be fair, he *is* a total commitment-phobe." He leans forward with his elbows on the table, lowering his voice. "But if you want to know my secret theory, I think he just hasn't found the right person yet. When he does, I have a feeling he's going to be more of an insufferable romantic than I am."

He grins, and I'm left feeling winded. With every revelation Henry has divulged about Jude, my questions have only deepened.

Thankfully, I don't have a chance to linger over them as our server comes to clear our plates and replace them with the final course. For the rest of dinner, we don't talk about Jude, even though the thought of him lingers like a well-dressed phantom at the edges of my mind.

It's not fair to Henry at all. By all my pre-Jude standards, it was the best date of my life. But as Henry and I leave the restaurant, the butterflies I've been urging to take flight all night may as well still be caterpillars.

He walks me to my car beneath the glowing string lights that crisscross over downtown Providence in a golden blaze, our hands in our respective pockets. Trading furtive glances, we're quiet as the perennial first date question mounts: *Will there be a first kiss, too?*

"I've been trying to think of something better to say than 'I had a really nice time' for the whole last block," he says, turning toward me when we stop in front of my Camry. "But it's the truth. I had a *really* nice time, Gracie."

He says this so earnestly and looks so handsome beneath the warm glow of lights, I could kick myself for not wanting to kiss him. Old me would probably be wondering if she could get away with casually asking how long he thinks two people should date before getting engaged. But somehow, in the few short weeks I've known him, Jude has taken the checklist of everything I've always thought I wanted and added things I've only ever felt with him.

I've tried denying it. Tried ignoring the quickly shifting landscape of my heart with every one of our conversations. But then he changed the chemistry of my brain with one single kiss. And in the aftermath, I now understand that it's possible to *know* someone is the worst person for you, while also feeling like you might just die if they never touch you again.

Which is why, despite all good sense, I tuck my hands a little deeper into my coat pockets and say, "I had a nice time, too. Now I get all of Jude's hype about you as his best friend."

I try to say it warmly, but the moment the word *friend* leaves my mouth, I see a crestfallen flicker of disappointment in Henry's eyes.

"I do pride myself on not sucking as a friend," he says. "But I have to admit, I'm interested in more than that with you, Gracie."

Once again, Henry proves to me that there are still men in this world who have the courage to lay it all on the line. My instinct is to try shoving down all the doubt Jude has sown and snap this man up before anyone else discovers him.

But the truth is, I'd hoped this date would make me feel swept off my feet, and instead, I spent nearly our whole time together thinking about his best friend. And even if I have no future with Jude, that's not the way I should be starting a relationship with anyone else.

I force myself to meet his hopeful gaze. "I really like you, too. But I'm just not sure we have that kind of spark, Henry," I say quietly. Apologetically.

His expression falls as he fixates blankly on a point in the distance. When he looks back at me, his gaze is determined. "Listen. I'm not usually pushy, and I'd never want to make you uncomfortable. But not every relationship has to start with fireworks. Sometimes slow and steady is the best way to start something that lasts. And given that you're a wedding planner, I'm guessing you're interested in finding that one person to do life with. Marriage, a mortgage, maybe some kids, right?"

I shift on my feet, wondering if he's aware that he's just spoken my love language with perfect fluency. "Of course I'd love to find that person," I say.

He nods eagerly, like I'm finally catching on. "Me, too! So just hear me out—we can go as slow as you want. If you need to put me in the friend zone for a while as we get to know each other, that's fine. I'm basically the mayor of the friend zone. All I ask is that you don't close the door on the possibility of more."

Maybe he's right. Just because my feelings for him aren't the all-consuming kind, it doesn't mean that passion couldn't develop, right? They say what burns hottest also burns fastest. I've had enough of flaming out, and given the impossible circumstances with Jude, I don't know what else could possibly happen with us. Maybe all I need to get over my ridiculous crush is a little time. So, with a deep breath,

I look at Henry and say, "Okay. Let's just take it slow. I promise not to shut the door."

He grins like I've just agreed to move in and file joint taxes with him. When we say goodbye, I don't pull away when he gently kisses my cheek. I swear to myself I will give this wonderful man the chance he deserves and ignore all my unreliable gut feelings. But for the rest of the drive home, I can't help wondering if I'm just leading both of us on.

21

JUDE

Four Weeks Before the Wedding

S*o this is what it's like to go mad.* As I pace around a second-floor guest room at Larkwood, pretending to catalog antiques and artwork for auction, what I'm really doing is coming up with another reason to look out the window. Uncoincidentally, it provides a direct view of Gracie's cottage, which is still dark. For the sixtieth time in as many minutes, I tell myself I just want to know she's made it home safely. When she gets back from her date with Henry, I will *not* go down and visit her. I won't interrogate her. I won't push her up against a wall until she's making those breathy little whimpers I drew from her at the cake shop, and—

Snap.

The tip of my pencil breaks clean off from pressing it too hard. "*Goddamnit.*"

From her perch on the back of a couch, Taco hisses at me. Frankly, I deserve it. I roll my forehead against the cold glass of the window. *She's on a date with your best friend, remember? She wants him, not you.*

I keep having to remind myself because for one suspended moment, with her hands tangled in my hair, I thought everything had changed. It had for me. But then she'd gasped his name. *Henry.*

It's difficult to exhale around my guilt. Telling him I'd kissed Gracie was one of the most shameful conversations of my life, and afterward, I swore I'd stop thinking about her—unless it was to remind myself of the manifold reasons she's off-limits.

But I can't stop myself from replaying our kiss until the thought of her with Henry is a live wire, sparking and thrashing in my stomach. I run a hand over my scratchy face. A committed relationship is something I've never even let myself fantasize about. Wanting one now makes my skin feel like it shrunk in the wash—too restrictive for the immensity of this craving.

I'm stalking toward an old mahogany desk for a pencil sharpener when I hear it: the crunch of gravel.

Tossing my clipboard and broken pencil onto the polished surface, the window yanks me back like I'm a wolf on a leash. Her headlights flash by, and my feeble self-restraint vanishes. I'm already making my way out of the room and down the stairs, half-assed rationalizations circling my mind.

Because I have to know—did she have a good time with him? Did she agree to see him again? Or did she spend the whole night thinking about our kiss, too?

When I finally reach her door, I don't think; I knock, only realizing belatedly that I'm out of breath and lacking any reasonable excuse for being here.

The door opens, and she's there in a short floral dress that pays homage to every one of her curves. Her hair is up, exposing her long neck, and she's wearing rosy pink lipstick and black-winged eyeliner. What's left is one rattling thought: *she did it all for* him.

"Jude," she says, alarm suffusing her face. "Is everything okay?" She looks toward Larkwood, then back at me. "Nothing's on fire, is it?"

You mean apart from my brain?

"No," I assure her. "I'm not that lucky."

She makes an irritated sound. "You scared me. I've only been home for like nine seconds."

"Sorry—I was just passing by and saw you pull in."

Her eyebrows draw together. "You were just passing by my cottage at ten p.m.?" Her eyes drop down to my feet and back up. "In slippers?"

Fuuuck.

"They're indoor/outdoor," I lie, wishing the earth would have the decency to swallow me whole. "I've been going through Nana's things. Needed some fresh air."

"Are you sure you're okay?" she asks with a look of concern.

Jesus. With effort, I unclench my fists and try to focus on anything but my racing heart and my fucking feet.

"Yeah," I say, closing my eyes for a moment. "I'm just—" I let out a croak of a laugh and run my hand through my hair. "I just wanted to know you got home safe."

Her worried expression dissolves into something so soft, I have to assume it's pity. "Do you want to come in?" she asks quietly.

"What?" I say stupidly, positive I've misheard her.

"I mean, unless you have somewhere else to hop off to in those bunny slippers," she says with a smirk.

Too relieved to be embarrassed, I say, "Sure. I mean, yeah. Only if you don't mind the company."

She gives me an indecipherable look but doesn't say anything as she lets me in.

When the door is closed behind us, she immediately slips off her heels with a soft sound of relief. It's such a banal, everyday moment; but intimate, somehow. Like the man who gets to witness it should be the one who gets to run her a bath at the end of the day and take her to bed. But I'm not that man. I'm a fucking psycho in slippers, intruding on her privacy after a date with someone else. With Henry.

With effort, I force myself not to ask about it. It's not my business.

"Are you thirsty?" she asks as she pours herself a glass of water in the kitchen.

If she only knew.

"No, I'm okay, thanks."

As she walks back toward me, I search desperately for something other than the one question I want to ask.

"How did wedding planning go this week?" I finally settle on.

She gives me a beleaguered look. "It's been a lot. My checklist is doing this thing where it never shrinks, and I just found out that one of my usual day-of assistants will be out of town for the wedding."

"You'll have me," I say. Her gaze lifts to mine. "I can help with whatever you need."

Her shoulders drop a fraction. "I appreciate that. I wasn't sure if you were allergic to weddings and planned on making a last-minute excuse."

"It's fine, I'll have my EpiPen at the ready."

She snorts and takes another drink of water. Looking away, my gaze catches on the bolts of fabric in the darkened corner of her living room. "So, are you planning on making a dress for this thing? Something from another Audrey movie?"

"You mean with all my spare time?" she responds with a sardonic tilt of her brows. But then she drops her eyes to her water glass. "That was just for Agatha. I don't really sew anymore."

"Why not?" I ask, surprised. "Too busy dealing with men who are sabotaging your life?"

At this, she rolls her eyes, but there's no mistaking her sudden discomfort. After a moment, she says, "I used to have a bridal wear design business." Her shoulders give a tiny shrug, but she doesn't meet my gaze. "Obviously, it didn't work out. I've been paying for it ever since."

All at once, dots I hadn't realized I'd been collecting connect. Her perfectly tailored, handmade dress at the funeral. Her empty cupboards. Her desperation to cling to a rent-free home and a stable paycheck. If I thought I'd felt terrible before, it's nothing like the pit of quicksand sucking me into its depths now.

"There's no shame in that, Gracie," I say. "It takes courage to start a business."

She shrugs. "Or stupidity."

"Hope is never stupid," I argue, wishing she knew that it's been the driving force behind every major decision of my life—including my plans for Larkwood.

She smiles sadly. "I know. Why do you think I keep trying to change your mind about this place?"

I have nothing to say to that. I'm too busy mentally kicking myself in the nuts for hurting her like this. "Can I see them?" I ask instead. "Your designs?"

She gives me a disbelieving look. "You want to look at a bunch of wedding dresses?"

If you made them, yes.

"If it means not going back to sorting antiques? Absolutely."

"Okay," she says, her voice deceptively light. "I have some old samples in my closet if you want to see them."

Highly aware that neither of us has brought up her date tonight, I feel like I'm barely managing to balance on a tightrope as I say, "Lead the way."

We step into her darkened bedroom and within seconds, we're within tumbling distance of her bed. Not my plan, but the unthinking part of me that kissed her is clapping me on the back for my genius.

She turns her bedside lamp on before opening an antique armoire with a squeak. Taking out a heavy-looking garment bag, she lays it on the bed's soft blue duvet.

"They're not in line with the current trends or anything," she warns, unzipping the bag.

"Well then, I'm not interested," I say distractedly as she carefully pulls the first sample from the pile.

A classic silhouette in creamy satin pours out of the bag in a white waterfall, and my jaw goes slack. It's timeless but unique in the way she's used the natural ripple of the fabric to dictate the draping. It's easy—too easy—to imagine it on her.

"You made these?" I ask quietly.

She nods, passing me the hanger. I hold it up, carefully sliding my free hand down the silken bodice. She isn't just a talented designer. She's a master tailor.

"You used internal boning?"

Her eyebrows rise. "If I say yes, are you going to make a dick joke?"

I try not to laugh. "As long as you don't mind knowing that I'm *also* an expert on boning."

She ducks her head like she doesn't want me to see her smile, and I feel ridiculously pleased with myself. *See?* I can do this. I can crack stupid jokes, and make her smile, and never touch her again, and it can be enough. *It has to be enough.*

I return my gaze to the garment bag and lift another sample that's just as exquisite as the first.

"Your seams are invisible. Is this blind-hem stitching?" I ask, running my fingers along the edge of the supple neckline.

She's staring at my hand, and when she speaks, her voice is huskier than before. "I didn't realize lawyering required such an in-depth knowledge of garment construction."

I look up from the dress, embarrassed. "Sorry. I didn't mean to nerd out. Agatha brainwashed me into loving clothes."

Warmth suffuses Gracie's dark eyes, and she smiles. "Even purple sequin boleros?"

"Did I mention she was in a matching ballgown with a leg slit up to her nostrils?"

Gracie's smile goes megawatt as she laughs, and my heart feels bruised with every new beat. What the *hell* did that kiss do to me? Silently, I pick up the next dress, and the next, more in awe of her with each one.

"You're incredibly talented" is what breaks loose in a hoarse scratch when I'm finally able to speak. "*This* is what you should be doing, Gracie. Not running errands for a bunch of newlyweds."

Her smile disappears. "It's a lot more than running errands," she says. "Believe it or not, planning the happiest day of someone's life is pretty fulfilling."

Good going, dickhead. I close my eyes. "I'm sorry, that was a shitty thing to say." I meet her gaze again. "I guess my 'shriveled little raisin of a heart' hasn't fully rehydrated."

I'm relieved to see a reluctant smile tug at her lips. "It's okay. I've had my prejudices about your work, too." She pauses. "But Henry really went to bat for you tonight. He helped me see a new perspective, maybe."

"Jesus. I really don't deserve him, do I?"

"Definitely questionable after yesterday," she says softly, and it's the closest we've come to brushing up against the one thing we shouldn't talk about. But as usual, she sweeps away all my best intentions with one drop of her lashes.

"Did you have a good time with him tonight?"

She's shifted closer to me. I know I'm not imagining it because I'm halfway to drowning in her scent of honeyed flowers.

"I did," she says. "He's nice, charming, thoughtful. Everything I've been hoping for."

"That's . . . great," I despair.

"Really great," she agrees, but she doesn't sound convinced either.

"So did he get a kiss good night?" I ask, my voice a low, possessive rumble that's light years away from the casual tone I was aiming for.

Her eyes flick up to mine, and I hear her swallow. "No. We didn't kiss."

Her words are like a match striking up my spine. If I were a decent person, I'd be disappointed for my friend. But right now, with relief pounding in my veins, decency feels like a rope that just slid out of my desperate grip.

"I'm sure he wanted to," I say, speaking directly from personal experience.

Her lashes dip. "Before yesterday, I thought we would. But I'm not sure we have that kind of chemistry." When her eyes meet mine again, I know we're both thinking of the cake shop. Citrus and rose, dark chocolate and coffee. The dark flutter of her lashes when my mouth found her pulse.

"Not like us." It comes out hushed, like a secret only we know.

She shakes her head. I shift closer. "It didn't mean anything," she insists. "We both just got caught up in the game you started."

The words sting because it was the first time a kiss was more than nothing to me, and from the way she's looking at me, she knows it.

"Then what are we caught up in right now?" I ask, clocking the rapid rise and fall of her chest. "Why the fuck can't I stop thinking about that kiss?"

Her breath audibly catches, and I *know* she feels this, too. Unable to stop myself, I tuck a lock of hair behind her ear, fingertips lingering on her skin. Her eyes drift shut, and I'm mesmerized by the sheen of her eyelids and parted lips.

"We could try this, couldn't we?" I hear myself bargaining. "If we just stopped this bullshit over Larkwood and you let me pay for this cottage, we could—"

But I don't get to finish my desperate, punch-drunk words because her eyes snap open. "Excuse me?"

"Wait," I say as she takes a step back from me.

"I can't believe you," she says, shaking her head as though to clear it.

"Gracie, listen—"

"Trying to convince me to sell the cottage when you've got me so—" The color of her cheeks deepens as she cuts herself off. "Is this some kind of tactic? Is all of *this* just to manipulate me?" she demands, gesturing frantically between our chests.

"No, of course not," I say, stepping back, horrified. "I'd never do that to you."

"How can I believe you? You charmed Betty into doing what you wanted. You lied to the bartender to get her off your back."

"That was different—" I start to explain, but she keeps going, ignoring me.

"You told Henry to ask me out! You *promised* you wouldn't kiss me, and then you did it anyway. You said it wouldn't happen again, but here you are! Touching me in my bedroom! Making it impossible to think, or breathe, or—"

"Only because I can't fucking stay away from you!" It flies out of me, as reckless as it is honest. Her eyes widen, and I know I should stop, but hours of restless pacing, of beating myself up for being the shittiest friend, and replaying our kiss have frayed me to threads.

"Do you think I *enjoy* feeling completely out of control?" I demand. "That I want to spend all my free time doing wedding chores for your ex? Do you think I want to betray my *best friend*?" I ask, shoving a hand through my unkempt hair. "*No*. But apparently, nothing is too low for me if it means I get to be with you. To breathe the same fucking air as you and hope for some stupid excuse to touch you." The laugh that emerges from me is unhinged and desperate. "Even the way you glare at me has me up at night, wishing you'd just take it all out on me. Because I *know* I can't have you. But I'd rather be your villain than nothing at all, Gracie."

Her eyes are wide with shock, but confessing a fraction of what I've been trying to repress is such a relief that I can't begin to regret it. Not yet.

"Jude," she says, seemingly at a loss. "It's not that I don't— That I haven't thought about—" She stops, gathering herself. "Tonight, I didn't kiss Henry because I was thinking about you, and it didn't feel fair to him. But you and I don't *work*," she says, shutting her eyes like she's been around this merry-go-round from hell as many times as I have. "We want completely different futures for Larkwood. For our personal lives. And while Henry and I might not have . . . whatever *this* is, I promised I'd give him a chance. He wants to find love, and so do I, but we won't have a future together if I keep ending up like this with you."

Her words sober me enough to see with eye-watering clarity how selfish I've been. Because she's right—she and Henry deserve to be together, and I'm the fucking guy with the flash cards from *Love Actually*, trying to ruin everything. I lift a hand to rub my eyes, too ashamed and wrung out by guilt to look at her.

"God, I'm sorry," I say quietly. It's a moment before I can speak again. "I know you have no reason to believe me, but I won't visit again. Won't touch you again. You don't have to worry about me standing in the way," I swear, forcing myself to meet her gaze. "You and Henry deserve every happiness."

She gives a short nod, but there's no relief on her face. "And our deal? Are you still open to having your mind changed about Larkwood?"

My chest constricts. "I'm still planning to get rid of it," I say heavily. "My mind hasn't changed, but if you want to keep trying until the wedding, then we can keep going."

The disappointment radiating off her is palpable, but she nods again. "I know we're only four weeks away," she says, "but I want to keep trying to convince you."

"Okay," I say, determined to uphold my end of the bargain. "Just text me who we're meeting next and I'll be there."

"Okay," she says, looking down at her feet. "I'll walk you out, then."

With nothing left to say, I follow her out, and there's a finality to every step. Every burning question I had tonight was answered, but instead of providing any kind of solace, all that's left behind are scorch marks.

But somehow, they'll have to be enough.

22

GRACIE

Three Weeks Before the Wedding

Gracie: HALP.

Sofia: Bat signal received. What is your emergency?

Gracie: I went on my date with Henry, but then Jude came over and said things.

Sofia: Saying things is the worst. How dare he?

Gracie: I think he might like me in a "not just friends" way.

Sofia: Class, please welcome Gracie. She has a lot to catch up on, but she's trying her best.

Gracie: SOFIAAAAA

Sofia: When can you come by?

Gracie: Could I come over for Sunday dinner tomorrow? I really need some Morales family love. And Abuela's sancocho. 🙏

Sofia: Sure you don't want to just grab drinks? There's this new Dolly Parton–themed bar I've been dying to check out. 🤠

Gracie: Amazing, but can we please do Sunday dinner this time? I haven't seen your family in ages.

Sofia: If you insist.

Gracie: 💞

23

GRACIE

Three Weeks Before the Wedding

As I walk through the familiar front door of the Morales house, the smell of frying tostones greets me like an embrace. It's followed almost immediately by an actual embrace as Mrs. Morales bustles down the short flight of steps and opens her arms wide.

"Gracie, Gracie," she says into my hair when I lean down to hug her. She plants a kiss on my cheek, and I feel the knots in my back melt. Holding me out by the shoulders to examine me, she says, "It's been too long and you're working too hard."

"Guilty on both counts," I say apologetically. "How have you been?"

"Too blessed to be stressed," she answers with her usual mantra as she releases me and turns to Sofia. But this time, I can't help noticing the slight weariness she says it with, and a pang goes through me for not making more of an effort to visit.

After Sofia's mom has thoroughly examined both of us, we walk up the short flight of stairs and through the cozy living room where all our zombie movie marathons would secretly happen. When we get to the heart of the house—the kitchen—Abuela is there, stirring a large cast-iron pot I know contains her famous sancocho. She bangs the wooden spoon on the edge of the pot before turning to us with a wide smile. She hugs me, wine is poured, and sore backs have been thoroughly discussed before I finally notice who's missing from the kitchen. "Where's Mr. Morales?" I ask.

Sofia's brothers and sister come to Sunday dinner when they can, but her dad has always been the linchpin of the gathering. His wife is fond of complaining about his personality being too big for any room, but I've always found that his off-tune humming, inappropriate jokes, and endless anecdotes fill a part of my heart that's always been too quiet. My own father never has anything to say to me.

Sofia, her mom, and Abuela exchange glances.

"Let's sit," Mrs. Morales says too brightly, leading us to the table. I try catching Sofia's gaze, but she avoids me, grabbing a plate of steaming-hot tostones instead.

Trying not to panic, I blurt, "He's okay, right? His angina isn't acting up again?"

"No, no—nothing like that," Mrs. Morales assures me, but Sofia is looking down at her hands instead of digging into her food, and if there were any signal that *the end is nigh*, it would be that. "But we did want to talk with you."

"Okay," I say, trying to stay calm. But Sofia bites her lip, and her chin is puckered in the way that always precedes tears.

Mrs. Morales takes a centering breath and reaches her hand across the table toward me. I grab it like someone's just thrown me a rope down a cliff I'm dangling from.

"Héctor moved out. We're separating, Gracie."

"He . . . what?" I say stupidly. I heard her words and comprehend them, but registering them as fact is proving difficult. "I don't understand."

Her dark eyebrows press together as she squeezes my hand. "I know it's a shock. But believe me when I tell you it was the right decision for both of us."

I close my eyes and try to calm my racing heart as a million warm memories war with what she's just told me. I don't want to believe it. Mr. and Mrs. Morales have been my blueprint for a loving, supportive relationship for as long as I can remember. The glue holding my heart together feels like it's dissolving, but as I look into Mrs. Morales's tired, pained eyes, I can only imagine what *she* must be feeling. What Sofia and her whole family must be going through.

"I'm so sorry," I say in a choked whisper. "What can I do to help?"

She gives my hand one last squeeze before letting go. "It's enough that you're here. We've had some time to adjust."

My eyes find Sofia's, and I know she hears my silent question: *How long?* But then I remember the studio potluck and how wan she looked. Her words return to me like a gut punch. *"You don't have time to help me, Gracie."*

All at once, breathing becomes difficult. Guilt is a fist around my throat for missing this. For being so wrapped up in my own troubles that I didn't notice my best friend was going through something of this magnitude. I came here tonight selfishly seeking comfort after things went sideways with Jude, never questioning the stability of this foundation I've always relied on. But this whole time, it's been splitting beneath my feet.

"But I thought you were so happy," I say, eyes stinging as I turn back to Mrs. Morales. "I-I thought you loved each other."

I hate that I'm asking her for an explanation, but I can't stop the words from tumbling out of me. Nearly all my life, I've heard Mr. Morales retell their love story like the soundtrack to my own hopes and dreams. I've witnessed it myself in his over-the-top affection and the way they always seemed to know what the other was thinking. But Mrs. Morales's face betrays the smallest wince at my words, and my heart sinks lower. "We do love each other. But sometimes," she says softly, "love isn't enough."

Automatically, I shake my head, because this runs counter to everything I believe—everything that this family taught me when my own didn't want me. That unconditional love might be difficult to find, but when it arrives, it can be strong enough to build a life on. "But it has to be enough," I say weakly. "If love can't hold two people together, then what on earth can?"

Sofia and her mother both lower their eyes, but Abuela's voice rings through the sadness. "Growth."

Our gazes swing to her, where she sits at the head of the table, looking directly at me.

"She's right," Mrs. Morales says quietly. She gives me, then Sofia, a tired smile. "They say your children are your greatest teachers, and as I've witnessed you all try on and outgrow relationships, I've learned a great deal about what's possible. I've been figuring out what *I* want." Her features pinch together as her voice begins to shake. "I began recognizing patterns in my marriage that were never okay and asked for change. But Héctor was never a flexible man. He didn't *want* to grow with me."

Sofia grabs her mother's hand when a tear slips down her face. "It's okay, Mami," she says in a choked voice.

I wish I could speak words of comfort, too, but my body feels like a burning building without a drop of water in sight. Mr. Morales hasn't only been a father figure to me—he's been the model husband and father against whom I judge all others. But while I might be in shock, I don't doubt what she's shared. Instead, my mind scrambles to adjust my perceptions of a man I thought I knew until I'm left with two questions. How did I miss the fault lines when they ran deep enough to break everything apart—and just as importantly—why didn't Sofia ever confide in me?

At this last selfish question, shame curls my shoulders forward. I know I shouldn't make this about myself. Not when the family I love is hurting so badly. But there's a kernel of hurt lodged beneath my ribs that wishes she had told me sooner.

Finally, I manage to say, "I'm here for whatever you need. I want to help in any way that I can."

Mrs. Morales gives me a look filled with warmth. "Then eat with us. Keep loving us, Gracie, and know that we'll always love you, too, no matter how the shape of this family changes."

And so that's what I do. We eat tostones, sancocho, and fragrant rice, and I will myself to keep my emotions in check. At least until I can get Sofia alone and beg her to help me understand how the unthinkable happened.

When we've done the dishes, said good night, and asked for Abuela's *bendición*, Sofia and I leave the house, walking toward her car in the humid evening air. Neither of us speaks until the doors are shut and we're safely out of hearing and viewing distance from the house.

"Sof—" I begin, hardly knowing how to articulate the snarled knot of feelings pulling tighter in my stomach with each breath.

"I know," she says, looking up at the car ceiling and swiping beneath her eyes.

"How long have you known this was going on?" I ask, trying to keep the hurt from bleeding into my voice. I understand all too well what she's going through. Navigating my own parents' separation was one of the most difficult times of my life, and adding to her grief isn't something I could forgive myself for.

But a smaller, more selfish part of me wants to ask if she was ever going to bother telling me if I hadn't invited myself over for dinner. Even though, for most of my life, her family has been closer to me than my own.

I hear her swallow. "It's been coming on slowly. Maybe for a year now?"

A year. I didn't think it was possible to feel worse than I already did, but I was wrong. This time when I speak, I can't hide the tremor in my voice, wobbly under the crushing weight of disillusionment.

"Do Luis and Dariel know? Does Marisol?"

"Of course they know," she says off-handedly, and while I know I'm not her sibling—that of *course* they had to find out first—I can't fully pretend that being left out doesn't cut me to the quick.

Staring out at the dark, suburban street, I bite my lips together to stop the quiet cry threatening to escape. I *know* this isn't my family. But Mr. and Mrs. Morales took me under their wing when my own parents wanted nothing to do with me. Instead of locking me in spidery garden sheds or dumping out my carefully organized sewing box on the floor like my stepsiblings used to, Sofia and her siblings invited me to carve my name in their tree fort. *They* felt like my real family. Which is why I can't stop my next words.

"Why didn't you tell me?" I ask in a small voice as the sting of feeling like an outsider gets louder than all my best intentions.

Sofia looks at me from the driver's seat, and in the moonlight, the lingering tears in her eyes shine bright. "I think I've been hoping it would all just . . . work out. But then Dad packed his things a few weeks ago, and—"

"A few weeks ago?" I cut her off, stunned. "Before the potluck?"

"Gracie—"

"You promised you weren't keeping anything big from me," I say, losing my grip on what I should be doing right now—comforting my friend. Before I can stop it, my selfish question ejects itself from the dark little box I tried stuffing it in. "When were you going to tell me any of this? Were you just hoping I'd never want to come over for dinner again?"

"I don't know!" she shouts, pushing her curls back from her face.

"But you know how much your family means to me!" I say, feeling a dam break inside of my chest. I know I'm being unfair—I know she's hurting—but pain and panic boil over until I'm too worked up to stop the words burning inside of me. "Why did you cut me out of this?"

"I didn't cut you out, I was trying to shield you," she says, wiping a frustrated hand beneath her glasses. "You've always put us on this pedestal, thinking we're this perfect sitcom family when the truth is, there have *always* been problems."

"What problems?" I cry. "Up until tonight, your parents' marriage is what made me believe that true love and supportive partnerships actually exist!"

Sofia makes an exasperated sound. "Gracie, I love my dad, but he is a *narcissist*. He loves playing the family man and treating you like his second daughter when you visit because it makes him look good. But haven't you ever noticed that he doesn't listen to anything anyone says? How Mami fades into the background when he's around?" She wipes more tears away as anger suffuses her face. "Maybe you can't see it because he was always performing for you. All his stories, the jokes, the big smiles . . . he *wanted* you to see him as father of the year. But the truth is . . ." She takes a stilted breath. "The truth that we've all been coming to terms with is that he's emotionally abusive—especially to Mami."

The world is upside-down and inside-out. "But you've never said anything," I protest weakly, loathing myself for being unable, or unwilling, to see the truth, when the signs were always there.

"I used to try," she says in a strained voice. "But nothing compared to the situation you grew up in, did it? How *could* I complain to you, when your own family treated you like a burden they couldn't wait to get rid of every chance they got? I know how much you've relied on us for love and support. You'd get so shaken if I even hinted that something was amiss that eventually, I just stopped."

Shame opens up inside of me, deep enough to swallow me whole. *Did I really do that?* Overlook her pain in the face of my own, and make her feel like she couldn't confide in me?

"And lately—really, ever since Calvin broke up with you—I've been afraid to tell you anything," she goes on. "You said at the potluck that you want me to share what's going on in my life, but you've been so fragile and afraid of leaving your little hobbit hole that I honestly didn't think you could handle it!"

Hurt steals my breath from me, and I'm left rigid and humiliated. "Well, I'm sorry my life is such a fucking mess that you feel like you have to treat me like a six-year-old," I say eventually.

"That's not what I've been—"

"Yes, you have," I say, my fists clenched against my shorts. "I'm sorry you haven't felt like you could lean on me like I've leaned on you. I *hate* that I made you feel that way. But I never asked to be protected from your heartache, or your family's. Did you ever think that maybe I *want* to be needed? Instead of constantly feeling like the walking shit show in our friendship?"

Sofia looks like she's been slapped. "It was never my intention to make you feel like a shit show."

"Well, it's hard not to feel that way when we can't have a conversation without you pushing me to take a studio space. When you don't trust me to know what's best for my own life or feel like you can even confide in me."

At this, Sofia's eyes widen. "Your happiness is the *only* reason I keep pushing you to get back in a studio and sew again. I've known you since we both believed in Santa Claus, and I can *tell* when you're acting from a place of fear instead of joy. And this whole bullshit scheme to try convincing Jude to keep Larkwood?" she asks, circling a hand in the air. "It's fear central! I know you think you have some leverage with the cottage now, but you're deluding yourself if you think he won't figure out a way to get rid of the estate, Gracie!"

I want to run away. Just sprint down this quiet suburban street until I disappear into the dark. I think about last night, when Jude told me his plans for Larkwood haven't changed. *But he also agreed to keep meeting up for wedding planning tasks*, I tell myself to keep the panic at bay. *He said the meeting with Daphne had an impact.* Surely, if we keep going, I'll have another chance to change his mind, right?

But what if he's just running out the clock? an insidious little voice asks.

I don't want to believe it. We've grown closer than I ever expected, and I want to think his feelings have changed since getting to know me and some of my vendors. I want to believe I still have a hope.

"Maybe you're right," I finally say, wiping the moisture from my face. "Maybe losing so much has made me terrified of losing Larkwood, too. Maybe the smarter move would have been giving up on helping my friends and forgetting about Agatha's wishes." I release a shuddering breath. "But Jude agreed to keep an open mind, and I'm going to see it through to the end."

After a moment, Sofia nods stiffly. "Then I guess you'd better get back to Larkwood."

She starts the drive back to my car at her studio, and regret for every word I've said punches through me. We both lashed out, and now the inches between us may as well be a chasm I have no idea how to cross. I don't know how to tell her how much I love her, and how badly I want her to lean on me—especially after she just gave me the chance and I fucked it up. Some words simply can't be taken back. So instead, we let them settle like stones between us, quietly nursing wounds we never wanted to give. Desperately, I try to hold on to what's left of my faith in love.

But in the silence, I can almost hear a muffled snap in the very center of my heart.

24

JUDE

Three Weeks Before the Wedding

I thought I was having my son over for dinner, not a cardboard cutout."

I look away from an abstract painting of the ocean that I've been staring unseeingly at and bring my mother into focus. Dinner is done, and she's barefoot and curled at the other end of the living room couch from me, her attorney general armor left outside on the porch. She's smiling softly at me and holding her wineglass with worrying nonchalance over the cream-colored rug, until a touch of concern creases her brows. "Everything okay over there, Rabbit?" she asks.

At the old nickname, I quietly exhale, pulling my mind away from Gracie's rejection last night and into the present. I hardly ever get to visit my mom when she's off duty at home, since it would mean seeing my father, too. But he's in London for work, and I should be making the most of this rare pocket of downtime we've found.

"Sorry," I say, taking a drink from my own glass and hoping the biting tannins will lift the fog I've been in. "A lot on my mind."

She tilts her head, her auburn hair brightening to gold beneath the floor lamp above her. "Work, or the house?"

I lean back against the couch cushions, glad my mom can't hear my mind repeating Gracie's name with the relentlessness of an EKG machine.

"Both. But it's fine," I say. "I cut back my caseload, and I'm headed to Larkwood tonight. I've got a meeting with the art appraisal people tomorrow morning about that godawful hunting painting in the main dining room."

My mom places a hand on her chest and looks affronted. "You wouldn't be talking about the portrait of your hallowed ancestor, Great Uncle Rifle Dick, would you?"

I snort as I get a vivid mental image of the stout, red-faced man who presided over every family dinner, posing with his large, suggestively placed rifle. "The one and only."

She shakes her head and takes a sip of her wine. "I never knew why Mom insisted on keeping that one up."

"Are you kidding? That gun was one of her favorite dinner topics. '*Look at the flared tip, Judy—what do you think it symbolizes?*'" I say in my best Nana impression.

My mom lets out a cackle that's so reminiscent of my grandmother, it's almost like she's here with us. I'm grinning right back until, inevitably, questions rise inside of me that yank down whatever happiness was trying to emerge. *When was the last time she was this relaxed? Does she ever laugh when he's around?*

"Wow, I needed that," she says, but a moment later, her smile fades. "It's too easy to get caught up in the loss and complications and forget the good stuff." She pauses. "Sometimes it's hard to remember that things were ever easy."

I nod, thinking of how effortlessly Gracie pulls my most joyful memories of Nana from me like a lodestone. How much easier it's become to talk about her when I know someone else will understand.

"I'm trying to get better at remembering the good," I say, before adding carefully, "Talking about her helps."

My mom's gaze stays soft even though she sees right through my effort to open her up. "It's not your job to walk me through this," she says gently. "You're already taking on too much as it is, sorting through the house."

I lift a shoulder, my eyes breaking from her gaze. I know she's being sincere about the amount of work Larkwood adds to my already heavy plate. But running on a lower current is something we stopped discussing when it became too painful for her—why the estate and its future were left to me instead of her.

"I'm glad it's me," I say, knowing I'm toeing into darker waters. But I don't want to debate my plans for Larkwood again, and if I make my stance clear enough, there's a chance she'll drop it. The hand that's been idly swirling her wineglass stills.

"So, you're still going through with your plans?" she asks lightly, like this hasn't been a blistering point of contention since the moment Nana left Larkwood to me. My back tenses.

"I haven't changed my mind," I say, voice firm. Because yes, while Gracie has sown more doubt than I'd like to admit, I'm still convinced that my original plans are the best way forward.

She hesitates, then meets my eyes with the determination that got her elected to the highest legal seat in the state. My heart sinks. *Here we go.*

"You're being short-sighted," she says bluntly.

"There's nothing short-sighted about how far I'll go to get rid of it," I counter, keeping my voice level.

She sits up. "I understand you have misgivings. But I don't see why you can't just keep it in the family. I'd be happy to manage it."

"Right," I say on a half laugh. "With all your spare time."

"Then we could hire—"

"There's no *point*, Mom," I interrupt, frustration getting the better of me. "Your life is in Providence. Why do you want to hold on to something so—"

"Because Larkwood was my *home*, Jude," she says, voice sharp and eyes bright with a loss that never healed. "It was the place I grew up dreaming in. The place I felt safest. A place that meant everything to me before—"

She stops. Closes her eyes. In the silence, we both complete that sentence in our own ways. I only have secondhand knowledge of the desperate, misguided ultimatum Nana made to my mother: *Larkwood or him.* I was fourteen and already packed off to boarding school in Connecticut, where Nana insisted I'd be better off. But I know her plan backfired. Like so many women put in the same position, my mother felt no choice but to abandon her home and support system for a man who only used the opportunity to further isolate her.

"If you were to keep it," she goes on, "you could raise your own family there and make *new* memories. Future generations would be able to enjoy a legacy property without any of the . . . connotations you associate with it."

I stare at her as my heart starts punching out a hectic pulse I feel in my temples. "*Connotations?*" I repeat weakly. It's a politician's blanket word for all the suffering that happened in that house. I understand why she doesn't want to name it. But after weeks of struggling to keep the real story from Gracie and years of hiding it from Henry, it's intolerable that the one person I *can* be open with is trying to spin the truth into something more palatable.

"It's called domestic abuse, Mom."

At my quiet voice, her mask falls. Her gray eyes are suddenly older, lined from holding back more pain than any one lifetime deserves. "Selling Larkwood won't rid us of the past," she argues, voice constricted.

I bite my lips together and close my eyes. I don't want to hurt her, but I also can't help being frustrated by her rose-tinted phrasing. After a moment, I force myself to meet her gaze. "But it isn't just the past. You're still with him."

The set of her square jaw hardens, and every instinct I have says to backpedal. I know better than to push her into talking about this if she's not willing, but after the week I've had, I'm floundering—clumsily stomping on all the eggshells I usually tiptoe around for her.

"That's none of your concern," she says, and I can't tell if it's a laugh or a wail that I have to stifle in response. Concern for her safety and well-being has been the thesis of my life.

At whatever my face is doing, she hurries to explain, "You don't live under our roof anymore. You don't know how hard your father has worked to—"

"To what?" I cut in. Stop lights and emergency sirens scream to life in my brain, but the words shoulder their way past all of them. "Only bruise you in places you can cover up with a pantsuit?"

She flinches like I'm the one who's raised a hand to her, and regret is a monster that swallows me in one toothy gulp. We stare at each other, frozen, because I fucking *know* better. I know better than to take my anger at *him* out on her. None of this is her fault, but blood is still roaring in my ears. I'm on the verge of apologizing when she speaks. "I've told you, he doesn't do that anymore."

I've barely managed to wrestle down my anger when it seethes back to life at her quiet lie, rippling beneath my skin in sickening waves. It takes all my power to redirect it to the correct target. I *know* her words are born from a place of protection, but tonight, I feel pushed past my limits.

"No?" I ask, setting my wineglass down with a clatter. "So you've been seeing a couples counselor, he's in anger management, and you don't have to wear long sleeves at all your press conferences, like last summer?"

A dull red flush creeps into her pale cheeks. "This isn't a conversation I'm going to have with my child. You're not responsible for saving me, and villainizing your father isn't helping your case."

"My case for what?" I ask desperately. "Wanting to see my mother safe and happy for once in my life?"

She sets her own wineglass down on the coffee table a little too hard, and I know I've gone too far. "Is this how you are with your pro bono clients? Judging them for decisions you couldn't possibly understand?"

The question twists the blade that's been embedded in my chest since the first time I saw my father's hands become weapons. Of course I know it's complicated. I happen to know it takes, on average, seven attempts to leave an abuser for good. Many people, like the woman seated across from me, never try at all, and it's not because they're weak. They face the threat of retaliation. Concern for their children. Income and resource obstacles. Emotional dependency, and a thousand other reasons.

And in my mom's case, she's not only a survivor—she's the state's top legal official, married to a man whose reputation is bound up with her own. There's no playbook for leaving someone like that—not with camera crews outside her office just waiting for a scandal, or the political capital it would cost her just to ask for help.

She has her justifications for staying, and it's not my job to judge. Not when I've never experienced what she's been through. But remaining impartial? That's a *much* taller order.

"You're not my client, Mom," I finally say, trying to stop the burning behind my eyes. "And I'm not judging you. I'm trying . . ." I let out a ragged exhale. "I just want you to be okay. I'm sorry for lashing out."

She squeezes her eyes shut for a long moment. When she opens them again, the attorney general is gone, and I've got my mom again. "It's okay," she says, eyes sparkling. "I'm sorry, too. Sometimes I tell myself that my choices don't affect you like they used to."

I repress the urge to pick up one of the nearby throw pillows and scream into it. It's always my goal to alleviate her worry about me. But over the years, I've gotten so good at it that the only person who understands how deeply this situation has fucked with me is my therapist. And sometimes, a desperate, childish part of me wishes that someone else knew, too. Someone I could tell without paying them to listen, simply because they care.

Unbidden, I think of Gracie, and longing arcs through me. I thought I'd accepted loneliness a long time ago. But sitting here tonight makes me ache for the kind of closeness I've purposely repelled. The kind that's impossible to have while I'm forced to hide every part of myself that matters.

"I know it isn't true," she says quickly. "But I am telling you the truth about things getting better."

It's not the first time I've heard this story, but I force myself to let it go with a nod, leaning forward to put my head in my hands. We've both been boxing without gloves tonight, and I'm too exhausted to keep it up. Too tired to repress the wish that I was with Gracie instead.

Eventually, my mom breaks the heavy silence with a tentative, "So. The transfer of the estate."

With effort, I lift my head. I'm about to admit that I don't have it in me to discuss it further, but her eyes are so anxious, I keep quiet. "Everything is going smoothly?" she asks. "You've got the right team in place?"

I sigh, knowing what she's really asking. She's built her political career on squeaky clean optics, and getting rid of Larkwood is something she wants done as quietly as possible. "Yes, Mom," I assure her. "It's a small, discreet group, and they've all signed NDAs."

She chews her lip and stares at me like she's trying to find holes in my plan. "And what about your friends? Or girlfriends? You haven't breathed a word about this to anyone, right?"

The padlock I've kept around my mother's secrets gives a weary groan, but it's so welded over with age and rust, there's no point worrying it will open. If there's anything in this world I take seriously, it's victim confidentiality. And in the case with my mother, it's even more than that—our personal relationship is at stake. She trusts me to keep her secrets, and I always will. No matter how isolating it is. No matter what kind of love I have to sacrifice to keep this one safe.

"No, Mom," I say quietly. "No one knows except David."

She brings the tips of her fingers to her mouth, drumming nervously. "And he's under an NDA, too, right?"

"He's my therapist. He's under a legal oath not to divulge—"

"I'd feel more comfortable if he signed another NDA."

I close my eyes, praying for patience. "Okay. I'll ask again."

There's a stretch of uncomfortable silence. When I open my eyes again, she looks as diminished as I feel.

"Thank you," she whispers. "For your discretion. For keeping this in the family where it belongs."

At this, a surge of emotion tears through my exhaustion like it was never there. "It belongs *nowhere*," I say, fists clenching on my knees. *Not in this house, not at Larkwood, not in any home.*

"It doesn't," she agrees quickly. "Of course it doesn't."

"You don't deserve this," I tell her, voice shaking. "You deserve a life without fear."

It's such a stupid, callous thing to say. As if it were that simple. But I can't take it back, just like I can't stop my eyes from welling or my throat from closing up.

She shakes her head, voice catching as she whispers, "There's no such thing, rabbit."

I press my palms to my stinging eyes, unable to take a deep

enough breath. I know she's right, but I'd give anything to show her that things could be better. I'd give anything to show her a future with wide-open laughter and sweetness in safety. I'd give anything at all. *Anything.*

"I would keep it." The words escape in a low, fevered rush before I can stop them. "I'd keep Larkwood if you left him."

As soon as I say it, self-loathing hits the pit of my stomach, caustic as an acid bloom. This is almost exactly what Nana did, but worse, because unlike Nana, I *know* that bargaining with a victim of DV is never the right thing to do. But the desperate temptation of holding a bargaining chip this powerful has stripped me of all my rationale, until I feel just like a panicked child again, being told to *run*. To *hide*. *Fast as you can, Rabbit.*

But I don't want to run. I don't want any more secrets to keep. I want to make the same childish promises I used to. *I'll be good if you leave him. I'll stop crying if you leave him. I'll take care of you if you leave him.*

My frame is rigid on the couch despite my pounding heart. Her gaze is stunned, and I can hardly breathe because for the first time ever, she's not looking at me like my promises don't stack up against all the reasons she stays with him.

It's why, despite all my training and experience, I say, "You could live there again." I move closer to her, clumsily trying to capitalize on her moment of indecision. "I-I'd keep everything just the way it was. It would be like coming home."

I'm holding my breath when she finally says, "That's . . . that's a lot to consider."

"Yes," I say, ready to be agreeable.

Her eyes rove around the room we're in. It's beautiful, but it's not home. It never will be. Her gaze slides back to me.

"Can I think about it?"

I'm nodding. If I could nod my entire body, I would. "Of course." Somewhere, far in the background of my mind, I register the consequences of what this might mean. The deal I've worked so hard on for Larkwood would be lost. Guilt for those who would be impacted rushes through me, but I'm too wired for it to settle. Too drunk on a possibility I've hoped for my entire life. I see her smiling. I see myself with Gracie and Henry, fully unburdened from my secrecy. I reach for my mom's hand and grab onto it. "I need to know soon, though," I say. "Before August."

She bites the inside of her cheek, eyes wide as she considers a different future for the first time. We both know how much she'd be risking. But finally, she says, "Okay."

"Okay," I repeat. Whatever happens next is her choice. No matter what, I'll respect it. But as her gaze holds mine—warm and solid as the grip on my hand—I feel something bright and unfamiliar take shape in the center of my chest.

I think it might be hope.

25

GRACIE

Three Weeks Before the Wedding

When I get back to Larkwood after leaving Sofia, the grounds are dark, but a light coming from the main house draws my eye to an upper level. *Jude.*

Turning the car off, I swipe my fingers beneath my puffy eyes. Sofia and I have had fights before—you can't love someone that much without accidentally hurting them once in a while. But tonight feels different. The shock of learning her parents have separated—and the sting of how long it took her to tell me—has hardened into a painful knot behind my rib cage. But worst of all is the realization that I've been so insensitive to my best friend for *years*.

For nearly my whole life, every win or loss I've faced has been celebrated or soothed by her kindness. Foolishly, I thought if anything truly terrible were to happen to her, she would lean on me, too. But she was right not to trust me. When she finally opened up tonight, I made it about myself instead of supporting her.

A shameful lump forms in my throat. Somehow, I think she knew that would happen. Just like she knew how desperately I've wanted to believe her parents were soul mates—just to prop up my own hope for Happily Ever After. But after witnessing the pain around that table of women tonight, I can't help wondering if the kind of love I've dreamed of is only found in romance novels.

I lift my head from the steering wheel and look at my dark cottage through bleary eyes. For once, it doesn't feel like a refuge, but a bunker. A place to cower from hard truths like the one I learned tonight. But right now, I don't want to be alone. I want to be with someone who might actually understand what I'm going through—someone else who's decided that it's safer not to trust love at all.

The soft yellow glow from Jude's window blurs as tears well in my eyes again. I was so convinced he was wrong—that everyone could find their person if they just tried hard enough. But now, committing to anyone ever again feels like choosing delusion, and tonight, I'm craving a different kind of certainty. Even if it's only a flame destined to leave me in deeper darkness when it dies.

A sob breaks free from my chest as I open the car door. Before I can talk sense into myself, I'm running to the kitchen garden door. As usual, it's the one lock that never seems to get fastened, and I let myself into the dark kitchen. Feeling like a thief in the night, I mentally map where the lighted window might be and decide which staircase to take.

With my shaking phone flashlight, I carefully pick my way through the dark, cavernous rooms, ignoring the judgmental eyes of dimly lit portraits and statuary. Thankfully, I don't have to search for long before I see a radiant line of light coming from beneath a closed door. Every nerve ending in my body jolts to life.

I swallow hard. Last night, Jude laid it all on the line for me, and I turned him down for Henry. For everything I *thought* I wanted. If anything is going to happen between us now, it will be up to me to cross that line, and there won't be any going back.

I close my eyes and, for a moment, wish I could ask Agatha what to do. But then realize I already know exactly how she'd respond. *Who do you* want, *Gracie?*

And while the consequences might be anything but, the answer is easier than my next heartbeat.

Taking a deep breath, I knock on the door.

Immediately, I consider sprinting in the opposite direction. But before I can turn on my heel, the door opens, and Jude is there—but not any version of Jude I've seen before. His disheveled hair looks like it's been in one too many disagreements with his hand, and the glasses I suspect he specifically wears to break me down are slightly askew. But it's his outfit that instantly kills the volume on all my inner turmoil.

A plain white T-shirt stretches over a torso far more sculpted than I'm mentally, physically, or spiritually prepared for. His bare arms are exposed to me for the first time, but more pressingly, so are his tattoos.

The twin swallows are there, but there's also a patchwork gallery above them, disappearing beneath the sleeves of his shirt in a way that begs the question—*Are there more?* They're all done in the same simple black linework. I see glimpses of an olive branch. A grinning skeleton mid-escape from its closet. A pair of roller skates.

"Gracie." His surprised voice jerks my gaze upward. "Are you okay?"

"I'm sorry," I blurt, still half-distracted by the unexpected ink and gray sweatpants slung low on his hips. "I know it's late, but I saw your light on, and—"

And I chose your best friend over you. I'm probably the last person you want to see for the rest of your life.

Now that I'm standing here, it becomes painfully obvious: just like with Sofia, I've selfishly gone seeking comfort from someone I've hurt. *What is wrong with me?*

"I'm just going to go," I say, as shame blowtorches my face. "I'm so sorry I bothered you."

I'm turning away when he says, "Wait, no. Please stay."

I look back at him and see his outstretched hand, like he was reaching for my wrist. Immediately, he withdraws it with a look of contrition, and my skin prickles with the ghost of his touch. *Don't pull away*, I want to tell him. *I was wrong. Wrong about everything.*

But instead, I say, "Are you sure?"

His Adam's apple moves heavily in his throat as he looks at me, and I know he understands every layer of what I'm asking. *Are you sure you still want me after I turned you away? Even if it means jeopardizing our bargain? Even if it complicates your friendship with Henry?*

Guilt wraps me in its familiar embrace at this last thought, but Jude's gaze is dark and parched as it locks on mine. "Yeah," he says hoarsely. "Get in here."

And so, without looking back, I make my choice and step over the threshold.

The door closes behind me, and suddenly all I can hear is my own breathing as I lean back against it. Jude is looking at me like he's convinced this is some kind of stress-hallucination, and I don't blame him. I try to find my voice, but in all my desperation to get here, I didn't consider what I'd actually say if he let me in.

What comes out is a slightly choked, "Hey."

"Hey," he repeats, dark eyebrows slanting together.

He knows I'm upset—I'm not exactly hiding it. But before he can ask me what's wrong and I completely break down, I walk past him into the beautiful room. It has high, crown-molded ceilings, heavy green drapes, a sitting area next to an ornate fireplace, and most notably, a giant canopy bed. I avert my eyes, afraid it might throw back its covers in saucy invitation if I stare at it long enough.

But isn't that exactly why you're here? To let go of Forever and Always and learn how to be someone's Just for Now?

At the thought, leaden sadness and electric nerves tangle in my stomach. The truth is, even though I feel completely safe with Jude, I've never had a one-night stand. I've never even had a one-night *sit*, and I have no idea how to start one. Do I just kiss him? Tell him that if it's not too much trouble, I'd like to have sex with him on every available surface?

I hear his footsteps approach from behind, and nervous heat floods my face.

"So, where's Taco?" I blurt, turning around to face him.

He blinks at my super smooth attempt to avoid explaining why I'm here, and points to a darkened doorway by the fireplace. "Her room adjoins the bathroom."

Unexpected delight cuts through my anxiety. "She has her own *room*?"

"For my own safety."

"Stop pretending you're not completely obsessed with her."

The way his eyes move over me makes my stomach zip tight. "I never said I wasn't."

The atmosphere changes so abruptly, I feel like I've been sucked into a vacuum chamber. I go perfectly still as he approaches me, and all my awareness is tugged across the space between us. When he speaks, his voice is hoarse. "Why are you here, Gracie?"

His eyes hold mine as his simple question loops around me like a lasso. I could tell him that tonight, the Happily Ever After story I've been telling myself for years just had all its pages ripped out. That in the aftermath, I only wanted to be with *him*—someone else with love in ruins at their feet. But the dim lamplight is far too bright for that kind of truth, so instead, I whisper, "I didn't want to be alone."

He moves closer, but just like at his door, he stops short of touching me.

"What happened?" he asks, sticking his hands in his pockets like some sort of safety measure. My heart folds in half as I watch him keep his word not to touch me again. He doesn't know that right now, being held by him feels like the only way I'll be able to get through this night. But I can't get the words out. *Hold me. Touch me. Make me forget I ever wanted forever with someone, when I could have right now with you.*

"I'm so sorry," I finally say around the thick wedge of disenchantment lodged in my throat. "I just . . . would you—"

Stumbling slightly, I take one final step and close the space I've tried so hard to maintain. I press my face to the warm cotton stretched across his broad chest as grief and longing pull taut within me. He's frozen, and for one terrifying moment, I wonder if I've read the whole situation upside down and backward. But then his big arms come around me, one hand cradling the back of my head, and a silent sob tightens my chest and throat like a vise.

It's such a simple thing, being held. Simple, but magnificent in its power to transmute our pain from a burden to bear alone to a bond of kindness shared. It feels like a millennium since the last time I was in his arms, and I can't keep it together anymore. I lost something precious tonight, and it feels like the North Star has fallen out of the sky. I shake against him, hot tears squeezing from the corners of my scrunched eyes. He absorbs it all into his solid warmth, soothing me with gentle hands and whispered assurances that I'm not alone. That he has me.

When I finally lift my heavy head from his wet, mascara-smeared shirt, I know one thing: I don't want to stop touching him. I don't want his hands off me for a single second tonight.

"I want you." The words gust out of me, blunt and far too simple for everything he makes me feel. His eyes flicker with a warning look, and I hurry to reassure him.

"I swear I'm not looking for promises or forever," I say, before he can remind me that while he might be craving a physical connection, too, he doesn't do relationships. I know it all too well, and it's exactly why I'm here. "I just want something that won't break my heart for once," I explain. "Something simple."

Because I have to know how he does it. I need him to show me how he stems the loneliness without ever risking his heart.

He shakes his head, eyes hectic over my face. "I don't think I can do simple, Gracie. Not with you."

"I-I know it's complicated with Larkwood," I begin to argue. "I swear I won't expect you to keep the estate just because we—"

"That's not what I mean," he interrupts, seemingly unaware that he's pulling me tighter against him. "I don't think we want the same things."

"I told you—I won't ask for more than you can give. I *want* this to be simple," I plead. "No strings."

He looks at me like I've completely missed his point. "You deserve better than this. I'll only hurt you." It's a last-ditch attempt to scare me away from everything he keeps locked up, but I don't believe him. Even pitted against each other over Larkwood, he's never been anything but caring and concerned for me, and tonight, I need him more than ever.

"Please, Jude," I whisper, staring up at him. "Just for tonight."

His eyes drift shut. "Tonight," he repeats, sounding drugged. His fingers are toying with the ribbon ends dangling from my ponytail, and against my stomach, his body begins to betray how badly he wants this, too. But the soft grazes against my skin stop when he opens his heavy-lidded eyes to look at me. "But Henry. I can't do this to him. I can't do this to *you*. You two deserve to be happy together."

He lets go of me, jaw tight and resigned. Taking his glasses off, he tosses them carelessly on the chair behind us before rubbing his eyes. According to my vagina, it's just been treated to a striptease.

"Wait," I say, my hands desperate on his shirt. "You're right—Henry deserves to be with someone who can return all the love he has to give," I tell him, as remorse fans through me. "He's wonderful. Considerate. Everything I always thought I wanted."

I swallow, letting the truth leap from me. "But right now, I don't want perfect on paper. Right now, all I want is a box of matches."

Something deeper than hunger passes like a shadow across Jude's face as he tugs me close again. Sensation ripples outward from his grip and lights up every erogenous zone I have.

"You want to burn it all down with me, Gracie?" he asks, voice darker than any arsonist's. I press myself to what feels like an iron bar between us, lifting onto my toes to get closer to his mouth and every bad decision I'm dying to make.

"Please," I whimper. Something hot and desperate flares behind his eyes, and his erection flexes heavily against me. Heat pools between my legs as the shell of the woman I've been for the last three years burns away like a papery husk. "You like it when I say please?" I ask, and his exhale sounds punched out of him.

Still holding me to him, his hand comes up to trace my bottom lip with his thumb. Before I can so much as kiss it, it's skating downward, grazing the centerline of my chin. My neck.

"I like it when you say please," he says, voice low and grainy, "because it means you want me to take care of you."

His fingertips linger on the collar of my shirt and graze where it meets my skin, summoning goose bumps. My hands slide up, into the dense, soft hair at the back of his head, and I think of all the times I teased him for having a kink.

"Is that it, then?" I whisper, with a single, sharp thump of my heart. "You want to take care of my needs?"

At this, his lashes drop as his head tilts back, exposing the sculpted underside of his jaw. He nods at the ceiling. Takes a rough breath. "Every conceivable need, Gracie."

There's a surging ache low in my belly at his rasping words. At his confirmation, every time he's fussed over me comes back like the filter's been ripped off. His eager hands on my wet ankles in the rain. His insistence on feeding me. His chronic worry over my tires. Quietly finding venues for all my ex-clients, and even the expert way he unpinned my hair the first time I met him. My chest squeezes—it's so perfectly, essentially *him*, I wonder how I didn't guess before.

When he looks back down at me, there's embarrassment painted across his features, but all I can think is how desperately I want this part of him. To let go of my crumbling life for a night and accept all the care he wants to give me. I pull him down, gliding my nose against his, and I'm breathless.

"Then kiss me," I urge him. "Take care of me, Jude."

The short groan he makes sounds involuntary. When he finally gives in, every moment from this kiss to the last one feels like dead space between two pins on a map. Not worth the visit. He kisses me like it's all he's thought about—like it's all he'll ever think about again. When his tongue finds mine, he's impatient but thorough, dirty but adoring, and I can't stop the muffled whimper it drags out of me. I want to climb him. Be fused with him at every point of contact. But just as abruptly as it starts, he's pulling away, leaving me openmouthed and panting.

"We can stop," he says, breathless. "If you change your mind—"

"I won't change my mind," I say quickly, already knowing the real issue will be pretending I don't want this every night into eternity.

"But in case you do—"

"I'll tell you," I promise.

Whatever he finds in my gaze must reassure him because he nods, exhales, and says five words that hit my bloodstream like pure adrenaline.

"Then let's get you undressed."

26

GRACIE

Three Weeks Before the Wedding

Apparently, there's nothing like the suggestion of getting naked with someone new to turn my voice into a dog whistle. "Right," I squeak. "Okay."

Jude looks at me sharply. "Not okay?"

"No, no, definitely okay. Great, even," I insist, yanking my voice down to a reasonable octave. "It's just . . ." I bite my lip and look away. "No one's seen me naked in like, three years," I admit in a rush, cheeks heating.

For a moment he's silent. Like I've said something unbelievable. Then, "You have no idea, do you? What you do to me."

I chance a glance at him, and the longing in his eyes almost makes me forget to be nervous. It nearly makes me forget what planet we're on. Vaguely, I shake my head, unable to speak.

"Come here," he instructs, taking my hands in his. "I'll show you."

Walking backward, he leads me toward the couch that divides the sitting area near the fireplace from the rest of the bedroom. When he sits, he's still tall enough to reach my chest with his mouth. I know this because he's kissing my Peter Pan collar like it's the hottest lingerie he's ever seen in his life. He looks up at me, eyes like maple syrup in the sun, and somehow, they calm me and make my blood race all at once.

"If it's okay with you, I'm going to undo this button," he says, lifting one of his hands to circle it with the tip of his middle finger. I feel the touch like it's happened between my legs, and suddenly I'm nodding, heart thumping.

"And then what?" I ask, on my way to breathless.

He tilts his head, considering. "Then, I'm going to do the next one, and the next. And when I'm done, I'm going to take this prim little shirt off of you, and those tiny fucking shorts, too, and you're going to prove me completely wrong."

"Wrong?" I repeat, my breath picking up speed as he deftly releases the top button.

His fingers slip into my shirt and stroke lightly down my bare chest to the next button. With a flick of his fingers, it comes undone, and he lets out a difficult breath. His eyes find mine again.

"Wrong that I couldn't possibly think you're more beautiful than I already do."

I bite my lip as unexpected emotion wells in me. Soon, he's undoing the last button and slipping my shirt from my shoulders. It falls behind me with a soft rustle of fabric, and his gaze is everywhere at once, drinking in the sight of my bare skin in the golden light.

"Fuck me," he whispers to himself, eyes roving over my simple black bra.

"That is the intention," I say in a nervous attempt at a joke.

"It'll be the other way around tonight," he informs me, tugging my hips closer.

Heart vibrating, I watch his hands pull the drawstring bow of my shorts. The waist goes loose, but instead of pulling them down, his hands just fist in the fabric. His eyes close, and his breathing is labored, like he's been hit with vertigo.

"I can't believe this is happening," he says. "Tell me I'm not passed out with Taco standing over my lifeless body."

A breathless laugh escapes me. "If you are, then don't wake up and ruin it," I order, hands traveling to his messy hair.

He looks up at me, eyes hopeful. "Maybe she'll administer a medically induced coma."

I smile. "That definitely seems well within her skillset. Could you ask if she'll make it a double?" I say, sliding my greedy hands down his arms. I trace a linework milk carton pint. A paper airplane. I want to absorb their secrets through touch.

"I thought you hated it when I ordered for you," he teases. There's a tug, and then a push of fabric down my hips, and every frozen, neglected part of me starts to melt like it's been thrust under a broiler.

I close my eyes as his hands slide over my panties, working my shorts down over the curve of my backside. "Maybe you were just ordering from the wrong menu," I say breathlessly.

"Or maybe I've had a hard time believing our cravings were mutual," he counters.

My stomach flips, and even through the haze of need fogging my mind, it's not lost on me that Jude still somehow can't fathom why I want him. I'm about to recite a list with approximately 280 bullet points, but then my shorts fall to my feet. I'm stepping out of them and toeing off my flats when his hand drops between his wide-spread legs.

"Fuck," he whispers, eyes on my pale pink panties as he adjusts himself through his gray sweats. Heat spills through me, knowing he can see how wet I am. I can feel it, slick between the press of my thighs.

"I've dreamed of this," he says, voice threadbare as he touches the little bow on my waistband. "Even before we met, I think." He leans forward to press his nose to my skin. Inhales. "You were always out there, just waiting to wreck me, weren't you? My what-if."

My chest constricts, but it's too dangerous to consider the possibility that Jude might want more than what I came for. Admitting it would mean facing the part of me that still secretly aches for it, too.

"I'm pretty sure you just described a natural disaster," I say, wishing my voice weren't so unsteady.

His hand slides up my spine to undo my bra clasp, while he presses a kiss to the center of my chest. My stupid heart presses right back.

"I could have prepared for a natural disaster, Gracie," he murmurs, slipping one strap off my shoulder, then the other. "There was no preparing for you."

He leans back enough for the bra to fall from my naked chest, and my stomach swoops. His words plant feelings that don't belong within a ten-mile radius of a casual hookup, but I'm too slow to stop them from taking root.

"Tell me," I whisper. "Tell me what else you've thought about."

But he's staring at my bare breasts, and I know he didn't hear me. His large hands are on my waist again, tugging me forward.

"Jude—" I say, catching myself on the cotton stretched over his thick shoulders. He told me he swims, and I feel it in the shift of heavy muscle beneath my palms. A lock of his dark hair has fallen forward, making a swooping *C* over his tense brows. I'm about to touch it when his mouth brushes over my nipple. Once, then twice before sucking me deep. He groans into me, and my breath lodges in my throat, forgetting whether it should be coming or going. All my thoughts are reduced to sensory flashes. His tongue, teasing. My toes, curling. Fingers digging. Back arching.

"*Jesus*," he says under his breath as he releases me, sliding his mouth to the underside of the same breast, wet and urgent. The hand that isn't twisted in the side of my panties comes up to squeeze my other breast, and my hips spasm.

"You want to know what else I've thought about?" he asks, moving across my chest with hungry, sucking kisses.

Apparently, he *did* register my request—apparently, he registers every little thing about me, including the way I'm up on my toes when he gets a little rougher with me. I nod fretfully, so turned on I think I could lose it like this. "*Yes*."

But he still doesn't answer me. His teeth close around me, his tongue soothing the sting, and I gasp, the edges of an orgasm already fluttering just out of reach. His grip tightens on me. "So sensitive, aren't you?" he says with wonder in his voice. Like he can't believe how badly I've needed this. How badly I've needed *him*. "So fucking perfect."

"Jude," I say, my neck going limp when his fingers dip just below the waistline of my panties.

"I know, baby," he soothes, laying a kiss to my rapid pulse. But that sweet endearment in his deep voice only makes the ache worse. "Will you turn around for me?"

My limbs feel too loose, like I might collapse if I move too quickly, but I nod—too needy to be self-conscious anymore. Jude's hands are on my hips, turning me, and I hear his ragged exhale at whatever he sees.

"Oh, my fucking . . . *fuck*," he says unevenly. Heat blooms low in my belly, and the friction of my own thighs isn't nearly enough. I want his hands on me—in me—but when they finally land, they're not where I expect. Instead, he's tightening my loosened ponytail and fussing with the ribbon, muttering something about *little goddamn bows*, and I realize this is part of it for him. Undressing me, arranging my hair just the way he wants it until I feel so precious I need him to break me.

"Gracie," he says, my name raw as a scrape as his hands glide down my back. He tugs my panties so they ride higher over my ass. Tighter between my thighs. His thumbs glide along the bottom edges of the elastic, and I can't stop arching into his touch. "Fuck, I need you to bend over. Just—" He huffs a breath. "Would you be a good girl and do that for me?"

His words send a spike of need through me, even as I startle at the request—I've never done anything so vulnerable. Never. But I've also never felt so safe or so wanted. Without any more hesitation, I drop my hands to the gilded coffee table in front of me. Tonight, more than anything, I want to let go of my fixation on the future and give free rein to what feels good *now*. And what feels good now is letting him see *exactly* what he does to me.

"God, just look at you," he rasps. I whimper, rubbing my legs together in a futile attempt to ease the ache, but his hands find my ankles instead of where I need them most.

"Do you have any goddamn clue what these do to me?" he asks, brushing the delicate lines of ink I have, and who *knew* ankles were so fucking sensitive?

"I-I forget they're even there sometimes," I say, looking down to see his big hands wrap completely around each ankle. He squeezes. My vision blurs.

His laugh sounds painful. “Lucky you. They may as well be tattooed on my fucking brain.”

I flush with pleasure all over again as he unknowingly flicks the tiny thorn of shame and regret I’ve carried over them into outer space. But then he’s gently tugging my ankles apart, and I forget to tell him how much I like his ink, too.

“This all right?” he asks, rough and quiet.

If by “all right” he means life-destroying, then sure. Yes. I take two wobbly steps wider. At this point, if he doesn’t touch me, it’s a very reasonable concern that I might cry.

Thankfully, he seems to know it, and his hands start sliding up the backs of my legs. He stops just beneath the curve of my ass, and my thighs begin to shake. He makes a soft, sympathetic sound. “I’m going to take care of you now, okay?”

My breath is just as erratic as my nod. “Please.”

He groans as his hands slide up my cheeks. Squeezing. Parting. The hot press of his mouth lands on the edge of my panties. There’s a muffled *fuck*. A scrape of bottom teeth, a bite, and then his large thumb, straight down the molten center of me. I gasp at the touch, everything clenching, but his hands only grip my ass harder, spreading me.

“This,” he rasps, pressing his mouth to the soaked fabric. He sucks it away from my skin before releasing it with a wet snap. “This is what I think about, Gracie. All the fucking time.”

I’m on the verge of tears, knuckles white, needing more. “What else?” I beg. Because it’s not enough that his fingers are yanking my panties down with muttered profanities. Not enough when his tongue licks into me, or how he grunts at the taste. I need to be inside his mind, too—to grab hold of that linking thread between us before I completely—

But then his thumb slides beneath his working mouth, circles my clit once, and I’m coming. It’s fast, shallow, and so unexpected that I can’t make a single sound from my open mouth. I’m up on my toes, every muscle in me spasming like they’ve been slapped, and Jude is groaning into my pussy, pulling at my hip to get deeper.

I lose myself to the white-hot feeling of it—the wet, filthy noises he's making, and the slick pad of his thumb, rubbing me just this side of too hard. A cry tears from my throat at last, and I can't hold myself up anymore. My knees knock together, and I'm collapsing, until Jude pulls me backward, into his lap.

"I knew it. Fucking *knew* it." He's muttering like a conspiracy theorist, his chest heaving, hands stroking my hair. Meanwhile, my head lolls back onto his shoulder, knowing nothing. "So responsive, aren't you? My fucking dream girl."

Thankfully, he doesn't seem to expect any intelligible response. I'm only barely aware that he's maneuvering my drenched and twisted panties down past my knees.

They fall to the ground off my dangling legs, and it's nice. Nice to be utterly naked against the heat of his much larger, fully clothed body. Gently, he hooks his hands beneath my closed knees and arranges them over his own.

"I've thought about this, too," he says, and I gasp a little when, abruptly, his knees spread wide, taking mine with them.

"Jude, I can't—" I protest, but his fingers are already stroking through the utter mess I've made of myself, showing me that, actually, I can.

"When you let me drive you to the cake shop," he says, his lips against my damp temple, "you kept rubbing your thighs together in that goddamn skirt." His hips shift, and I become suddenly aware of the unrelenting press of his erection behind me. "It made me think you might want me half as much as I want you. But you were—"

He stops. Exhales sharply.

"What?" I whine, squirming against his lazy circles.

"You were being such a little brat," he scolds, voice low with some unholy combination of annoyance and hunger. "Telling me you wanted to be *friends*? Making me so fucking jealous of my best friend that my teeth ached?" His grip on my inner thigh becomes vise-like as a breath gusts out of him. "I wanted to reach under your skirt to feel how wet you were. Make you admit exactly how *friendly* you wanted me to be."

He pushes a thick fingertip into me, just to the first knuckle, and I flutter helplessly around him. "Is this friendly enough for you, Gracie?"

I bite into my lip with a moan, my feet locking behind his immovable calves as he spreads me wider. "N-no," I stutter, arching my hips up, nails digging into his forearms. "*More*."

"No more?" He tuts, and I could kill him for teasing me.

"*Jude*," I say, but it comes out in a feral growl I didn't know I was capable of.

He kisses the side of my head like I'm sweet, and then slides his finger deeper. When he starts rocking his thumb against my clit, I see stars for the second time.

"*Christ*," he bites out as his other hand presses on my low belly, holding me tighter to his lap as I buck. He's rock hard beneath me, immense, and I'm dripping in his hand.

"More," I whimper again, thighs shaking uncontrollably as I lift my head to look down at where he's still pumping into me. "Tell me more."

Another finger squeezes in, but I'm so swollen, it barely fits. I moan, circling my hips in his lap, and his chest heaves beneath me. "Tell you more?" he asks, voice unravelling. "You really want to know my dirtiest dreams, Gracie?"

"Please," I gasp as the hand on my belly slides up to my throat, gently gripping until my head falls back onto his shoulder.

He pushes his fingers deeper, reducing my breath to fragments. His exhale could be a curse, and I turn my head enough to lick the salty side of his neck. To see the edge of his profile, staring down at my writhing, sweat-sheened body.

"Fuck, I want—" His eyes slam shut as his hips and hands flex involuntarily. "I want to wash your hair. I want to put you in a bath and paint your fucking nails. I want to dress you in lingerie and rip it off. I want—" His entire body shudders, and I can't hold on much longer. His thumb is erratic on my clit, fingers pumping faster, and I'm going to come too hard this time, but it's not what scares me. What scares me is the torn seam in my chest, exposing just the barest sliver of how I feel for this man who desperately wants to take care of me.

And how badly I want to let him.

His voice is choked and feverish as he lays his whole palm over my pussy, fingers still tucked deep inside. He's pressing me down, grinding me against his cock, and I'm floating. "I want to buy you a new car and burn your old tires," he says against my ear, and the first spasms twitch through me. "I want to put diamond chains around your neck and wrists so everyone knows you're mine to spoil. I want to order you food every goddamn night and feed it to you," he pants, and I can tell he's losing control. "I want to take care of you. But most of all," he says, hand flexing on my throat as his voice turns into a growl I feel against my back. "I want you to *like it*."

My orgasm blindsides me like an avalanche. A total whiteout that knocks away my ability to breathe, or to even tell whether I'm tits up or buried upside down. It makes me question if I've ever even come before, if I wasn't coming with *him*.

His sharp grunt snaps my eyes open, and I look down to see his hand between my widespread legs, fucking me like my pleasure is the only thing that will get him off. It's loud, and wet, and when he bites my shoulder, my cry is uncontrollable. He groans into my skin, teeth sinking deeper, and I know he's coming, too. It's too much and nowhere near enough—not when I can't see him lose his careful control. Not when my heart is beating backward to get closer to his. But maybe it's better this way. Maybe if we were heart-to-heart and sharing exhales, I'd be in deeper trouble than I already am.

When we're both spent, twitching and gasping with aftershocks, I don't think I could move if someone dangled ten million dollars an inch from my face. I'm draped over him like a corpse, and somewhere in the static of my mind, I consider the very real possibility that I've passed away. *It has*, I decide, *been a good life*. If he sells Larkwood, I'll just become the resident ghost, moaning for more.

I'm only half conscious when he rearranges my limp body in his arms. When he carries and then tucks me into the softest bed I've ever felt, I only realize I've dozed off when he wakes me with a soft, "Gracie. Angel. Can I clean you up?"

I nod, unable to keep my eyes open, and hum in pleasure at the soothing heat of a warm washcloth between my legs.

"You did so well," he tells me in a low voice, kissing my bent knee. His praise curls into me, soft and addictive.

"*Me?*" I say weakly as he finishes and sits me up enough to take a sip of cool water. "Pretty sure I'm not the one who deserves a gold star here."

"I don't want a gold star," he says, turning off the bedside lamp and climbing in behind me. He tucks us under the covers and pulls me against him. "I want you to fall asleep so I can confirm that you snore."

"I don't snore!"

"Of course you do," he murmurs, finding my hand to hold in the dark. "Like a chainsaw."

I laugh, but it morphs into a yawn. "And I gave that impression . . . how?"

His voice is muffled against the back of my neck. "No one can be this perfect."

My heart stutters. When I came here tonight, I told myself I wanted something simple. Being with Jude was supposed to be my way of proving that I can have the sort of no-strings hookups that ward against heartbreak. If I were following my own rules, I wouldn't be staying the night. But right now, my legs have the structural integrity of a pair of Slinkies, and my will to leave his embrace is even weaker.

Because tonight was anything but simple. It altered me in ways I'm only beginning to process. So much so that I don't even question the last thought I have before drifting to sleep.

That maybe "simple" isn't what I want at all. Maybe, I want to be tied up in all his strings, just so he can unravel me like a pretty little bow.

27

JUDE

Three Weeks Before the Wedding

Somehow, even only semiconscious, I know I've never had a better night's sleep in my life—until my usual alarm of claws presses threateningly into my exposed foot. With difficulty, I resist kicking Taco away, knowing from experience that she'll only dig in deeper. *Dammit.*

I don't want to get up. Not when the source of all my bone-deep contentment is still lying half-sprawled across my chest. *Gracie.*

An irrepressible sigh escapes me, because now, I guess I'm a sigher. I fucking knew I was in trouble the first time I saw her at Nana's memorial, but I had no idea how bad it would be. Even after she became the one person I want to share every secret with—I told myself it was fine. There have been so many obstacles between us that I was convinced nothing would happen beyond our kiss.

But then last night . . .

I fucking sigh again.

Last night.

It changed everything. I couldn't have been more worn-out and heartsick after dinner with my mom. But then Gracie knocked on my door, tear-stained and needing *me.*

My idiotic heart works itself into a knot of pride and longing, while farther south, desire slides into my belly, so thick and hot, I have to close my eyes.

I exhale. My specific . . . proclivities have never bled into my everyday life before. Usually, when I've been with other women, whatever caretaking I do is artificial. Scenes have clear beginnings and endings. But with Gracie, there are no boundary lines around the ways I wish I could take care of her. And last night, she finally let me have a fraction of what I want from her. She chose *me*, and I was too shell-shocked to question it. Even if it meant betraying my best friend.

I wince as the guilt I've been staving off throws a brick directly at my chest. I wish it would throw another. After our first kiss, I looked Henry in the eyes and told him I wouldn't touch her again. But now, my fingertips are being cradled by the soft dip of her spine, and her dark hair is spilling over my shoulder like ink I want to make permanent. It's too much to believe.

But somehow, impossibly, she's here. And so is my *fucking* cat.

Taco sinks her claws a little deeper in warning, and I acquiesce. Pressing a kiss to Gracie's messy bangs, I gingerly begin to slide out from under her. She makes a quiet moan that goes straight to my dick when I manage to extricate myself, but she doesn't wake. Taco, pleased that I've obeyed her commands, sits on the foot of the bed, cleaning her paws like they've been sullied.

I glare at her in silent communication. *You couldn't let me enjoy five more minutes of the best night of my life?* She glares right back. *No.*

Grumbling, I get up and stalk to her bedroom. She's only ever affectionate with me while I'm feeding her, and pathetically, I usually eat it up. But right now, I've got Gracie in my bed—a woman who has single-handedly turned my whole personality inside out, ripped out the seams, and resewn it into a shape meant to hold someone. To hold *her*.

Which is why I don't linger over the opportunity to pet my evil cat. Once she's eating, I hurry downstairs to make coffee and breakfast for Gracie. With any luck, it'll help coax the reason she came to me last night. Or at the very least, give her strength for everything we didn't get to do last night.

When I make it back up to the room with a rummaged breakfast, I toe open the door and find Gracie awake and . . . *petting Taco*?

Trying not to drop the tray, I cross the threshold like I'm entering another dimension. Gracie's dark hair is down now, messy around her pale shoulders, and the early morning sun paints her every outline like a brush dipped in light.

The door squeaks, and she looks up at me briefly before smiling back at Taco. "I can't believe you said she was mean!"

"Did I say mean?" I say faintly. "I meant despotic."

"I think the word you're looking for is *purr*-fect," she coos, scratching Taco behind the ear.

"Please just be careful," I warn, approaching the bed. "Her favorite snack is human flesh."

But even from here, I can hear Taco's purr. Naturally, it stops the moment I sit down. Taco takes one look at me, decides I've ruined everything, and runs off the bed with the feline version of *harrumph.*

As Taco leaves, Gracie turns her full attention to me and notices the tray. Her eyes light up for one unguarded moment before her smile falters. Almost as if she's just realized her natural reaction was the wrong one. I stand stock still, mentally repeating the word *Fuck* until she finally says, "You made breakfast. Wow!" But her tone sounds more like "You're proposing on the first date. Wow!"

Internally, I flinch. Of course I remember what she told me last night. *I want this to be simple. No strings.* But after what we shared, I thought things might have changed for her, too.

Christ.

I know better than to be disappointed. She's only protecting herself, and if I had any self-restraint, I'd be respecting her boundaries instead of making hearts in her fucking latte.

Summoning all my natural God-given apathy like a muscle reflex, I shrug and walk to the bed. "I was starving," I say as she sits up, carefully holding the sheets to her chest. "Want some?"

"You really didn't have to do all this, but thank you," she says, picking a grape. I watch it disappear into her mouth with a flare of satisfaction before meeting her gaze.

"I may have had ulterior motives," I admit, hesitating. "I was hoping we could talk about why you came over last night."

"Oh," she says, clutching the latte she just grabbed to her chest.

I give her an apologetic look. "Look, I'm the last person who's going to complain about your visit, but you seemed pretty upset when you showed up. I want to make sure you're okay."

She blinks down at her coffee, shoulders rising slightly. "I appreciate it, but we don't have to talk, Jude. I told you last night that this can't be anything more than . . ."

She lowers her lashes, too shy to say it.

"Fucking?" I finish for her, as disappointment snakes through me. Because apparently, we've slipped into an alternate universe where the hopeless romantic wedding planner wants commitment-free sex, while the cynical divorce lawyer wouldn't necessarily be opposed to having her initials branded on his ass.

She glances up at me but stays silent.

"Jesus," I mutter, shaking my head. "Just because we didn't do it on rose petals doesn't mean we can't talk. You're not some random woman I met on the internet, you're—" I cut the word off in the nick of time. *Everything.*

"Well, unlike you, I've never done this before," she snaps, setting her coffee down. "I don't know the rules. You show up with breakfast in bed a-and I don't know what to think."

"*You're* calling the shots here, Gracie. You told me you wanted something simple, and I promise I'll try. But if you think you can show up to my bedroom, let me do things to you that I'll be replaying for the rest of my natural life, and then expect me not to ask why I got so lucky, you're dead wrong."

She closes her eyes and exhales. "I'm sorry. I know last night was out of character for me. I honestly feel like I barely even recognize myself right now."

"You don't owe me an apology or any specifics," I tell her. "I just want to know that you're okay." *And fix everything if you're not.*

Her eyes hold mine, like she's trying to decide something. After a moment, she says, "Do you have anyone in your life who can handle any storm you bring to their door? Like a safe harbor?"

The question catches me off guard. Automatically, I think of my therapist, David, but I somehow doubt Gracie is referring to someone who invoices me. Next, I think of my mother, but while we're close, that's not our dynamic at all. So instead, I give her the most truthful answer I've got.

"Nana was that person for me. She and Henry, of course," I say, with a stab of guilt.

At the mention of Henry's name, she winces before nodding. "Agatha always made me feel safe. She opened her home to me when I needed it most."

My stomach tightens as I think of my efforts to kick her out of it. "Is this when I should ask if I'm the asshole?'"

The hint of a smirk lifts her lips. "Are you asking me, or the universe at large?"

"I don't think an answer from either of you is going to be very good for my self-esteem."

Her smile is no more than a flicker that doesn't reach her eyes. "I had another safe harbor besides Agatha," she says, and I'm alarmed to see the rapidly gathering distress on her face. "But last night—" Her brow crumples, and she looks down at her hands, twisted in the covers.

I curse softly. "Is it your mom?" I ask, remembering that she doesn't have a close relationship with her dad. "Is she okay?"

The short laugh that emerges from her is serrated as she wipes both hands beneath her eyes. "No, it's not my mom." At my look of surprise, she says, "Is that unexpected?"

I rub the back of my neck. "Well, don't sic Taco on me, but after you mentioned not having a relationship with your dad, I kind of assumed you're the much-beloved daughter of a strict but supportive mother who secretly wishes you worked in accounting. Am I wrong?"

A sad smile lifts her lips. "Now that's a hoop I could've jumped through for her."

I frown. "I didn't realize there were any hoops too high for you."

"Well, unless I wake up tomorrow with hitherto undiscovered athletic prowess or a penis, I think I'm sort of destined to be a disappointment for both my parents. Or at least an oddity."

My eyebrows team up with my frown to make a scowl. "You're not an oddity."

"My small army of zombie plush toys would suggest otherwise."

"You're not a disappointment either," I say, my blood heating.

"I appreciate the reassurance, but none of my parental baggage is relevant to this conversation. I didn't mean to shock you with my childhood wounds."

"Trust me, there's nothing you could say that would shock me," I mutter without thinking.

There's a stretch of silence, and when I glance up at her, she's staring at me like she's just seen the outline of a sea monster glide beneath the ice we're standing on. Trying to pivot, I say, "So, since they're clearly not a safe harbor or even a wet cardboard box, who did you rely on growing up?"

At my barely civil tone, she looks away but doesn't contradict me. "I think I've mentioned my best friend—"

"Sofia."

"Right," she says, seeming surprised that I remembered her name. "Well, her family—" She stops for a beat and bites her lips together. It's a moment before she can continue. "They kind of raised me?" she says unsteadily.

"And are they okay?" I ask, trying not to become visibly upset that she needed to be taken care of by her best friend's family.

Her eyebrows scrunch together. "Not really. No. Last night I found out that Sofia's dad moved out. Her parents are separating because, apparently, he's been emotionally abusive for years." Her voice cracks slightly, and without thinking, I grab her hand.

"It's obviously devastating on that level alone, but I also can't stop thinking that I should have *known* somehow." She wipes a hand beneath her eyes. "How did I never notice anything was wrong while they were suffering for so many years? How could I be so insensitive?"

Her quiet anguish punctures my composure, spilling cold rage toward this man I've never met.

"Don't blame yourself for not seeing it," I tell her with the conviction of someone who has witnessed countless victims and their loved ones torture themselves with misplaced guilt. "Emotional abuse can be extremely covert, and if no one confided in you about it, it's probably because they weren't ready to talk about it. Sofia and her family might only be coming to terms with the truth now." I close my eyes. "Processing something like that doesn't come with a road map."

"You're right," she says, voice wobbling. "I know she's still adjusting, but I got *so* upset that she didn't tell me sooner. Sofia said she was shielding me, but I can't stop thinking of how I've put her dad on this pedestal all this time. How badly that must have hurt."

At this, I can't help interjecting, "Don't punish yourself for wanting someone to trust and look up to, Gracie. If anything, it sounds like you were being emotionally manipulated, too."

A tear slips down her cheek. "Yesterday, I never would have believed it. Compared to mine, I always saw Sofia's parents as having this, you know . . ." She waves a hand and rolls her eyes. "Fairy-tale love story. They made me believe happily ever after was possible, but now it all just feels like . . . bullshit."

Her voice is so bleak, I'm robbed of any words that might comfort her. Last night, her belief in love was broken, and instead of trying to fix it with someone like Henry, she decided to give up hope with someone like me. My heart becomes an anchor in my chest.

"And I know this is so selfish," she goes on, "but instead of supporting my best friend when I finally had the chance, we had a huge fight. The things we said to each other . . ."

She covers her mouth with her hand, unable to say more. Instead, she turns toward me and burrows her face into my neck with a quiet sob.

"You were in shock," I say, holding her closer. "You were in no state to help anyone. I know when the dust settles, you'll talk with her. You'll support her however she needs you to."

She lifts her head to gaze up at me. "I don't know if I deserve another chance," she says. "I don't even know how to begin to fix it."

At this, I can't help thinking of Henry and my own selfishness. "For a friendship like that . . . you have to try." I brush a tear from her cheekbone. "I know if she gives you the chance, you'll repair whatever's broken."

"And what about what's broken inside of me, now?" she asks. "For as long as I can remember, I've wanted to find my soul mate. That one person who'd make a map of my heart." She shakes her head. "It sounds so stupid to say out loud. You've been right all along, Jude. It was just a fantasy."

"Don't say that," I whisper, taking her damp face between my hands and pressing a kiss to her bangs. "If anyone's heart deserves to be charted, it's yours, Gracie."

The words slip from me in a knee-jerk compulsion to comfort her. They're too honest, but she's so overcome that she doesn't register the truth beneath them. That I wish it could be me.

"It's too risky," she says, shaking her head as I release her. "It's why I came here last night." Her dark eyes lift to mine. "I wanted you to show me how to be happy with just this."

"Just this?" I repeat, as an ache for *more* nearly suffocates me.

"Something casual," she explains, tracing a finger over one of my swallows. "I've never been good at guarding my heart, but you make it look so easy."

Do I? When I can finally respond, my voice is a husk. "I guess practice makes perfect."

At my tone, her expression shifts into something apologetic. Shy. "Am I wrong? It's just . . . you called yourself a one-night-stand expert once, and that's exactly what I need right now. A break from constantly hoping my next kiss will lead to forever."

Her words scrape me hollow, but her eyes are so determined that I can't tell her the truth. That keeping everyone at arm's length has been easier than breathing—until her.

"If that's what you need, then that's what I'll be. One emotionally stunted asshole, at your service."

It's supposed to be a joke, but I guess my delivery needs work because her eyebrows knit together before she tentatively reaches for my hand.

"For the record, I don't think you're an asshole. Or emotionally stunted. But maybe . . ."

She bites her lip, hesitating. "At dinner, Henry mentioned you might understand what it's like to be hurt by your family. Is that why you're so good at protecting yourself?"

God. Not for the first (or hundredth) time, I wish I could tell her everything. But it's just a selfish impulse to feel less alone. The fact is, I'm not a victim, and I'm not about to give Gracie a fucking sob story. Not when I'm the only person my mom trusts with the truth. There's simply too much at stake.

"Whatever I've experienced is incidental," I finally say, but even this barest admission is more than I've ever said to anyone outside David's office.

"In other words, 'don't worry about me,'" she says softly, pressing a finger to the cleft in my chin.

I capture her hand and kiss her fingertips. "Exactly. I've given you enough to worry about."

"So the caretaker doesn't like being taken care of."

My mouth is on her wrist now, slowly moving up her inner forearm, hungry to give her the one thing she wants from me. The one thing I'm good for. "If you've got the time, I've definitely got some aches you could take care of."

She makes a soft sound but then freezes. "Shit. *Time*."

"Just a construct," I murmur into her skin.

"No, no," she says, sitting up quickly. "What time is it right now?"

My brows pull together. "Around seven, I think?"

"*Nooo,*" she groans, but before I can ask what's wrong, she spills Wite-Out on all my thoughts by practically falling out of bed naked, glorious in the morning sunlight.

"I have to go—I'm so late!"

"What are you late for at seven a.m.?" I say after managing to sweep two brain cells together.

"It's this thing for my mom's birthday party," she explains, rushing to pull on her clothes. "She wants the Patriots' mascot there for the kids, which, obviously, I couldn't make happen. But I found a guy with a retired costume in Woonsocket, and unfortunately, this was the only time he could meet."

"Wait, I thought you said you weren't close with your mom," I say, trying to parse this new information. "Why are you planning her birthday?"

She's rebuttoning her shirt at light speed with a hair tie in her mouth as she mumbles, "It's complicated."

The words are so familiar, I nearly have to laugh, despite knowing what kind of mountains they can blanket. But instead of interrogating her, I put a mental pin in it and get out of bed.

"Can I help with anything?" I ask as she steps into her shoes. "Do you want food for the road?"

But she's paused midmotion, staring at the lower half of my body. I glance down at my boxer briefs and white T-shirt, but apart from the semi I'm already sporting from her tumble out of the sheets, nothing's out of the ordinary.

"No," she squeaks. "I'm fine."

At her flustered response, a rough, empty sort of satisfaction curls in my stomach. I may be the worst thing for her, but at least I know she still wants me anyway. "In that case, I guess I'll see you later?"

She visibly swallows. "Yeah. Later."

And with that promise, I lead her to the door as anticipation spikes my bloodstream. Because I may not be able to give her everything she deserves, but I can certainly give her what she wants—and pray it'll be enough for both of us.

28

GRACIE

Two Weeks Before the Wedding

The best way to completely ignore the feelings you accidentally caught during the best sex of your life? A bone-crushing workload.

Is it fun? No. There's nothing fun about trying to organize the final details of a two-hundred-person black-tie wedding while your stepsisters keep sending you hostile texts about buying discount shrimp in bulk and storing it in *your* freezer until *their* party. But the silver lining is that I've barely had time to shower in the last week, much less ruminate on the fact that Jude Larkwood stole the heart right out of my chest.

It's a highly inconvenient revelation. So much so that given the choice between actually processing it and playing freezer Tetris with seven trays of shrimp cocktail, I choose the shrimp. But thankfully, I have something far more important to focus on today: Sofia.

In the almost week since I had dinner at her parents' house, I've only called once (reasonable) but texted five times (admittedly less reasonable) before finally getting a message that read: "I love you, but I need some space."

Seeing those words crushed the air out of my lungs, even if I understood why she sent them. So, in an effort not to be an asshole *again*, I told her to take her time.

It's why I was so relieved and anxious when she texted yesterday, asking to come do a last run-through of the photo spots Calvin and

Brooke requested. It's a chance to support her the way I should have after dinner, and this time, I don't plan on squandering it.

Leaving the cottage, I spot her almost at once. The sight of her slight figure coming toward me with her big camera fills me with so many feelings, I wish I had an overflow bucket for them.

"Hi," I say when we stop in front of each other. I offer a tentative smile, but she doesn't return it. She looks exhausted.

"Hey."

At her lifeless tone, the impassioned speech I had planned shrivels up until all that's left is the through line. "I'm sorry," I say, my voice wobbling under the weight of my regret.

She stares at me with red-rimmed eyes. "I'm sorry, too."

I shake my head. "You have nothing to be sorry for. I shouldn't have expected you to tell me about your parents sooner, or *any* time before you were ready. I should have been grateful to be told at all." My breath catches. "I should have supported you the way you've *always* supported me. Without question."

"Friends confide in each other," she argues. "When you told me I was being overprotective, you were right. I think my whole family has done that with you since you were little, and it's not fair. I should have trusted you to be able to handle it, and I didn't think about how it would make you feel to be left out."

My throat tightens. "You *never* owe me information that you're not ready to share. And even if you were ready to tell me sooner, it's not exactly easy to confide in someone who keeps running away from their own problems. I know I haven't exactly been a pillar of strength lately. For myself, or for our friendship."

She frowns, looking offended on my behalf. "You're a lot stronger than you give yourself credit for, Gracie."

I think about the last week—the way I've buried myself in wedding tasks to avoid facing what happened with Sofia and my feelings for Jude. I think of the megaton of frozen shrimp cocktail I bought just to avoid my family's discontent.

"I don't know about that," I say. "But I do know you had every right to tell me about your parents' separation on your terms. Not mine." I swallow down the jagged lump of guilt that's been stuck in my throat all week. "I said I wanted you to share the big things with me, but lately, I haven't been the kind of friend who's earned that kind of trust. Even when you gave me the chance to support you after dinner with your family, I blew it. I made it about myself." I shake my head, nose stinging. "I'm so sorry I let my own insecurities get in the way of seeing the bigger picture, and for not being there when you needed me most."

Sofia's eyes are brimming as her chin crumples up. "It's been a really hard week without you," she says shakily.

"You're telling me," I respond, my own eyes blurring.

I don't know who makes the first move, but then we're in each other's arms, hugging like we haven't seen each other in a year. She smells like cinnamon and home, and I realize Jude was right: some loves can survive any tear if you're brave enough to stitch them together again. You just have to try.

When we release each other, she has the same relieved smile I know I'm wearing, too. "How's your mom?" I ask.

We begin walking the grounds, vaguely heading in the direction of the ceremony site that Calvin and Brooke chose, and she tells me about Mrs. Morales's new pottery class and the way she pretends to be scandalized by the romance novels Sofia keeps dropping off. When I ask about her father, she's less sure about her feelings but tells me her new therapist is helping her sort them out.

"And what about you?" she asks me as I unlock the front door of Larkwood and we head to where the cocktail hour will be. "You never got to tell me about your date with Henry. What else happened during our Frism?"

"Frism?" I repeat over the sound of our shoes on the polished marble.

"Friend schism."

I smile faintly but hardly know how to begin explaining that the date with Henry seemed tailor-made for a lost version of myself. Or how the discovery of her parents' separation sent me into an emotional tailspin that led directly to his best friend's bedroom.

With an uncomfortable twist in my chest, the rejection I sent to Henry this week comes back with painful clarity. A few days ago, he asked me out to dinner again, and (after hyperventilating on the edge of my bed for a while) I responded that while I'd really loved getting to know him, I couldn't date him anymore. His two-word response ("I understand.") has haunted me ever since—and not just because of how guilty I've felt.

Saying no to Henry felt like closing the back cover on a story I've been telling myself my whole life: that I would find my Happily Ever After with someone exactly like him. But now, I'm not sure those kinds of endings really exist. Not when every man I've ever put my faith in has now officially broken it.

Except for one, who I'm desperately trying not to put my faith in at all.

We're walking into the billiard room when low voices coming from a far corner stop my steps. It's Jude and a tall woman my mother's age with dark skin, a close-cropped haircut, and bold red lipstick. They're standing by the large green marble fireplace, both in suits sharp enough to slice through the tightest alibi.

It's a shock to the system to see him back in his armor after the last time I saw him, half-dressed and sex-rumpled, but somehow, he looks just as good. Better than good—*essential.* All week, I've kept our communication to a minimum, afraid he'll realize that my insistence on staying cool and unattached was nothing but wishful thinking. But then his eyes meet mine across the room, and my heart starts flapping in my chest like a homing pigeon that just spotted its nest.

"*Shiiit,*" Sofia whispers. "*That's* Jude?"

I swallow hard. "Yeah," I manage, before he and his guest begin walking toward us, looking like the intro sequence of *Law & Order*.

"Why do I feel like I'm about to be sentenced to twenty years of incurable horniness?" Sofia whispers out of the corner of her mouth as we watch them.

I elbow her as discreetly as I can as they get close enough to greet us.

"Gracie," Jude says, his eyes locking with mine before Sofia delicately clears her throat. Blinking, he turns his focus on her. "And I'm assuming Sofia?"

He holds out a hand, and she takes it. "Live and in person. And you must be the infamous Jude Larkwood I've heard so much about," she says, just *asking* me to step on her foot.

"My doctor keeps telling me to cut back on the infamy, but it's a work in progress," he says, earning a reluctant smile from Sofia. "Ladies, this is my friend and estate planning attorney, Dr. Samara Kincaid. She's been helping me sort out some loose ends here at Larkwood."

Estate planning? Planning for what exactly?

"Just Samara," she says with a smile, shaking our hands in turn. "Sofia, it's lovely to meet you. And, Gracie, I've rarely heard Jude speak so highly of anyone."

Jude looks down at his polished Oxfords while I swallow my surprise. "I didn't realize he knew another Gracie," I say, trying to make it sound like a joke instead of a peek into my bottomless well of self-doubt.

Samara looks at me with slight confusion. "You're the estate's wedding coordinator, right? The one giving him grief for cutting off an income source for local vendors?"

"Damn right she is," Sofia says, radiating pride.

I should respond, but a question is snapping at me like a rubber band against my throat—is she helping him plan the sale of the estate?

Samara smiles. "Then yes, you're the Gracie he's mentioned. Keep up the good work. I've known Jude since he was just a baby law student, and I know how stubborn he can be. But it's always important to consider both sides of the coin."

"So does that mean the possibility of keeping Larkwood is still on the table?" I blurt.

Unease flickers through Samara's eyes before she looks at Jude. He clears his throat.

"Uh, yes. It's still on the table," he says, but there's an unspoken charge in the air. Something has shifted, and I can't tell if "still on the table" means it's a lovely centerpiece or on the very edge, about to crash to the floor. Either way, I can't help my relief at his words.

There's a soft ping, and Samara looks down at her watch. "Unfortunately, that's my signal to get going. I'll see myself out, Larkwood.

Don't get too distracted and forget to send me that paperwork over the weekend," she says with a small smirk.

"Of course," he says with a guilty glance my way. "Thanks for coming all this way, Samara."

"I'm sure it won't be my last visit," she says warmly, before bidding us farewell.

Tentative relief is still working its way through me, except now that Samara is gone, there's no buffer between Jude and my very outspoken best friend, who has no idea what's developed between us.

"Nice place you've got here," Sofia says casually, looking around the opulent room. "Very broligarchy chic."

Jude smiles pleasantly. "Only the finest accommodations for the Mouth of Hell."

A surprised laugh jets out of Sofia, before he says, "Gracie tells me you run a community arts space in downtown Providence. Is it KILN?"

Sofia's eyes light up. "Yup, that's my baby."

"My office isn't far from there. I keep wanting to go to one of the open studio nights you put on, but I'm always afraid I'll stick out like a sore thumb," he says, gesturing down at his impeccable suit.

"You should come with Gracie!" Sofia exclaims, before turning to give me a frozen smile and unblinking stare that clearly says *I THOUGHT YOU SAID HE WAS AN ASSHOLE.*

"Or you could just grow an ironic mullet," I suggest, trying to divert attention away from myself. "Then you'd fit in perfectly."

"Hey now, there are only two—fine, *three*—mullets in the building," she says. "But hopefully when a space opens up, you'll join us and improve the ratio."

"You want Gracie to rent a studio?" Jude asks, looking from me to Sofia. "For her bridal wear designs?"

"Desperately. But only if that's what she wants to do, of course. Right now she's still holding on to the hope that *you'll* change your mind about selling." She gives him a harassed look. "Please. Just put my friend out of her misery and tell her you're not keeping Larkwood, so she can move on."

Jude looks at me with a faint smile of exasperation. "I've tried, but if you think she'll listen to me, then you're giving me way too much credit."

Emotion clogs my throat, making it difficult to breathe. "Then you're saying there *isn't* a chance of saving Larkwood?"

He stares at me, his expression unreadable as my stomach pulls taut. "I thought there wasn't a chance of keeping it. But now . . ." He shakes his head slightly. "I don't know. I'm considering every side of the coin like Samara suggested. Even its edges."

If hope has been a tightly furled bud in my chest all this time, it explodes into full bloom now, petals crushed against my rib cage in their expansiveness. I nod, unable to break eye contact with this beautiful man who has his own wounds but is slowly unfurling for me, too.

"Wellll, I hate to rain on this lovely little pheromone swap," Sofia says, reminding us that she's had a front-row seat to this exchange, "but as romantic as a vague maybe is, we should finish up this photo run-through, Gracie."

Flustered, I look at Sofia, who is staring at me so pointedly, she may as well be holding a harpoon.

Jude nods and checks his watch. "I'm sorry for keeping you. I need to get back to Providence anyway."

"But you're coming back, right?" I ask before I can stop myself. It's Friday—the night he and Taco usually arrive for their stay, and it would be pointless to deny that I haven't been secretly hoping for a repeat of last weekend.

The regret in his gaze tells me his answer before he says it. "I have to stay in the city this weekend. But if you need anything—"

"No," I say, suddenly embarrassed. No matter how unruly my feelings have become, I told him I'd keep this casual. "I don't need anything."

Disappointment flickers in his eyes before he schools his expression into something impassive. "You have my number just in case. Sofia, I'm so glad I met you at last."

She gives him a long, assessing look. "Ditto."

When he leaves, my friend turns to me slowly, and there's nothing that can prepare me for what she says next.

"Gracie, when were you going to tell me he's in *love* with you?"

29

GRACIE

Two Weeks Before the Wedding

I may not have much experience with one-night stands or casual flings, but I can already tell I suck at them. Ever since yesterday, when Sofia lobbed the *L*-word like a grenade into my plans to stay emotionally distant from Jude, I've felt like a little kid who just heard the *F*-word whispered on the playground for the first time. I can't stop silently repeating it, even though I *know* it's forbidden.

I sigh and tie a Patriots ribbon around yet another favor bag for my mom's birthday. Obviously, I know Jude doesn't love me. We've only spent one night together, and even though we've gotten closer than I ever expected to, there's still so much he keeps from me.

The morning I woke up in his arms, I was an open, highly distressed book for him. But when I tried getting *him* to open up, not only did his walls go up, but he also installed some piranha-infested moats, just for good measure. Sighing, I try to refocus on my boring task *without* spiraling.

I'm filling another cellophane bag with Patriots shot glasses, daydreaming about dumping a tray of frozen shrimp down the back of my stepsister's shirt, when my phone rings. With alarm, I see that it's my old college friend Maya, who is also the pole-dancing instructor I booked when Brooke begged me to help her flaky maid of honor "throw something together" for her bachelorette party. Which is tonight. *Shit*.

"Hello?" I answer, but immediately pull the phone away from my ear at the blaring sound of Beyoncé's "Single Ladies." "Maya, is everything okay?" I ask, raising my voice.

"Gracie! Oh, thank God," she shouts. "I'm so sorry to bother you, but this group you booked me is completely out of control, and I need help getting them out of here. I don't want to call the cops, but they've already damaged property, and my bartenders are too slammed to help me."

What? All at once, a vision of Brooke swinging around a stripper pole in a perfectly pressed pencil skirt has me standing up from my chair so fast, I nearly knock it over.

"Oh my God, I'm so sorry," I sputter, already rushing to grab my coat. "I'm heading out now, but I'm about forty-five minutes away." *If I speed and run every red light.*

"*Forty-five minutes?*" Maya repeats, sounding panicked. "Gracie, these women are one high kick away from a head injury."

I close my eyes as frustration with Brooke tangles with dread. I'm a wedding planner, not a bouncer! But Maya's asking for help and I'm the one who sent this group to her. *But I'm not there.* Immediately, I think of texting Sofia, but she's hosting a KILN event tonight. I'd call Calvin to pick up his pregnant wife-to-be, but he's in Boston for his own bachelor party. There's only one person left who makes sense.

Every conceivable need, Gracie.

At the memory of his words from last weekend, my face goes hot. I somehow doubt breaking up drunken bachelorette parties was how he imagined taking care of me, but the simple fact is, I need his help.

"I'm going to call a friend in Providence and ask him to come right away," I tell Maya. "Just hang on tight."

"Thank you, Gracie—please just *hurry*."

"I'm on my way."

I don't know what I'm expecting when I finally pull up to the popular bar and dance studio that Maya and her wife, Eve, run together. Women in bridal party sashes and handcuffs? Flames licking out of the windows? I hope I'm only catastrophizing, but when I rush through the front door, somehow, it's just as bad as I've feared.

My eyes lock onto what everyone in this loud, crowded bar is staring at: a blond woman wearing four-inch heels and a MAID OF DISHONOR sash, wobbling on top of the bar with her eyes closed in rapture. She's holding a plastic fork like a microphone and singing along to that song from *Dirty Dancing*—"(I've Had) The Time of My Life"—seemingly unaware that everyone is shouting at her to get down.

When a maraschino cherry is pelted at her head and she doesn't even register it, one voice rises above the rest.

"*Kaylie. It's time to get off the bar.*"

With a spike of mortification, my gaze lands on Jude, who's standing just below the woman, hands lifted for her to grab onto. But instead of taking them as an offer of help, she only stretches out a dramatic hand to him like she's reaching across time and space for her long-lost love (while diligently avoiding actual contact). Staring passionately into his eyes, Kaylie belts out a particularly flat note that makes every surrounding spectator wince, myself included. Jude, however, stands his ground.

"*Kaylie, it's time,*" he reiterates over her song.

It's the wrong thing to say.

She nods fervently, and as the music approaches its famous crescendo, Kaylie's eyes go wide. "I'm going to jump!"

There's a chaotic mix of shouted no's and people scrambling to get out of the way. I see Jude mouth the word *fuck*, but he also solidifies his stance.

A second later, Kaylie and her plastic fork are flying, her swan's song on her lips as she leaps from the bar. It's clear from her peaceful expression that she has complete faith in Jude's ability to gracefully catch and lift her above his head, just like the movie scene. But there's nothing graceful about this. I watch in horror as her boob makes first impact with Jude's face in seeming slow motion. The surrounding crowd makes a collective "oof" as the rest of her collides against him in a loud thud.

He's knocked back a step, but a moment later, a cheer goes up as Jude sets her down and extricates himself from her grip. Hair a mess and still looking winded, he puts his hands on Kaylie's shoulders and begins firmly guiding her toward the back of the bar, where the dance studio is connected. Pushing my way through the crowd, I try to follow, but they've gone through the door before I can reach them.

When I finally make it to the closed door, I brace myself for what I'm about to walk into, nervously adjusting Kit on my shoulder. But when I step inside, everything is calm, even if the room is a total disaster. At least two broken glasses are swimming in spilled cocktails on the floor, one of the floor-to-ceiling mirrors has a huge crack in it, and the big costume cabinet in the corner looks like it's vomited sequins and feathers across the entire room. Something that looks like *actual* vomit sits in an ominous puddle in another corner.

Maya is walking around, passing out water glasses to the eight women sprawled across chairs and the floor, one of whom is blatantly unconscious. Jude is still guiding Kaylie, urging her to sit down next to a friend.

"Gracie!"

I turn and see Brooke, calling from where she's seated on a bedazzled throne I'm pretty sure is used for teaching lap dances. She has an ice pack on her head and attempts to stand, but Maya is already putting a hand on her shoulder.

"Just sit," she says in the hollow voice of a burned-out kindergarten teacher.

Brooke, with her BRIDE tiara askew and something orange splashed down the front of her white athletic wear, looks dangerously close to tears as I approach. When I pass Jude, I exchange a look that I hope communicates my eternal gratitude. I have no idea what Saturday night plans he'd been in the middle of, but the fact that he dropped everything to help me with this disaster is just *great* for keeping my feelings for him in check.

Kneeling to get on eye level with Brooke (who, I forcibly remind myself, is still a client and therefore beyond reproach), I say, "Brooke, what happened? Are you okay?"

Maybe it's the gentleness of my tone, but she breaks down completely. "I'm so sorry," she sobs, letting the ice pack drop to reveal a sizeable lump at the top of her forehead. "We were all having the loveliest time, but Marina kept sneaking in shots—I wasn't drinking, of course," she adds, rubbing her still-flat stomach, "but then Katherine lost a shoe and broke the mirror, and then Charlotte and Jessie got into a fight, and—and I tried breaking it up, but I couldn't *stop* them."

From a corner of the room comes a loud, guttural snore, and we both look at where Kaylie is now passed out against a wall, legs splayed on the floor. I turn back to Brooke, who looks horrified.

"Don't worry about them, it's all going to be okay," I say, trying to calm her down. "Would you like any Tylenol for your head? A granola bar?"

She nods, suddenly childlike. "Cal was right. You take care of *everything*."

Happy not to feel the stab of pain this definitely would have given me a mere month ago, I open Kit and find what she needs. "Take these. In the morning, we'll assess the damages and—"

"Of course, I'll pay for any repairs," she promises, ripping into the granola bar. "Just please don't tell Cal, I'm too embarrassed."

I make a zipping motion over my lips, deciding to let her discover the quail egg growing on her forehead on her own. "Not a word."

"Gracie, you're a—what's the American term? A lifebuoy?"

I stand back up, suddenly concerned she might be concussed. "Do you mean a lifesaver?"

"Yes, exactly," she says, eyes wide. "A *lifesaver*."

"Just rest and don't forget your Tylenol. I'm going to talk with the owner."

I make my way over to where Maya and Jude are talking in hushed voices and stealing exasperated glances at Kaylie.

"Maya, hey. I am *so* sorry about all this," I say in a low voice. "I never would have booked them with you if I had any idea they'd cause such a mess."

She pulls me in for a tight hug. "It's okay. I'm just so grateful you sent in the cavalry. Jude and I go *way* back."

"No way!" I say, wondering if I'll ever stop being surprised by how small Rhode Island is. "How? When?" I ask, looking between them. But Jude only shifts uncomfortably, rubbing the side of his jaw. Immediately, I feel like an idiot. Is "go way back" code for "slept together"?

Maya rolls her eyes. "Do you remember that motherfucker I married right out of grad school? Bobby?"

I grimace at the unexpected turn of conversation, because it's somehow worse. Maya was a grad student when I was just a sophomore, but we became friends while working part-time at the school café together. Bobby was our supervisor.

"Yeah, I remember him," I say darkly.

She nods and takes a breath. "Long story short, things got rough. I didn't have any money for a decent divorce lawyer, but a friend put me in touch with this amazing organization that helps women out of bad situations, and Jude took on my case, free of charge."

She smiles up at him, emotion warming her gaze, and he returns it with a subdued nod. "It was my pleasure to help."

She laughs. "You mean it was a pleasure to make that man shit bricks in court?"

His full lips tug up at one corner, and there's a glint in his eye that almost looks predatory. "That, too."

Maya lets out a big exhale and does a little shimmy of her muscled shoulders like she's shaking off the mere mention of her ex. Meanwhile, pieces of a puzzle I've been trying to solve blindfolded don't fall into place, but I start to feel their edges. *Is this the kind of pro bono work he does?* When Henry mentioned it, I imagined him helping low-income clients with basic divorce filings or offering free advice at legal clinics—not this.

"Anyway, thank you for everything. Helping me calm everyone down, organizing rides, playing doctor," Maya says with a pointed glance at Brooke, who's adjusting the ice pack on her forehead with a wince. "And for risking life and limb for *that* one," she mutters, jerking her head toward Kaylie as she burps in her sleep.

"It was nothing," Jude says.

She rolls her eyes before giving me a flat look. "These women were mid–*Coyote Ugly* on top of my bar when he got here. *She* refused to get down," Maya tells me, not knowing I just witnessed the whole debacle.

"It was my dishonor to catch her," Jude says dryly, eyeing her rumpled sash.

Maya snorts while I send up another prayer of thanks for his willingness to help.

"Listen, I really need to get out front and help Eve—this class was supposed to end an hour ago." She shakes her head and looks at me. "Would you two mind just staying here until they're all in cars? I don't trust them not to set something on fire."

"Of course," I say, feeling winded from this whole night, but maybe especially from the possible revelation about Jude and his work. "I'll see if I can get a cleaner to come first thing tomorrow morning. If you could also let me know how much to charge Brooke for damages, I'll get on that right away."

"Thanks for everything, Gracie. Jude, we should catch up sometime. Free dance lessons whenever you want," she says with a wink before hurrying out to help her wife.

After she's gone, Jude and I look at each other fully for the first time all night. In his pristine joggers, soft black T-shirt, and damp waves, he's completely out of place amongst the wreckage, and all I want to do is crush myself against him. He must have the same thought, because the next moment, I'm up against his warm chest, breathing in clean cotton and the faint scent of chlorine.

"Thank you," I whisper, hardly able to get the words out around the swell of gratitude in my chest. "I'm so sorry I ruined your night."

"Ruined? How many people can say that they've successfully re-created the flying leap scene from *Dirty Dancing* with a wasted stranger?"

"I think calling that successful might be a stretch," I say, a reluctant smile pulling at my lips.

"You wound me," he deadpans, but his eyes are moving over my face like he hasn't seen me in months.

"Well, even if your form *does* need work, I couldn't be more grateful," I say, my voice softening as I stare up at him. "Thank you for dropping everything for me."

"You never have to say thank you for letting me take care of you," he says quietly.

My stomach flips, but before I can argue that catching drunken, bar-leaping strangers on my behalf definitely warrants thanks, there's a loud chime from a nearby phone. We turn to see Kaylie jerk awake, before blearily unlocking her screen. She elbows the friend next to her and says, "Ride's here, Becca."

Jude and I go at once to help them to their unsteady feet, and for the next fifteen minutes, it's like supervising school pickup as we get these women safely into cars and off our hands. The last person to leave is Brooke, who we've convinced to visit the ER to get checked for a concussion.

"Please, just let me know how much Maya needs for repairs," she says one last time from the window of her ride. "And I'm so sorry again for everyone's behavior and—"

"Just take care of yourself tonight, Brooke. We'll talk tomorrow once you've rested up."

The car mercifully drives off, and I let out a massive sigh of relief. "Oh, thank God that's over."

The sidewalks are crowded despite the late hour as groups of people migrate toward eerie music playing from the river. It's a summertime Saturday night in Providence, which means one thing: Waterfire—a weekly spectacle where bonfires are set ablaze in the middle of the river.

Without deciding to, Jude and I begin slowly walking, too, swept along by the crowd.

He shrugs. "I don't know. Definitely livened up my Saturday night."

"That tells me nothing," I say as we round a corner and see our first views of the fire-lit river and thousands of people gathered along the banks. "Based on that hair extension hanging from the ceiling fan, you could have been skydiving and had a less lively time."

"And where in the skydiving-to-bachelorette scale of liveliness do you think clipping Taco's nails would fall?"

My eyes widen. "I'm honestly shocked she let you."

A group of teenagers dressed as fairies runs past giggling, and Jude pulls me to his side when I'm clipped by a wing. "'Let you' implies that I was successful in the attempt. I gave up and went for a swim instead," he says, hand sliding to my waist.

I laugh while my heart spins in my chest until it's dizzy. He doesn't let go. "I bet I could do it in less than five minutes," I boast.

"If you did, the world would have one less set of deadly weapons to worry about," he says, leading us toward a tent and the intoxicating smell of kettle corn. "Hungry?"

When I nod, he buys me a bag of popcorn approximately the size of my torso. But I don't argue. I'm too busy fighting against a current of pure fantasy—that this could be more than casual.

I know it's a ridiculous thought. *I'm* the one insisting on no strings, and the number of barriers between us could block an extinction-event asteroid. But with his hand on my waist, it's hard not to feel wanted. Adored, even. It makes me think the most dangerous thought anybody can have about an emotionally unavailable man—*maybe I can fix him. Maybe I'll be the one who opens him up.*

"My place isn't too far from here," he says. "And I don't mean to brag, but my couch is *really* comfortable."

Electricity leaps in my stomach. "Is this just a ploy to get me to cut your cat's nails?"

He smiles. "Less ploy, more plea. But only if you think saving a man from being sliced to ribbons in his sleep is a worthy cause."

In the firelight off the river, his eyes are nothing but trouble. The kind that blurs hesitation into desperation, until I'm ignoring every instinct shouting that I'm about to fall even deeper. Instead, I meet his gaze and say, "Lead the way."

30

GRACIE

Two Weeks Before the Wedding

"I've gotta say, I'm a little disappointed there aren't more whips and paddles," I comment when Jude lets us into his downtown apartment. It's in a building tall enough to have a beautiful bird's-eye view of the river, and modern in a way that seems like a conscious F-You to Larkwood's Gilded Age maximalism. But that doesn't mean it's cold. Everywhere I look, the clean lines of the space are softened by furniture that seems designed to promote cuddling, and rugs thick enough to make snow angels in.

But you're not here for cuddles, I remind myself firmly. *You are here for kinky, commitment-free sex with the hottest man alive. And to trim his cat's nails.*

He smirks, and I grip my giant bag of popcorn tighter. The last time I ran to Jude, I was emotionally spiraling. Now that I'm (relatively) level-headed, it feels more like an active decision to be here, and I'm not sure where that falls on the morally gray scale. Because even though I ended things with Henry, it's hard not to feel guilty for hurting someone so genuinely kind, and for potentially setting fire to his friendship with Jude.

"Don't tempt me to redecorate," he says, pulling my attention back. He drops his keys and things into a tasteful bowl on a tasteful entryway table before taking off his tasteful sneakers. I do the same, suddenly deeply aware of my messy gremlin cottage with all its zombie tchotchke and romance novels. This is the home of a functioning adult with an actual budget for things like furniture, art, and probably more than one set of sheets. Sheets that, if I can stop overthinking *everything*, I could potentially get wrapped up in.

"Hey."

Jumping slightly, I look away from his spotless, open-concept kitchen and up at him.

"Hey," I say, leaning back against his front door.

"You're nervous," he says. Not a question.

I consider denying it. Consider flashing my boobs to distract him. In the end, I sigh. "Maybe."

He looks at me for a moment before reaching down to grab the hand that isn't clutching my mammoth bag of popcorn. At his touch, my shoulders melt.

"We don't have to do anything tonight if you don't want to. We could watch a movie, or I could walk you back to your car."

He says this so earnestly, it would be a shame to laugh in his pretty face.

"No, that's not it. I definitely want—" I stop, toes curling under my feet.

His thumb strokes down mine. "Then what is it?"

I wince. "It's just . . . are we doing the right thing?"

He takes a slow breath. Runs a heavy palm over his still-damp hair. "When it comes to right or wrong, there's no 'we' in this, Gracie. You haven't done anything wrong. But I . . ." He exhales. "No. I'm definitely not doing the right thing."

My heart sinks.

"Because of Henry?" I ask, my voice little more than a whisper.

He nods. "He's a big part of it."

"I ended things with him this week, but I didn't mention you." I hesitate. "Have you talked to him?"

He shakes his head, guilt etching creases around his eyes. "He keeps avoiding my calls, and it's not something I want to tell him over text. But I'm meeting him for lunch this week."

My throat moves in a dry swallow. "And you're going to tell him about us then?"

"Yeah," he says softly but decisively. "He deserves the truth, and you don't deserve to be kept like a secret."

My heart flips over, beating upside down. "And you don't think we should stop this?" I say as his hand lets go of mine to trace up my arm.

His eyes close briefly. "I definitely think we should stop this," he says, and my disappointment is a physical weight in my stomach. But then he shifts closer. "I just don't think I can." My breath hitches as his eyes find mine, blown out and hungry. "Do you want me to stop, Gracie?"

It's wrong—for a thousand reasons, I know this is wrong. Jude and I are tied up in a bargain that could end disastrously, and *nothing* about this feels casual. But if I just keep telling myself this is meaningless, then I can ignore how loudly my heart is shouting the word *Liar*.

Breathless, I shake my head. "No. I don't want to stop. I want—" But I can't say it. Can barely look at the dark cotton strained across his chest, much less his face.

He tips my chin up, forcing me to look at him anyway. "Tell me."

At his order, the bones of my knees turn to water, and the words are out before I can stop them. "I want to kiss you. I always want to kiss you."

It comes out petulant, but I think he understands how frustrating it is to be completely consumed by the thought of someone else's mouth. He moves in slowly, his hard thigh pressing between mine until I'm forced onto my tiptoes, back against the door. His thumb sweeps over my bottom lip, tugging it down until I'm openmouthed and squirming.

"That's it?" he asks, his soft voice in complete contrast to how firmly he's pinned me. "Just a kiss?"

I try nodding, but his grip on my chin is tight. I never want him to let go. When he lowers his mouth to mine, the moan that escapes me is too loud for just a kiss. I flush hot with embarrassment, but then his tongue is pressing into my mouth, slow and decadent, and I moan all over again. When his hands grab my hips, angling me just right against his thigh, I drop the bag of popcorn and hear it scatter everywhere. But I don't care—can't think at all when he starts working me against him, my skirt rising like mercury in a thermometer.

"Are you sure that's all you want?" he asks, breaking away to stare down at me. His grip tightens, stopping my needy movements.

"No," I pant, as whatever shreds of hesitation I felt before go up in greedy flames.

"Then what," he asks, pressing me harder against him, "do you *want*?"

I whimper, squeezing my legs around what feels like a tree trunk, but the words won't come out. I can't tell him what I think about when I slip the cake shop Polaroid out from my bedside table every night—I can't. I shake my head.

He makes a soft sound with his tongue like a tut. "I like how shy you are. But I need to know you really want this."

My breathing comes in staccato gulps, my hips struggling to move against his iron grip. "I do," I promise him, voice thready.

He makes a sound like he doubts it. "Do you want to show me instead? Can I lift this skirt and see what kind of mess you've made all over my pants?"

I clench so hard, I know he feels it. The blush staining my cheeks could heat a house in the dead of winter. But I'm nodding anyway, sucking on my bottom lip since I can't have his.

His dark lashes flutter at my consent as his hands slide to the hem of my bunched and pleated skirt. For a moment, all he does is run his fingers over the edge, and I can feel my pulse in my stomach. But then he slides it up the rest of the way and whispers a harsh, "*Fuck*."

I look down, and my simple white panties have been displaced, only half covering me. They're so wet, they're transparent. His charcoal joggers are slick and dark beneath me, and his hands are hastily tucking the hem of my skirt into my waistband. Self-consciousness curls in my stomach, but then he starts moving me again, and the back of my head hits his door.

"Fuck, you're so pretty like this," he says, yanking my hips forward.

His thumb finds my clit, still caught under my panties. When he taps it three times, I jerk against him. When he moves the fabric aside and starts stroking me in earnest, I come for the first time, keening through my teeth. When I can remember my own name again, I want to make embarrassed excuses. Tell him I've never been this way before. That I've always been—

"Made for me," he whispers, eyes glazing over. "It's like you were made for me."

His rock-solid cock nudges against my thigh, and every late-night wish I've made while gasping into my pillow comes back to me in a hot rush.

"I want to see you, too," I pant, hands going to his flexing biceps, my eyes drinking in every line of ink that disappears under his taut black sleeves. "All of you."

His gaze stutters up to mine, like it's the last request he expected. Like he couldn't possibly imagine me wanting *that*, in the whole realm of what he's willing to give me.

"Please," I say breathlessly, and it really is the magic word. Something shifts in his eyes, and then he's picking me up, throwing me over his shoulder.

"Jude!" I gasp. But then I see the flex of his muscular ass as he walks us deeper into his condo, and I shut all the way up.

Based on the shift from wooden floors to creamy stone tiles, I take it we've entered a bathroom. A low, warm light goes on before he sets me on my unsteady feet.

"Wait here," he tells me.

No problem, I think. I'm too horny to walk in a straight line anyway.

He moves toward an obnoxiously large shower with a built-in bench. As he does, he grips behind the neck of his shirt and pulls. In one fluid, panty-scorching movement, it comes off, dropping to the floor in time with my jaw.

He's opening the glass door of the shower and turning it on, but all my attention has been stolen by the thick shift of muscle beneath smooth skin. Vaguely, I notice he doesn't have any tattoos on his back, and feel I should be applauded for stringing a single thought together.

Until he turns around.

Until he casually shoves down the waistband of his pants and boxer briefs in one artless movement before stepping out of them. As he removes his socks, something hot starts dripping into my stomach. It might be my brain.

I swim a little, he'd said. Like he enjoys the occasional dip. Not like he could qualify for the Olympics just from the wingspan of his lats alone. But his almost aggressive beauty becomes peripheral when my gaze drops below the sporadic gallery of tattoos spanning him from chest to hips.

My mouth goes dry. I'm doing calculations. Equations so improbable and worrisome that my gaze jerks back up, almost wishing I hadn't seen. Because we're not going to fit together, and suddenly, I'm light-headed. I need to sit. To lie down. Possibly in a coffin. I need—

"Come here."

His voice is low. I barely hear it over the shower, but it's like he's tugged on a rope wrapped around my waist as I stumble forward.

"I thought you said you wanted to see me," he says with a quiet chuckle when I reach him.

"I did," I say. "I do."

"And how's that going with your eyes closed?"

I take an unsteady breath. "I'll look. Just give me a mi—"

He kisses me. Pulls me against him, and my hands are on his bare, hot skin. He's heavy and thick against my stomach, and it's too much. *He's* too much.

"Oh-m'God," I say, but my mouth is crushed against his, and it comes out smothered. His hands are tugging. Unbuttoning. Slipping. Before long, I'm topless against him, skirt and panties around my ankles, and *God*, it feels so good to be naked against him at last. My mouth seeks his warm skin, teeth sinking, and his sharp grunt of pleasure permanently lodges itself in my long-term memory bank.

Clumsy in our haste, he walks me backward into the shower, and the hot jets of water make me gasp against him. I open my eyes and come face-to-face with my own bite mark on his large pectoral. Right over a simple linework tattoo of a heart-shaped diary lock—the kind I used to have as a little girl.

"I'm sorry," I say, kissing the mark. Sucking it.

"Fantastic," he pants, pushing my wet hair back from my face. "Want to make it up to me?"

I look up at him, and he's so mind-wipingly beautiful like this—with a million sparkling droplets clinging to his high cheekbones and long lashes—it's indecent.

"More than anything," I answer him breathlessly. I drag my hand lower. "How's this?" I ask.

His head falls back with a groan when I slip my hand around his cock for the first time. There's precum gathered at the tip, and when I spread it over the broad head, my hand feels so small. Insignificant.

"*Fuck*," he whispers thickly, watching me work my hand down his length, stomach muscles rippling under the sheen of water. I wet my lips, suddenly starving for him, but he covers my hand with his.

"Baby, wait. Please," he says hoarsely. "There is something else. Do you think—" He stops, exhales roughly, and this time, it's his turn to look bashful. It turns me on beyond belief. "Could I just—"

I take in his flushed cheeks, and the way his gaze skims over my hair, and a memory slots into place. Heat forces its way into my abdomen, where I'm rubbing him against my wet skin. "You want to wash my hair?"

His eyes find mine, almost furtive. "Only if you'd like it. We don't have to," he's quick to say, voice tight. But his cock flexes against my hand and stomach in protest, his slick throat moving in a hungry bob. And that's when I realize he's ashamed of this part of himself. Ashamed of his urge to take care of me like no one else has ever wanted to.

A lump inexplicably forms in my throat, and I press up on my toes to reach another tattoo, this one below his collarbone. An iron poker. "I love your hands in my hair," I say. "Remember the first time?"

He exhales hard. Twists to pump shampoo into his hand like he's envisioned this exact scenario a million times. "You mean that time I nearly got a boner at my grandmother's funeral?" he says flatly. "I try not to."

I laugh, mortified, but it turns into a garbled moan when his fingertips sink into my hair, working soapy circles into my scalp. My neck becomes a noodle.

"God, your hair," he says, voice desperate. "You have no idea." Suds spill down my breasts to my stomach, where he's hot and slippery in my grip, thrusting involuntarily.

I'm drunk on his touch, and the words slur out of me before I can catch them. "I bet you say that to all the girls."

My regret is instant, and my hands still. I shouldn't care if he's done this a million times with other women. I said no strings. But then he responds with a broken laugh.

"Christ, no. I've never—" He blinks rapidly, hands slicking shampoo down my wet back.

Something leaps in my stomach, and my hands flex possessively around him. "You've never what?"

His thick lashes shudder, his breath catching. "Being with anyone else has always felt like playing house—not the real thing," he confesses. "They leave in the morning, and it's easy—so fucking easy to get on with my life." Water sluices down the muscles flexing in his chest as his voice turns helpless. Frustrated. "But I can't with you. You're all I ever think about, Gracie. Talking to you. Touching you. Just fucking looking at you. But even when you're right in front of me, it's never *enough.*"

This last word is almost a growl, and when he wraps his fist in my sopping hair, I groan, unable to tell him that my heart is covered in his fingerprints, too.

"There are no other partners," he says, as I bring my arms around his waist, closing the space between us. "Not since I saw you in that church and everything fucking stopped. I've been right here in this goddamn shower every night, imagining *this*. Over and over and over again."

At his confession, and the hard, wet roll of his hips, I suddenly feel so empty, my stomach aches. "I've touched myself, too," I tell him, voice hushed beneath the roar of the water.

He curses, and a hard tug against my scalp sends a bolt of need down my body. I gasp as I'm forced to look up at him, my lips dripping with hot water.

"How often?" he demands, slowly pulling me along as he walks backward.

"Every night," I gasp, nipples pinching tight. "Sometimes in the morning, too."

His exhale sounds painful. "And you think of me sometimes?"

I could laugh. Or sob. "E-every time."

He lets out a sound that's half-curse, half groan, and then lowers himself to the bench. He sits with his head back, long legs thrown wide, and his veined hand gripping the base of his erection tight. "Sit," he orders.

I swallow. After weeks of opposing him at every turn, it's shockingly easy to just do as he says. To hope he might tell me how good I've been again.

With his help, I straddle his lap. We're both breathing hard, looking down at the small gap of space left between us and the almost comical size difference in our anatomy. It's absurd, really. To think this might work.

"Jude," I say, and I can't help the desperate, miserable little laugh that comes out of me. Because when it comes down to it, this is all I've wanted. *Him*, as close as possible.

His hand lifts to my worried face, stroking my damp skin. "Do you trust me?"

It feels like a loaded question. But I find myself nodding, hoping he has some kind of solution for this particular issue. Maybe he's consulted NASA.

"I do."

He exhales. "Good. Then I want you to touch yourself."

I frown. "Isn't the point of doing this together that we *don't* have to touch ourselves?"

"What did you literally just tell me six seconds ago?"

I huff out an annoyed breath. And I guess it's good to know we're still capable of bickering on the brink of finally having each other. Relenting, I slide my hand between us. At the first stroke of my fingers, Jude's mouth parts in silent awe. His knuckles brush against my hand as he gives himself a tight pump. Another. And I stand corrected. This is the best idea in the world.

Pleasure coils tight within me under his feverish gaze. I can't stop watching his hand on his cock, memorizing his every movement. When he squeezes more precum from the tip, smearing it over himself, a soft moan escapes me.

"Faster," he demands, eyes trained on my hand.

I whimper, breasts shaking as my fingers work harder, the spray of water hot on my back.

"Shit. *Yes*, just like that," he urges me. "Need you dripping if you want this."

"Jude," I gasp. His thumb strokes over my aching nipple and I arch, thigh muscles tightening, and I could easily come apart like this. Just from watching rivulets of water shiver between his contracting stomach muscles. From the brush of his swollen cock against his hollow navel. From his eyes on me. *His eyes*. They hold me like a fist when I meet them.

"Show me how wet you are," he orders, breathless. "Fuck yourself and show me."

His words are lightning down my spine. I dip two fingers inside myself, eager to please, before holding them up for him.

"*Christ*," he swears, grabbing my wrist none-too-gently. When he pulls my fingers into his hot mouth, tongue sliding between them as he sucks me clean, I nearly fall off the bench. I nearly fall off Earth itself. It's instinct to rise higher on my knees. To seek friction against him as I pull my fingers free.

"Yes," he grunts, grabbing my ass to work me against him. I brace myself on his wet cheekbone. His unshaven jaw, and the strong cleft of his chin. He's so beautiful, so caring, it could break my heart to a thousand pieces. Tears slip down my cheeks as I choke back gasps.

I'm clumsy, hands shaking, and I don't mean to—not exactly—but the fat head of his cock slips lower, pressing against my opening. His eyes are wild on me. "Condom," he blurts.

"Do we have to?" I whine, hips fretful. "I'm on birth control."

His eyes squeeze shut. "You're going to kill me, Gracie. *No*. We don't have to. I'm clean."

I believe him. If he told me he'd rather eat his own foot than harm me, I'd believe that, too. And so, I lower myself on him. Or at least, I try. With a tight push, the first few inches slip in and his eyes roll back.

"Jude," I pant, gripping his shoulders like I mean to keep him from passing out. "*Please*. You're not—" I press harder. "It's not *working*."

My voice is edged with panic, and with effort, he opens his eyes. Beads of condensation roll down his neck, over his fluttering pulse. "It's okay," he rasps. "I'll teach you how to take me."

His hand slides down, almost lazy in his haze of pleasure. When his fingers find my clit, his touch is so gentle that the lack of friction is all I can focus on. My wide eyes lock with his.

"Jude—"

"I know, angel," he pants. "Relax for me."

I take a shuddering breath and begin to move, desperately searching for more than his skimming touch. But he's barely touching me, torturing me with fleeting grazes, until a frustrated whine breaks from my throat. He's doing it on *purpose*.

"You're almost there," he promises.

"Liar," I breathe, rocking him deeper as pleasure begins eclipsing discomfort.

He shakes his head with a half-smile, chest muscles bunching with every labored breath. "You can take a little more," he promises, and somehow, he's right. With a needy roll of my hips, he slips deeper with a whispered curse. When he lightly smacks my clit, soothing it with his thumb and soft words of encouragement, the building pleasure landslides into desperation.

"That's— *Yes*," he groans. "So proud of you, baby. Keep taking it."

I gulp down his praise like water, unable to stop moving on him. Rising and falling until my thighs are burning. I'm not going to last, and he knows it.

"I can't," I cry, tears mingling with the water on my flushed face. But his hands are so steady, so adoring, I know he has me. If he makes me shatter, it's only because he wants to put me back together again, and again, and again.

"You can," he rumbles, mouth dragging down my neck. "You take me better than anyone else, Gracie. All my bullshit. All my walls. You knock them down faster than I can build them."

My eyes squeeze shut as the ache for him reaches a peak that's almost violent in its intensity. Not just for his body, but for everything he keeps from me. Until I wish I could crack open his chest and force myself inside. "It's not enough. You never give me enough," I hiccup, gulping down my cries as my whole body begins to shake. "I want everything, Jude."

The curse he aims at the ceiling is guttural. "Lean back for me."

He guides my hands to his knees, and the change in angle is devastating. I feel him flex hard behind my belly button, so deep and thick I can't breathe. Can't move. But then his hips lift into me as his fingers finally give my clit the pressure it needs, and I've exited my body. When I'm finally able to swallow enough air to make a sound, it's his name—long, desperate, and punctuated by the thrust of his hips.

"F-fuck, I'm losing it, Gracie," he warns me, lashes trembling as his thighs flex hard and fast below me.

"*Please*," I beg him. "Please."

He scoops me forward, till I'm crushed against him. I burrow my face into his straining neck as he cries out, his powerful hips unrelenting beneath me. We're so tangled up, dripping with water, sweat, and our own need for each other, it's hard to tell where one of us begins and the other ends. And it's fine. More than fine. Because I never want to be untangled from him again. Never want to live a life that doesn't include the salt of his skin in my mouth, or the bruising grip of his hands again. I never want to live without him at all, and if he doesn't already know it, then he will soon enough. Because he might not want to keep me as a secret, but the truth is that I'd let him keep me any way at all.

31

GRACIE

Two Weeks Before the Wedding

I survive the shower, but barely. Jude is padding toward the kitchen, looking a little too pleased with himself. Meanwhile, I sit on an ice pack.

It's not the only thing he insisted on. After cleaning us both up and wrapping me in a towel, he convinced me to raid his perfectly curated walk-in closet. He didn't have to twist my arm. In my nosey perusal, I found a soft and faded Yale Swim sweatshirt next to a Yale Law shirt and gave him approximately ten solid minutes of shit for it. (An outraged "You '*swim a little*'?" followed by "I bet breaststroke was your specialty," and "Do you have a 'Yale Breathing' shirt, too?")

Eventually, he'd shut me up by whipping my towel off and pulling the hooded sweatshirt in question over my head backward. He wrapped his arms around me and kissed me through the hood until I was laughing so hard I threatened to pee in his closet.

But now that we've reached a truce, I've agreed to trim Taco's nails if he'll watch a zombie movie with me.

"Do you want a drink?" he asks, opening a cupboard. "Snacks?"

"Tea sounds great," I say. Being agreeable comes with the bonus of watching him move around the kitchen shirtless in his gray sweatpants.

He lifts an eyebrow. "Sure you don't want something stronger for the job ahead? I have some straight vodka around here somewhere."

I hop off his counter and wander over to where a collection of Judge Judy bobbleheads lines one of the big windowsills.

"Tempting. But I think it's probably best to keep all my faculties intact, thanks," I say, picking up one of the figurines. This one is wearing Judge Judy's signature robe, but instead of a gavel, she's holding a peanut butter and jelly sandwich. Guilt flickers through me. "A gift from Henry?" I ask as Jude puts on a kettle.

His hand pauses midreach toward a neatly arranged caddy of tea options, before he finishes the movement.

"He gets one made for me every Christmas," he says without looking at me. After a moment, he adds, "That, and the most surprising sex toy he can find."

I can't help my laugh. "Too bad you don't display those."

"You're more than welcome to my silicone tentacle collection if that's what you're into."

My smile doesn't last as worry settles in my stomach.

"How do you think he'll take it?" I ask, carefully placing PB and J Judy back on the sill. "When you tell him about us, I mean."

"Badly," he says in a quiet voice, leaning his head back against the cabinets and closing his eyes.

I walk to him, letting my hands rest on his tense stomach. "I can't help feeling like this is all my fault," I say. "I went on a date with him. I gave him hope."

Jude's eyes open, searching my face. "None of this is your fault. You went on one date and ended things before it went anywhere." He looks away, his throat moving in a tight swallow. "After what happened with Sofia's parents, it makes sense that you got scared. You had every right to find someone to fuck around with instead of starting something serious. But if I'd been a better friend to Henry, I wouldn't have touched you. Not after I told him I wouldn't."

My breath feels like glue in my lungs. "So you regret it?"

He looks up at the ceiling, and the exhale he makes sounds helpless. "I should. God knows I should." He stares back down at me. "But I could never regret you, Gracie. Not for one second."

A soft ache spreads through my chest. Last week, I ran to him in panic, thinking he'd keep me safe from the lie of Happily Ever After.

When he unearthed all the feelings I've been denying for him instead, I tried burying them again in endless work. But tonight, he dropped everything to help me. Made my opinions about shower sex do a three-point turn in the opposite direction. And every new second I'm with him, it gets harder to deny the truth: this doesn't feel like fucking around at all. It feels like all I'll ever want again.

"I don't regret it either," I whisper.

He pulls me against him, cradling my face against his warm skin, and even though I don't have any answers, I do know that I want this hug to last until I'm seventy-five.

When the tea is made, he leads me to the big sectional in the living room with cloudlike cushions. I sink into it with my chamomile tea and let out an involuntary sigh. The living room, like everywhere else, is neat but welcoming, except for the coffee table. It's covered in paperwork and his open laptop.

"Sorry," he says, shuffling the papers together and closing his screen. "I was working earlier."

"I thought you were trying to hog-tie Taco before you gave up," I say, taking a sip from my steaming mug.

"Part of the process," he says. "Sometimes if I work on the couch, she'll cuddle me from over there."

He points at the chaise end of the couch with an enticingly fluffy white blanket.

"I hate to break it to you, but I don't think it counts as cuddling if there's more than a football field between you."

"Shows what you know," he says, sitting close enough beside me to make my heart start skipping rope. "She has a very large personal bubble."

I roll my eyes. "Where is she, by the way? Doesn't she know her manicurist is here?"

"It's flattering that you think I'm privy to her comings and goings. She could be speaking at the UN for all we know."

I snort into my mug. "Must be hard leading a less accomplished life than your cat. Is that why you were working so hard on a Saturday night?"

He runs a hand through his damp hair and doesn't look at me

when he says, "I'm working on something pretty urgent. It's why I couldn't stay at Larkwood this weekend."

"Oh," I say as my mind feels around for those loose puzzle pieces again, thinking of what he did for Maya. "Is it for a regular client or pro bono?" I ask tentatively.

He interlaces his fingers like he can prevent them from fidgeting. "Pro bono."

I bite my lip. After pushing me away so many times before, now I can practically see when his emotional force fields come up. But for better or for worse, things have changed between us. I've never been more intimate with anyone in my life, and as a result, he was able to get me to open up at my most vulnerable. Now I'm wondering if he's needed the same thing all along.

After a moment, I decide to take a chance and climb onto his lap. He looks surprised but doesn't argue when I settle and face him like I did in the shower.

He squints at me. "I think I've seen you here before."

I want to roll my eyes, but they get stuck on a tattoo of a sweet little teddy bear next to his hip bone. It might be the most erotic thing I've ever seen. I brush my thumb over it, and his stomach muscles contract like I've pressed a magic button labeled SIX PACK. It's disgusting. I hate it.

"Do they mean anything?" I ask, eyes traveling over the collection of seemingly random images. I touch a wasp on his ribs. A small breath shudders out of him.

"Yes."

I wait patiently, but apparently, that's all I'm getting. "Seriously?"

His eyes slide away. "It's stupid."

"Your fourteen Yale shirts would beg to differ."

This pulls an exasperated laugh out of him, and my grin can probably be seen from space. "Come on. Tell me."

His expression sobers as he meets my eyes. In the loaded silence, every tiny hair on my body rises like leaves before a storm.

"They're cases," he finally says, like those words are two highly volatile chemicals he's weighed with the utmost care. "The ones I need to remember."

My body stills. I look at the tiny diary lock. The roller skates. *The iron poker.*

My stomach gives a sickening lurch. After a moment, I manage to say, "What you did for Maya . . . are those the kind of pro bono cases you usually take on?"

Slowly, he exhales, like he knows his answer will open doors he's been trying to barricade. My eyes dart to the skeleton on his bicep. Its frighteningly unhinged smile as it gleefully leaves its closet. "Yeah," he says quietly. "DV advocacy is my specialty."

It takes my brain a second to catch up. *DV. Domestic Violence.* My heart slowly sinks to the bottom of my rib cage. I think of all the times I accused him of being the destroyer of Happily Ever After. How I assumed he was a divorce lawyer because of some personal grudge against romance. I think back to what Henry said about Jude on our date. *He's the most morally solid person I know. Honorable, even, if such a thing still exists.*

"God, I'm such an asshole," I say, my throat closing up.

He shakes his head. "You're not. You didn't know."

But I'm barely listening because my mind is still looping over what Henry told me on our date. *I've known him a long time, and I've never heard a single story about his childhood.* My pulse becomes a drumbeat in my ears.

"Why?" I whisper.

His brows crease. "Why what?"

"Why is it your specialty?"

His hands, which had been rubbing soothing circles on my legs, stop. Something like panic flares in his eyes.

"Don't ask me that."

He says it like a plea, and I bite my lips, torn between wanting to respect his privacy and trying to reciprocate the gift he gave me—someone to trust.

"If you want to tell me," I say softly, without any kind of demand attached to it, "I'm here to listen."

His careful expression falters for just a second before it's back in place. "I'm not the victim here. You don't need to worry about me."

The way he says it is measured and final. But there's also a specificity to his tone that feels like a breadcrumb trail to other conclusions. Someone *is* a victim. *Whatever I've experienced is incidental.* My chest begins to cave in.

"And I'm not Sofia's mother," I respond, tears stinging my eyes. "But it doesn't mean that what she went through doesn't break my heart," I say, tracing a small, three-leaf clover on his ribs. "That it hasn't left a mark on her family."

His eyes meet mine, more vulnerable than I've ever seen them. "I can't talk to you about this," he whispers. "Not yet."

I nod, finding his hands. He twines my fingers with his, and it seems to calm him. He takes a steadying breath, and the thread that connected us at Agatha's memorial solidifies. It becomes a chain that could hold the weight of the planet.

His lashes cast downward. "I hate keeping secrets from you."

My eyes spill over. For whatever he endured or had to witness. For my best friend, her family, and every person tattooed on his carefully disciplined body. "I hate that you have to," I say, my voice choked.

"Shh," he says, pulling me to him. I collapse forward on his chest, and he just holds me, kissing my hair, like I'm the one who needs comforting. If he could, I think he'd take care of the whole world.

I'm not sure how long we stay that way, but at some point, he lies me back on the couch, before coming down on his side against me.

"What happened here?" he says, taking my hand in his. He lifts it to press a kiss to the small cut on the side of my ring finger.

"Nothing. Just being clumsy."

He frowns. "How did it happen?" he asks, like it's his topmost concern.

I shrug, a little embarrassed by the way I was spending my Saturday night before Maya called. "I was curling ribbon for these favor bags for my mom's sixtieth birthday party."

"Don't you have enough on your plate without a birthday party to plan?" he asks.

"Ahh yes, the eternal question. Why *am* I such a pushover?"

"You, a pushover?" he asks. "Are we discussing an alternate dimension?"

"It's just the way I am with my family," I admit, brushing a damp lock of his hair from his forehead. "And pretty much everyone else who means something to me."

Except for you, I think. For better or for worse, I've never felt the need to sugarcoat myself with him.

His gaze softens like he can hear my thoughts. "You don't seem to have a problem standing up to dastardly divorce attorneys."

I shrug self-consciously. "Standing up for the people I love is easy. Saying no to them, though . . ." I grimace. "It's why I said yes to planning this party."

His eyebrows pull together. "And does your family understand how much time you're sacrificing to organize it for them?"

I snort. "Definitely not. But that doesn't mean I haven't stopped trying to get them to luh"—I cut the word off just in time—"preciate me."

He gives me a look that says I'm fooling no one. "We all crave some luh-preciation from our families sometimes. Especially when you're being so neroic."

I cover my face with my hands and groan. "Some polite, selective amnesia would be great, thanks."

"Are you kidding? You had me at grelpful, Gracie."

"Stop, or tonight's about to turn into a Nora Ephron film festival," I threaten.

"Better than zombies," he mutters.

I gasp in outrage, and he kisses my open mouth to stop the coming diatribe. When he releases me, I'm dizzy and disarmed.

"So, you said yes to planning this party, even though you have zero time for it?" he prompts.

"Yes, and in case you're preparing to lecture me on drawing healthy boundaries, I'll have you know that Sofia beat you to it about twenty years ago and hasn't stopped since."

"What makes you think I know a goddamn thing about healthy boundaries?" he asks, tugging on the drawstring of the sweatshirt.

"You seem pretty good at them to me."

He looks at me, and the smile that lifts his lips is heartbreaking. "Sometimes. But when it comes to family, I know all about forgetting your best intentions when you think they might finally change."

My throat tightens. "And you don't think that could ever happen?"

His features flinch into something bleak. "From my experience, no. But hope doesn't really give a shit about the facts, does it?"

I brush his hair back from his forehead. "It's why we have to keep trying," I say, unsure if I'm talking about our families, my wishes for Larkwood, or this reckless craving for more with him. "They say miracles do happen."

He squeezes my hand. "When is your mom's party?"

Wincing, I say, "Same weekend as the wedding."

He closes his eyes briefly. "Of course it is."

"But I'm so close to finishing everything. I just need to drop off the favors this week and—"

"Will you tell them you won't be going to the party, or doing any other planning?"

I laugh weakly. "I thought we just went over this. The word 'no' vanishes from my vocabulary with them."

"What if I came with you?" he offers.

I blink. "Come with me?"

He shrugs. "I'm pretty good at glaring people into submission."

"I don't know . . . it's my mom's sixtieth. If I make sure everything goes perfectly, then maybe—"

"They'll suddenly sprout new personalities despite thirty years of evidence to the contrary?"

"What happened to folding in the face of hope?"

"I only do that with *my* family, silly. You should know by now that I have no problem being an asshole to everyone else."

I snort against my will. "Or charming them into doing whatever you want."

He lowers his eyes to where our hands are entwined on my borrowed hoodie. "I know *yes* can feel like the best shortcut to some overdue respect," he says, gliding his thumb over mine, "but there's a lot more power in the word *no*. And even if they don't see it at first, kindness, too. Saying no allows people to take responsibility for their own lives. Saying yes just denies them the opportunity to grow."

"You make it sound like I've been the one holding *them* back," I say, feeling a little defensive. "You don't know how clear they've made it that *this* is how I'm expected to contribute since I don't—"

I stop, emotion tightening my chest.

"Since you don't what?"

I take a breath. After sharing so much with him, I feel overexposed. But tonight, he told me about his tattoos and his DV work. His walls are still firmly in place, but he trusted me enough to remove a few bricks. So, I say it.

"Belong." I'm quiet for a moment. "When my parents separated and suddenly had their new, perfect-fit families, I sort of became that extra IKEA bolt—related, but confusing and unnecessary."

"So you made yourself useful," he says quietly.

I nod, unable to speak. Jude's hands are gentle but insistent as he pulls me closer. When I'm lying against his chest with his arms wrapped around me, every nervous voice inside of me settles. Maybe a cookie-cutter relationship isn't in the cards for us. But I'm starting to think that finding someone who clearly sees the most jagged pieces of your heart and still wants to gather you close matters more than fitting any mold.

He kisses the top of my head. "You shouldn't have to do a job that belongs on payroll to feel seen by your family. If you never stop, you'll never find out if they'll show up for you."

"But what if they don't? I didn't have anything to offer them growing up, and they were happy enough to pass me off to Sofia's family every chance they got."

Jude's arms tighten around me. "If they don't want to know someone as giving, talented, and hardworking as you, then they're fucking idiots, Gracie. At a certain point, all you can do is step back and grieve. You lean on the people who *do* luh-preciate you."

Is it possible to shrink a duplicate of this man down to pocket size and carry him around with me everywhere? There's no judgment or frustration in his tone—just understanding paired with a clear (if difficult) path forward.

"What do I owe you for the therapy session?" I ask.

He smiles faintly. "You could say yes to letting me come with you."

"You'd really come with me to my mom's house?"

"It's not in the bowels of Mordor, is it?"

"Are you saying you *wouldn't* journey with me to Mordor?"

"Lately, I've been going every weekend."

I smack his shoulder. "Hush. Lucky for you, she's just in Pawtucket."

He chuckles, and at that moment, Taco saunters in, lightly hopping onto the coffee table. She sits and stares unblinkingly at me with her bright yellow eyes as though to say *Well? I'm here for my appointment.*

"And how was your UN address, Madame President?" I coo, reaching out a hand to let her sniff me. "Did they accept your plan for world domination?"

Just like last time, she headbutts my hand and begins to purr when I pet her.

"Oh sure," Jude says, rolling his eyes at Taco. "Just ignore the guy who picks up your poop every night."

"The heart wants what it wants," I say simply.

Jude disentangles from me and gets off the couch. "For that, now you're definitely clipping her nails."

When he comes back to Taco lounging on my lap, he makes a sound of disgust and hands me the clippers and a bag of treats. The job is easy enough, and when I'm done, she shakes her fur and leaves like she's grown tired of our company.

"I don't get it," he says, watching her graceful retreat into a dark room.

"You're nervous around her. She can tell you think she's going to lash out, so she does."

"So, you're saying if I just act like she's going to be well-behaved, then she will be?"

"Couldn't hurt to give her the benefit of the doubt."

"Maybe trust doesn't come easy for me either," he says.

Understatement of the century, I think, with a flash of anger toward whoever lies at the root of his guardedness. I study him for a moment before grabbing one of the soft throw blankets from the back of the couch to drape over us. Tonight, after every confession he groaned into my wet skin and our conversation afterward, it's unfathomable that I used to see him as cold and unfeeling. Unthinkable that I could get to know him and not fall for him, no matter the risks. I put my head on his shoulder as he brings his arm around me.

"I read once that zombie movies help with trust issues," I say.

"Huh. Can't say I've seen that particular study. Was it on bullshit.org?"

I elbow him, refusing to admit I'm making this up. "It was very in-depth! Something about bonding through fear . . ."

He snorts before grabbing a remote from his coffee table. "Well, if there's anyone I'd be willing to bond with through fear, it's definitely the person brave enough to trim Taco's nails. I bet you'd be amazing in the apocalypse."

I pretend to wipe a tear away. "I don't think I've ever received a better compliment."

The giant flatscreen mounted to the wall comes to life, but he doesn't start searching for anything. Instead, he takes a breath. "And what if I told you I hate violent movies? Would that be a dealbreaker for you?"

He doesn't look at me as he says it, but all at once, my chest is flooded with a force so large and protective, it's hard to breathe properly.

"Then I'd say we should watch *Corpse Bride* instead," I say, tangling my fingers with his beneath the blanket. "And I'll hold your hand, just in case."

"But what if that's not enough?" he asks, looking away from the screen to meet my gaze. "What if I need you to stay the night?"

Somewhere in that last request were the words *I need you*, and they glow a little longer than all the rest. I may not be able or willing to put a label on what this is between us, but I do have a word for how it makes me feel. *Safe*. And more than anything, I want him to feel the same way.

"Then I guess it's my turn to take care of you, Jude."

32

JUDE

Two Weeks Before the Wedding

"Hey, hon, I'm a few minutes away from my lunch meeting. Everything okay?" my mom says when she picks up my call.

Damnit. I thought she might be open for lunch, but I guess a phone call will have to do. Gracie left my place an hour ago, and I've been watching the clock until I knew my mom might be free.

"Yeah, everything's fine," I tell her, standing up from my desk. "But I wanted to ask you something."

"Shoot," she says, sounding distracted. I hear a distant blare of a horn, and then her muttered, "*Okay, okay*, I'm moving," as she fights traffic.

I rub a hand over my face. "Maybe this isn't the best time," I say, even though every molecule in my body is vibrating with urgency.

Last night, Gracie opened me up in ways I've never been with anyone but my therapist. My small slipups were a far cry from the total trust she shared with me, but somehow, she intuited enough to see the rough shape of what I keep from everyone. It should make me feel panicked. But instead, I feel like I've lifted my head above water for the first time in years.

"No, it's fine, I'm listening," my mom says. "What's up, honey?"

Fuck it. I should wait for a better moment, but I can't. "I met someone."

The words fly out of me, as freewheeling as a boomerang destined to smack me in the forehead on its way back.

"Oh," is her belated, surprised response. I run a hand through my hair as she recalibrates her expectations for this call. "That's great to hear." A beat. "How serious is it?"

The careful question betrays her concern. My mother didn't become attorney general for lack of intelligence or an inability to spot danger. At the same time, I know she wants to see me happy, and *that's* the chip I'm resting all my hope on. I weigh my words before answering.

"I could see a future with her. If I'm free to be honest with her."

She's quiet, and I know she understands what I'm getting at. I've safeguarded her secrets for years without question—even if it's meant keeping whole parts of myself locked up from the people I care about. But with Gracie, that muzzle has never chaffed so badly.

"But you're not officially with her?" my mom asks, seeing right through my intentionally vague language.

Shit. "Not technically. Not yet. But only because it wouldn't be right. Not when I have to keep so much from her."

She hesitates, and I can practically see her worried expression in the silence. "You know I don't want to ask this, sweetheart, but how long have you known her?"

My teeth sink into the side of my cheek. "I met her at Nana's funeral."

My mom sighs, and my hope stumbles. "Jude, no," she says, her voice apologetic. "I love that you've found someone, and I'm sure she's wonderful if she's captured your attention like this, but I've had assistants longer than that who I still don't trust to get my coffee right. Have fun with her, but please—keep family business within the family."

She pauses, and I know what's coming. "If anything were to get out, it would put all of my initiatives at risk. You *know* what's at stake."

I pinch the bridge of my nose hard, forcibly reminding myself of why she's afraid. Of course her work is important. But there's a line between protective and paranoid, and after so long, it's become completely blurred. "I trust her, Mom. She'd never spread gossip."

"I didn't say she would. Not intentionally. But is she trained in confidentiality like you are? Or does she have a few best friends she shares everything with over mimosas? Will *those* friends understand how damaging it could be if it came out that I—a woman who has based her *entire* career on protecting and opening doors for other women—has been involved with—"

Her escalating voice cuts off. I press my forehead to the cold glass of my window. Her concerns, as much as I don't want to admit it, are valid. Her hard-won position has given her the ability to do immeasurable good for women in similar circumstances, and risking that power isn't something she's willing to do. And I get it. But for the first time in my life, those risks seem worth taking.

"I trust her," I say again with complete conviction. "She wouldn't breathe a word."

Her sigh is resigned, and something in my jaw pops. "I'm sorry, Jude. You want me to tell you I feel comfortable with this, but I don't. Not yet. If you end up engaged to this woman a couple of years from now, we can revisit this topic then."

"Mom—"

"I have to run," she cuts me off, but there's a tremor in her voice. "The governor's waiting, and these days, he's got a stick up his ass the size of a redwood tree."

I run a hand down my face and look up at the ceiling in the hope that it might do me a fucking favor and crash down on me. I have never *once* asked her permission to tell someone. Not even Henry. Being instantly shot down after years of silence and loyalty feels like more than a slap in the face. It makes my willingness to cooperate feel less like a choice and more like a cage.

I close my eyes, willing my heartbeat to slow. I remind myself of everything at stake for her. For her constituents. That this isn't about me. It's enough to calm me down and ask the question I've been keeping in the direct center of my chest.

"And what about my terms for keeping Larkwood?" I say, reminding her of her promise to consider leaving my dad.

There's a loaded pause that has me bracing for impact. "After you and I spoke, I decided to take some space from your father. We haven't been speaking."

Shock pins my pacing feet to the ground where I stand. "Really?"

"It's only until he comes back from Europe, but it's been . . . a change of pace. I will say that."

I bring a hand up to rub my suddenly tight chest, hope blooming inside of me like a dandelion through concrete. If she leaves him—*really* leaves him—it could change everything.

"That's . . . really great to hear," I say. "I'm so proud of you, Mom."

There's a long silence on her end. "But I've decided it's not the best timing for something more permanent," she finally says.

As quickly as it rose, my hope falls back to earth, skidding and burrowing until it's deep underground. "But you said—" I start.

"I'm sorry," she interrupts, voice tight with emotion. "I know how you feel and how much you want things to change. I know how difficult this is for you."

"Do you, though?" I ask, before I can stop myself. It's such a selfish fucking question—God knows I've only been through a fraction of what she has. But with dashed hopes and nothing to show for my Hail Mary, my anger flares hotter than my grief, burning everything in its path. She sighs like she can feel it, and in the background, I hear the sounds of her car shutting off and the rustle of her jacket and keys.

"I'm your mother," she says, and I can hear the exhaustion in her voice. The guilt. "Of course I do."

She hangs up, and I only realize how hard I've been gnawing the inside of my cheek when I taste blood. *Goddamnit.* I stalk to the bathroom to rinse my mouth. It's only when I get there that I see a lipstick heart on the mirror. It's small, almost like she was unsure if she should draw it or not. On any other day, it might have given me hope for a future together. But right now, all it seems to symbolize is everything I stand to lose if I can't find a way to open up to her.

Beyond it, my normally pale face is flushed, my lashes wet. *When the fuck did I start crying?* Quickly, I turn on the cold tap and wash away the evidence of how badly I wanted that call to go differently. How badly I've wanted my life to go differently. The icy water makes my face ache, but I can't stop scooping it up in my trembling hands, wishing it would numb everything. The anger at her. At my father.

But most of all, at myself, for being stupid enough to think things could ever change.

When I finally look up, my collar is sodden, my hair dripping, and I'm shaking, but the heart is still there. I don't know what the future holds. But one thing that's as clear as my own determined reflection is that Gracie will be part of it.

33

GRACIE

Two Weeks Before the Wedding

If someone had told me six weeks ago that Jude Larkwood—the one-man welcome committee to my own personal misery spiral—would be supporting me as I stood up to my family, I'd have asked if the zombie apocalypse was truly upon us. But as we pull up to the small, gray-brown house livened up with yard inflatables of every conceivable New England sports team, there's no denying that he's by my side—and letting me hold his hand in a death grip.

"I'm glad you're relaxed," he says as he turns the car off. "Family confrontations are so much easier when your extremities aren't throbbing with adrenaline."

I look down at my hand wrapped hard around his and try letting go. He pulls it back with a tut and kisses my knuckles.

I sigh. "Can you remind me *one* more time why leaving everything on the doorstep isn't a better plan?"

The other night, after watching *Corpse Bride*, he convinced me to bring not only the DIY favors today, but everything else I've been storing for my mom's party. In theory, dropping it all off will clearly communicate to my family that I'm done doing this thankless job, *and* allow me to get rid of the life-size Tom Brady cutout whose eyes seem to follow me around my cottage. Now, however, I'm convinced a Molotov cocktail through my mom's window *might* feel less aggressive.

Jude turns in his seat to look at me. "You're going to be fine.

Everyone in that house is an adult capable of respecting your boundaries."

"That's highly questionable."

"Let me rephrase: Everyone in that house is *technically* an adult who *should* be capable of respecting your boundaries. And if they can't . . ." He shrugs. "It's not your fault that their emotional intelligence peaked in middle school."

I stare at him. "You know, if the lawyering thing doesn't work out, you could always be one of those hot self-help influencers."

"'Hot' as in popular, or 'hot' as in good-looking?"

I cup a hand to my ear. "Did I just hear the *zzz* of a fishing rod?"

"Just trying to figure out the job qualifications for my new career."

"And if I think you're hot, apparently."

"Pretty sure I got the answer to that question when you licked my armpit last night."

"I did not lick your armpit!" I say in outrage, snatching my hand from his. "That ice-cream cone is on your *ribs*."

"You of all people should know I don't mind a kink. My armpits are all yours, Gracie."

"Oh my god, are you stalling?" I ask when it occurs to me how long we've just been sitting here. "Because if you're suddenly rethinking this whole plan, you should know I'd *much* rather lick your armpit than go in there."

"Absolutely not. Just trying to restore feeling in my nerve endings," he says, flexing his hand. "Wouldn't want to fumble a teenie-weenie."

I laugh, despite my nervousness. "That's a good start. Any sports jargon you can slip into the conversation will win you points."

He bats his lashes. "The only points I'm here to win are for you, Gracie."

I roll my eyes, trying not to let my heart melt down to my toes, when the front door opens. My stepsister Brianna stomps out in flip-flops, staring at Jude's SUV. She's wearing her signature outfit of shiny basketball shorts, a championship-something T-shirt, and a frown. Jude gives me one last reassuring smile before opening his car door. "Come on. Time to knock it out of the park, slugger."

"Oh my God," I say, half in exasperation, half in actual prayer.

As I get out, I wave to Brianna on the porch, hoping my smile doesn't read too much like a rictus of terror. Meanwhile, Jude opens the back hatch to start unloading.

"I think I can grab Tom," he says, shifting a box in his arms to grab the cutout.

"And deny me my shield?" I whisper back, shooting an arm out to pull the cardboard man toward me. "I don't think so."

"What is she going to do, tackle you?"

"Not if it might damage Tom," I say, carefully maneuvering him out of the backseat.

I've just gotten him out, along with a five-gallon helium tank, when I turn to see Brianna standing directly behind me. I yelp, and the next few seconds are a nightmarish blur.

I fumble the tank, and in my desperation to catch it, smack her hard in the face with Tom, whose cardboard head bends all the way backward. She gasps, which turns into a scream when the tank, which I do *not* catch, lands directly on her nearly bare foot, before bouncing loudly down the driveway.

"God*damnit*," she roars, slapping Jude's car right beside me.

I gasp and hide behind Tom's flapping head while Brianna grabs her injured foot, cursing loud enough to wake the dead.

Jude appears, physically putting himself between me and Brianna, and while he doesn't stop a careening van with his palm, I still feel like I'm suddenly living out all my teen *Twilight* fantasies.

"Please back away from Gracie," he says in a voice so calm and at odds with Brianna's that it catches her attention.

"And who are you?" she snaps, giving him a once-over.

"The person helping Gracie transport all the supplies she's been kindly buying and storing for you. Now would you mind helping us carry some of this inside?"

Brianna's frown deepens, but surprisingly, she stalks off to retrieve the helium tank before heading back inside.

"So, was that Brianna or Josie?" Jude asks pleasantly, as though my stepsister greeted him with a plate of warm brownies and a hug.

"Brianna," I say, taking a calming breath. "Jude, listen—"

"No, I'm not having second thoughts," he says, brushing a stray piece of my hair into place. "In fact, I'm only more convinced that you should go in there and say your piece. And then maybe set Tom Brady on fire."

"He did make a pretty good shield," I point out.

"Here's a thought: maybe you shouldn't *need* a shield from your family."

I sigh. "Okay, let's do this."

When we've finished loading everything onto the kitchen counter, Jude is properly introduced to my mom and stepsisters. Standing shoulder to shoulder, they're stiff and uncomfortable as he shakes each of their hands in turn. But it's no problem for Jude. Apparently, awkward silences are his comfort zone.

"I hear your teenie-weenies are a slam dunk, Mrs. Bowen," he says, purposefully not meeting my gaze while my mom makes a half-hearted offer to whip some up.

"If only," he responds regretfully. "But I'm on a strict diet—I'm sure Brianna and Josie know how it goes. Is it true you both played Division One volleyball? I swam a little in college."

I try not to gawk as, somehow, with sheer civility, he turns my loud and demanding family into paragons of politeness. My jaw may as well be on the floor when Brianna asks us if we'd like some water or coffee.

"Water would be great, thanks, Brianna," Jude says. "Gracie?"

He looks at me, and I realize that up until now, I haven't uttered a single word to anyone. With every nicety he's delivered, Jude has created the best possible baseline for laying my boundaries. And yet, my brain is the *Wheel of Fortune* on fire, spinning every possible lie I could give instead. *Sorry, my cottage flooded! Sorry, I'm getting a nose job the day of your party! Sorry, I've decided to sell all my earthly possessions and flee into the woods!*

"Honey, what can we get you?" my mom asks. "I've got some coffee milk if you want that instead."

It's the "honey" that jolts me out of my freeze state. It's the first time she has *ever* called me that, and I have the unnerving feeling of having accidentally walked onto a studio set with actors playing my family. "I'm okay, thanks," I say as Brianna hands Jude a water glass.

"Let me know if you change your mind," Mom says. After a moment, she glances at the pile of boxes and slowly thawing shrimp. "This is more than the favors we thought you were bringing," she comments.

This is it. But I'm a kid frozen on the high dive for the first time, looking down into what I'm sure are shark-infested waters. Jude and I rehearsed what I want to say and even anticipated their reactions. I'm not unprepared, I'm just . . . scared. Terrified of taking away the one thing my family values me for. Without it, I'm that superfluous little girl again, replaced by her new siblings. The college student who clung too hard to the first man who showed any interest in her and later couldn't let him go when it was time. I'm the woman doing the same thing now with Larkwood and who, at this rate, will probably end up completely alo—

My inner thoughts stop circling the drain when Jude's hand reaches for mine. I grab on tight. When I glance at him, he gives me a small nod filled with confidence and the assurance that I'm *not* alone. Not today.

I look at my mom as I take a deep breath and say, "I'm dropping everything off because I can't do any more planning. I also can't come to the party because I have a wedding to coordinate that weekend."

For a moment, the only sound in the room is my pounding heart, which I'm sure can be heard by every dog in Rhode Island. Then Josie says, "What do you mean you can't do any more planning? The party's next weekend! You can't hit us with a curveball like this—who's going to decorate, and pick up the grill, and make the balloon arch and—"

"I'm leaving you my planning binder," I cut her off, pointing to where I left it on the kitchen table. "It's got the contacts of all the vendors I've used, and my master checklist. As long as you stick to the schedule, you should have no problem getting everything done on time."

"But I'm coaching all week, and Josie has back-to-back clinic clients," Brianna says. "We don't have time to sit around making balloon animals!"

The anger that my fear has kept at bay flares to life. "Trust me, neither do I."

"Then what? Are you expecting *Mom* to plan her own party? You're an *event planner*," Josie says, enunciating those last two words like I'm not fluent in English. "This is what you *do*."

"And would you be willing to use your clinic hours to give me PT, whenever I asked, free of charge?" I shoot back, starting to see red. Jude gives my hand an encouraging squeeze.

Josie's face flushes. "It's not the same thing. This is just a party."

"If it's 'just a party,' then it shouldn't be a big deal to tie up the last details." I look at my mom while Josie and Brianna exchange dumbfounded looks. "Mom, I'm sorry I can't make it to your party this year. If you want to go out to lunch to celebrate sometime in August, I'd love that."

My mom puts a hand on Brianna's shoulder, stopping whatever she's on the verge of saying to me. She looks at me like she's seeing me fully for the first time in years. "Of course I understand. Thank you for everything you've done so far, Gracie. We'll take it to the finish line."

Surprise, gratitude, and some other hard-to-name emotion pile up in my throat like a three-car collision. I think it might be pride.

"Well, it was lovely to meet one of you," Jude says, pulling me against his side, "but we should get going. Happy early birthday, Mrs. Bowen."

And before my stepsisters can protest, he guides me out of the kitchen and out the front door.

With each step closer to his car, I have to repress the urge to either punch the air in victory or throw up. By the time he's opening my door for me, I'm not sure my feet are even touching the asphalt. When Jude gets in, I turn to him and shout, "*Did I really just do that?!*"

"Yes, you *fucking* did!" he yells back, and then he's pulling me into a hug across the center console, kissing my temple repeatedly.

I pull back a little to look at him and realize I'm shaking with excitement, nerves, and the feeling of unadulterated freedom. "Thank you," I tell him. "Thank you for helping me get rid of all that goddamn *shrimp*."

He laughs, grinning so widely that I see his elusive nose-scrunch. "Your real motivation, revealed at last."

"I can think of far worse motivations than an oversupply of discount shellfish."

He lifts a hand to the side of my face, and I can't stop myself from leaning my cheek into his palm. "I'm so fucking proud of you," he says. "I wish I were half as brave."

His eyes are so sincere and breathtaking in the sunlight, that for a moment, I wish I could let myself fully acknowledge the truth: I'm falling in love with this man. Even if he can't share his whole story with me. Even though I know he's keeping secrets. Even if time is running out for our arrangement, and the fate of Larkwood and my future hang in the balance. The simple fact is, being with him feels like stepping into the warmth after shivering for years. And when he smiles, saying, "Come on. I know a place with *great* shrimp cocktail," my heart tries to leap from me, completely certain he'll catch it.

34

JUDE

One Week Before the Wedding

This morning, as I was walking into court for the emergency hearing I motioned for, I got a text from Henry that read: "Congrats, Judy, you're the official new owner of your least favorite place on Earth! Still on for lunch today? You're buying."

Somehow, I managed *not* to release an existential groan in front of my nervous client. Not only did his message cement something I've been dreading my entire life, but I'd also forgotten about lunch. Quickly, I texted back, "In court. Nick's 1:00 p.m." and then turned off my notifications. Unsurprisingly, it was much harder to shut off the intrusive thoughts about Larkwood and coming clean to Henry about Gracie.

Thankfully, I managed to keep my focus on my client, but now that the hearing is over, all the worries I compartmentalized have crawled back out of the box I stuffed them in. But I don't have time to spiral.

I rush into Nick's ten minutes late and find Henry at our usual table near a big window, waving me down. Trying not to look like I'm walking to my own execution instead of lunch with my best friend, I accept his handshake and quick back-slapping hug as he stands to greet me.

"Hey, man! I was starting to get worried you'd been eaten alive by your client's respondent."

I unbutton my jacket as I sit, remembering my client's full-body relief when I told her it would just be us and the judge today. "Nah, no respondent, it was ex parte. Sorry I'm late."

He waves my apology away. "The wheels of justice are slow, blah, blah, blah. I just hope you saved some room for lunch. I ordered the fried squash blossoms, and you're not allowed to make me eat them by myself."

Henry's eyes won't meet mine. To anyone else, he might sound completely normal, but there's an artificial brightness to his voice that has me on edge. Is it because of Gracie? She said she ended things with him, but despite my efforts to call and text, he's been evading me since it happened.

The server comes to take the rest of our order, interrupting my thoughts, and I tack on a gin and tonic at the last second.

Henry raises an eyebrow at me. "Is that a celebration G and T or an 'oh god, help me numb the pain' G and T?"

I lean back in my chair, tossing my menu onto the table. "Can it be both?"

"I guess we could call it a 'Good and Tragic' instead."

I snort. "Perfect."

"And so, the tragic half of it"—he takes a sip of water—"I'm assuming it's mansion-shaped and filled with secrets?"

I resist running a hand through my hair. Becoming the official owner of Larkwood was never going to feel great. But at the very least, I have a plan to get rid of it. After learning my mom's decision to stay with my father, I've resettled on my original plans for Larkwood's future. I just need to find a way to make Gracie understand.

"Judy?"

I look up from the fork I've been nudging into place. "Sorry," I answer. "There's actually something else on my mind."

Henry nods like he's been expecting it. "Gracie."

Jesus, am I that obvious? Can he see my heart beating for her right through my shirt, or did I black out and get her name tattooed on my forehead?

"Yeah," I say, throat dry, glancing around for our server. *Where the hell is my "Good and Tragic"?*

He tilts his head, considering me. "She really wanted to change your mind about selling it, man. When are you going to tell her that she didn't?"

It's not what I expected him to say, but my guilt has a whole collection of knives, and this one slices through me, quick and bloodless.

"This weekend," I say quietly, not above praying for a miracle that she'll forgive me.

"And how long is she going to have to move out and find a place to live?" he asks. "Seems like you're getting pretty down to the wire if you're planning on selling in early August."

"I'm not going to let her be homeless," I say, sharper than I intended. "I have a plan."

No matter what happens, she'll be okay. I'll make fucking sure of it. But the look he gives me—like he doubts I could ever care for Gracie the way she deserves—dives directly beneath my skin and starts burning me from the inside out.

"Well," he says, "I know she's probably got friends she could stay with, but I'm going to offer to let her crash with me, just in case." His brows knit together as he exhales. "She ended things between us, but it doesn't mean I'm not concerned about her. And if it leads to a second chance . . ." He shrugs. "I wouldn't be opposed to that either."

Fuck, fuck fuck. A sick, empty feeling in my chest swallows any response I could make. By some miracle, the server arrives at that moment with my drink. He also has a platter of fried squash blossoms, but the smell turns my stomach. I reach for my drink instead, taking a long pull.

"Thirsty much?" Henry asks, laughing uneasily when I put the half-empty glass down.

"Hen, listen," I say, leaning forward. "I said I had a plan for Gracie, and I do. I was actually going to ask her to stay with me while she finds a place of her own."

At first, Henry can only stare at me. Then he smiles like he's just cottoned onto a really bad joke. "Right, okay," he says, plucking a blossom from the platter and taking a bite. "Fuck that's delicious," he mutters, before wiping his hands and mouth with his napkin.

"I'm not kidding," I say, carefully watching his reaction.

"I didn't say you were," he responds, and this time, there's no trace of levity on his face. "I know you feel bad for leaving her in a tight spot," he says. "But I'm pretty sure you have a better chance of growing a second dick than getting her to stay with you. Never stop dreaming though, bud."

Stomach churning, I say quietly, "I think she might, though."

Henry takes in my expression, and his jaw flexes. "What are you talking about?

At my miserable silence, he goes still. "You didn't." He stops. Lets out a short, sharp laugh. "Jesus. You didn't actually take my advice seriously, did you?"

I blink at him. "What advice?"

"Back when I first told you about the cottage going to Gracie. I said if you wanted it so badly, you should just seduce her." He shakes his head, disbelief flickering across his face. "It was a fucking joke, man."

Heat rises in my chest, so hot my vision blurs around the edges. I refuse to even dignify that accusation with a response.

Slowly, clearly, I say, "Things have changed between Gracie and me. We've gotten closer."

Henry's eyes pinch closed as he brings a hand up to rub his forehead. He nods to himself, like this is exactly what he should have expected. "You mean you fucked her," he says in a quiet voice. "*That's* why she ended things with me."

I will myself not to get upset. *Of course he's angry*, I tell myself. *You* knew *he'd be angry.*

"It's more than that," I say as steadily as I can.

"Okay," he says, tossing his napkin on the table. "Let's forget for a moment that you knew I liked her and that you promised you'd stay away. Are you trying to tell me that you're suddenly *capable* of something more than sinking into whatever warm body you find for the night? Because that would be news to me."

Pressure begins building in my body, slow but unstoppable. It takes everything I've got to stay calm when I say, "I didn't know either, but this is different. This could be something more."

"Christ," he says under his breath, looking out the window. "Just like last time."

"Excuse me?"

He looks at me, and there's exhaustion in his eyes. "*Priya*. Remember that name?"

In the seconds it takes for my mind to scramble in this unexpected direction, Henry rolls his eyes and lets out a laugh that feels like a slap. "Of course not."

"No, I do remember her," I say, grateful to have landed on the memory, even if it took me a second. "Priya Agarwal. Our TA from Property Law. Fucking brilliant."

"But not brilliant enough for you to actually date her. To give a shit about her feelings."

I frown, trying to remember the details of a hookup that happened years ago. Vaguely, I remember her being disappointed when I said I wasn't looking for something serious, but in my mind, we'd gone our separate ways amicably. Was I wrong?

"I'm sorry, but what does Priya have to do with anything?" I ask, getting frustrated.

"I was *crazy* about her, that's what," he says. "But, of course, she didn't have eyes for anyone but you, did she?"

I'm at a loss, feeling more and more like a dick every passing second. "I'm sorry." I shake my head. "I wouldn't have slept with her if I'd known, Henry."

"But you *did* know," he accuses, pointing at me. "You knew it, but I told you to go ahead if you felt like it could turn into something real. So you did, even though it never went anywhere because it *never* does. And now you're doing the same goddamn thing with Gracie. Except this time, you didn't even ask me. And now, you're going to fuck around until you get bored, or you're too threatened by actually feeling something, and then who the hell do you think she's going to come running to?" Henry's eyes are wide and distraught. "Who do you think *Priya* came running to, begging to know the way to my best friend's heart, while you moved on to the next girl? Gracie doesn't *deserve* it, Jude. She deserves someone who can love her and—"

"I do love her," I blurt, loud enough to make people at nearby tables look around at us. But the pressure that's been steadily building inside of me finally reaches a boiling point. "I love her, Hen," I say hoarsely, heart pounding at the admission. "That's got to be what this is, right?" I ask him desperately. "Feeling like I'm dying when she isn't with me? Feeling like I'm dying when she is, because I *know* she isn't mine?" He's staring at me like I've suddenly started speaking in tongues, and maybe I have.

"You . . . love her," he repeats slowly.

"I'm sorry," I say, wishing he knew how much I meant it. "I'm so sorry about Priya, and what a clueless, insensitive prick I've been to you. You're my best friend, and I've never wanted to hurt you, but yes. If there's any chance Gracie might feel a fraction of what I feel for her, then I'm going to try to make it work."

"And you actually think she'll want you after the bomb you're about to drop on her?"

I shake my head, wincing. "I don't know. I don't know if there's any hope. But even if she hates me after all of this, I'm not going to leave her high and dry." I swallow hard. "I'm going to take care of her."

"And has she told you this is what she wants? Has she said she feels the same way?"

I shake my head, wishing I had a different answer to give. "No. She has even less reason to trust me than you do. She's protecting herself, but I *know* she feels something for me, too."

"And did you ever think that maybe you should just leave her the hell alone?"

I rub a hand over my eyes, hating myself for the truth. "I tried. I knew she'd be better off with you—you're everything she deserves. But I was too fucking selfish and she—" I stop, not wanting to hurt him more than I already have.

"She wanted you, too," he finishes for me.

Henry is staring at me like he's never seen me in full color before. I don't have it in me to tell him how little he actually knows.

"You have to promise me that you're not going to throw her away," he says eventually. "You've already put her through enough, Jude."

"I swear it," I tell him. "I'm hers for as long as she'll put up with me."

Henry shakes his head and looks down at the cold squash blossoms. I catch a faint, disbelieving breath of laughter from him. "Jude Larkwood in love. Is it as terrifying as you always imagined?"

I sink both hands into my hair. "So much worse."

Henry leans forward on his elbows, bitterness still lacing his voice. "Want some advice?"

"Anything."

"Be honest with her," he says. "You think you have to protect everyone with your secrets, but hiding things from the people you love, even when you think you have the best intentions . . ." He leans back in his chair and suddenly looks exhausted. "Let's just say I know from personal experience how hurtful it is not to be trusted."

"Henry—"

"Don't apologize. I know this is a you thing and not about me. But Gracie hasn't had years to adjust to your bullshit. She won't understand, and your secrets *will* hurt her if they haven't already. So . . . just be honest. As honest as you can."

He told me not to apologize, but all the years of keeping him in the dark are pressing down against me like the heel of a boot. I want to tell him how close I came to telling her everything—about Larkwood, my past, and my present. But in the end, I couldn't. Just like I've never been able to tell him.

"Okay," I say, throat constricted. "I promise to try, and I am sorry. For everything."

He nods, and if he has anything more to say on the subject, I don't find out, because at that moment, our server comes back with our main courses.

"Were the zucchini blossoms not to your liking?" he asks, looking at the nearly full plate.

Henry gives him a tight smile. "They were great. But my poor friend here is too lovesick to eat a thing."

Our server gives me a sympathetic look. “We’re all waiting for *that* vaccine. Can I get you another drink?”

“Make it two,” Henry says, and I’m so filled with gratitude for his willingness to sit with me—to somehow forge a way past this—that I hardly register his next muttered words. “I think I need one more than he does.”

35

GRACIE

Wedding Day

This morning, when my eyes snapped open two hours before my alarm, I knew there was no point trying to go back to sleep. I got up carefully, trying not to disturb Jude, who showed up last night with pizza, wine, and a deeply appreciated "How can I help?"

After letting me read my entire coordination schedule to him (twice), he forced me to relax and get some sleep. Eventually. But now that Wedding Day has cometh, I've had the energy and hyperfocus of an overcaffeinated bomb squad all day.

I take a breath, glancing at the grandfather clock behind the milling wedding party to make sure we're still on schedule. Somehow, despite having to work within this ridiculously short time frame, everything I've planned has gone off without a hitch today.

Well, almost everything.

Checking to make sure that Phoebe is still distributing bouquets and that none of Brooke's bridesmaids are sneaking shots or trying to leap off the furniture, I pull out my phone.

Gracie: Please let me know when you have the cake and you're on your way back.

Jude: That's the third way you've phrased the same request in under 10 minutes. Impressive.

Gracie: JUDE.

Jude: I will let you know when the cake is secured. Unclench your jaw.

I note with annoyance that my jaw is, in fact, clenched and make an effort to relax it. This morning, when Valerie told me there had been a family emergency and no one was available to deliver the cake, I was on the verge of panic. But then a pair of large, warm hands were smoothing my shoulders down my back. *I'll take care of it*, he'd said against my neck. Exhaling, my jaw loosens, and my phone vibrates.

Jude: See? Isn't that better?

I shake my head, a reluctant smile tugging at my lips.

Gracie: Good to know you're not beyond planting a Nanny Cam, perv.

Jude: I would never.

Gracie: Sure. Just tell me which potted plant I should flash.

Jude: Stop before you melt Siri. I'm trying to be a safe driver here, Gracie.

Gracie: 😇

Jude: Does your dress fit? It's all I can think about.

I catch my reflection in the polished glass of the intricately carved bookcase I'm standing next to, and my cheeks heat. This morning, I woke up to a pile of iconic black-and-white boxes that had *no* business gracing my shabby kitchenette table. When I insisted there was no way I'd be accepting a gift so outrageous, he gave me the saddest puppy eyes to ever puppy.

"Just try them on, at least," he'd said.

"This is ridiculous. I don't need gifts like this."

He'd laughed. "I think we can both agree that this is a gift for myself."

"Just because you have the money to be a sugar daddy, doesn't mean I *want* a sugar daddy," I'd argued. "I love the way you want to take care of me, but this might be too much."

This had sobered him. "The last thing I want is to make you uncomfortable. If *you* don't get pleasure out of this, then I don't either."

It was the lack of pressure and his sincerity that made me reconsider. In the end, I agreed to try it on as an experiment, but *only* after he'd left to get the cake. When I finally lifted the lid of the largest box with trembling hands, there was a note inside.

Not a Gracie Holland original, but I hear they make an okay LBD.

Heart in my throat, my brain connected the dots—this wasn't some random luxury brand but the one responsible for *the* iconic *Breakfast at Tiffany's* dress I'd tried re-creating for Agatha's funeral. I carefully folded back the tissue paper and was confronted by an oil spill of blackest silk.

My chest squeezes as I take in the perfect silhouette in the reflection of the bookcase. I knew it would be beautiful—how could it not be? But what I didn't expect was how cherished I would feel in it. Or how desired. I smooth the fabric over my hips as warmth builds low in my belly. I think of the last and tiniest box, which held another note.

To match your other bows.

Flushing, I realize I haven't responded to him and still have a wedding to coordinate. I fire off a quick text back.

Gracie: You should be thinking about the CAKE. Get back soon, I miss you. ♥

"Gracie, hey."

Turning quickly, I see Calvin coming toward me with a grin stretched across his face. He looks incredibly handsome in his tux, but all the heartache I anticipated feeling on this day is nowhere to be found. Instead, there's only regret for spending so much time pining over someone I thought was too good for me, when all along, he simply wasn't *right* for me.

"Hey, Cal," I respond, smiling.

"Wow," he says, giving me a once-over. "You look beautiful, Gracie."

"Thank you," I say, barely feeling an echo of what those words would have meant to me just a couple of months ago. "How are you feeling? Ready for the big walk?"

He puffs out his cheeks and lets out a big exhale. "More than ready, thanks to you. I don't know how you managed to pull something like this off in so little time, but it's more than we ever dreamed of. Even Brookey's parents haven't found something to frown at."

I wave a hand like the last two sleep-deprived months of my life were a joyful skip through the park. "It was my pleasure."

The smile on his face tightens a little. "I'm sure it wasn't. In fact, I'd be willing to bet my left ass cheek that it was one giant headache from the word go."

"Just the left one?" I ask with a smile.

"Fine, both," he says.

I give a modest shrug. "It was a lot of work, but I've had help," I say, my mind sliding to Jude. "All of the vendors really pulled through for this."

Calvin looks down at his polished wing tips. "Yeah, but I don't just mean the work."

I'm silent at this, and he looks up sheepishly. "I guess what I'm trying to say is, sorry for asking you in the first place."

"Oh," I say faintly.

He rubs the back of his neck. "I knew it was out of line, but honestly, I had been looking for an excuse to get in touch, and at the time, it felt like two birds with one stone." He presses his lips together. "It was . . . dumb. I know. Especially after the way I ended things with us and then kind of . . ."

"Disappeared?" I finish for him, stunned to be getting any kind of apology at this point.

"Yeah," he says heavily. "I know it's not an excuse, but you were always so . . . intimidating."

My eyes bug. "What?"

He shrugs. "It's true. You know I've never strayed from the playbook. Went to school where my parents went. Took the job they set up for me. But you were never afraid to have these huge, creative dreams and make something of yourself. It made me feel . . . I don't know. Small, I guess. And sometimes—" His sandy eyebrows come together as he frowns. "Sometimes, it made me want to make you feel even smaller. I hated that about myself, so . . . I left."

I swallow hard. If I'd had even an inkling of this two years ago, or enough self-worth to shake off his rejection instead of internalizing it, where would I be now?

Not at Larkwood, a little voice whispers through me.

I shake my head to clear it. "Why are you telling me all of this now?"

He takes a deep breath and looks over his shoulder to where the wedding party is taking selfies across the room. Brooke hasn't come down from the bridal suite with Sofia yet, but I know he's thinking of her.

"One thing about Brooke," he says slowly, "is that she doesn't mind calling me out. I tried pulling the same crap with her at work, and she wasn't having it. I think, over time, I started waking up. I've wanted to apologize to you for a while now, and I guess today kind of seemed like the last chance to clear the air?"

He says this last bit like he's asking for permission, and I'm not going to lie—there's still an itty-bitty part of me that still wants to blame him for my choice to give up on Grace & Veil and go into permanent hiding beneath my Snuggie. But it's a squeak compared to the much louder part of me that's finally accepting my own role in all of this.

So, I take a breath and give him a smile that feels like sweet relief as years of baggage drop from my shoulders. "Thanks for saying all of that. I'm more than ready to move on as friends, Cal."

The surprised grin he gives me is so boyish and genuine, I don't stop him when he comes in for a hug. "Thanks, Gracie. You were always too good for me."

"Not true," I say against his shoulder. "We learned exactly what we needed from each other, and no one can ask for more than that."

He lets out a relieved exhale as someone from across the room calls his name. I gently pry him off me and whisper, "Come on. Let's go get you hitched."

The ceremony is perfect. Fluffy white clouds skim across the balmy blue sky, and every rose in the garden is in full bloom. Brooke and Calvin are gorgeous together, even if Brooke's makeup doesn't *quite* cover up the still-healing lump on her forehead.

Standing in the same portico where I once crumpled in Agatha's arms, it's incredible to me that I feel so much peace now. I only wish she were here to witness it. Despite all odds, I not only found the closure she wanted for me, but also the love she predicted I'd find where I least expected it.

My stomach fizzes like champagne when I think of Jude, racing back to me. Today, the charade we've been playing is finally coming to an end. But for once, I'm not afraid. He's seen how important Larkwood is to the vendors who rely on it. And while we still might not see eye to eye on the issue of Agatha's legacy, I'm beginning to believe that I've proven to Jude that love *can* be found. It might be rare and precious, but that only makes it more worthy of celebrating. Hopefully, right here at Larkwood.

At the sudden swell of cheers and whistles, I look up to see Calvin and Brooke, sharing their first kiss as a married couple. My heart is so full for them, and for my own future, too, but my moment of reverie is over.

For the next hour, Phoebe and I move like two coordinated blurs, and in what feels like .3 seconds, it's time to get everyone to the ballroom for dinner. I'm so busy that I've completely forgotten to worry about the cake or even pester Jude until a passing server says to me, "There's a delivery for you in the kitchen."

The bolt of nerves that shoots through me is so fast and electric, I'm surprised I don't leave burns on the parquet floor as I take off. When I reach the door, my stomach is a merry-go-round on warp speed as I smooth my dress. I've never felt so beautiful or more nervous. But somehow, every racing thought and task on my to-do list disappears when I see him.

He's leaning against the kitchen island in the tux I asked him to wear to "blend in." But looking at him now, it's obvious that "blending in" isn't going to be an option.

My breath catches as I take in the perfect cut of his black jacket, its peak lapels pointing like arrows to how unreasonably broad his shoulders are. Below his black bow tie, the crisp white V of his shirt draws my gaze down his impossibly long body, all the way to where his slutty bare ankles are crossed, one over the other. And suddenly I understand. If I could afford to dress him like this every day, I would. I'd go bankrupt just to see him like this again and again.

"Baby," he whispers, his voice perforated as a shooting target as he slowly straightens from the island.

My eyes jump to his, and I'm swallowed by his gaze in one famished gulp.

"It fits," I say pointlessly. Then, flushing a little, "Everything fits."

He nods, throat moving in a swallow. "Will you turn for me?" he asks.

I nod, stomach clenching. When I start to rotate, he says, "Slower."

My breathing ticks up as I hear him cross the room. When I'm faced away from him, I feel the whisper of his touch at my bare nape. Slowly, a single fingertip trails down my completely exposed spine, and goose bumps rise like every inch of my skin is calling out for his attention.

His lips brush my ear as my eyes flutter shut, nipples tightening to an ache. "Jesus, Gracie. How am I supposed to do anything but need you right now?"

His low voice sends a shiver through me as desire gathers hot and fast between my legs. Needing to see him again, I turn around as he captures my hips.

"It's not too much?" I ask uncertainly.

"It's way, way too fucking much," he rasps. Pulling my hips closer, his fingers dig into the silk. "There's a butler's pantry," he says in a coarse rumble. "I just need five—no—fifteen minutes. No more than thirty. Please."

His hands and lips are the world's greatest salesmen, but the mention of minutes abruptly reminds me that hiking my dress up in a closet is definitely *not* on today's strict timetable of events.

"Jude, the *cake*," I say, swinging so quickly from horny to anxious that my body feels like a torch dunked in ice water. "We have to get it to the caterer. Guests are already eating dinner."

"Cake," he agrees slowly, like all the brilliant brain cells that help him carry out complicated legal procedures have been reduced to swirling dust motes. "Should I not have brought it to the kitchen?"

I reach up and place a finger on the cleft of his chin like a reset button. "This isn't where catering sets up—they have their own mobile kitchens parked in the back," I say, wanting to kick myself for my oversight. Of course he wouldn't have known that.

But apparently, his chin cleft *is* a reboot button of sorts, because his eyes are instantly less dazed. "Right. Okay, I know a shortcut, but I'll need you to hold some doors open for me."

"Of course."

"And let me feed you cake later."

"Sure."

"And let me fuck up your pretty lipstick."

"Jude, the *cake*."

He makes a frustrated growl before grabbing the gargantuan wedding cake box on the kitchen island. Somehow, we make it to the catering vehicles without a single hormone-fueled mishap, but from the way I felt his eyes on my backside the entire time, it was probably a near miss.

The cake is delivered just in time. Sofia takes photos of Calvin delicately forking a bite of chocolate cake into Brooke's mouth, and Brooke smashing Battenburg into Calvin's. I'm able to spare Jude one heated look as memories of our first kiss ricochet between us before one of the babysitters hired for the event rushes up to me.

"Gracie, I'm so sorry, but one of the toddlers threw up carrot puree all over a rug." Her eyes dart to Jude and then back to me as she panic-whispers, "*A very fancy-looking rug*."

I turn to grab Kit, but Jude gets to it before I do. "There is no way you're cleaning up orange vomit looking like that," he says, slinging Kit over his shoulder like an old pro. As a server passes by us, he stops him with a hand on the shoulder. "Can you please bring this woman a plate of food and make sure she eats?" he asks. "She organized the whole event tonight."

The young man looks from Jude to me with wide eyes. "Of course."

"She's going to need slices of both cake flavors, too. *Big* slices."

The man smiles. "You got it."

Jude reaches into his inner breast pocket and takes out a silver money clip. "Could you also send up some food to the childcare providers?"

After the server accepts his tip and sets off, Jude looks toward me. "When I'm back from cleaning, do you want me to start distributing checks to the vendors first, or make sure everything is ready to go for the sparkler send-off? I could also check in with the chauffeur from the classic car rental place. I'm pretty sure he's napping in the Rolls out front."

For a moment, all I can do is stare at him. I know he's asked me a question, but in the face of his sheer competency and willingness to show up for me, the dozens of plates spinning in my mind crash to the ground.

"Gracie?" he prompts, raising an eyebrow.

"Uh, yes. I mean, distributing the vendor checks would be great," I say, hastily reassembling my thoughts. "Phoebe is already handling the send-off, but could you also talk to the lighting guy about the individual dances? Brooke specifically requested no blue spotlights to avoid 'looking like a corpse,'" I air quote.

"Got it. Distribute the vendor checks. No corpse lights," he says, before looking at the babysitter, who's been watching him, mouth slightly ajar. "Will you show me to the vomit?"

I guess I'm not the only one who gets hot and bothered by a helpful man, because she practically curtsies as she nods and begins quick-stepping away. Jude gives me a look that makes my heart flutter like the pages of a romance novel. "I'll find you later."

I nod, and then he's gone.

Somehow, I do manage to pick at my heaping dinner plate between my final check-ins with Phoebe, the band, the videographer, the oyster shucker, and the portrait artist who will be painting the newlyweds' first dance. Every time I pass Jude or Phoebe, I give them a fresh list of tasks, but I'm still a spinning top in constant motion. I don't find a moment for a full breath until the lights lower and Angie from The Love Notes invites everyone onto the dance floor.

Sofia gives me a wordless high five as she quickly passes me with her camera, snapping candid pictures of the dancers. She knows the heavy lifting of the event is over. Unless someone breaks an ankle doing the Electric Slide (yes, it's happened before), I can relax a little until my end-of-night tasks kick into gear.

"One dance?"

I turn at the low, familiar voice, and he's there, his gaze just as soft as the band's slow-dance rendition of "Fly Me to the Moon." As a wedding planner, I never dance at my clients' receptions. But Jude is looking at me like he's been waiting for this moment all night, and as I glance around the joy-filled room, I know no one will miss me for a few moments.

"I can't dance with the guests," I tell him.

He smiles and takes my hand. "I know the perfect place," he says, leading me to the very same potted plant I got caught in when we first met.

When he tugs me out of sight behind it into a small, shadowed alcove, my breath catches as he pulls me flush against his body.

"If you're trying to be romantic," I say, staring at the bladelike leaves, "we could always just pretend we met somewhere less deadly."

"And sacrifice authenticity?" he chides as his warm hands find the bare skin of my lower back. "I'll accept the risks."

"Even crushed toes? Agatha never made me learn the waltz," I warn, automatically looping my wrists behind his neck.

The swirl of pink and orange lights is muted in our shadowed corner, but his smile is bright. "No doubt one of her only major life regrets."

I tilt my head back to meet his eyes as the music pulls us into swaying movement. "At least we're dressed for the occasion," I say as his solid warmth begins to permeate my thin silk. "She would have loved our outfits."

"Mm, I think she would have preferred if we were both wearing something . . . louder."

I smile. "Maybe she was onto something. I'd love to see you in that purple sequined bolero sometime."

He points a thumb over his shoulder. "I could put it on now if you want," he offers. "It goes great with the gold lamé leotard she gave me for my birthday last year."

I grin up at him as he turns us in a slow circle. "And have you upstage my dress? I don't think so."

"Audrey Hepburn herself couldn't upstage you in that dress." His hand slides low and gives me a rough squeeze. "She doesn't have the ass for it."

I would laugh if his grip weren't deep-frying all my abilities beyond mouth breathing.

"Do you like it?" he asks, trailing his fingers up the curve of my cheek to the small of my back.

My eyelids dip as I arch into his touch. "Yes," I breathe.

"Good to know, but I meant the dress," he says with a chuckle.

My face becomes a magnet for all the blood in my body. "I knew what you meant," I lie.

"So that's a yes," he says carefully, but I can hear how much he wants me to agree. To tell him that yes, I enjoy receiving as much as he loves giving.

"I like it," I confess.

I feel his physical reaction in the flex of his hands and his short exhale against my bangs.

"Thank you for wearing it," he says, like I've endured a hardship.

"It's the least I could do," I tell him. "You've helped everything go perfectly today."

He shakes his head. "I'm just the vomit squad. This whole event . . . everyone's happiness . . ." He looks beyond my shoulder at the party before finding my eyes again. "That's all because of you, Gracie." He shakes his head. "No cynic would stand a chance in this room tonight. You could pull love from a stone."

Love. The word is heavy and jewel-bright in my mind, spinning in time with our own slow rotations. My heart begins to rise, crowding my throat as it pulses with a question I'm suddenly too afraid to ask directly.

"So maybe weddings aren't quite as despicable as you imagined?"

His hands pull me closer as his eyes roam over my face. "You make it easy to imagine spending the rest of my life with one person."

"Jude," I whisper as my arms tighten around his neck. He kisses me, and it feels like the rebirth of every part of me that wanted to stop believing in love. For the first time in *so* long, I feel something like real hope radiate in my chest. That maybe love isn't just for people in movies and novels—but finally something warm and solid I can hold onto for myself.

I tilt my face, needing him to know how close I want him. I feel the vibration of his groan in the ends of my hair as our kiss slides into something too feral for a polite jazz standard. Somewhere in the back of my mind, I know I'm being unprofessional. I'm on the job. But he just gave me the closest thing to a love declaration I've ever received, and unless there's a major accident, no one is going to miss me for a few minutes. And so I break free and say the only two words I can manage: "The pantry."

36

GRACIE

I can't stop pacing when I make it to the walk-in pantry before Jude, who said he'd check in with Phoebe before we temporarily disappeared. I've never played hooky like this before, and even though no one will miss me for a little while, I still feel jumpy.

Taking off my earpiece to turn on speaker mode (just in case someone *does* break an ankle on the dance floor), my mind is whirring with all the end-of-night tasks still ahead of me. According to wedding planner math, I definitely don't have time to be getting frisky in a butler's pantry. Unless—

An idea comes to me like my hardwired efficiency and horniness had a brainchild. Without giving myself time to second-guess myself, I slip my hand to the discreet side zipper of my dress and pull. The garment slithers off me like it's my most devoted collaborator in this scheme to get laid as quickly as possible. Carefully stepping out of it with my heels, I'm bending to pick it up when the door to the pantry opens.

My head snaps up as Jude drops the handle, and the door swings open. The kitchen beyond him is dark, but the soft light of the pantry illuminates the mute shock on his face. Reflexively, I bring the dress up to hide behind. Stepping in quickly, he closes the door behind him.

With the click of the latch, the air in the room undergoes an immediate reconfiguration. Molecules rearrange into something far less oxygenated as his eyes rake over me. There are three, maybe four steps between us, allowing him to take in everything from my neat chignon to the pointed toes of my shiny black stilettos. In between, there isn't much else. Sheer black stockings held up by tiny satin bows and an equally sheer black garter belt. Matching black panties and every single trembling ounce of my vulnerability.

"I know you like undressing me, but we have to be quick, so—"

"Drop the dress," he says quietly. At his shift into a tone that my body has begun associating with earth-scorching orgasms, I shiver. Let the silk slip out of my hands, where it's been blocking my naked chest.

"Come here," he commands gently. Breath becoming thready, I slowly walk toward him, carefully stepping over my discarded dress and all the unchecked wedding tasks that have fluttered from my mind. When the click of my heels stops in front of him, he lifts a hand, and I notice for the first time that he's holding a crystal plate with two slices of cake.

"You didn't eat your dessert," he notes. "Why not?"

I look away, embarrassed. I could say I was too busy, but that's not the full truth, and he'll know it. So, I try for honesty.

"I was saving it. You made me promise to . . ." Somehow, I say the rest, but it's a mumble that sounds a lot like *lulu fumu*.

He crooks a finger beneath my chin with his free hand and tilts my head up. "What was that?"

I raise my eyes to his, taking a shaking breath. "You made me promise I'd let you feed me cake," I repeat.

"Mm," he says, like he's glad I've recalled my promise. His thumb strokes the underside of my bottom lip. "You're good at following instructions, aren't you?"

I try not to whimper as I'm flooded with heat. I nod.

"Is that because you like being told what to do?"

I clasp my hands in front of me, twisting my fingers together. This is all so new to me, it's hard to articulate. I do enjoy being told what to do, but it's not my end game, either. It's more . . .

"Or do you just want me to tell you what a good girl you've been?"

At this, my thighs press together against the corkscrewing heat between my legs. My lips tremble, a breath shuddering out of me.

"That's what I thought," he murmurs, caressing my cheek. "At first, I was sure I was just imagining it. That shake in your thighs whenever I praise you," he trails off, eyes moving to my lips. "But you crave it, don't you? You'd plan your ex's wedding. Bend over backward for your thoughtless family. Strip down in a pantry when you should be working, just to please me. To get a *little* affection."

Shame prickles the inside of my stomach. What does it say about me that he's right?

He must see my expression fall, because suddenly he's cradling my face, tilting it back up to his. "Baby, no," he says, his eyes steady on mine. "Shame on *them*. Shame on everyone who took, and took, but never returned your generosity. Who never appreciated your kindness and talent. They never chose you, Gracie." His deep voice catches in his throat. "But I do. I want to choose you every day until you can't believe you were ever scared of this."

I'm overcome. Overwhelmed by this outpouring of love. Because that's what this has to be, right? My heart isn't just beating—it's sprinting right toward him, ready to dive.

"I choose you, too," I say in a rush. "Even the parts you can't show me yet. I trust you, Jude."

His Adam's apple bobs as his eyes search mine, and all the hunger that's built between us over the last two months reaches a precipice I'm ready to jump from.

"You want to give me your trust?" he repeats softly.

I nod, eager to prove myself beyond words of declaration. I can hardly take a full breath as I watch him lift the crystal plate and break off a small piece of frosted pink Battenburg with his fingers. He holds it aloft between us.

"Open your mouth."

I do it without thinking, hungry in ways I've never felt before. He makes a quiet, pained sound as he slips the piece of cake between my waiting lips. I moan, half from the sweetness, half from his lingering fingertips, sticky with frosting.

"Fuck yes," he whispers, pushing them deeper. "Suck them clean."

I whimper and do as I'm told, hollowing my cheeks as his lips part, watching me from under heavy lashes. An unexpected surge of gratification twines irrevocably with desire. Knowing praise and affection lie on the other side of whatever task he gives me is like pressing an untouched dopamine button at the very base of my skull. I could almost cry from how simple it is. From how clearly he saw this unslaked thirst in me.

When he draws his wet fingers from my mouth, I reopen my eyes, vision glazed. He's staring at me like I'm not the only one in the middle of a life-changing sexual revelation. "Is this how you need me to take care of you, Gracie?" he asks, dropping his hand to the level of my breasts before circling my right nipple with his wet fingertip. It's already as hard as possible, but at his feather-light touch, I gasp. "You need me to give you a to-do list? Reward you for every check mark?"

I arch into his touch, seeking more pressure as he lightly trails his fingertip across the slopes of my breasts to the other side. "Yes," I pant, dying for him to tell me what to do next.

"Open up," he says. "You haven't tried the chocolate yet."

My jaw drops instantly, and he repeats what he did with the Battenburg. This time, I can't help the way my lashes flutter as I swallow, whimpering around his fingers from the taste.

"You like this one better?"

I nod as best as I can.

"Why?" he asks, removing his clean fingers from my mouth to drag them down my neck.

I squirm in my heels, uncomfortable from how wet my panties have become. "It tastes like you," I say breathlessly. "Like your mouth when we first kissed."

He lets out a strained breath. "Would you like to taste more of me?"

"*Please*." I moan, wanting nothing more than to rip his perfect tux to shreds and get my mouth all over him.

"Do you remember what else I asked you to let me do?" he asks, placing the plate on a nearby shelf.

My brain is a scrambled egg, but there's no forgetting words that felt like a hot slap between my thighs. "You asked to fuck up my pretty lipstick," I recite dutifully, wanting a little kiss on the forehead for my efforts.

"That's right," he says, his voice ragged as he brushes his thumb beside the corner of my mouth. "Is that something you'd like to do on your knees?"

My legs collapse like a fawn's in my hurry to drop in front of him, my tights doing nothing to protect my knees from the cold, hard tile. But somehow, I like that feeling, too. I like everything about this, but nothing so much as the way he groans when I stroke him through his trousers. Fumbling in my haste to release him from the extra layers of his buttoned jacket and black silk cummerbund, I earn a grunt when I finally free him. At my touch, his shoulders fall back against the door with a loud thud.

"*Christ*. Look up at me. Let me see those eyes," he says, grabbing the plate off the shelf again. Hands skimming his heavy length, I watch him drag a finger through a thick dollop of light pink frosting before saying, "Stick your tongue out. Keep it soft."

I follow his instructions, and then his finger is swiping creamy frosting on my tongue until I'm coated and salivating. It's so hard not to close my mouth and swallow, but then he murmurs, "A little more. You're doing such a good job," and my toes curl from the affection in his voice. I open my mouth a little wider, pleading with my eyes.

He drinks me in, like he just needs a moment to burn this image into his core memory bank. Finally, he nods with a shaky exhale. "Put me in your mouth. Want to get you messy."

I hum with relief when I finally sink my mouth over his first jaw-stretching inch. I take more and more until there's not enough room for him and all the frosting. Within one greedy minute, it's everywhere, slick and sweet and delicious. I feel it dripping down my chin as his palm cups the underside of my jaw, squeezing it open.

"H-holy shit." His whole body shudders with the whispered curse, and I'm drunk on this power. He's barely holding it together, his breath coming in sharp staccato bursts as he says, "Just a little deeper, sweetheart. That's . . . that's it— *Fuck* you take it so well."

I moan around him, his words urging me past the threshold of personal comfort. I want him so deep I can't breathe. My eyes are streaming, my hands and face sticky with frosting, but I can't get enough. I want to be his—to show him how much I'm willing to give if he'll just love me the way I love—

"*Gracie*." My name is a groan as he lets go of my jaw to quickly grasp the side of my hair. He pulls me away, leaving me empty and panting.

"God, just look at you," he breathes. "Such a fucking angel on your knees for me. Come here."

With his help, I stand on wobbling legs, grateful when he pulls me against his heaving chest. He cradles my face between his hands and groans again, eyes mapping the tracks of my tears and swollen lips. "So gorgeous," he whispers, bending to lick stray frosting from the side of my mouth. "So giving." He sucks my sticky lips and tongue, kissing me so deep, my insides liquify.

"Please," I whisper, my hands shaking as I undo his bow tie. His top shirt buttons. If he doesn't touch me soon, I'm going to weep.

He caresses my cheek, and his eyes are so tender, so sympathetic, that I think he understands. "I know it hurts," he says. "Turn around, and I'll make it better."

Shakily, I turn, and he repositions us so that I'm facing the door. With a firm and steady hand between my shoulder blades, he urges me forward until my cheek and hands are pressed against the cool wooden surface.

"Okay?" he asks, sliding his hand down my spine in a well-meaning caress. But nothing is soothing right now—nothing is going to ease this ache except feeling him inside me.

I nod fretfully, arching my spine. "Need you now," I breathe, wanting him to go quicker.

But his hands are skimming the sheer mesh of the garter belt, fingers tracing down to the straining clips holding up my stockings. I feel him slide his fingers beneath them, pulling the garter straps out before snapping them back against my ass. I gasp at the small sting, and he grunts his approval. And then his thumb brushes the hot, liquid center of me—just a whisper of pressure against my panties, and my knees nearly buckle.

"Oh God," I exhale, squeezing my eyes shut.

"Shh. It's going to be okay," he promises as his fingers slip beneath the soaked fabric. For long moments, all I can do is writhe against his touch, pressing my hips back, wordlessly begging for more.

"Goddamn," he whispers over the wet sounds filling the pantry. "It's going to be so easy to stuff you full tonight, isn't it?"

I sink my teeth into my bottom lip, nodding fervently as he slides my panties down to the tops of my stockings. The cool air makes me feel even more exposed, but then Jude presses himself against me. I moan at the feeling of his broad underside sliding against me, side to side. Smacking me wetly.

"*Jude*," I whine, moving my hips in a desperate wiggle.

He groans and finally—*finally*—pushes his way inside. I gasp, fingers turning to claws on the door as he mutters an inarticulate curse. He was right—I'm so ready for him that he's able to push in most of the way, but the intrusion is still a shock to my body. I lift onto my toes with a squeak, panting as Jude covers my hands with his own. His head drops beside mine.

"I'm sorry," he pants, peppering the side of my face with kisses. "You okay?"

"Yes," I exhale, weaving my fingers through his on the door, relishing their comforting warmth. My body quickly adjusts to the unbelievable feeling of being joined with him, and soon, the ache that's plagued me all night begins demanding friction. "More," I beg against his mouth.

He makes a noise like he's dying and flexes his hips against me. Carefully. Gingerly. Working himself in with short, rough exhales until I feel his crisp white button-up against my fevered skin. His hands are crushing mine against the door, every vein articulated, and for a moment, all I can do is try to breathe around the slight burn and ear-ringing pleasure of being this full. Until slowly, he pulls back, leaving every inch he fought for so hollow I'm crying out. When he presses back in with one smooth push, my eyes roll back, spine arching. But soon enough, his slow, cautious pace goes from being nearly too much to just a tease.

"Harder," I whine, pressing back against him.

He shakes his head, his hair a caress on my cheekbone. "I'll hurt you."

"I'll like it," I promise.

"*Fuck*," he growls. Grip tightening on my hands, he drives into me like he's needed this, too. My jaw falls open, and I want to tell him how good it is, but I have no breath. He rolls into me again and again, his movements so fluid and demanding, I feel like the water he loves to lose himself in.

"So perfect for me," he says, panting and desperate. "How'd I get so fucking lucky? Tell me how to deserve you."

Tears well in my eyes as the relentless, delicious pressure builds inside me, his sweet words crystallizing in every chamber of my heart. "I love you," I cry, squeezing my eyes shut as the naked truth accidentally rockets out of me.

"God, Gracie," he pants as he quickly pulls out and spins me around so that my back is against the pantry shelves. In a moment, his hands are dropping low, and he's ripping my panties to get them out of the way. They dangle in tatters above one stocking, trapped by my garter straps, but it seems good enough for him. He quickly shucks his jacket, letting it crumple to the floor. With his bow tie loose and his hair falling into his wild eyes, he looks as undone and desperate for this as I am.

Lifting me quickly, my thighs wrap around his hips while my elbows shove backward onto the shelf. A stack of metal mixing bowls close to the edge fall to the ground, clanging and scattering wildly, but I barely register the sound as he pushes into me again. I cry his name, eyes squeezing shut, and it's all I can do not to come apart.

"Look at me," he demands, grinding his hips in a way that makes stars pop behind my closed eyes. Dazed, I lift my lashes, and it's worth the effort to see his miracle of a face staring at mine.

"It was never casual for me," he confesses, voice threadbare. "It was never just hooking up. It was never *anything* but loving you. Even before I knew what to call it, I loved you, Gracie." He exhales hard, lashes shuddering. "You have my trust. My everything. Anything I have to give is yours."

I can't respond with more than a sob as he drags his hungry mouth down my neck, pushing me to my limit with every rolling thrust. This love we've found is rushing in, filling every hollow part of me until I'm a dam on the edge of bursting. He kisses my gasping mouth, salt and sugar, and I want it all. The dark and the light, the spoken and the unspoken, as long as it's with him.

His hand finds my tipping point, stroking me past the point of all control. I break open with a strangled cry, and he follows, growling his release as a conduit opens between us. An irrevocable feedback loop of trust and knowing. Knowing that if everything else falls apart, there will *always* be this. The feeling of being chosen. Of being loved beyond all reasonable doubt.

37

GRACIE

I love you, you love me, I love you. When I wake the next morning, those words have been scrolling like a quiet ticker tape in the recesses of my mind all night. I crack my eyelids open, half wondering if all the stress and buildup to the wedding finally sent me into a series of extremely lucid sexual hallucinations in which I repeatedly professed my love for Jude Larkwood. But the dark riot of his hair against my pillows and the heavy, sleep-softened planes of his body in the streaming morning light seem to confirm that last night *wasn't* a dream. Even the part where he said he loved me back.

The memory sparkles in my chest (yes, it *sparkles*) before fanning outward to the tips of my fingers and toes. It's not the first time someone has said those words to me—Calvin used to say them, but only after I'd say it first and always casually. *Love ya, too, babe!*

But last night, Jude made his feelings on the matter clear, which is probably why I was incapable of being stressed after we'd cleaned ourselves up and gone back to the reception. It's why I can't stop grinning like a lunatic at him while he's still unconscious.

Creep alert, Gracie.

Reluctantly, I force my gaze away from his serious profile. How does he look like he could read a deposition in his sleep? I sigh. There's no way I'm falling back asleep now, but as my stomach gives a growl, I decide to return the favor of breakfast in bed.

I sneak out of the bedroom as quietly as I can. As usual, I have nothing to write home about in my own cupboards, but after spending quality time in Larkwood's pantry last night, I know I'll be able to make something there. With a small thrill, I pull on Jude's white button-up, despite the red lipstick all over the collar and suspiciously lower places.

After scrawling a quick note to him, I leave the cottage and jog across the garden to the kitchen door. As usual, it's unlocked, but when I walk in, a surprised yelp makes *me* yelp and I nearly fall backward out the door.

"Oh my God, Gracie. I thought you were Ronald McDonald."

My heart is still convinced that my esophagus is a far safer place to be than my chest, but it's just Henry. Henry . . . who is probably the last person I want to see while wearing another man's lipstick-covered shirt. Especially his best friend's.

"Ronald McDonald?" I repeat with a nervous laugh, willing my pulse to slow. "That's a pretty specific conclusion to jump to."

"Well, if he were your worst childhood fear, your mind would probably jump to him, too."

"Your worst childhood fear was being set upon by the McDonald's clown?" I ask, momentarily distracted.

"Set upon? You make him sound like a roguish highwayman with a penchant for petticoats and virgins."

"And that's less terrifying *how*?"

"Good point." Henry shudders. "Sorry I scared you. I've been texting Jude all morning. We usually meet at the pool on Sundays, but he never showed. I got worried Taco finally assassinated him and came over, but . . ." His eyes move to each lipstick stain on Jude's shirt like he's mapping crime scene evidence. "Looks like he just had a change of plans."

My arms cross, uncross, and cross one more time as I try (and fail) to cover up the deep red stains. Jude told me that he let Henry know about us, but in the crunch leading up to the wedding, I haven't had a chance to talk to him about how it went. But from the hurt outlining all of Henry's features, it couldn't be more obvious how he feels.

"I'm so sorry for how everything happened," I say earnestly, wishing I could ease all his disappointment. "Everything with Jude just happened so unexpectedly."

He tries to smile, but it comes across as a grimace. "I wish I could say I was surprised, but it's nothing new at this point."

"Nothing new?" I repeat.

Henry frowns down at his keys on the butcher block counter. "Oh, just the well-established pattern of the women I'm interested in falling head over heels for my best friend instead."

His words stun me. Up until this second, I had imagined Jude's sex life as having a traceable app history and being as far from the realm of "personal" as rubbing two bodies together gets. The revelation that it somehow ever intersected with Henry's love life—that my situation with the pair of them isn't unique—makes my heart stumble.

He loves me, I tell myself. And while I feel terrible that Henry is hurting from my unrequited feelings, I remind myself that I did give him a chance and didn't feel a spark. I tried *so* hard to ignore what I felt for his best friend, but in the end, our connection consumed me. It consumed Jude, too.

I take a breath. "I'm sorry this isn't the first time something like this has happened, but I promise it was never my intention to hurt you."

"I'm not the one you should be worried about getting hurt," he says, his face somber.

At his insinuation, I wrap my arms tighter around my middle. "He cares about me," I say, trying not to let him see the hairline fractures he's creating. "He told me he loves me."

"Loves you?" he repeats, eyebrows raised. "Wow, he really went there."

His surprise slides in between my ribs like a knife, but I force my voice into something confident. "Believe it or not, yes, he does."

He must sense from my tone—or maybe it's the way my chest has deflated from its newest puncture wound—that he's hit a nerve.

"Shit, Gracie, I didn't mean to imply that you're not—" He exhales. "It has nothing to do with you. It's just, I've known Jude for nearly half my life, and I don't think he's *capable* of letting himself love someone, no matter how wonderful the woman in question is."

"Then why on earth would he say it if he didn't mean it? You're his best friend. You of all people should know how capable of love he is," I argue, some of my fear spilling from me like a jostled cup.

"I never said he wasn't capable of love; I said he would never let himself have it," he says, frustration creeping into his tone. "If you haven't noticed, his whole personality is keeping people at arm's length. He thinks he's protecting everyone he loves from whatever the hell happened to him here, but if you think I'm any closer to knowing what that was, my current working theory is that he got probed by fucking aliens."

I don't want his words to make me doubt Jude, but questions are wriggling in. Yes, he's guarded, but hasn't he also trusted me with those hidden pieces of himself? Hasn't he shown me glimpses?

As if Henry hears me think it, he asks, "Has Jude actually told you anything about himself? About his past?"

I'm about to retort that yes, he has. Just the other night, he told me about his DV work and his tattoos.

But only because you pushed him, a small voice argues. *And even then, he only told you the barest minimum.*

I bite my lip, searching for solid proof against Henry's assumptions. But that same night, when I *finally* felt like Jude was going to open up, he only shut me down again. *Don't ask me that. I can't talk to you about this. I hate keeping secrets from you.*

But he does keep secrets. And no matter how badly I want solid ground to stand on, my argument comes out so weak that I wonder if I even believe it myself. "His actions speak louder than any painful secret he could tell me," I insist. "He cares about me, and he'll open up when he's ready."

"His actions," Henry repeats quietly, shaking his head as he leans his weight on his hands. "So I take it he hasn't told you his plans for Larkwood yet?"

A sharp-edged chunk of ice seems to surface in my stomach like a glacier. "He's going to keep it," I say, wishing I sounded more assured. "We're talking about it today."

Henry pulls a hand down his face, looking at me like I'm a seven-year-old about to find out there's no Santa, Easter Bunny, or Tooth Fairy in one fell swoop. "Gracie, he's selling. I talked to him a few days ago, and that's his plan. It was *always* his plan."

I shake my head. "No, that's not right. Last night he said—" I stop, panic tightening my throat. "He promised—"

"What did he promise, exactly?" Henry asks, but his tone isn't vindictive. It's tired.

The answer bounces around inside me like an echo in an empty room. *Nothing. Nothing. Nothing.*

"Listen," he says gently. "I do think he cares about you. But there is nothing—*nothing*—he cares about more than getting rid of Larkwood." His gaze is sympathetic. "I don't want to say that he'd make big, empty declarations to achieve his ends, but if he were backed into a corner and desperate . . . I don't know. He *really* needs your cottage, Gracie."

I take a step back from him. "No," I say, like that simple word could banish every poisonous possibility Henry has forced me to consider. "No, he wouldn't do that. That would be . . . no," I stammer, unwilling to consider it.

When we made our bargain, he agreed to keep an open mind. He went on every errand I asked him to and *told* me that meeting Larkwood's vendors had opened his eyes. But more than that, I've seen him undergo a change of heart—not just about me but about love itself.

I may have misjudged him at first, but now I *know* Jude. He's shown up for me in ways that I thought only Sofia and her family ever would. He helped me find the confidence to stand up to my family. He dedicates a large portion of his life to helping people out of terrible circumstances. He's a *good* man, and nothing Henry could say is going to shake—

"I know it's hard to hear, and honestly, I blame myself for suggesting it in the first place," Henry goes on, absently massaging his opposite shoulder.

"Suggest what, exactly?" I say, my voice pulled tight enough to snap.

Henry lifts his eyes to mine in a slow, guilty rise. “It was just a stupid joke. I had no idea he’d seriously consider it. But I guess I underestimated the lengths he’ll go to get rid of this place.”

I don’t *think* steam has started shooting from my ears, but Henry clearly picks up on my nonverbal request for him to spit out whatever he’s thinking. He sighs, dropping his hand back to the counter. “It was the day I told him Agatha left you the cottage. He was spiraling over getting you to sell it to him, and I . . .” He shrugs uncomfortably. “I suggested he just seduce you for it.”

It’s like the words have been printed on the bottom of a falling anvil. I comprehend them, but when they really hit me, all the air is evacuated from my lungs. I don’t have a moment to catch my breath before Henry plows on.

“At first, he just rolled his eyes and told me that wouldn’t work because you hated him. I didn’t think anything of it again until I’d heard you’d gone out for drinks and sung freaking karaoke with him.” He shakes his head incredulously. “I thought to myself, if *anyone* could pull off that one-eighty, it would be Jude.”

My heart is limping quickly in my chest, desperate to get away from the onslaught of mounting evidence that everything I thought I knew about Jude was a lie. I’m trying not to cry—I don’t want to shed a single tear until he either fesses up to gross emotional manipulation or presents me with irrefutable counterevidence. But even if he does, it wouldn’t completely heal the grief of finally knowing I’m losing Larkwood, even after all my efforts to change his mind.

“I have to go,” I say, turning away from Henry.

“Gracie—”

“Please,” I say, stopping for a moment and closing my eyes. “I need to talk with Jude, and then I need some space.”

“But your deed to the cottage—I was going to drop it off this week,” he says.

I swallow, resisting the burning pressure building behind my eyes. “Don’t bother. Jude can have it.”

38

JUDE

The moment the cottage door opens, I look up, eager as a dog left alone too long. I've been holding the note Gracie left me, anticipating her return, but immediately, I can tell something's off. It's the troubled downturn of her mouth before she realizes I can see her. The inward curve of her shoulders, like she's trying to negotiate between curling into a ball and remaining standing. When she finally spots me, standing in her living room wearing nothing but yesterday's boxer briefs, she startles.

"Jude—"

"What's wrong?" I ask, voice rusted from sleep. "Is Sofia okay? Your family?" I ask, casting around for something that might cause her to look this pale and distraught.

She looks down at her feet as she toes off her sneakers. "They're fine."

Her voice is clipped, and those two words are all I need to know that, somehow, I've fucked up. Somehow, despite all my caution and premeditated plans, I've hurt her. *But when?* She's wearing my shirt, which means something must have happened after she left the cottage.

When she finally looks up, her eyes are wary, and the realization hits me like a brick to the jaw—she's scared of me. Whatever's happened has put her on her guard, and I suddenly feel far too large and far too naked for this situation.

"Do you want me to leave?" I blurt out. "You don't need to explain. I'll go right now if you need me to. We can talk when you're ready."

Confusion and hurt spasm across her face, almost like the simple courtesy I've offered suddenly doesn't match up with what she's expecting from me. She crosses her arms over her middle. "No. We need to talk. But maybe—"

Her eyes jerk briefly down toward my mostly naked body.

"Of course. Do you want to change first?" I ask, eyeing my button-up covered in her lipstick.

She quickly looks down like she forgot what she was wearing and then nods once before walking to her bedroom. When the door closes, it may as well be a giant boulder rolling into place. The message is clear: *I don't trust you anymore.*

Trying not to panic, I close my eyes, willing all the years of therapy to penetrate the seething swirl of *what-ifs* trying to suck me under.

I do the breathing exercises. I remind myself of what I can and can't control instead of desperately grasping for a way to fix a situation I'm not yet fully aware of. By the time Gracie's door opens again, I feel slightly less like my head's on fire. When she holds out my shirt and the rest of my crumpled tux, I take it with numb fingers and quickly pull on my clothes while she averts her eyes.

"I'm decent," I say as I finish buttoning my shirt.

She turns back to me, and the leaden disappointment in her eyes stops my fidgeting, my breathing, and possibly all organ function. "You're getting rid of Larkwood," she finally says.

For a moment, my mind goes blank. But then, like a television switching from static fuzz to a high-definition channel, I see every single one of my missteps leading to this cliff edge. Every time I could have been more honest with her. *Fuck.*

"Yes," I whisper, too bewildered to even ask how she found out. "I was going to tell you last night, but then—" I stop. I don't need to give her a recap of how out of my mind with love and lust I was.

Her mouth tightens. "Last night, you said that anything you had to give was mine. And while I never expected you to keep it for my sake, I *was* stupid enough to think that you'd changed your mind." She shakes her head. "I thought you were beginning to care about my friends more than your own greed, or whatever reason you have for doing this. I even thought something had shifted in your opinions about Agatha. That you were finally coming to respect what she wanted because love didn't seem *quite* so ridiculous to you anymore. But I guess I should have read the fine print."

At her accusations, even my unbuttoned collar begins to feel suffocating.

"Of course I feel like shit for cutting all the vendors off. For cutting *you* off," I say quickly. "You showed me exactly what was at stake by closing Larkwood's doors, and if I'm being honest, you did make me question what Nana wanted. But you have to believe me when I say that she knew I'd be desperate to get rid of it. She made her peace with that when she left it to me, but I *still* weighed every option like I said I would," I tell her, as frustration, guilt, and defensiveness claw for dominance just below my sternum.

"You have no idea how many times I've considered keeping it—and not for any noble reason, either. I've spent so many nights thinking about throwing away this opportunity for the estate *just* to make you happy."

My breathing is unsteady, heart racing. Obviously, I can't tell her that I also offered it to my mom in a rash, misguided gambit, but it doesn't matter. Gracie's staring at me like she sees every one of my careful omissions like they're bullet holes in my story.

"It was never just about my happiness, Jude! Agatha—"

I shake my head, impatience flaring. "This was never just about my grandmother or the vendors," I cut in. "Deep down, we both know the real reason you've been trying so hard to save Larkwood, Gracie."

Her lower lip trembles, but her eyes hold steady. "Then go ahead. Say it."

"You're *afraid*. Too scared of getting hurt again to try living in the real world. But staying cooped up in this cottage for the rest of your life isn't going to protect you from anything. Not from failure, not from heartbreak, not from grief. You're clinging to the delusion that staying here isn't the worst possible thing for you, when what you *should* be doing is moving on with your life."

"And what makes you qualified to know what's best for me?" she snaps. "Is this just another part of your caretaking thing, or are you *really* that self-absorbed?"

Weaponizing my kink against me is a low blow, and from the flash of regret in her eyes, she knows it. But she also isn't wrong. Maybe it is self-absorption, but after repeatedly weighing all the options, I *know* my decision is for the best. Even if I'll never be able to explain it to her.

"I'm sorry." The words slip from me, inadequate but honest. "You may not agree with my decision, but I've settled on it. Larkwood will no longer be a wedding venue, but I promise to do everything in my power to cushion the blow when you sell me the cottage. I want you to be okay—more than okay. I've *never* wanted to hurt you."

She lets out a hollow laugh. "No? Not even when you were discussing seducing me to get what you wanted? Maybe I should congratulate you on such a job well done."

Incredulity draws my arms across my chest. "What the hell are you talking about? I would never—" But I stop as understanding clicks into place.

"You spoke with Henry," I say. My eyes close. Henry's willingness to throw me under the bus hurts, but I can't muster any anger. The truth is, I deserve this. I deserve it for thinking I had any right to love and friendship when all I can safely offer back is a watered-down version designed for hurting people.

"Yes, I spoke with him," she says, her dark eyes sparkling with unshed tears. "He was surprised you had the nerve to follow through with his suggestion, but I guess he knows better than I do how desperate you were."

"Seducing you to get your cottage was *never* my plan. I tried staying away from you, Gracie. You *know* I tried," I say, wide-eyed and anguished. "But in the end, you came to *me*, and I'm sorry I wasn't strong enough to say no. I'm sorry the way I want you grinds all my common sense and decency to a pulp. No one knows better than me that I don't deserve you—that you don't deserve to be with someone who shouldn't be with *anyone*. But for me, knowing you *is* loving you, Gracie."

My heart is beating like I've just swum a hundred meters with a refrigerator strapped to my back. Her glossy eyes spill over, and it takes everything in me not to close the space between us.

"I want to believe you," she whispers. "When I'm with you, I feel how much you care. How much love you want to give me. But how am I supposed to trust you when you won't confide in me? When even your best friend hardly knows you beneath all the secrets you keep? Am I just supposed to accept that you'll never let me in while I give you everything?" She shakes her head. "Love can't stand on half a foundation, Jude."

Eyes and nose burning as tears force their way past my control, I can only nod. She's only saying what I've known to be true all along. She deserves the full truth, and I can't give it to her. Not without betraying a confidence I've protected my whole life.

"You're right," I croak. "I'm sorry I ever let it go this far. You were right about my greed. My selfishness." The word slices out of me, sharp and bitter as a lemon rind. "I let myself have you, knowing it would hurt you, and everyone else I care about."

I wipe impatiently at my eyes, but it only brings her devastated expression into clearer focus. I take a strangled breath, trying to pull myself together. To say goodbye. "I'll hire an intermediary to handle the cottage sale. You won't need to communicate with me at all. I hope . . ." I swallow hard. "I hope you find someone worthy of loving you, Gracie."

She doesn't stop me as I walk to her front door. Doesn't say my name as I shove my feet into my untied shoes. Says nothing at all as I pull open her door and leave. And it's better this way.

Because I don't deserve a single word.

39

GRACIE

There's nothing that says "rock bottom" quite like moving into your mom's basement. In the last few days since I threw some essentials into a duffel bag and left the cottage, I've grown slightly more accustomed to my new life as a squatter. To her credit, my mom didn't bat a lash when I showed up and asked to stay, not even after how our last conversation went. Maybe it was the fog of shame and despair rolling off me or the tear tracks on my face, but she wordlessly took my bag, sat me down in the kitchen, and promptly made me a grilled cheese sandwich with a glass of coffee milk. I didn't realize how emotional I could get over my childhood comfort foods, but the simple kindness of it felt like a cushion to break my fall.

And after what happened between me and Jude, a soft place to land was exactly what I needed.

I know I could have called Sofia. Sharing a bed with her definitely would have been more comfortable than the rusted torture rack masquerading as a pullout couch that I'm currently sleeping on. But after our fight, coming to her with *another* life crisis didn't feel right. She'll always be my person to confide in, but right now, she's the one who needs my support.

On a more shameful level, I can admit that I'm not quite ready to face up to the fact that she's been right all along. Right about what a coward I've been, and right about the futility of changing Jude's mind about Larkwood.

At the mere thought of him, the fist-size knot of pain I used to call a heart clenches tight. With effort, I cram the hurt down, just like I have every other time it's tried to surface since watching him walk out of my cottage. *Can't you give me a minute to worry about my best friend, please?* I think at it viciously.

Compartmentalization complete, I sigh. If Sofia's impending *I-Told-You-So* wasn't enough to make me want to crawl into a body-size bag of potato chips and eat myself into a shame coma, I also know what she would suggest I do with my career now, especially since my financial circumstances have changed.

Yesterday, I received an email from Jude's real estate agent with a cash offer for the cottage that made me refresh the page just to be sure it had loaded correctly. The sum would not only clear my debt but also provide a decent nest egg for savings. *Or* (extremely) hypothetically, let me invest in a new business venture.

Either way, it was seeing that number in black and white that finally allowed me to grasp what Jude and Sofia have been trying to show me all along: taking his offer from the start would have been the smarter move. But even after failing to save Larkwood, I still can't bring myself to regret fighting for my friends' jobs, or Agatha's legacy. It was the right thing to do, even if it cost me more than I ever expected. Now that it's all over, I just need to figure out what I'm going to do to escape the fate of becoming a permanent basement dweller.

Cheek in my palm at the kitchen table, I halfheartedly click on a job posting titled "Assistant Banquet Manager" at a discount hotel chain. It's one of many similar search results on the job site I've been scouring for event planner listings. It pays next to nothing but comes with benefits, which is something I've never had before. I mentally weigh this against "Night shift event cleanup," which is listed as one of the job's "key responsibilities." Was there ever a clearer euphemism for puke patrol?

And just like that, I'm thinking of Jude at the wedding, valiantly marching off to manage the toddler vomit situation for me. Maybe some women imagine their heroes on galloping white steeds or walking onto front lawns with boom boxes. But for me, there might be nothing more romantic than seeing a man sling a bag of cleaning spray and stain-removal wipes over his shoulder. I'm replaying the moment in slow motion, embellishing it with a nonexistent indoor breeze that ruffles his dark hair when I catch myself.

Dammit. Over the last few days, my mind keeps producing these memories like it hasn't gotten the memo: fantasizing about Jude isn't something we do anymore, and that *includes* fantasies of pouring spoiled milk on his perfectly vacuumed Mercedes floorboards and kidnapping Taco.

"How's the job hunt going?"

I look up as my mom breezes through the kitchen entryway, dropping her keys, purse, and lunchbox onto the counter. She's dressed in her signature tracksuit, her no-fuss short black hair damp from a shower.

I sit up from a slouch that could be classified as a wilt. "I learned that a few of the bigger grocery stores offer benefits *and* employee discounts on food. Could be worth applying for."

She nods, starting to gather ingredients for her after-school protein shake. "Not a bad option. Nothing in events, though?"

I shrug. "A few hotel positions. But they all want a hospitality degree."

She makes a *pshh* sound, scooping peanut butter into her single-serving blender. "With all your experience at Larkwood? You'd be a shoo-in."

After years of showing little to no interest in what I do for a living, her newfound encouragement has been as surprising as it's been touching. "Thanks, Mom," I say quietly.

She throws me a quick, slightly forced smile as she continues to bustle around the kitchen. It's been like this ever since coming home. We've never had an easy time connecting, but after cutting off my party planning services, she's been making an effort to try. It seems obvious in hindsight, but by making myself unavailable in the ways she'd come to expect and rely on, all that's left is *me*. For as long as I can remember, that's never felt like enough—but with every tentative new question she asks and supportive smile she gives me, I'm starting to question those old insecurities.

"Loud noise," she warns, before switching on the blender.

The familiar wail fills the kitchen, and I turn my attention back to my screen. Staring at the Upload Résumé button for the assistant banquet manager position, I try to imagine the next year or two of my life in this job. Setting up armies of folding chairs for accounting seminars and cleaning up wedding after-parties isn't my dream job, but it also isn't something to stick my nose up at. It would offer a modest income and health insurance, and after the sale of the cottage and the elimination of my debt, that's all I really need.

The blender stops, and my mom comes over with two glasses. "Here, I made you some, too."

She sits down with me at the table, and I close my laptop as she slides a glass of thick, grayish-brown protein smoothie toward me.

"Thanks," I say, even though the drink has the same visual appeal as liquified cardboard. I take a small sip to be polite and am surprised to taste bananas, peanut butter, and chocolate.

"Good?" she asks.

I raise an eyebrow and take another sip. "Never judge a protein shake by its color, I guess."

"The P.E. teacher's golden rule," she says, before giving me another hesitant smile. "I'm sorry the job market's so grim. I've been hearing about it everywhere."

"I'm sure something will turn up," I say, with 0 percent confidence.

Her hands wrap around her glass, and she glances up at me. I still can't splice this nervous version of her with the confident, outspoken woman she is with my stepsisters and stepdad, but I resist trying to fill the silence. After a second, she says, "Have you thought about reopening your business again instead? The one with the dresses?"

It's the last question I expect from her, not least of all because her opinion on my chosen education and career path over the years has been definitive: "Too expensive, too impractical."

"Um, I hadn't really considered it."

Liar, liar, rock-bottom sweatpants on fire.

"Well, you *should* consider it," my mom says, some of the confidence coming back into her voice. "I may have never understood it, but you've always had a creative spark, and talent like yours shouldn't go to waste." She snorts. "Can you imagine if Tom Brady had quit football just because he got drafted as a second-string? He never would've discovered he was the GOAT!" She looks at me with a level of sincerity I've only ever seen from her when she's wearing a giant foam finger. "For all we know, you could be the GOAT of dresses, Gracie."

I stare at her, gobsmacked. My shock is the only reason I have the nerve to say, "Mom, the last time my bridal design business came up, you and Josie cracked up when Brianna called it my 'real job allergy.'"

Her features pinch together. "Did I?"

"Yes. You also laughed at graduation when Josie congratulated me on my degree in 'Glitter and Glue.'"

She runs a hand through her still-damp hair, making it stick up in spikes. "Can't say I'm very proud of how things have been between us," she says, looking down into her smoothie. "I'm sorry for laughing."

I swallow down some smoothie, hoping it'll cool me off. "Thank you."

She shakes her head, then laughs emptily. "You know, sometimes I used to think there was an accidental baby switch when you were born. That somehow, I'd gotten the child of some brilliant, famous artist I had no business raising." She lifts her eyes to mine. "Your ability to create beauty out of scraps and thread and anything else you touched should have been a joy for me to watch, but instead . . ." She presses her lips together hard. "It just made me feel out of my depth. Like I'd never be able to give you what you needed."

She raises her brows and exhales. "And then, of course, Joel, Bri, and Josie came into my life, and I could understand them. They were just like me. They made it a little too easy to tell myself that you weren't interested in us anyway. That you were happier being left alone to do your own thing." She looks down at her hands as years of neglect get pulled to the surface like a splinter. "I'm sorry, Gracie. I was wrong."

For long moments, I don't know how to respond. My first instinct is to brush it off and tell her it's okay, but it's *not* okay. It was never okay. I spent my whole life internalizing her dismissiveness, believing it was the result of my own deficiencies. If I'd never met Sofia, her family, or Jude, I might never have seen any shortcomings besides my own.

But because I did meet them, I know it's well within my rights not to accept her apology. I could tell her it's too late for any kind of reconciliation. And maybe it is. But there's something to be said for a genuine apology, no matter how late-coming or insufficient it is. An apology can be a bridge to a new place. Or, at the very least, a rickety rope swing.

"I think I really needed to hear that," I say eventually.

My mom's eyes are glistening when she says, "And I think I really needed to have my ass handed to me. The other weekend when you and your boyfriend came over and told me you weren't going to finish planning the party, you could have knocked me over with a feather. It woke me up. *Shook* me up, really, and you better believe I've had a talk with your sisters about the way they treat you." She ducks her head, brows swooping downward. "The way *we've* treated you."

There's so much I could say. So much to respond to, but I can't seem to move beyond two syllables.

"He's not my boyfriend." The words slip past my numb lips.

My mom raises one jet-black eyebrow. "You sure about that, muffin? He seemed very . . . protective of you."

The nickname, which I haven't heard since before I could tie my own shoes, makes me look up at her. And maybe it's the way she's giving me her complete attention for once, or her apology, or that long-lost endearment, but all my resistance to truly registering what I've lost finally crumbles. Agatha. My job. My home. My faith in Happily Ever After. But somehow worse than any of that, *Jude*. The involuntary sound that breaks loose from me is half sob, half moan.

I drop my face into my hands, and a few seconds later, a pair of strong arms I haven't felt in years wrap around me. I sink into my mother more completely than I have since before her divorce, breathing in her Irish Spring–and-chalk scent. From the way her chest and shoulders start shaking against mine, I can tell she's wondering the same thing as me: How did we let ourselves get here? At what point did our fear of being honest with each other become a callus too thick to feel past?

"Tell me what happened," she says into my hair. "Tell me everything, and then I'll sic Brianna and Josie on him."

A watery laugh emerges from me, but it's short-lived. I wipe my eyes as I pull away from her. After the last two months of foolish desperation to keep Larkwood, I could close my eyes and point at any number of dumpster fires to start this story with. But at the center of my misery, there's a pulsing red dot. An ache that goes deeper than anything else.

In a choked whisper, I tell her the truth. "I still love him, Mom."

She reaches out and takes my hand. "And does he love you, too?"

I try blinking back the freefall of tears down my face. A few days ago, the answer would have come to me in a surge of joy and disbelief: *yes*. But now, nothing is certain.

"I-I don't know. He said he did, and I'd give anything to believe him, but there's just so much he keeps from me," I tell her, my stomach clenching as I circle closer to the crux of why I can't be with him.

"He's lied to you before?" she asks, her voice getting sharper.

"Not outright. Not as far as I know," I answer. "But he's never fully opened up, either. He shows me bits and pieces, but when it comes down to really knowing him, he always has his guard up."

I don't mention my lingering anger over the fact that he's going through with a sale that will be incredibly profitable for him, at the expense of Agatha's legacy. It's just too overwhelming to explain, so instead, I say, "In some ways, he's the most selfless person I've ever met. He treats all the damaged parts of me like they're just as precious as the polished pieces. But because there's so much he *doesn't* share, I have no explanation for why some of his decisions seem so selfish."

I rub my forehead as a headache begins to throb above my eyes. "I can't be with someone who doesn't trust me with their own rougher edges. If I'm going to give my whole heart to someone, I can't settle for only half of his in return."

My mom nods. "I know it's hard to let go of a love that isn't good for you, sweetheart. Doing the right thing is hardly ever easy, and you've been doing a lot of that lately." She squeezes my hand. "But if Jude is as selfless as you say he is, and these decisions he's making have an explanation he's been too afraid to share, then he'll *find* a way to open up to you."

I rest my forehead in my hand. "I don't know, Mom. He doesn't even open up to his best friend, and they've known each other half their lives."

"We'll just have to see, I guess. The ball's in Jude's court," she says, letting go of me and lightly slapping her hands onto her knees. "The big question is, what's going to give *you* the comeback you need?"

"Am I being coached right now?"

"Damn right. About time you had a little help from me." She gives me a sudden, quizzical look. "Speaking of help, what does Sofia have to say about all this?"

I take a sip of my smoothie, delaying my answer. "I, uh, haven't talked to her about it yet."

My mom's eyes widen. "But you two are inseparable. Did something happen?"

I want to brush off her question with a breezy *No, of course not!* But I've already told her everything else—why not this, too?

"Things are better . . . but we're recovering from a rough patch," I say. As succinctly as I can, I tell her about Sofia's parents splitting up, the disillusionment I've been wrestling with ever since, and my fear of reopening Grace & Veil, despite her encouragement.

"I just haven't been able to bring myself to tell her what happened," I admit. "She's going through something *so* hard right now, and I don't want to add to her plate again while she's the one who needs support."

My mom takes a big swig of her smoothie, nearly finishing it. "Then don't add to it," she says simply, setting her glass down. "You can still tell her what happened without being needy. Just handle your shit so she doesn't have to. You're an event planner, aren't you? Make a five-year plan for yourself and make sure it brings you *joy*. She's your best friend. Seeing you happy and fulfilled—or at least on your way there—will go a long way in calming the waters."

I nod, amazed by my mom's unexpected wisdom and grasp on to the idea of a five-year plan like a life raft. "I can do that," I say, already imagining the color-coded spreadsheets I'll make. Unsurprisingly, there's no sign of the assistant banquet manager position in my fantasy, but there *are* fresh bolts of fabric and dusted-off lists of manufacturing contacts.

My mom smiles at me like she can see the wheels turning in my mind. "See? That's not too hard. But I am sorry about her parents, Gracie." Her smile becomes pained and self-conscious. "I know you're close with them."

My racing mind sobers at once as I realize it's been over a week since I checked in with her about her family. "I need to call her."

She nods. "Yes, you do. Check on her, but also make sure you confide in her. She would want you to."

I swallow hard. "I will. Thanks, Mom."

Her eyes are sparkly with unshed moisture. "Anytime. Just do me a favor."

"What's that?"

"Get back in the game, Gracie. Find a studio space and stop pretending that sewing isn't the one thing that's always made you happiest. No one likes a chickenshit."

I smile with tears in my eyes and lift my smoothie glass. "To not being a chickenshit."

My mom clinks her glass to mine. "That's my girl."

And as rickety as it is, the rope swing holds.

40

JUDE

Hi Jude,

Congratulations—the owner just accepted your offer on the cottage. Time to pop the champagne! You mentioned hiring a proxy to be present at the closing in your stead. Send me their contact information, and I'll get the ball rolling. Thanks!

Swiping the email away from my real estate agent, I wait for the relief to hit. *She's going to be okay*. But somehow, even the knowledge that I've been able to give Gracie a financial cushion barely makes a blip against the hollow roar of loss that's been drowning everything else out since we parted ways. Money won't buy her forgiveness, it won't give her the truth she asked for, and it definitely won't make me more qualified to be in a relationship than a parasitic fungus.

I exhale, shoving down my self-loathing, which I'll flop around in later. The only thing to be said for the last few days is that they've been punishingly busy. As it turns out, discreetly getting rid of a historic estate is fucking complicated. I've even had to step back from my pro bono work just to attend all the necessary meetings between the prospective owner's leadership team, the escrow company, financial advisers, my estate attorney, trustee manager, and a goddamn partridge in a pear tree.

But today, I'm at Larkwood because while I've somehow managed to go through the entire estate and label my grandmother's possessions into keep, auction, or donate categories, there's still one room I haven't touched.

I stop in front of the door, which has been closed ever since she passed. I had tentatively hoped that Gracie and I might be able to tackle this overwhelming task together. My rib cage contracts when I think of how it would have bonded us.

But that possibility is gone now. Not only did I break her heart, but I've also robbed her of a last goodbye. Stomach twisting, I open Nana's door, knowing I deserve whatever pain waits inside.

But when I cross the threshold, the familiar scent of Chanel No. 5 envelops me like a hug. Pieces of the room that lost their wonder through familiarity seem to glow anew. The signed Broadway poster for *Funny Girl* in its pride-of-place above the fireplace mantel. The carelessly flung dressing gown on the green fainting couch. The space is as warm and eclectic as Nana was, and despite the tears burning behind my eyes, I can't help feeling comforted.

As I scan the room, wondering where the hell to start, my eyes catch on a bright yellow piece of paper on the mantelpiece. Something about it is familiar, and as I cross the room, I see it's a card I made her as a child. On the front is an unfortunate drawing of a dolphin that looks almost indistinguishable from a penis, complete with a graphic spray of water from its misplaced blowhole. Below this, in toiled-over lettering, are the words:

Too Nana
Luv Jude
Happy Bichday

The surprised laughter that escapes me is almost painful after days of frowning. Of *course* this is the childhood relic she'd display. I pick it up, surprised to find that it's heavy. My heart kicks in my chest. Inside is an envelope paper-clipped to the back side of the card, labeled in Nana's perfect cursive: *Jude*. Stomach leaping, I quickly remove it.

Taking out the letter with trembling hands, I walk distractedly to the fainting couch and open it.

Dear Judy,

So you found your card. How long did it take you to work up the nerve to enter my haunted chambers? If I were a betting woman (and I am), I'd say it probably took long enough for you to be kicking yourself right now, wondering why you waited so long. But unfortunately, this bet isn't one I'll be cashing in on because if you're reading this, I'm already dead.

Sorry for the morbidity (actually, I'm not sorry—who doesn't love a juicy postmortem letter?). But I know you probably have some pressing questions, and as I'm running short on time in both the day-to-day and existential sense, I'll hop to it.

Question 1: "Nana, will you curse me with male pattern baldness for getting rid of Larkwood?"

How dare you ask such a thing. For one, have you seen your hair, boy? Doves would fall from the sky, and baby angels would weep at its loss. Secondly, no: I'm dead! If I played my cards right (and I'm certain I did), I'm butt naked in a heavenly hot tub with Cary Grant, Paul Newman, and Omar Sharif as you read this. Trust me when I say the fate of Larkwood is the last thing on my mind. But I can understand your concern.

Yes, I often and loudly proclaimed that turning Larkwood into a wedding venue was the best decision I ever made. Yes, seeing it play a starring role in so many new love stories brought me incredible happiness. But most importantly, it helped me achieve what I've always wanted for the estate: to be a place of hope and new beginnings after so much darkness.

And while I suspect we'll have very different ways of accomplishing that goal, I left Larkwood to you, Judy. You're the one who gets to decide what happens now, and because of who you are—the most caring and selfless man I have ever known—I know that whatever you do will be eye-wateringly moral and kind.

Question 2: "Then why the fuck did you leave Gracie the cottage, Nana?"

Oh, I can't wait to answer this one. As I prepare to shed this fabulous mortal coil, one of my only regrets is knowing I won't ever get to see the nuclear bomb detonate behind your eyes when you see Gracie Holland for the first time. I can imagine how it'll transpire, though. Naturally, you'll be at each other's throats when you discover she's my wedding coordinator and she finds out that you're planning on terminating her job. But because of the cottage, you'll be at a stalemate unless you can find a way to work it out. And therein lies my absolutely delicious reasoning for putting you in this pomme de discorde.

After three years of getting to know Gracie, I've come to the irrefutable conclusion that you each have something that the other desperately needs. After being badly burned in love, Gracie has retreated from the world and become stuck in her past. She needs someone as pragmatic as you to shake her loose and show her that not every person she shares her tender heart with will be careless with it. And you, my sweet, guarded grandson, need someone to fall head over heels for.

As someone who's known you since infancy, I can say with zero hesitation that despite the unromantic airs you put on, you have more love to give in your pinky finger than the rest of us combined. And while siphoning it off toward worthy causes is a noble endeavor, it has broken my heart to see you deny yourself the experience of receiving love in return. You are worthy of that kind of love, Jude—no matter what you tell yourself—and I do hope meeting Gracie will open you up to it.

Question 3: "Nana, why didn't you tell me you were dying?"

Oh, sweetheart. Something tells me you already know the answer to this one, but I'll spell it out for you anyway. It has been one of my life's greatest heartbreaks to watch you grow up bearing the burden of so much grief and worry over things beyond your control. No child should have to witness what you witnessed, just as I never should have had to see my daughter and grandchild shoulder so much pain.

More than anything, I wish your mother and I had found a way to close the rift between us, despite her choices. It's why I've also written her a letter, in the hope of telling her that a single moment hasn't passed since she was born that I haven't loved her with all my heart. You'll find it in my dressing room, beneath her old teddy bear. Please give them both to her.

And so. Knowing the kind of pain you have both endured, withholding my diagnosis was the least I could do to spare you from any further suffering. Let me assure you, Jude—there was nothing you could have done to extend my life or make me more comfortable. You have been the axis around which all my hope and love spins outward. By simply existing, you've already done more than you know.

And now, off to my nail appointment. Can you imagine me showing up to the Pearly Gates with chipped polish? Heaven forbid. Literally! But I'll leave you with this: It's a beautiful thing to protect the ones you love. But when protecting them means sacrificing your own well-being, it's time to stop. Your mother is a grown woman, Jude. She can handle more than you think, especially if it means seeing you find happiness. And with any luck, my meddling will help you do exactly that.

Kisses from the hot tub,
Nana

P.S. You'll find a letter for Gracie in my jewelry case. Give it to her. And if you've fallen just as hard as I suspect you have, you may want to consider giving her something else in the box, too.

When I finish reading, I let the letter drop onto the couch beside me, only to immediately pick it up again. It wasn't enough to read it once. Having my grandmother's words and wisdom fill my mind when I never thought I'd hear them again leaves me feeling glutted and hungry at the same time. I scan greedily back over the section where she explains the most elaborate, Machiavellian matchmaking scheme there ever was, and shake my head as a hoarse laugh escapes me.

Wiping my eyes, the unexpected joy of finding this message mingles with grief and, more than anything, the crushing urge to share these words with Gracie, along with her letter.

My eyes drop to words that got stuck in my chest as I read them. *It's a beautiful thing to protect the ones you love. But when protecting them means sacrificing your own well-being, it's time to stop.* Resistance automatically swells in me, ready to shoot down any attempt to prioritize myself over the secrets I've guarded for so long. I swallow down another choking lump in my throat. But it's not just my heart at stake this time—it's Gracie's, too.

Exhaling with difficulty, I stand, pulling my phone from my pocket. A plan crystallizes in my mind like it's been there all along, waiting for permission to be put into action. But if I want any chance of pulling it off and repairing the damage I've done, I'm going to need help.

Staring at Henry's name for just a moment, I tap on it to call.

"Jude, hey."

He sounds nervous, but my stomach relaxes at his willingness to pick up my call at all.

"Hey," I respond, hoping he can't tell I've barely stopped crying.

"You sound sick," he says.

I take a shaking breath. *Honesty*. "Nah. Just having a good old-fashioned emotional breakdown."

"Shit. Jude, listen," he says, in a miserable rush. "I know I fucked up. I don't have an excuse—I just saw Gracie in your shirt and that lipstick and—*God*. I was so jealous and pissed, but as soon as I cooled off, I couldn't believe what I said to her about you. I'm so fucking sorry."

I shake my head, even though he can't see me. "I'm not mad," I answer truthfully. "I appreciate the apology, but she was always going to find out that I'm not keeping Larkwood. I should have told her first."

"Yeah, but I didn't need to plant any evil fucking seeds in her mind, did I? I told her you were seducing her for the cottage!" He lets out an exhale like he's been dying to get this off his chest. "That wasn't just low, it was subterranean."

"I won't argue with that," I mutter.

"Exactly. So why the hell are you giving me the time of day?"

I look up at the luminous clouds painted on the ceiling, promising brighter days to come. "Because I need to tell you some things I should have shared years ago, and if you're willing, I need your help."

"Of course," he says, and then goes quiet, like he knows I need the space to open this door between us.

"You've never made me feel like I had to share the parts of my life I'd rather keep hidden," I begin. "You've always just accepted my boundaries without question, but I'm starting to understand how one-sided that must feel. Like I simply didn't trust you enough." I close my eyes. "But I do trust you, Hen. The only reason I've never shared those pieces of myself with you is that they weren't just mine to share.

"In my family, I've been given the kind of trust that has always outweighed my own wish to confide in you. I've even rationalized that I was doing you a favor by not burdening you with all my issues." I take a breath. "But I know it's not fair to shut you out either, which is why today, I'm going to get permission to share those things with you and Gracie."

I impatiently rub my blurring eyes. "You're two of the most important people in my life, and you deserve to be trusted. I'm starting to see that I deserve to tell you, too. But before I can, I need you to help me get Gracie back," I say, the words catching in my throat. "I love her, Hen. I can't lose her when I'm finally ready to tell her everything."

"Jesus, Judy," Henry says, his voice as choked as mine. "Just tell me what to do, and we'll ride at fucking dawn."

I close my stinging eyes as relief and gratitude radiate through me. "Can you rent a moving van and be here as early as you can tomorrow?"

"I'm on it. Are we talking a U-Haul or like a Mack Truck?"

A smile that's nearly painful breaks across my face. "A U-Haul's great. Thank you, Hen. For everything."

"Don't thank me till you've got your girl back."

I press my lips together, praying to Nana that it's not too late. "Okay. See you tomorrow."

We hang up, and without giving myself time for doubt or fear to sink in, I move on to phase two of my plan.

Swiping to my contacts, I call my mom.

41

GRACIE

Gracie: Hey, are you around for a visit this week? Miss you + I have a surprise.

Sofia: Get out of my head, Gracie, I was just about to text you! Can you come to KILN tomorrow at 3? You know I live for a good surprise. 😉

Gracie: I'll be there!

42

GRACIE

I'm no stranger to romance novels. Yes, I may love a zombie horror flick as much as the next girl, but when I'm really in the dumps, I gravitate toward stories with a guaranteed Happily Ever After. This week, I let myself get lost in the latest Margot Bradley rom-com, consuming every page like the hope and laughter they provided would inject helium directly into my heavy heart. I understand that Happily Ever After rarely works out in real life, and it certainly hasn't for me—*yet*. But over the last few dark days, I've realized HEAs don't belong exclusively to romantic love.

They can be found in the burgeoning trust between an estranged mother and daughter. Sometimes, they can only be achieved by *ending* a relationship. But they can also be found in the friendships that carry you through it all, even if you have to face the occasional *I Told You So*.

I take a deep breath as I hoist Randy under my arm and grip the bag of doughnuts with my other hand in front of KILN. There might not be room for me, but Sofia did say she'd be willing to cram me in a broom cupboard if I ever wanted to give Grace & Veil another shot. And over the last few days of finalizing the sale of my cottage and making an aggressively detailed five-year plan, I think I'm finally ready to try again.

I push open the door, and Sofia's waiting for me in the entryway with a smile.

"I brought doughnuts," I say by way of a greeting, holding up the bag.

Her jaw drops as her eyes catch on the large, bedazzled box beneath my other arm. "Screw the doughnuts, is that *Randy*?"

"Hey, these are Knead Doughnuts—if you can't appreciate them, I'll just have to eat them all by myself."

Her eyes slide reluctantly away from Randy to the grease-stained paper bag I'm holding up. "Okay, fine, bring them over here," she says, walking toward a bright yellow metal bench beneath the community bulletin board. "*With* Randy."

We sit down and I dig into the crinkly bag, handing her the cinnamon brioche doughnut I know she'd happily sell state secrets for.

"Ohmigahh," she says around the huge bite she takes, eyelids fluttering.

"So now that I've got you high on butter and sugar . . . how's everything with your mom? Is she still going to that pottery class she liked so much?"

Sofia smiles and gives me the update about her family, putting up with all of my questions until she finally says, "Okay, okay, now you, Gracie. We still haven't debriefed about the wedding! Don't think I didn't see Jude following you around like a lovesick puppy."

At her words, pain skips across my chest like it's wearing knives for heels, but I manage to hold it together as I fill her in on everything that's happened since the wedding.

She grabs my hand when I get to the part I can barely stand to think about, much less admit out loud. That it's over between Jude and me. "I'm so sorry, Gracie," she whispers.

I nod, squeezing her hand back. "I fell in love with him, Sof. But in the end, he couldn't share enough of himself to be in a relationship." I bite my lip, trying to blink away the tears rising in my eyes. "But even if it didn't work out, he helped me learn how to be braver. To start protecting my time so that I can show up for the people I love."

"Gracie—" Sofia says softly, but I shake my head at her placating tone.

"I know I have a habit of hiding from anything that hurts too deeply. I ran away from my whole life when things fell apart with Calvin. I gave up on my dreams when Grace & Veil stumbled. But I'm done making excuses, and I'm done being scared," I tell her.

Turning, I hoist Randy and place the glittery box between us. "If you have a broom cupboard available, we're ready to move in. I'm going to try again, and this time, I'm not going to take you or your support for granted."

At this point, Sofia's eyes are just as watery as mine. When she throws her arms around my neck, her half-eaten doughnut crumbling in my hair, I feel like we've been two misaligned gears finally locking into place.

"You'll *always* have a place here," she says in a choked voice.

"You forgive me for taking so long to listen to you, then?"

"Of course I forgive you. I knew you'd come to your senses eventually." She lets go of me, her brown eyes swimming. "Grace & Veil shall rise again; more pretty and powerful than ever it was before."

"I'll settle for profitable," I say with a laugh, wiping stray doughnut crumbs from my hair before sobering. "Thank you for always believing in me, Sof."

"Well, duh. And as it happens, I have a little surprise for you, too."

"Oh?"

She takes another huge bite of her doughnut and grabs the bag as she stands. "Follow me."

When we reach the door of the studio where the potluck was held, I give her a quizzical look. But she just opens the door with a smile, and at first, I can't fully process what I'm seeing. Instead of printmaking tools, the space is filled with beautifully familiar furniture and sewing equipment.

Everything has been arranged so thoughtfully, with ample workspace in the back and a small showroom and fitting area near the front windows. It feels like home, but somehow so much better. Wonder and disbelief expand in my chest, filling me to the point of bursting when I hear the other door to the space open.

"A little more to your left—*ow*! No, your other left, Judy! Are you *sure* you passed the bar?"

And just like that, my heart is a racehorse, flinging itself forward again and again against my chest. I watch Jude walk backward through the door, holding one end of my serger. He and Henry are both breathing heavily as they carry the heavy piece of equipment, but I'm pretty sure my lungs are working harder. Quickly, I turn to Sofia, who's grinning at me like my approaching cardiac arrest is her greatest triumph.

The guys finally get the table in place, and Jude turns to survey the studio, pushing back the hair that's fallen across his brow. When he sees me, he goes completely still.

Every cell in my body begins pushing forward, urging me toward him, but I resist, frozen in place. I want to cringe away from the pain of seeing him again. From his wide, amber eyes to his beautiful, nervous hands, every one of his features feels like a relentless thumb pressing into my bruised and tender heart. But I can't look away. I never could.

"Gracie," he says, taking me in with eyes just as starved as mine. After a moment, he slowly approaches. Yearning arches through me as he gets closer, unthinking and wild before logic catches up.

I spent years with a man who never gave me all of himself. Jude's brand of withholding might be different from Calvin's, but I refuse to be with someone who makes me beg for scraps of trust and honesty. Even if it means fighting upstream against all the love still flooding through me, I'm not taking any more steps backward.

"Welll, I think Henry and I are going to eat some doughnuts," Sofia announces. "Just text if you need me, Gracie," she says, giving me a significant look that says she *will* show up with armor and a sword if necessary.

I give her a shaky nod. "Okay."

Sofia gives me an encouraging smile before looking up at Henry, who I'm delighted to find is staring at her in a dazed, hit-in-the-head-with-a-mallet sort of way. When she gives him a shy smile and immediately averts her eyes, I'm *almost* distracted from my impending conversation with Jude. Almost.

But then they leave, and all that's left is him and the ache of holding back a river's worth of love and longing. "What are you doing here?" I manage, wishing the giant windows didn't turn his eyes into pools of sunlit honey, deep enough to drown in.

He takes a quick look around the studio, pushing his hair back. When his gaze lands on mine again, he says, "I thought it was obvious. I'm grand-gesturing you."

My brows pinch together. "But this was Sofia's plan," I say uncertainly. "This is *her* grand gesture to out–grand gesture *me*."

He shakes his head. "While she did provide some strategic assistance, I retain full proprietary rights to this grand gesture."

"But . . . how?" I say, feeling dazed. "This was a printmaker's studio."

At this, he looks a little embarrassed. "After Sofia mentioned how badly she wanted you to rent a studio space from her, I couldn't let go of the idea. I was still undecided about keeping Larkwood at that point, but I thought you might want a space for personal projects. Even if you just wanted to sew a giant quilt with the words JUDE SUCKS."

I can't quite stop my smile until I think of the softspoken printmaker I'd met at the potluck. "But the artist who was here before—you didn't threaten him with legal jargon to get the space did you?"

This pulls a smile from him. "No, I just got lucky. When I reached out to Sofia, she told me a studio was opening up, and this was it."

I close my eyes as the full impact of what he's done settles into me. "But Sofia never said a word."

"Uh, yeah," he says with a chagrined look. "That was harder to manage. But in the end, I convinced her that you'd know soon enough anyway and that it was, ah, more romantic as a surprise."

At one point in our relationship, I definitely would have asked if even *saying* the word *romantic* meant breaking the blood pact he'd surely made when becoming a divorce lawyer. But now, his efforts to make me feel cared for come as no surprise. In some respects, it is romantic. On the other hand . . .

"But, Jude," I say, slowly. "This wasn't your decision to make. This is *my* life. What if I hadn't wanted a studio?"

At this, he nods, brows furrowing. "You're absolutely right. Which is why I leased it for only a month. It's not up to me, Sofia, or anyone else whether you reopen your business, or ever sew again for that matter." He captures my gaze. "And if you give me the chance to explain some things, and you still don't want any of this," he says, and I know he isn't only talking about the space, "then I'll understand."

"Jude," I say, as the exhaustion and pain of the last week creeps into my voice. "No matter how generous or thoughtful this might be," I say, looking around my dream studio come to life, "I can't do this with you anymore. You sold Larkwood despite how many people depend on it. You sold Agatha's home and legacy. But somehow, what hurts most is that you can't even tell me why. I've shared *everything* with you, but you haven't given me any of that trust in return." I bite my lips together for a moment as tears well in my eyes. "I never needed a grand gesture. I just wanted to know you."

He closes his eyes for a moment. "And that's exactly what I want to give you. The whole truth, if you're willing to listen."

I'm not sure he really understands what I'm looking for, but I nod anyway, hope flickering like a damp matchstick in my chest.

He exhales. "First, I know you're upset about Larkwood's vendors. I have been, too. But there's an upcoming auction for all the artwork and antiques I've been sorting, and the proceeds will more than cover the income they'll be missing out on from this season. It'll bridge the gap and give them time to find new venues."

I stare at him, stunned. "Was this your plan all along?"

He shrugs. "It wasn't a sure thing until I'd gone through all the appraisal work, but I'd hoped it would work out this way."

I can't respond. Two solid months of stress and worry begin lifting from me like I've been wearing a lead suit. He goes on.

"As for not keeping Nana's legacy, I understand that not knowing why has been painful and frustrating. I can't tell you how badly I've wanted to explain everything, and today, I finally can. I'm going to tell you my plans for Larkwood, but first, I need you to understand that this information is still extremely sensitive. If it were to get out, it could cause safety issues for the people involved."

Surprise rocks me back, and nonsensically, my mind jumps to

Henry's working theory about alien probes. "You're not about to tell me you're involved in some kind of government UFO coverup, are you?"

The surprised smile on his face is brighter than all the light pouring in from the windows. "No," he says on a laugh. "That would be so much cooler than what it is." His smile fades. "Can you agree to keep what I tell you to yourself?"

"Yes, of course," I say without hesitation.

"Then the first thing you should know is that I'm not actually selling Larkwood—I'm donating it." As these words are released, his shoulders drop a full two inches.

"Donating it?" I repeat incredulously.

He nods. "You haven't heard of Pathways, have you?"

I shake my head slowly. "No, I don't think so."

He nods. "They're a local organization that provides safe houses for women leaving dangerous domestic situations. I do nearly all my pro bono work through them, and they've been looking to acquire a new safe house location by August. They're who I'm donating Larkwood to, but keeping the transfer as discreet as possible has been essential for their clients' future safety. No one can know what it's being used for, apart from the organization and the community we serve. As far as the public's concerned, it will be sold to another private owner."

The silence in the studio following this is profound. Slowly, my blood begins buzzing until there's a roaring in my ears like a thousand bees have taken up residence in my mind. My heart. I think of my friend Maya from Brooke's bachelorette party, whose gratitude toward Jude went far beyond the help he offered her that night. I remember the urgent pro bono case he'd been working on when I visited his apartment for the first time. His panic after I pried the truth about his tattoos from him and I edged too close to the truth. All this time, I've been so worried about what Agatha would think if she knew Larkwood was being sold, and what the vendors would do without the estate. But now I finally believe what Jude has been saying all along—this is more important.

Without meaning to, I step closer. The night I came closest to understanding why this cause is so close to his heart, he wasn't ready to tell me details. I don't want to pressure him, but if he's trusted me enough to reveal his plans at last, then he might be ready now.

"When you told me about your tattoos and pro bono work," I begin carefully, "you made it clear that it was personal."

At the opening I give him, his lashes drop in a wince of emotion. I'm holding my breath, prepared to be gently turned away again.

"It is personal for me," he finally says. When he forces himself to look at me, there's a quiet anxiety behind his eyes that makes me want to close every space between us. "I decided to donate Larkwood to Pathways because . . ."

He pauses, and his expression is open, scared, and determined all at the same time. "Because I grew up in the kind of situation that Pathways helps women and children out of."

"Jude—" I whisper, feeling the barely glued cracks of my heart split open. He shakes his head.

"You have to know that if it were simply a matter of being discreet about the donation, I would have told you. I've wanted to tell you everything from the first time you let me kiss you. Earlier than that, even." The regret in his gaze robs the oxygen from my lungs. "But it would have meant sharing my past and my current reality, too, and that's not my story alone."

"Your 'current reality'?" I ask as the back of my neck prickles.

"My mother is still in the cycle, Gracie. She never went to a safe house," he says quietly. "I continue to live in fear and worry over her safety, but she made her choice a long time ago."

A quiet breath racks his chest as a tear slips quickly down my face.

"I've spent my life doing everything I can to be in the best possible position to support her, but the awful truth is that most victims will never leave their abusers. It's never their fault, and it certainly isn't my mother's. If anything, her job just adds further challenges."

He swallows hard. "Because of her position in the public eye, and how the truth might risk all the advocacy work *she* does, she's always needed absolute privacy when it comes to our . . . family matters," he explains, as the V between his brows deepens. "I'm the only person she trusts with the truth, and because I know how important victim confidentiality is . . . because I love her, I've never felt free to share any of this with anyone. Even Henry."

Jude. If my heart could wail his name, it would. All this time, the pieces have been there—razor-edged mosaic shards I couldn't connect. Now that he's arranged them into the full picture, every moment I was frustrated by his lack of transparency comes back to snarl at me.

I think of how I quietly judged him for never confiding in Henry, but now, all I can imagine is how painful it must have been to keep these secrets for so long. Another tear runs down the side of my face. I told my mom that Jude was the most selfless man I'd ever met, but I had no idea. No idea at all.

"But that's not fair," I say, impatiently wiping my face. "Having to keep all of this to yourself without any kind of support—no one deserves to carry something like this alone!"

His face is drawn as he argues, "I'm not completely alone. I have a therapist who knows my situation, and his support has been . . . everything."

"But having to keep this from Henry," I say, breathless from the fractures that keep spreading like fault lines in my chest, "your mother couldn't agree to let you have *one* friend to confide in? After all this time?"

"She has every reason to be protective."

"Yes, of course, she does. I can't even fathom what she's been through. But *you* deserve protection, too," I say, my voice breaking. "Everything you do is in the service of others. Keeping your mom safe, donating Larkwood, all your pro bono work . . . the way you care for me," I say, my voice sliding higher as my throat tightens. "You deserve to be taken care of, too. More than anyone I know."

"Gracie," is all he's able to say as I move closer, drawn to him across the space and anything else that might separate us. When he lifts his hand to brush away my tears, his warm palm is better than any homecoming I can imagine.

"Does she know?" I ask. "That you planned on telling me?"

He nods mutely, lips parted as though he can't believe he's touching me again. I step closer, wishing I could shield him from all the pain he's ever known and silently carried.

"When you left me," he says, making my rib cage want to crumple, "I forced myself to accept that it was for the best. You were right to leave someone who couldn't be open with you. Who would always be in constant fear of sharing too much. But then, I found these."

He reaches around to his back pocket and pulls out two small envelopes. I immediately recognize the handwriting, and my mouth parts in a silent gasp. "Letters from Agatha?"

He nods. "One for each of us. Do you want to read them now?"

At this, my heart becomes a kite in my chest, freewheeling and wild. I let out a breathless, "Yes, of course!"

He doesn't make me wait. My hands are trembling when he hands them to me. I look up at him, fresh tears already welling. "I don't know which one to read first."

A corner of his mouth lifts. "Says the woman who once spent thirty minutes snooping in my sock drawer. Go ahead."

Letting out a choked laugh, I take out his letter, which is soft around the edges like it's already been read about fifty times. The truth is, I do want to save my letter for last—if only because it means holding on to her final, unknown words for a little longer.

Unfolding the paper, I begin to read and promptly start to cry. And laugh. And gasp. And cry some more. By the time I'm done reading, my chest feels like it's been asked to hold twice its capacity for love and grief.

"Jude—" I begin, hardly knowing how to express my desperate urge to become a living shield against anything that might try to hurt him. Or how to apologize for my own misjudgments and assumptions. Or how to digest the ludicrous fact that Agatha successfully set us up from beyond the grave.

But he shakes his head. "Read yours."

Nodding, I hand him back his letter before opening mine.

At the sight of my name in her elegant hand, I can't help my shaking exhale.

Dear Gracie,

If you're reading this, then I believe it's safe to assume you've been missing me for a little while now. Darling, I already miss you, too. But with my departure, one of my greatest comforts is knowing that you've finally met my outrageously handsome grandson, Jude. And if you agree, I believe a big, glittering I-Told-You-So is in order.

If he's let you read his letter (and I'm assuming he has because I did an excellent job raising him as a gentleman), then you already know about my romantic meddling. And while I'm not sorry in the slightest (I do love a side of drama with my champagne), I do sympathize with the growing pains you must have endured after meeting each other. I understand how dearly you've relied upon Larkwood to stay in your beloved comfort zone, and conversely, how deeply Jude has yearned to remove it from his life.

It was never going to be an easy needle to thread. But as I've said to you before, I have always believed that Larkwood was meant to be a place of hope and new beginnings—no matter if it stays a wedding venue or transforms into something new. Above all, I hope that it has become a means to a fresh start for both of you—together. Because (as you know) I'm nothing if not a romantic.

As someone who has known and loved you both, having to wait until the right time to introduce you has felt like holding two halves of the same heart in separate hands. And maybe I'm wildly mistaken. Maybe you both still despise each other—wouldn't that be a twist? But something tells me that if Jude is with you as you read this, he's staring at you with every ounce of the—frankly, alarming—amount of love he's capable of. And that you're giving it right back.

Which is the only reason I'm able to say goodbye to you now with a smile. There's no earthly way of expressing how dear you've become to me, but I'll rest easy knowing you and Jude have found each other. I only ask that you give him one last kiss for me and eventually name a grandchild after me—a middle name is fine. I'm only kidding, of course.

Love eternally,
Agatha
P.S. Or am I?

When I finish reading on a sound that's somewhere between a laugh and a sob, I lift my eyes to Jude's. And just as his grandmother uncannily predicted, he's staring at me like my tear-stained face is the light source for all his future happiness. His love swims in my bloodstream, as permanent and necessary as oxygen, and I know I'm incapable of reflecting anything less back to him.

"She knew," is what I finally whisper, knowing he'll understand.

He nods, his smile soft and a little tired. "Of course she knew I'd fall in love with you, Gracie. How couldn't I?"

There's a feeling in my chest like invisible hands are reaching toward him. I step closer. "She called us two halves of the same heart."

He closes his eyes for moment, swallowing hard. "We should probably get that checked out."

I smile through my tears, bringing my hands up to loop behind his neck. When he looks at me like he still can't believe I could want him after all the immeasurable good he's done—I try not to crumble under the weight of how long he's isolated himself.

"Is Agatha's letter why you talked to your mom about confiding in me?"

He lets out an exhale and nods. "In the end, it wasn't really a choice. Even though I swore I'd move on after you left, losing you for good felt"—his Adam's apple works heavily—"unbearable. Her letter gave me the final push I needed."

His hand moves to my jaw. "So I called my mom and told her that I love you," he says simply. "I told her that if you'll let me, I want to spend the rest of my life loving you, Gracie. And somehow, she listened. She gave me her permission to tell you everything." His eyes search mine. "But the only question is, will you let me? Will you let me love you the way you've always deserved, for as long as I possibly can?"

In a final splitting crack, my heart seems to burst in my chest, and I realize all the time I thought it was breaking, it was just expanding. Failing to contain all of this love. It rushes through me until a single word breaks loose.

"*Yes*," I say through my tears. "I love you, too," I try to tell him, but he's already kissing me, and I feel it—the same dam breaking in his chest, concrete walls crumbling and washing away until we're in the torrent of it together. Suspended and weightless in this sweeping love that we no longer need to hold ourselves back from.

When he pulls back slightly, his smile is too beautiful to smother with another kiss. "So that's a yes," he says breathlessly.

"Yes," I say, my smile so wide it hurts.

He caresses the side of my face. "And you realize you technically just agreed to a lifetime arrangement."

A wild thrill leaps through me. "I didn't realize I'd signed any kind of contract."

"That could be arranged," he says huskily, gaze darkening.

I lightly smack his chest with a nervous laugh. "You can't just say stuff like that to a wedding planner! We take lifelong romantic contracts very seriously."

His lips press to mine, featherlight and adoring, before moving to my jaw, making me shiver. "Who said I wasn't serious? You of all people should know how deeply I've always respected the institution of marriage."

My laugh is breathless as I cling to his broad shoulders, never wanting this moment to end. I shake my head with wonder. "Jude Larkwood, talking marriage. I never thought I'd see the day."

He rests his forehead on mine. "Gracie Holland, there is no ceremony I wouldn't go through, no contract I wouldn't sign, and no vow I wouldn't make to call you mine."

My eyes flutter shut as his words sink into me. “Then I guess I’m yours,” I whisper.

His lips find mine, and this time, it’s the turning of a page. The release of something old. The start of something new. The beginning of forever.

Epilogue

GRACIE

One Year Later

"I really don't understand why I have to—ow!"

"Sorry!"

"—Wear face paint. I'm already in costume."

"You're literally in the same suit you wore to court today," I point out to Jude, who is looking supremely grumpy about this turn of events.

When I first told him I wanted to host a Halloween costume party at my studio for the KILN community, he seemed enthusiastic. ("And exactly *how* little is your costume going to be?") Then when I informed him that we would be going as Emily and Victor from *Corpse Bride*—our favorite comfort movie—he seemed agreeable enough. ("Convenient. I'll just go as myself.") But tonight, when I sat him down in my studio and broke out my makeup kit, he was less than thrilled. ("Isn't my pallor already ghostly enough?") It took some strategic lash-batting and a perfectly timed "Please," but he never really stood a chance.

"I added a vest and changed my tie," he argues, like his perfectly tailored three-piece suit actually counts as a Halloween costume. "You know I never wear a full Windsor knot."

"How daring of you," I say with a laugh, softly blending dark shadow around his eyes. It gives him a haunted look that somehow looks absurdly attractive on him.

"My skin feels like it's vacuum-sealing my skull," he says as I touch up the dark hollows I've blended beneath his cheekbones. "Is that normal?"

I roll my eyes with a smile and put down my makeup brush. "There. Done, you big baby."

I get up to find a mirror, and the ethereal white dress I made for the occasion swirls around my legs in a rustle of feather-light chiffon and tattered lace. Jude's darkened eyes follow me across the room like he can't tear them off me, and my stomach gives a little skip beneath the corseted bodice. I'd be lying if I said that wearing a wedding dress in front of him—even just a ghoulish costume version of one—doesn't make my heart race a little. And maybe it's fast to be thinking along those lines. But the truth is, starting our lives together has been easier than breathing.

What started as "temporarily crashing" at his place turned into "why move out if we spend every free moment together anyway?" It made things simple, and lately, simple has been hard to come by. Especially after one of my bridal wear designs unexpectedly went viral six months ago, and life became too busy to even think about moving—and too full of reasons to stay.

There are still hard days. He's gotten two new tattoos since I moved in, and sometimes I'm terrified that my fledgling business will fail all over again. But neither of us ever feels alone now. His mother and I have grown close, and my mom and I go on monthly runs, exchanging smoothie recipes like our own protein-rich version of a love language. Sofia and Henry are also thriving in their relationship (perhaps a little *too* well, if I'm going by our extremely competitive couples' pickleball record), along with Mrs. Morales and her new boyfriend.

As someone who has spent nearly her entire life craving a supportive family, it's the kind of abundance I've always dreamed of. But at the heart of all my joy is Jude. Through every up and down, his care for me is as constant and unwavering as mine is for him. Which is why—even though I may no longer be in the business of planning weddings—there's one more I'm secretly *aching* to organize.

"Here," I say, returning to where he's leaning against one of my pumpkin-strewn worktables, looking like the X-rated fanfic version of Victor in his quote-unquote "costume."

He takes the hand mirror and holds it up to inspect his handsome face, contoured in gray scale. "I look—"

"Ready to be the rake of the underworld?"

He puts the mirror down and lets his gaze travel over my own carefully painted features. After watching a few tutorials online and doing a couple of practice runs that involved yelling at some false lashes, I feel beautiful in my dramatic makeup and light blue complexion.

His eyes lift from my bubblegum pink lipstick to meet my gaze, hungry in a way I haven't seen before. "I look ready to propose to my beautiful corpse bride."

My heart goes still at what could simply be a reference to the central plot point of the movie, or something else entirely.

"Technically, Victor only proposes accidentally," I say, my voice suddenly breathless in a way that suggests I've gone on a quick sprint around the earth.

"But we all know it was the best move he ever made," Jude says, stepping closer to me.

"I think he might disagree, considering he marries someone else in the end," I point out.

"Well, it's a good thing that, unlike Victor, I'm not a completely useless imbecile."

I laugh, but it lodges in my throat like a baseball when Jude slowly drops to one knee. I watch, dumbstruck, as he pulls out a black velvet box from his jacket pocket.

"How does the vow from the movie go again?" he muses. But I can't answer. I'm frozen in place, even as my heart begins to gallop in every one of my pulse points. Mouth dry, I watch as he lifts the box. "'With this hand, I will lift your sorrows. Your cup will never be empty, for I will be your wine.'"

My heart is a wild creature in my chest as he opens the box, and I see Agatha's most spectacular diamond ring flash like a living flame as it's exposed to the light.

"'With this candle,'" he continues, "'I will light your way in darkness. With this ring, I ask you to be mine.'"

"Jude—" I whisper, still half-convinced this is some kind of cosplay fantasy and not real life.

But he finds my gaze, removing all doubt from my mind when he says, "Gracie Elizabeth Holland," with more tenderness than my name has ever been uttered with.

"From the first moment I saw you caught in that horrible plant, I knew I would be fighting a losing battle against falling hopelessly in love with you. Every day since has made me wonder how I ever lived without you. Please—will you make me the happiest man alive by being my wife?"

My eyes blur as I nod and say the only thing I *can* say in response to this. "Of yes. I mean—of course. *Yes*," I stammer, completely overwhelmed. The grin that stretches across his beautiful face is miles wide as he slips the stunning ring onto my finger.

"The perfect headline for our engagement announcement," he says, standing up and pulling me to him. "She said 'Of yes!'"

I laugh, unable to be embarrassed when he's staring at me like this—eyes alight like I really have made him the happiest man who ever lived.

"I could always take it back, you know," I threaten emptily, unable to believe that I found him. *My person*.

"On what grounds?" he asks in mock outrage.

"On the grounds of needing my future husband to up his pickleball game. Henry and Sofia are *killing* us."

At the word *husband*, his hands on my waist flex possessively. "Noted, but I'm afraid you'd be in breach of clause 87b of No-Take-Backsees," he tells me in a voice more heated than his joke warrants.

"Well, we wouldn't want that," I say softly as he tips me back.

"No, we wouldn't."

When he kisses me, it feels better than any promise. It's a proposal—to share a future more beautiful than I ever could have planned.

ACKNOWLEDGMENTS

When I first started working on *Not That Kind of Proposal*, I'd already heard the rumor that an author's sophomore novel is the hardest one they'll ever write. Naively, I thought, *pshh*. I'd written my first novel while battling breast cancer, and what could be harder than that? (See acknowledgments from my first, much-easier-to-write novel, *Any Trope but You.*) As it turns out, the whispers were right. Without the support of so many incredible people, this story would definitely still be languishing in my drafts folder. So, without further ado:

To my team at Atria, thank you for your unwavering support and for being unreasonably good at your jobs. To my publicist, Camila Araujo, thank you for working tirelessly to get the word out about my stories in such a crowded space, and for being a professional magic maker. To my marketing manager, Zakiya Jamal (another rom-com author you should *definitely* be reading), thank you for being incredibly kind on top of being intimidatingly talented. Thank you to my wonderful copyeditor, Shelly Perron, for having such an eagle eye. And of course, an extra (extra!) special thanks to my editor, Elizabeth Hitti Musicant, without whom this book simply wouldn't exist. I knew when we worked together on *ATBY* that I'd found someone truly gifted to partner with, but collaborating on *NTKOP* with you somehow inspired newfound levels of admiration. Thank you for lending your sensitivity and extraordinary talents to this very personal book, all while planning your own wedding (which I know Gracie would have been in awe of)!

An enormous thanks to my sensitivity reader, Dr. Kelly O'Connor, for reading this novel with your expert perspective and clinical background in trauma, healing, and resilience in violence-exposed populations. It was an honor to have your time and wisdom! And to Emilia Rhodes, thank you so much for helping me cut words when I desperately needed an extra pair of scissors.

To Jessica Mileo, my incredible agent whom I brag incessantly about to all my writer friends, thank you. You keep me steady when I need it most, and there isn't a day that I'm not grateful to have you in my corner. Likewise, to my wonderful UK co-agent, Louise Lamont, thank you for having my back at the drop of a hat—I can't wait to gush with you about Captain von Trapp IRL someday!

Sending another huge thanks across the pond to my entire UK team at Zaffre Books. To my editor, Melissa Cox, thank you so much for betting on me—I want so badly to make you proud! To Enisha Samra, Georgia Marshall, and Florence Philip, you all have the uncanny power to make me smile every time one of your emails hits my inbox. Thank you for constantly going above and beyond to support me—I couldn't be more grateful.

To my wildly talented cover illustrator, Sandra Chiu, thank you once again for drawing the cover of my dreams and putting up with all my "can we make Jude hotter" requests. I think we can all agree he's at maximum hot now. To Davina Mock-Maniscalco, Min Choi, and the entire production and design team, thank you for turning my messy Word doc into this absolutely gorgeous book.

Special, massive thanks to the readers, librarians, and booksellers who embraced *Any Trope but You* with their whole hearts. Your excitement for *Not That Kind of Proposal* has been the wind in my sails, and you're the reason I keep writing when it feels too hard.

To my friends and family who supported me during this transformative year, there aren't enough words to encompass my gratitude. You sent life-giving texts when I was on deadline. You made my debut pub day so special when I was too pregnant to walk straight. You brought my family food when we were too tired to cook (or even order DoorDash). Special thanks especially to my mom and dad, Sandra and Tom, my beloved goddaughter Luzannette Cortez, and to my dearest friends Eden Campbell, Regina Verret-Foster, Meghann Utrata, Laurie Palagyi, Christine McIntire, Elizabeth MacInnes,

Kate Strait, Jill Lydon, and Meaghan Chemelski. Thank you also to my incredible romance author community—there are so many of you who help me make sense of this job, and I'd be lost without you.

To my children, Georgie and Roman, you are sunshine on my face and moonlight in my heart—it's never dark because of you. And to you, James. Thank you for being the embodiment of "men written by women." You make it so easy to stay in love.

ABOUT THE AUTHOR

Victoria Lavine is the internationally bestselling author of *Any Trope but You* and *Not That Kind of Proposal.* Her love of romance novels started in high school with a crate of old bodice rippers and a wink from her local librarian. Now, she writes her own Happily Ever Afters when she's not enjoying the great state of Maine with her husband, daughter, and son; taking orders from her two cats; or coming up with excellent reasons to make her next latte.

Atria Books, an imprint of Simon & Schuster, fosters an open environment where ideas flourish, bestselling authors soar to new heights, and tomorrow's finest voices are discovered and nurtured. Since its launch in 2002, Atria has published hundreds of bestsellers and extraordinary books, which would not have been possible without the invaluable support and expertise of its team and publishing partners. Thank you to the Atria Books colleagues who collaborated on *Not that Kind of Proposal*, as well as to the hundreds of professionals in the Simon & Schuster advertising, audio, communications, design, ebook, finance, human resources, legal, marketing, operations, production, sales, supply chain, subsidiary rights, and warehouse departments who help Atria bring great books to light.

EDITORIAL
Elizabeth Hitti Musicant
Emilia Rhodes
Natalie Argentina

JACKET DESIGN
Min Choi
Sandra Chiu
James Iacobelli

MARKETING
Zakiya N. Jamal

MANAGING EDITORIAL
Paige Lytle
Shelby Pumphrey
Sofia Echeverry
Abby Borchers

PRODUCTION
Laura Wise
Allison Har-zvi
Shelly Perron
Davina Mock-Maniscalco

PUBLICITY
Camila Araujo

PUBLISHING OFFICE
Dana Trocker
Suzanne Donahue
Abby Velasco

SUBSIDIARY RIGHTS
Nicole Bond
Sara Bowne
Rebecca Justiniano